BEAUTIFUL DECEIVER

"How lovely. And thoughtful." Maura took the roses and inhaled a deep breath from their fragrant depths. This time the smile she gave Garrett added sparkle to her eyes. "And totally unnecessary. I am perfectly fine as you can see."

That he could.

She wore a simple blue dress that brought out the blue hints in her eyes and set off her long dark hair as it curled invitingly down her back. That her feet were bare only added to her innocent allure. She looked so young and pure, unaware of the appealing picture she presented.

How could this current appearance be real, given all she had revealed this afternoon? Could this be a deliberately seductive pose from a woman who knew her sensual enticements?

<u>BOOK YOUR PLACE ON OUR WEBSITE</u> AND MAKE THE <u>READING CONNECTION!</u>

We've created a customized website just for our very special readers, where you can get the inside scoop on everything that's going on with Zebra, Pinnacle and Kensington books.

When you come online, you'll have the exciting opportunity to:

- View covers of upcoming books
- Read sample chapters
- Learn about our future publishing schedule (listed by publication month *and author*)
- Find out when your favorite authors will be visiting a city near you
- Search for and order backlist books from our online catalog
- Check out author bios and background information
- Send e-mail to your favorite authors
- Meet the Kensington staff online
- Join us in weekly chats with authors, readers and other guests
- Get writing guidelines
- AND MUCH MORE!

**Visit our website at
http://www.kensingtonbooks.com**

Luck of the Devil

Emily Baker

ZEBRA BOOKS
Kensington Publishing Corp.
www.kensingtonbooks.com

ZEBRA BOOKS are published by

Kensington Publishing Corp.
850 Third Avenue
New York, NY 10022

All Kensington titles, imprints and distributed lines are available at special quantity discounts for bulk purchases for sales promotion, premiums, fund-raising, educational or institutional use.

Special book excerpts or customized printings can also be created to fit specific needs. For details, write or phone the office of the Kensington Special Sales Manager: Kensington Publishing Corp., 850 Third Avenue, New York, NY 10022. Attn. Special Sales Department. Phone: 1-800-221-2647.

Zebra and the Z logo Reg. U.S. Pat. & TM Off.

ISBN 978-0-8217-7793-9

First Printing: May 2005
10 9 8 7 6 5 4 3 2 1

Printed in the United States of America

THE LEGEND OF THE GREEN DRAGON

In the days of old three kingdoms reigned in Ireland and the King of Desmond held three knights pledged in fealty beyond other clansmen. The Black Knight, the White Knight and the Green Knight, called Green Dragon for his emerald ring—a carved dragon on a field of gold—and for the dragon-hilted sword he bore.

Time passed. The age of the High King faded. Titles changed and families dwindled until only the Green Dragon's fealty remained—to obey his lord, protect his people, and serve the cause of justice.

Those who protect the legacy, the legacy protects in return—passed from man to man, season to season, generation unto generation. Ring, sword, and responsibility belong to the man destiny chooses.

"Thus we are arrayed and armed."
—rallying cry of the Green Dragon and his men

Prologue

County Wicklow, Ireland, 1816

"Fer the love of God. I paid the rent last Thursday."
Raucous laughter rose over Da's tense protests as
Bridget's gaze froze between gaps in the barn boards.

"Ask his lordship," Da repeated. "I paid in full!"

Bridget watched the nightmare scene unfold before
her. Mam's screams rose high into the night air as the
men dragged her from the cottage in her night rail.
Only Mam, she noted, holding her breath along with
an unsaid prayer. The littles must have gotten out
through the root cellar. They must have. Bridget
clung to the litany.

A Dia, let it be so.

She pressed her fist against her mouth, her throat
tight as she fought back the screams building inside
her, and huddled farther back in the corner by the
broodmare. One of the brigands clamped his hand
over Mam's mouth to stifle her objections as they
tossed furniture into the yard and set it aflame.

"Leave her be, ye bounder. I paid already. There's
no need fer this." Da struggled against his captors'
meaty grasps. He broke one arm free and took a wild
swing, connecting with one intruder's hard jaw
enough to rock the man back on his heels.

Get 'em, Da. Bridget swallowed her cheer as fear kept

her rooted in the corner, unable to look away. *Untie Bess and get her out through the backdoor.* Da's orders about the mare rushed through her mind, but she couldn't turn away from her father and mother, from the injustice taking place in her own front yard.

Two of the ruffians pummeled Da to the ground in short order. Bridget winced, and a moan welled inside her. Hot tears streaked her cheeks. Still rubbing his jaw, the tallest of the band got in several kicks before being waved off by a man still on horseback. Da coughed and lay still.

Her heart dropped.

The rider leaned down and spat at Da's bare feet. "You paid late. That's need enough." *English.* He was dressed in finer clothes than the others, and his arrogance was as unmistakable as his speech. The others were a rough lot. This one alone sported the kind of mask worn by the quality when they attended His Lordship's annual Christmas ball.

"Let this be a warning to you, Clancy, and to all your neighbors. Pay on time or pay a penalty."

"This here's the only woman about the place. They musta gotten the girl out as we rode up." Light from the blazing furniture glittered wickedly across the leering face of the man holding Mam. She struggled to break her mouth free of his restraining hand while he used the other one to paw at her bosom.

"Too bad about the girl." The Englishman shrugged. The brute of a stallion he rode pranced close to Da. Bridget gulped, fearing the worst, but he seemed to have lost interest in her father. "I have no use for crones. Release this one."

Mam ran to Da's still form and fell weeping upon him before turning back to their tormentors. "Shame on ye fer attacking an unarmed man." Her voice came dark and tear-laden. "We're good tenants. Ask anyone. His Lordship will hear of this."

The Englishman threw back his head and laughed. "We'll seek our sport farther on, boys. Although this one's almost feisty enough to be of interest."

He wheeled his horse about and snatched a burning fagot from the bonfire. "Torch the barn. So all might see and heed this warning—"

"No!" A small figure rushed from the darkness beyond the cottage, his shout overriding Bridget and Mam's horrified protests.

Paddy. Bridget pushed to her feet. *No!*

"Get off my Da's land," her brother bellowed with all the bluster of his angry twelve-year-old heart. The handle of a broken hoe filled his fists. "Leave here now or the Green Dragon will make ye wish ye had. Ye'll pay."

Please God let them overlook him. Please God let them not hurt Paddy.

The words cycled through Bridget's head as her fingers fumbled with the sorrel mare's rope. She watched Paddy swing his makeshift weapon at the Englishman. The brigand knocked the blow aside, reached down, and scooped up her squirming brother.

"Did you hear that boys? The Green Dragon here swears we're about to pay."

"Green Dragon?" The tall ruffian pulled Paddy from the Englishman's grasp and held him up. "Looks more like the Green Tadpole ta me."

"Put me down." Paddy swung at the thug but couldn't connect. The others roared with laughter.

Mam jumped onto the man's back. "Leave my boy be."

A whistled note split the night air from beyond the fire. The sound of horse and harness, riding hard, pounded closer and closer up the lane.

"Enough of this circus." The Englishman spun his mount and headed toward the barn, flaming stick still in hand. "We've got company. Raze the barn and let's get out of here."

With a mingled roar his men followed him across the yard, brandishing torches. Her own imminent danger hurried Bridget's fingers. She finally got the knot loosened as the brigands reached the barn. She wound the rope around her hand and forced herself to concentrate on getting the mare out of the barn and not on what was going on outside. She had to get Bess out. Da had already sold the foal she carried to pay his back rent. Bridget was the eldest. He was counting on her. She couldn't afford to think about his prone figure on the ground outside, to be distracted by her fears for Paddy or Mam or even the little ones.

She threw her shawl over the mare's head as the first lick of flames caught the straw in the loft. *No more time.* Smoke filled the air as Bess fought being led deeper into the barn's depths. Bess's panicked whickers joined the crackle and pop of the rapidly spreading fire. Mam screamed. The sound of pistols fired outside. Bridget persisted and finally tugged the terrified horse to the paddock door. She reached for the latch.

The door swung outward before her fingers touched it.

Smoke billowed past her in a hot rush joining the cool air in the back meadow. The flames behind her roared. A figure loomed in the doorway. Bess whinnied and reared. Bridget screamed and fought to hold on. There was nowhere to run. A strong arm scooped her up and held her fast.

"There now, my girl." This time the cultured voice was low and soft. *The Englishman.* Bridget tried to kick her captor but only succeeded in flailing the air

"I have you, *muirnín*," he continued, unaffected by her efforts. "You only need to be brave a moment more, then we will be outside. You will make a fine, strong mother."

As Bess quieted enough to be led outside, Bridget realized the man holding her in his iron grip was not speaking to her and he was not the English raider at all. His voice and accent carried the mark of education, sure enough, but his use of Gaelic held the lilt of a native Irish son.

He set her on her feet and pulled the shawl from Bess's head, then released the mare's guide rope so she could escape into the night. "She will not go far; her time is too near."

He turned toward Bridget. She took an involuntary step backward. The flames from the barn added menace to his stance as the light cast shadows and highlights along his tall frame. His coat and trousers were fashioned much like Da's Sunday suit, only less coarse. But it was the mask that stopped just beneath his nose that made her shiver as her teeth chattered together.

"There now, sweeting." He held his hands out, open palmed, and smiled. It was a nice smile—kind, but not too broad—topping a strong jaw and clean-shaven chin. "You have been very brave. Do not quaver now. I am a friend. One of many."

He paused and cocked his head. "And from the sounds of things, the rest of my friends have made short work of those bullies."

Sure enough, the chaos on the other side of the barn had subsided. She could hear only the creak and roar of flaming timbers. "Mam. Paddy?"

She started forward. He caught her shoulders and stooped to bring his gaze level with hers. "They were fine when I headed back here. Stand away from the barn, but wait for me. I'll go have a look."

His voice was calm and soothing yet carried enough command to have her nodding ready agreement.

"Good girl." He smiled and released her. She

caught the flash of a large ring on his right hand as he turned.

She backed up about twenty paces and watched in horrified fascination as the fire consumed her family's barn. The flames and smoke reached high into the sky . . . *so all might see and heed this warning.* That's what that Englishman had said. His warning would probably be seen three villages away. She shivered despite the heat from the burning straw and timber before her.

It seemed an eternity passed as she watched the fire.

"Bridget?" She startled at hearing her name and turned to find yet another stranger standing just within the circle of light from the fire. " 'Tis safe to come back, lass. Your mam seeks you."

She darted around the barn. Mam still knelt on the ground beside Da. Her curls tumbled over her soot-covered nightdress, and tears streaked her cheeks. One man appeared to be tending Da's wounds. Three more were trying, to little avail, to throw water on the raging barn fire. Several other figures lay unmoving on the ground. The man who had summoned her and the man who had rescued her from the barn were in deep consultation. All the men of this bunch sported the same half masks.

"Mam, Mam. Where's Paddy?"

"I sent him after yer brothers and sister." Mam spread her arms wide as Bridget ran forward.

She waited until she was safe in her mother's embrace before daring a look at her father. "Is Da . . . is Da . . . ?" She couldn't finish the question.

"I believe your father will be fine given a day or two's rest and no heavy lifting for a week or so after." The man wrapping Da's chest with pieces of linen looked up. "He has some cracked ribs and some great bruises from the blows he took."

"The worst is the blow ta me pride." Da tried to sit up but groaned and collapsed. Relief poured through Bridget to hear his voice. *Praise be.*

"Nonsense." The man from the barn joined them. "There is no a man alive that could take on eight armed brigands and come out looking any better than you, sir. You are a lucky man."

"Luck?" Da gestured toward the barn with his chin. He closed his eyes and swallowed hard.

"Aye." The man squatted beside him. "You are alive. You have a fine, brave family. What you lost this night can be replaced."

Da opened his eyes once more and stared at the man for a moment in silence.

"I know ye speak true. And I'm grateful fer the help ye gave us." Da looked from the man to Mam. Bridget had never seen so much hopelessness in her father's gaze. "But I barely made the rent last quarter. How're we ta build a barn, feed our wee ones, and save fer next time?"

"I got Bess out Da. At least her babe and her are safe."

"He's right in that way, Bridgie." Da held out his hand to her. She grabbed his fist and laid her cheek on it. "Ye're a good girl. Ye and yer brother. And yer Mam. Ye all stood up fer what's ours."

"And this should help with the rebuilding." The man took a small pouch from his coat and dropped it in Mam's lap.

She unwrapped the leather tie from the top of the green velvet square and burst into tears as what was surely a fortune in coins spilled onto the ground. Bridget gasped.

"We canna take charity, sir. Ye've done enough." The barn roof creaked loudly and collapsed in a shower of sparks as Da struggled to sit upright and refuse the gift.

"Nonsense—" Their rescuer waved him off.

"See I told ye the Green Dragon saved us." Paddy's excited assurance drew all their attention. He ran forward carrying their baby sister. Their three little brothers trailed behind. All of the children's eyes were rounded with wonder and a measure of fright as they took in the strangers, the burning barn, and finally Mam and Da.

The Green Dragon?

The pieces fell into place for Bridget. Green velvet pouch, green mask, timely rescue . . . She'd always thought the tales of his exploits were the same as the stories of Sidhe and the Fian of old—exaggerated myths and not much more.

"I aim ta be jest like ye when I'm growed." Paddy skidded to a halt and looked up at the man who had helped get Bess from the barn. The littles ran to Mam and clung to her.

"I want ta help ye get rid of the English. I want us ta be free and strong," Paddy continued, ignoring Mam's sharp intake of breath and the worried frown she cast her eldest son.

"The best way you can help to see that freedom comes about is to learn all you can from your Da and keep this farm going." The Green Dragon smiled at Mam and cuffed Paddy lightly on his cheek. His signet ring, gold with a carved emerald dragon, flashed in the light cast by the barn fire.

Paddy frowned and looked away, trying to swallow his disappointment without embarrassing himself into tears, trying to understand.

"If we Irishmen lose our way of life in the struggle for freedom, what have we won? You think on that while you grow." The Green Dragon's voice was gentle, soothing—the tone he'd used on Bess in the barn. "For now, you can help your sister and mam get your da back to the house. You will have quite a mess to clean up come morning. I cannot stay and help so I am counting on you. Can you do that, lad?"

Paddy's shoulders had straightened during the last. He looked up. "Aye, sir, I can."

"Good man." The Green Dragon signaled his men. They melted into the darkness. "Take care of your family and your land and I will always consider you one of my strongest allies."

The Green Dragon looked down at Da. "Like I said, you are a fortunate man. Good luck to you."

"Thank ye." Mam and Da spoke as one.

He'd already vanished into the night.

"Bridget?" His voice drifted back through the darkness.

She straightened and strained to see. "Aye?"

"You are a rare fine lass, and brave into the bargain. Stand proud. Listen for the song of the redstart and one day I'll be there. *Sonnas ort!*"

Hooves pounded in retreat as Bridget stood staring off into the dark. She hugged his wish for her happiness to her heart.

"*Beannacht ort.*" She whispered her blessing for him, knowing he was already beyond hearing her.

The redstart's song. "I'll remember."

Chapter One

Dublin, Ireland, 1820

"I love you," Freddie gasped against her neck as the final echoes of his most recent passion quivered away.

He thought he meant it, too, poor dear.

Maura bit back a sigh and stroked the sweat-dampened curls at the nape of his neck without comment.

What the Honorable Edmond "Freddie" Vaughn lacked in finesse as a lover he leveraged into energy and enthusiasm. Her body thrummed from his attentions as she tried to concentrate on the moment—on the man in her bed—not on the disastrous consequences awaiting any response she might fashion to his rash declaration.

There simply was no safe answer save the physical. She trailed her fingers across his spine and felt him shiver against her. The only safe answer.

Half an hour later she sat before her mirror brushing her hair while he dressed. Lamplight caressed his trim form as he slid finely tailored trousers up his legs and shrugged into his proper linen shirt. She should feel flattered by his claims of affection; Freddie had much to recommend him beyond his physique, social standing, and rapidly improved prospects. He possessed an honest innocence and sweet thoughtfulness she felt almost honor bound to protect, especially

from his own intentions. He was so very young, for all
he was her elder by two years. It was only natural for
him to fancy himself in love with the first woman with
whom he'd carried on a sustained liaison.

She should be flattered, but all she felt was dread.

His gaze caught hers in the mirror, and she stopped
her brushing.

"Let me." He stepped over to the dressing table and
took the brush from her hand, laying his brocaded
waistcoat and crumpled cravat next to her perfumes
and powders. Gently, but firmly, he stroked the silver
brush through her dark hair, keeping his gaze locked
with hers in the mirror. The intimacy of the moment
and the intensity of the look in his eyes hitched her
breath despite her determination to remain indiffer-
ent to his appeal.

"I meant what I said." His serious tone belied the
tousled carelessness of his sandy brown hair. "I do love
you. Marry me."

He relinquished the hairbrush and slid his fingers
into her hair, sculpting it back, tenderly tracing the
curved rim of each ear before resting his hands on
her shoulders. His hands looked dark against the
ivory silk of her wrapper. The heat of his palms
warmed her flesh while the fervor in his gaze chilled
her.

He meant every word. Every socially damning word.

He might be young, but he was not so naïve as to be
unaware his proposal pushed the boundaries required
by their relationship, let alone the social reprisals he
would subject himself to with such a choice. She
couldn't help wondering what might have happened
had she been different. Freddie might be easily duped
by a greedier woman than her.

"Freddie—" She took up his cravat, stood, and
turned to look at him.

He put his finger on her lips to still her protest as

he drew her to him. "I know you do not think I am
sincere. Or that I know what I am saying. But I do,
Maura."

His lips brushed hers in a kiss both tender and demanding. A shiver of uncertainty raced through her.
It would take too little effort to let herself pretend to
love him back, to believe he might be able to mantle
her in the respectability she had lost years ago, to
leave this part of her life behind and start fresh.

But she knew better. The impossibility of that wish
struck new pain nonetheless.

"You are so beautiful." Freddie's breath fanned her
cheek. His hands drew her closer still. "Come back to
bed. Let me show you how much I can offer you. Let
me spend the night and make love to you until tomorrow dawns and your doubts are nothing but yesterday's shadows."

"Nonsense." She forced a lightness to her tone she
didn't feel. "You have nothing to prove that you have
not already shown me."

None of her lovers ever spent the night. Not the
whole night. It was a small measure of control and distance she strove to maintain.

She brushed her fingers over his cheek to take any
sting out of her words, pushed back from the security of Freddie's embrace, and flung the cravat about
his collar. "You have always been generosity itself with
both your attentions and your financial rewards."

He frowned, raising a dark brow at her bald statement regarding the true nature of their arrangement.
She persisted nonplussed, smiling up at him as she
tried to make light of the tension tightening his shoulders. "As for spending the night, did you not tell me
you were escorting your mama and younger sisters to
your grandfather's estate in the morning?"

"Damn tomorrow," he offered with the enthusiasm

of his youth. "I only wish to talk about us, about tonight. About what I have asked you. Let me stay."

She twisted his cravat into the waterfall arrangement he preferred. "Her Ladyship will not take kindly to any tardiness caused by your dawdling in bed with your mistress until all hours."

She looked up through her eyelashes and pulled her lips into a pout with just a hint of feigned regret. It was an expression that seldom failed to win her whatever she desired. "Could we not discuss this when you return to Dublin?"

"Ever the practical one, eh?" He hesitated a moment longer, as if searching for the magic words to make her acquiesce to his demand. Then he pressed his lips into a line and reached around her for his waistcoat. She took it from him and helped him get into it, then fastened the buttons for him. Her fingers smoothed the fabric over his tapered chest and firm abdomen.

"I will miss you," she admitted, not certain whether she meant during his journey or when he eventually left her to continue on with his life.

He smiled then, a spark of hope lighting the depths of his soft brown eyes. "Mother plans to stay at Clancare Manor for the better part of next month, but I will be back within the next fortnight despite Grandfather's threat to saddle me with the Barony of Stanhope."

"So the *Ard Tiarna* plans to make a true lord of you." She handed him the carved-gold studs for his shirt cuffs.

"The High Lord can try." Freddie shrugged. "He wishes to saddle me with lands to tend and a wife to bear his next set of heirs as soon as he can manage. He thinks it is time I settled down and began my training to be his heir."

"Perhaps he is right." She concentrated on threading the end onto the studs for him as relief over the clue he had provided for this urgency soothed her anxiety.

Rebellion against the heightened expectations thrust on him, so unexpectedly and recently, explained his rash proposal. The immediacy of her dilemma eased. She had no need to act in his best interest and end things between them just yet. Freddie would come to his senses on his own, or his grandfather would pull in the reins soon enough.

"Only if I may have the wife of my choosing." Freddie's tone carried a note of resolution she'd never heard before. "Only if I can have you, Maura Fitzgerald."

She had absolutely no idea what to say at that moment, so she released a long sigh.

Freddie cupped her cheek. "We'll talk when I return. Perhaps you would do me the honor of hosting a few of my friends for an evening of cards and allow me to stay the night then."

"Perhaps." She nodded, promising nothing but not dashing his hopes altogether. She was not ready to bid final farewell to the new Lord Stanhope.

He smiled broadly. "That's a heartening answer. Give me a smile and a sweet kiss to linger over while I am away."

She wrapped her arms around his neck and gave him the soul-searing send-off he expected.

The Ogham stone's edge grated against Garrett's soul as much as his shoulder as he kept watch under the light of the full moon over Saint Marnock's well across the grouse.

Even within the cloak of night this meeting site was too exposed, too risky. But his recent absence from the city had left him little choice. He'd had no time to investigate the possible reasons behind this late-night appointment or to change the location. Keeping it, or not, were his only options.

In the distance, high golden moonlight spilled over the ruins of a medieval church once dedicated to a Cistercian monk and the lone, silhouetted figure pacing the clearing between them. The only sound was the pounding of the Irish Sea on the distant strand. A hint of salt carried on the wind mingled with the taste of anticipation on his tongue.

Damnation, where was Sean?

So much depended on timing, on their both being in place. The rough edge of the ancient pillar's incised lines scraped his ear and tore a hiss from him. The messages these lines were meant to convey were wrapped in almost as much mystery as the summons that had brought the Green Dragon and his most trusted lieutenant to this coastal meeting.

A high-pitched trilling sounded from what had once been the roofline of the church. The redstart's song, at last. It was time to begin.

He followed the line of the dunes to the place he'd noted earlier as the best approach for crossing to the well unobserved. When the admiral turned and headed once more away from the view of Velvet Beach far below, the redstart's call sounded again. The way was as clear as it ever would be. Garrett moved as quietly as he could toward the strangest meeting he'd ever been asked to attend.

Several minutes later, the admiral paced back toward the appointed spot, his gait uneven from the stiffness he bore in one battle-scarred leg and the walking stick he used to compensate.

"Halt where you are, sir." Garrett gave the warning.

The older man stopped immediately.

A heavy cape swirled around his mast-straight figure clad in the dress breeches and high boots of a naval officer. Beneath his ancient tricorn hat, he did not appear either surprised by Garrett's presence or concerned at being alone on a deserted hillside with the man considered by some to be one of Ireland's most notorious criminals—the man he had spent nearly a year of his retirement trying to catch. After all, he'd summoned the Green Dragon to this spot.

"If you have assured yourself I am alone as promised, I would prefer speaking to you man to man, not man to shadow." The crisp command of years spent on a quarterdeck came with unmistakable disdain.

Not for the first time, Garrett wondered what had forced this old salt to issue his urgent invitation. That much at least he was surely about to discover, along with the cost. There was always a cost where the English were concerned. He stepped away from the well. "Good evening, Admiral Fuller. State your business."

For the stretch of several minutes, the admiral remained silent, assessing Garrett as his keenly observant gaze took in his mask, the rural simplicity of his attire, the brace of pistols in his belt, and the knife he held in his right hand. The only reaction Garrett could discern under the muted light and shadows supplied by the moon was a small tick in the admiral's cheek.

He fought the urge to squirm under the mariner's intense scrutiny. The sooner they could get their business concluded the better, but he had no intention of betraying his unease over this whole matter. Finally, the man's chin raised ever so slightly, then dropped. He'd made up his mind.

"Why are we meeting, sir? Why here?" Garrett pressed.

"Why here?" The admiral looked over his shoulder at the church ruins. "Marnock was a sailor, you know. Not much is known about him save that he is rumored to have inspired your Brendan into making his own voyages of discovery. Brendan is supposed to have journeyed over the seas to the New World even before that Spanish fellow—"

"Italian," Garrett corrected. He had no patience for delaying tactics.

"What was that?" The admiral turned back to face him.

"Columbus was Italian."

"Quite right." The Admiral nodded. "I knew you must possess a superior education. No common criminal could be so elusive based on luck alone.

Garrett's impatience grew. "Admiral Fuller, you did not request this meeting to fish for clues regarding my identity, nor to exchange information on my country's seafaring legends. Pray get to the point and explain your summons."

The admiral pressed his lips together. "Right again. Still, this does not come easily to me."

He paused, and several more moments passed as he clenched and unclenched his fist on the balled head of his walking stick. "This concerns my daughter."

His daughter? Garrett knew of her. Jane Fuller made quite a splash in Dublin's social circles when her widowed father retired last year and brought her with him to take up the Irish estates he'd been granted as recognition for his valor and long, distinguished career in the king's navy.

"You have a daughter?" Garrett forced a casual, almost bored incredulity into his voice despite his heightened senses at the mention of Miss Fuller.

"Do not feign ignorance." The admiral fixed him with a hard look. "She is my only child and she is missing. Went berry picking with her maid on my country lands and never returned."

Awareness prickled Garrett's spine. "How long?"

"Nearly two weeks."

Two weeks? He'd been away from Dublin for a little more than a fortnight, yet there had not been a whisper of this on anyone's lips upon his return. Something as salacious as the disappearance of an admiral's daughter, no matter how discreetly handled, would have slipped out. Perhaps this was an elaborate trap after all. "Why seek me out and not the authorities?"

The admiral held his peace. The tic returned to his cheek. His fist continued to clench and unclench the head of his walking stick. The only sound was the rustle of the marram grass spikes along the dunes from the breeze rising off the water behind them.

Garrett puzzled a moment more over the admiral's reluctance to continue, then expressed his thoughts aloud. "Unless you think she has run off with a beau and you want her back before the scandal breaks."

"Quite right," the admiral admitted, his shoulders slumping ever so slightly. "One of her suitors—a bounder if I ever saw one—has been absent from Dublin for almost the same time."

Garrett's gut knotted. "Who do you suspect?"

"Talbot. Sean Talbot."

Damnation.

Sean Talbot. That explained the location for this meeting at least. But hell, he'd assigned Sean the job of appearing to court Jane Fuller in the first place. Now he'd made his own man a target.

"The Talbots are one of England's staunchest allies in these parts." Garrett could not tell the admiral just how far off the mark his suspicions were. Sean had been with him for the duration of Miss Fuller's absence. "I would think you would be pleased at her making such a match."

"The Talbots are a savvy lot. I am sure they have many allies—" Was there a veiled threat behind the admiral's statement? "—still they claim to have no inkling of the blackguard's whereabouts or activities, or any mention of my daughter."

"Surely there may be others who expressed an interest in Miss Fuller's hand? I had heard she was hardly an antidote."

The admiral snorted and reached into his pocket. He proffered a folded piece of paper. "Although my money's on Talbot, here is the list of her admirers. You will see it is rather extensive. My daughter is an heiress thanks to her mother's family. That makes her a very popular young lady."

Garrett unfolded the list. There were a number of names. Most he recognized either from his own social contacts or from Sean's reports. This project was going to require a major commitment of time and men. "What do you expect from me?"

"I want you to bring her home, at any cost," the admiral stated baldly. "I have no intention of allowing any fortune hunter to take advantage of her innocence in order to line his pockets. Especially not for a lifetime."

At any cost.

Garrett thought for a moment. Having the admiral on his side, instead of against him, could became one of the Green Dragon's most valuable assets. But if this should fail, the man would no doubt prove a bitter enemy. "I am not an assassin. No matter the price. If I locate her, I will not make her a widow or remove her from a situation of her own choosing."

"Yes, yes. I know your reputation." The admiral waved his hand in the air. "Very noble. You help the downtrodden, taking from the rich and giving to the poor and all that other Robin Hoodish rot."

"Robin Hood?"

"A legend from near my boyhood home. We all wanted to play a champion of the people like Robin Hood at one time. Then we grew up and began to live in the real world." World-weary experience tightened the admiral's tone. "Are you prepared to assist me or not?"

Garrett twirled the knife in his hand a moment longer before sheathing it. "I am prepared to attempt discovering if your *daughter* is in need of assistance. The parties who delivered your request to me mentioned something about an exchange. Would you care to elaborate on your offer before we proceed any further?"

The ghost of a smile skimmed the hard planes of the admiral's face. "Legend or not, everyone has his price."

"Jane is missing?" The intensity in Sean's voice surprised Garrett a half hour later as he recounted his meeting.

"Aye." He offered his friend the flask he'd pulled from his pocket as they watched the admiral's distant figure walk stiffly down the Port Marnock Road toward the carriage waiting for him over a mile away.

"He has put out that she is down with measles and recuperating at his County Meath estate, but the girl has been gone for nearly two full weeks."

"Sounds like an elopement." Sean tossed back a healthy dram of whiskey. "What does he think has become of her?"

"He is certain she eloped with you."

"*Diabhal.*" Sean took another draft and scrubbed his chin with the back of his hand.

"Aye, the devil indeed. At least it explains the location for this meeting."

"He went to Malahide Castle?"

"Aye. Your elder brother claimed no knowledge of your marriage or your whereabouts. I doubt the admiral believed him on either score."

"The Talbots have not resided at Malahide for nearly seven centuries without gaining a reputation for knowing how to play most games to our advantage." A mix of bitter irony and reluctant pride twisted through Sean's tone. "Tell me what happened."

The admiral had disappeared around the bend in the road. They'd be here at least another half hour waiting for the all clear sign. "We might as well sit while we sip," Garrett said.

They settled themselves against timeworn stones of the church walls. It was eerily quiet. Mist from the Irish Sea spilled across the moon's golden light. The breeze no longer shook the marram grass spires. "Seems the girl went berry picking with her maid and never returned—just over ten days ago. The irony is he sent her to the country because he thought she was spending entirely too much time mooning over you."

Sean snorted. "Jane Fuller is hardly the mooning type. Only a doting father could think such a hummer. She is maddeningly headstrong and entirely too outspoken for her own good." He took another swallow from the flask. "I pity the man who ends up saddled with her."

The tone was right, but anxiety glinted in Sean's eyes.

"Aye." Garrett capped the flask when Sean handed it back. He might need to keep his thoughts clear. No matter his friend's protest, the news affected Sean deeply. "So I gathered from your reports this past season."

"But you say both Jane and her maid have not been heard from? For nearly two weeks?"

"Aye."

"*Diabhal.*"

Garrett let the import of the admiral's dilemma sink in with Sean a few moments more.

"Do you think he made the connection between me and you?" Sean leaned his head back against the stones and exhaled.

Garrett shook his head. "As far as he is concerned,

you are as you appear, a wastrel and a gambler. Something his daughter said led him to banish her."

"Jane told him about the kiss?"

Kiss?

"If she did it is more than he shared with me." Garrett shifted forward so he could look directly at Sean
in the gloom. "And more than you have imparted as
well. Especially during our recent travels."

Sean looked away; his jaw worked for a moment.
"The incident seemed irrelevant to your purpose in
having me play at courting her."

Garrett sighed. Sean knew better than that. Everything, significant or seemingly insignificant, could
prove relevant to their cause. He struggled to keep his
frustration from showing. From the looks of his friend
there was nothing he could say that Sean was not already using to upbraid himself. "What happened?"

"Harold Jameson took her for a turn in the Hamilton's gardens during their daughter's come out last
month. I happened to be out there enjoying a cheroot when he decided to press his attentions."

"So you intervened?" Rumors of Jameson's unsavory interests had followed him from Belfast when
he'd slithered into town some two years ago. So far
they'd failed to pin anything firmly in his corner, but
the activities of the Orangemen and their compatri-
ots had taken a decidedly twisted turn since the English dilettante arrived in Dublin.

"Only afterward . . ."

Garrett brought his attention back to the story at
hand. "After what?"

"She slapped him hard enough to knock him off
balance." Sean's admiration seemed clearer than his
retelling of the event. "The admiral must have taught
her Gentleman Jackson's right hook."

"And then you intervened and hit him, too?"

"Not exactly." For the first time since he'd learned

of Jane Fuller's disappearance, some of the tension eased in Sean's voice. "You know the Hamilton's fountain at the heart of their maze?"

Garrett suppressed a shudder as he recalled the massive casting of Lady Hamilton depicted as Aphrodite arising from her scallop shell with her long locks mercifully covering her modesty. "Aye."

"Jameson tumbled over the edge and pulled Jane . . . Miss Fuller . . . in with him."

"And that's when you hit him?"

"Aye. I helped her escape to the carriages unnoticed and sent for her aunt. I have not seen her since."

"What are you still leaving out?"

Sean shrugged. "She was soaking wet. I gave her my jacket and may have brushed my lips against her temple as I bid her farewell. It was meant as a comfort only. She is not much older than my sister, after all."

"Well, I suppose Jameson will have to go to the top of our list. And you will need to keep a low profile while you work to locate Miss Fuller. Especially while you make inquiries in Meath."

"You trust me to investigate Jane's disappearance?"

"Of course." Garrett hoped his instincts were right on this count. "You obviously have a personal stake in finding the girl—"

"I—"

"—whether you acknowledge it or not." Garrett waved off the protest forming on Sean's lips. "Besides your appearance back in Dublin without her will only alarm the admiral. Perhaps enough to rescind his offer."

Sean leaned forward. "What offer?"

Despite his failure to report the Jameson incident, Garrett trusted Sean to carry out his mission, especially once he knew how much hung upon the outcome. "The admiral has promised to use his influence to free five men currently held under suspicion of sedition."

Interest tightened across Sean's features. "Did you agree?"

"So far little can be proven against these men. Two of them are more important to our people's future than our English brothers suspect. It is their freedom that brought us to Kerry. Rather than confirm this to the admiral, I said I would make inquiries, then get in touch with him to discuss suitable recompense for my trouble."

The admiral had not been pleased to link his daughter's fate to an undetermined cost, but Garrett had given him no other choice.

"So finding Jane is key to the *Ard Tiarna*'s directive." As usual Sean cut straight to the heart of the matter. The Talbots were nothing if not astute.

"Precisely. Take Liam with you. Your inquiries will go much more quickly if there are two of you." Garrett knew Sean understood that the reason behind this job was to be kept between the two of them. The fewer of his men who knew what was at stake, the safer the prisoners on Green Street would remain.

In the distance, the redstart's call sounded. Garrett counted to ten, and it sounded again.

Sean scrambled to his feet and dusted his trousers. "So while I am off to County Meath with Liam, what will you be doing?"

"Attending a card party." He'd intended to send Sean to the event hosted by the *Ard Tiarna*'s grandson, along with one of their host's former schoolmates. Both men possessed enough social cachet to have all but the worst foibles overlooked and were welcome everywhere in the city. Stanhope was falling in with a bad lot, and his grandfather wanted his interests diverted.

"A card party? I'll be making discreet inquiries in the countryside and you will be forced to endure a night of fine cigars and finer brandy." Sean reached down and held out a hand to pull Garrett to his feet. "Talk about the luck of the devil."

"Hardly." There was nothing lucky about either assignment. "You know part of the High Lord's charge consists of babysitting his grandson. This party is being held at the home of the lad's mistress—a mistress he told his grandfather he intends to marry. I'm to size her up and calculate how much it will cost the earl to buy her off."

Sean shook his head. "Stanhope escorted Mrs. Fitzgerald to the theatre last month. She is both beautiful and charming. But for her circumstances she would make a very presentable countess. It will take quite a bit to buy her off, I'd wager, given the new baron's devotion to her, and his prospects. Still, if he keeps her in the style she dresses, you will have a delicious meal and good spirits along with a fair night's entertainment. Not too tough a night while I am encamped in County Meath."

Garrett shrugged. The *Ard Tiarna* had been very clear on this point. His grandson must not marry his mistress, charming or not, a fine hostess or not. Garrett was to spare no effort to separate the lovers.

They started down the road toward the men and horses awaiting their return.

"One benefit for tomorrow, I should also have a chance to learn more about your friend Jameson. He is on Mrs. Fitzgerald's guest list."

He could feel Sean's gaze shoot toward him in the darkness. "The extent of your contacts never ceases to amaze me."

He could almost see Sean's eyebrow cocked with amusement. Good. He wanted his friend's mood lightened enough to face what lay ahead.

Chapter Two

"You can't be serious, man. They were caught in the garden?" Percy Masters's outburst squeaked far outside the bounds of well-bred enthusiasm. The sound echoed back from the high bas-relief ceiling, down along the dark green and cream etched walls. Maura tried to suppress her wince.

"I am serious as a magistrate."

"Well, I am just stunned. You simply must be jesting."

"Not a whit."

This entire scandalous on-dit seemed especially witless. Maura let out a slow breath and forced her attention to the task at hand. Percival Masters, one of Freddie's old school friends and more constant companions, had been going on like this for what felt like an eternity. No matter how much high-pitched, disbelief-ridden urging he managed to infuse into each squeal, he received the assurance of the opposite in the amused, slightly bored tone that seemed to be Harold Jameson's preferred method of utterance.

She bit back a sigh before directing Gerald to hand Freddie's guests the libations they had requested. Straight brandy for Mr. Jameson and a somewhat watered-down version concocted for Percy. Freddie had warned her to temper the alcohol afforded Percy unless they wanted trouble. Gerald shuffled across the room bearing his tray to attend the knot of gentlemen discussing the horse meet they'd attended last week in Kildare and the latest exploits and outrages attributed to the Green Dragon.

Not for the first time, Maura wished Freddie had chosen that side of the drawing room to occupy rather than this cozy corner. Her maid kept her fully informed, with breathless hero worship, of whatever the latest tattle regarding this legendary defender of the poor and oppressed. In Teresa's eyes the Green Dragon was clearly destined for sainthood at the head of his band of brave comrades. Hearing another side to the exploits attributed to him would surely prove more entertaining than listening to Percy and Jameson's lame repartee.

Percy saluted her with a blend of lust and respectful admiration as he sipped his refreshment. She turned to Mr. Jameson. His glance met hers briefly as he also raised his tumbler filled with an excellent vintage of the burnished liquor Freddie had procured for the evening.

Jameson was new to the circle of friends and acquaintances she had previously been called upon to hostess at Freddie's game nights. This man was older. More sophisticated. She couldn't help wondering what had possessed him to accept an invitation to spend his time with these younger men. Freddie was so intelligent and his breeding offered him any number of opportunities, but he had come into so much so quickly these past two years that there was a real danger of his head being turned.

Percy laughed again, his voice rising in volume and fullness to prompt the beginnings of a headache in her left temple.

Jameson's gaze held hers as he sipped the brandy. "Thank you for your hospitality, my dear. His Lordship is fortunate in his choice of friends."

His eyes were dark and unreadable for all their light shade of hazel. He missed little even while he dismissed her as beneath his station if not quite beneath his notice. What was he thinking behind those strangely light and dark eyes? Worse, what was he plotting? She was glad he had already stated his intentions to leave early, much to Percy's chagrin. She might not be overly fond of Percy or his interest in entertainments of a questionable nature, but she could tolerate him because of his youth and his general lack of true malice.

The word slithered through her. Was that what Harold Jameson made her think of? Malice? And plots? She hoped the two did not go together in connection with Freddie or Percy, for both their sakes.

"Come on, man, you cannot start such a tale then leave us hanging as to the outcome." Percy prodded again as Jameson sipped his brandy with an almost dreamy, contemplative air. "Tell him he simply must finish his story at once, Mrs. Fitzgerald."

"Of course." Jameson swirled his drink, inhaled its aroma, and took a slow appreciative sip before continuing. "However, I wouldn't presume to share such a tale in the presence of your . . . lady." His gaze slid to Freddie. Though said with a suggestion that he respected Maura's position in Freddie's life, unrespectable as it may be, his tone clearly labeled the last word a question.

The tiniest flicker of shame etched her nerve endings and traced the length of her spine. She straightened her shoulders and resisted the sudden urge to either run from the room or tell Harold Jameson exactly how soon he could leave instead. Ire burned low in her stomach. She seldom allowed disgrace for the direction her life had taken to affect her. She made the choices she made to provide for the ones she loved. What man in this room, given the same choices and circumstances, could swear he'd have done otherwise?

Not one of the men in her life had ever treated her as less of a lady because of her choices. She knew without glancing back into Jameson's all-seeing eyes that such was not the case with him. He meant to sting her with his tone and words. She forced the tension out of her shoulders, determined not to give him whatever satisfaction he sought with his goading.

"Let me freshen this for you, my lord." She stood and scooped Freddie's nearly full tumbler from the table between their chairs without looking at any of the three men involved in this conversation.

She prayed Jameson had no idea how directly his barb had hit its target as she stepped over to the sideboard liquor cabinet. Toward what end would a near stranger make her a target, save to test the depth of Freddie's attachment and protective instincts regarding his mistress. She suppressed a shiver of apprehension at the thought.

She poured a small draft of whiskey from a cut-crystal decanter, then added water from the matching pitcher to Freddie's tumbler. He seemed uncharacteristically enthusiastic about this card party, as though he expected something much more than cards to come of the evening he'd arranged to honor Percy's birthday, specifically at Percy's behest. Whenever Percy was involved in some scheme or other, she worried about Freddie. Adding Jameson to the mix only increased her worries.

She drew a slow breath and turned to hand Freddie his drink, deliberately curving her lips into an intimate smile to hide her thoughts. Now was not the time or place to appear to remonstrate her lover over his associations. If she had any hope of exerting influence on the direction the new Baron Stanhope's life was taking, she needed to play the role he re-

quired of her tonight—gracious hostess willing to
fade into the wallpaper to give him the chance to
shine with his friends.

Freddie's gaze locked with hers as their fingers
brushed. She could see him struggling between his interest for whatever Jameson intended to share and his
desire to keep her as close to him as possible. After all,
he believed he loved her, and this was the first time
they'd seen each other in over two weeks. Sympathy
collided with her worry and anger. She was probably
overreacting to the entire situation. There were too
many other things crowding her thoughts for her to
worry about one sanguine gentleman bent on insulting his host's mistress.

"If you gentlemen will excuse me, I need to check
on supper preparations now that most of the guests
have arrived." They awaited but two of the night's
gamesters, and her reason for withdrawing was legitimate enough at this point. "That should leave you
free to converse as you see fit."

"Of course." Freddie's grateful smile rewarded her
for her tact. She waved him to keep his seat as he appeared ready to rise.

"About time." Percy swallowed the last dregs from
his glass. His cheeks flushed red to match the tip of
his nose as the realization of what he'd just said struck
him. "Oh, my dear Mrs. Fitzgerald. I did not mean
you. I am just too eager to hear the end of Jameson's
frolics in the countryside. He is a master of the tease,
and I simply must gain release from his thrall."

"No offense taken, Mr. Masters. I entirely understand."

"Dare I hope that I have *you* in my thrall as well?"
Jameson raised his glass ever so slightly. His gaze did
a quick but thorough slide down the length of her
body and back as her position shielded his lascivious
interest from Freddie and Percy in their chairs.

He lingered over her breasts, and she regretted her decision to wear this gown. One of Freddie's favorites, it was a soft, rose watered silk, low cut in the bodice with a tiny froth of lace that fluttered with each breath. It managed to appear demure and risqué at the same time. Now it made her feel as though she were all but naked in front of this man she was beginning to heartily dislike.

"I'm afraid not." She attempted to keep her tone light despite the anger—laced with a touch of fear—arcing through her again. None of the men Freddie had brought to her home before had ever treated her with such avid interest or thinly veiled lack of respect. She prayed Freddie was not paying too close attention lest his evening be ruined.

"Oh, you are such a jester." Percy gushed. "Mrs. Fitzgerald is entirely devoted to our dear Fred . . . Stanhope, here."

"Of course she is." Jameson shifted his position as he turned his attention to the two men. "I've said it before, Stanhope. You are a lucky man."

"I could not agree more." Freddie beamed with pride as his gaze locked with Maura's before going back to his guests. He apparently had not been paying attention to the undercurrents in Jameson's conversation and attention to his hostess. She wished she could feel relieved, but it only added to her unease. He really was very naïve.

She kept a polite smile fixed to her face with effort as she turned and headed toward the pocket doors promising her escape.

She slid the doors open on their smooth, well-oiled runners, her mind already fixed on the details of the supper they were about to serve. The hour was late enough that most of Freddie's guests had completed their dinner or other obligations and made their way here for a night's entertainment. They'd begin with a

light supper followed by hours of whist, faro, ribald
stories, and drinking once the last invitees arrived—
Lord Longford, another schoolmate of Freddie and
Percy's, and one of his friends, whose name escaped
her.

She turned as she exited, closing the doors on her
company. As she spun to head to the kitchen she collided with a broad chest and strong shoulders cloaked
in dark, superfine wool and striped Marcella.

Her breath caught, dragging in the sensual warmth
of sun-kissed hawthorns in early May. For a moment
fraught with the man's effort to keep her from falling
flat on her face, she was held firmly by a pair of iron-
strong hands against a granite chest.

Despite being off balance she felt oddly safe. The
loud hammering of her heart in her ears and the sudden tight, tense awareness deep in her chest startled
her almost more than being thrown off center so unexpectedly. Deep inside her a primal awareness usually reserved for the bedchamber roared to life.

" . . . Lynch, Mrs. Fitzgerald."

Teresa's words from a few feet away in the foyer
barely registered as the man slid his hands down her
arms to grip her elbows just below the hem of her
long gloves. He shifted his weight ever so slightly and
put an inch of air between them.

She was still too close to him. All she could tell was
how very tall he was. Tall with dark, wavy hair. Green
eyes to steal a woman's soul without a second thought.
Her thoughts and supper plans scattered into meaningless bits. *Eyes of green to steal a woman's soul and hair
of midnight ebony*—weren't they the lyrics to a song her
mother used to sing?

"I beg your pardon." His voice was deep and mel-
low, tasting impossibly of distant green hills and ancient pride. The sound rushed along her nerve
endings like the fine brandy she'd just served the men

in the room behind her—soothing and intoxicating at the same time. She hadn't moved, but still she needed to catch her breath as if she'd just run the length of the street outside.

"Are you all right, lass?" His softly voiced question held intimacy, as though he too felt something of the overwhelming sensations coursing through her, as if this unexpected swell of profound connection was something neither of them would want anyone else to recognize.

"I'm . . . I'm fine, thank you." She blinked and struggled to remember who and where she was.

"I didn't realize there was anyone out here and I . . . I'm terribly sorry." Heat scorched her cheeks as she fumbled her way through this inarticulate apology.

"Mr. Lynch?" Was that the name Teresa had been attempting to announce just now?

"Indeed. Garrett Lynch, grateful for your hospitality, Mrs. Fitzgerald." He took her cue without batting an eyelash. "I am here at Lord Longford's invitation. I'm quite certain it is I who owe you an apology, since you can hardly have been aware of my presence in your foyer."

"Oh yes, Freddie mentioned you as someone Daniel . . . Lord Longford hoped would join us." She smiled, finding her emotional footing a little bit more as she mentally went over her guest list.

"Lord Longford is but a few minutes behind me. He is escorting his mother home from dinner at her sister's." He returned her smile, causing a devastating effect on the backs of her knees. Surely he was aware of the charm. If only she were a little less so.

She'd referred to Freddie by his given name just now, a faux pas even the rawest of debutantes would never make, although her visitor had the grace to let it go unremarked. Some hostess she was proving to

be, nearly mowing him down and then behaving
worse than a green girl.

What on earth was wrong with her? She'd been a
mistress for almost as long as she'd been a woman.
None of her three lovers had ever caused her to
waver, aside from the obvious, from the standards her
mother had instilled in her. Surely she could manage
one guest, no matter how attractive, without totally
losing her composure.

As if he knew her thoughts and wished to prove her
wrong, Mr. Lynch released her elbows at last, sliding
his hands lightly down her arms. His fingers lingered
against her wrists. A simple touch, yet somehow as intimate as if he made love to her right there in the
doorway.

She couldn't move from her place in front of him.
He remained much too close. His eyes smoldered as
they looked into hers. For the barest moment, she
drew in his scent again as her senses reeled.

"Fast, but steady." His voice spiraled heat through
her middle. He nodded, then squeezed her hands
gently and continued to hold them, lightly, softly, as
though he knew he shouldn't retain the contact but
couldn't quite give it up. "Very good."

"Yes." She couldn't have named what she was agree-
ing to.

"Missus?" Young and inexperienced, Teresa was still
hovering near the door where she'd been stationed to
take Gerald's place as the footman served her guests.

The realization of her maid's presence helped
bring Maura out of the intoxicating trance she
seemed to have fallen into just as Garrett Lynch finally released his hold of her hands.

"Yes, Teresa." She smiled and peeked around their
guest's massive shoulder to set the nervous maid at
ease. "Please check with Mrs. Kelly and Cook about

the preparations for supper. I believe we are shy but one of our company at this point."

"Yes, ma'am." Teresa bobbed a quick curtsey while managing an appreciative sideways glance at their new guest one last time before scurrying down the hallway. The admiration shining in the girl's face only confirmed Mrs. Kelly's policy regarding the female help and limiting their contact with the men entertained on nights such as these.

Maura couldn't really blame the girl, despite the fact that her last glance had been outside the boundaries. Garrett Lynch was a riveting sight. And now she was alone in the hallway with him. If only Mrs. Kelly's dictates could extend to her mistress as well. However, this was her home to order. Her life. She straightened her spine and favored him with her best smile. "Mr. Lynch, please come with me."

"My pleasure." The words were said very softly, respectfully. Either he didn't know the true nature of her liaison with Freddie or he didn't care. The thought struck home deep inside her, warm and comforting like an unexpected caress. For the second time this evening she was considering her position in society. This was much more pleasant than the last, but the realization disconcerted her just the same.

She slid the pocket doors open once more.

Percy slapped his knee as tears poured down his face. Freddie was squinting and laughing almost as hard. Jameson, as before, appeared bored and totally unaffected by either the jest he had just delivered or the humor enjoyed by his audience. Even the men clustered on the other side of the room stared. The sight disturbed her almost as much as Jameson's too-intimate perusal of her body.

It took several seconds, but the small cluster looked toward the doorway at last. That Jameson noticed first, then said nothing, failed to surprise her. She definitely didn't care for this man.

She favored Freddie with a broad smile. "My lord, Mr. Garrett Lynch has arrived."

She stepped aside to allow the tall, unsettlingly handsome man behind her to enter the room.

"Baron Stanhope, a true pleasure." Garrett bowed with an elegant bent knee in his doeskin pantaloons. "Lord Longford sends his regards. He is but a few minutes behind me."

He straightened. Still very tall, still darkly handsome with startling green eyes, but somehow not the same man who had held her so intimately and seemed to touch her soul with the simple brush of his fingers.

His gaze swept hers ever so briefly. Humor twinkled in the depths as though he shared some private jest.

"Ah, Lynch." This first greeting from Jameson. "It will be a pleasure to best you at faro again this evening."

"The pleasure will be all mine, Jameson." Mr. Lynch answered enigmatically. Apparently the two were already known to one another.

"Longford speaks very highly of you, Lynch. And your reputation as a gamester precedes you." Freddie stepped forward with his hand extended. "I hope you will find your evening enjoyable."

"Garrett Lynch." Percy pushed to his feet and wiped away the telltale tears as Freddie shook Garrett Lynch's hand. "I've seen you play. You are the very devil of a card player. When Stanhope here mentioned you might be joining us, I very nearly changed my mind about participating. But who could resist the opportunity to see two such elbow shakers at work? Jameson here is acquitted as being a knight of the elbow himself don't you know."

Percy bowed politely enough to take any sting out

of his words. Jameson, on the other hand, offered what could only be described as a smirk.

"Percival Masters." Freddie offered the late introduction.

"A pleasure, indeed, Masters. I'm sure we both look forward to our play later, if only so you can judge for yourself if either of us deserves such high-flying praise." Garrett Lynch offered a wry smile and a slight bow of his head.

"Do sit gentleman while we await Longford's arrival." Freddie invited. "There will be time enough for banter once we lay out our cards."

"Can my footman offer you some refreshment, Mr. Lynch?" Maura asked as the other men returned to their seats and the conversation from across the room swelled once more.

"Nothing for me at the moment, thank you. It promises to be a long night and I'd like to keep a clear head while I get acquainted with the company."

His refusal surprised her. Sobriety was hardly the order of the day at events such as this. But what disturbed her was the curious flip her stomach performed when he turned his attention to her as he answered.

The pocket doors slid open, and Teresa nodded to her. Their last guest had arrived and supper was about to be served. Good. The sooner this night was over, the better.

"This way, gentleman." Maura rang a small bell from the table behind her. She indicated the foyer. "It is time you share a light repast and then begin your evening's entertainment. I believe I will leave you to both so you may converse and enjoy yourselves more freely."

Freddie guided the other gentlemen out of the drawing room and called a greeting to Lord Longford in the foyer, where Gerald awaited the guests to usher them toward the dining salon. Most of the gentlemen took the opportunity to thank her for her hospitality as they exited. Jameson actually made an attempt to follow Percy's example and kiss her hand, then had the audacity to chuckle when she pretended not to understand his gesture and reached behind her to return the bell to its resting place. The thought of him touching her was too much, and he seemed to realize it.

Garrett Lynch on the other hand almost seemed to put on a mask and fade into the woodwork. One minute he'd been there, and the next he'd slipped out with the rest of the company.

Freddie paused at the doorway and slid his fingers between hers, linking their hands. "I'm sorry if you were overset earlier. Jameson's story really was too ribald for such delicate ears. I'm glad he thought to treat you with such respect, even if he phrased it badly."

He leaned down to brush his lips against hers. Sweet, thoughtful Freddie. Respect was the last thing on Harold Jameson's mind when it came to her. That much was clear to her, at least.

"I have a gift for you." He slid his hand into his pocket and drew out a small box. "Because I missed you and in gratitude for this night."

"There is no need . . . "

"A present is not given out of necessity, Maura." He interrupted. "Open it and tell me if they please you."

She took the box from him and found two perfectly matched, diamond drop earrings inside.

"Oh Freddie," was all she could manage. They were beautiful indeed, but it was at times like this she felt most like the scandalous member of the demimonde she had allowed herself to become. The shame of her fallen status always stung.

Her first instinct to tears was not the reaction he was looking for however, and she leaned into him and let him kiss her slowly. She would indeed miss him when she let him go. But he already cared for her much too deeply. The tender passion of his mouth on hers and the expense of this gift proved that much. His recognition that Jameson's shabby treatment had been awkward for her touched her more deeply than his gift.

The dangers of letting him stay with her too much longer were clear. Time might let him fully convince himself he loved her as much as he thought he did. Time might let her believe his love would be enough to sustain them both. Neither was true.

"I wish you could join us." His breath caressed her cheek. His hands on her arms as he held her close failed to produce the cascade of sensations she'd experience when Garrett Lynch had steadied her earlier.

"I'll be within easy reach," she promised him. "I'll be in my private salon while you enjoy your cards with your guests."

"And perhaps when they have departed you will show me how those earbobs look on you. I bought them because they reminded me of the stars in your eyes."

"Perhaps." Part of her melted, despite the odd hurt his gift had engendered. He hadn't meant to remind her of her status as his mistress. He'd been trying to pay her a compliment.

"Good. It will be too long of an evening without you." He kissed her again and sighed, releasing her with clear reluctance. "Why did you let me plan this evening so soon after my return to the city? We could be spending the time together engaged in much more pleasurable pursuits."

"Why? Because you asked it of me, my lord." She laughed to lighten the moment and stepped out into the foyer, bringing him with her. "And I am ever given to trying to please you. In all things."

"I'll hold you to that."

Chapter Three

After three hours of play, Garrett Lynch had indeed proven himself to possess the devil's own luck, just as Percy had said. His winnings tallied higher and higher according to Gerald, who reported periodically to Mrs. Kelly, who in turn imparted news of the party to its hostess.

As Lynch's winnings mounted, Jameson's mood darkened. And the brandy, port, and whiskey flowed more heavily. Tattle-mongering with the servants was not the usual bent of a hostess, but how else was she to monitor what was occurring within her walls without actually being present? Besides, she hardly ran her household, or her life, by conventional means.

While her guests had been deep in play, she had been deep into ledgers with her spectacles perched on the end of her nose and a hot pot of good Bohea tea at her side. If one or two of her investments came through, she should have her books in good enough order to remain independent for at least several years, albeit with some reduced circumstances. Freedom beckoned.

Voices in the foyer drew her away from the columns of figures at last. It was Freddie asking Gerald to summon Mr. Jameson's carriage.

"Aye, sir."

"These experiences are more liberating than you

could imagine," Jameson was speaking low and persuasively to someone as he waited.

Her stomach knotted. No good could come of this tête-à-tête. Was it eavesdropping when the conversation carried clearly into the room one had occupied for the bulk of the evening? She was certain the gentlemen did not realize she was only a few feet away with a cracked door between them—although the light spilling from the doorway should have provided a clue that she had not retired upstairs just yet.

"Far more, yet at the same time less, intimidating than stories that circulate," Jameson continued. "I am quite certain you would . . . enjoy the entertainments we could offer. Young men with certain appetites and excellent families are always welcome."

"Then it is as Percy said. You are a member of the Devil's Club?" Freddie spoke in a somewhat shocked tone.

A chill raced over her arms at the mention of the name.

"Others call it that." Jameson's offhand tones spoke again. "To us it is a rite of passage, a commitment of gentlemen."

Gentlemen! A second chill followed the first. She drew her silk shawl tighter over her shoulders

"A rite of passage," Percy sounded more than a little foxed. "I told you it was something like that, Stanhope, old man."

"Yes." Freddie did not seem convinced, but the very fact that he had suspected this man was somewhat unsavory and had allowed Percy to bring him here made Maura's stomach swirl. "But—"

"Have no fear, my lord. You'll only need to participate once to realize the chances our little society offers for freedom and invention—A place for men to truly engage in, and savor, the sexual fantasies a man is privy to in the deepest recesses of his soul. The sort of experimentation unwelcomed by one's wife, or even one's mistress, can be indulged with women who play the game to the hilt."

The nagging worry that had been her companion all evening in regard to Harold Jameson surged in a hot wash of concern and dismay. The lascivious temptations he alluded to would seem all too enticing to a young hellion like Percy Masters and perhaps even Freddie. No wonder Percy had been so intent on anything the man wanted to say. He'd no doubt hoped all evening the invitation she had just overheard would be forthcoming.

Oh Percy. She'd like nothing better than to shake that nodcock and give him a long lecture about what entailed proper behavior for a gentleman in his position and what did not.

"Well, I say old man, that is very decent of you," Percy gushed. "Wouldn't you say, Stanhope? Or perhaps I should say indecent." Percy laughed at his own sally.

"I really cannot desert my guests," Freddie protested.

"Perhaps we can continue the party at your club, Jameson," Percy prompted. "What say you?"

"Well," Jameson did not sound at all pleased by the suggestion. "Perhaps some of the gentlemen might be appropriate for an invitation. We must be discreet. Longford might prove acceptable and one or two others."

"I know just who to tap. Let me handle it for you."

It was time for her to intervene. She rattled the heavy brass handle on the salon door and swept into the foyer with an elaborate rustle of skirts and a startled look on her face. "I'm sorry, I had no idea anyone was out here. Are you leaving us so soon, Mr. Jameson?"

"Unfortunately, my dear." He favored her with a look that told her he saw right through her timely en-

trance. "Not only do I have that further engagement
I mentioned, but my pockets are quite to let thanks to
Lynch's savvy play."

"Not that this has not been the veriest of good
times—Jameson here may be spiriting some others of
your company away from you, dear Mrs. Fitzgerald.
I'll just nip back to the faro tables and see who might
be interested." Percy slid open the pocket doors and
slipped inside without noticing the look of consternation on Jameson's face.

Freddie moved to stand beside her. A look of relief
and admiration lit his eyes as he took her arm in his.

"If you have already spoken to my footman, your
carriage should be along momentarily, Mr. Jameson."

He lifted a brow at her. "Thank you, Mrs. Fitzgerald.
I appreciate your . . . attentions. I hope you will favor
me with future invitations, despite my inability to see
the night through. Just as I may endeavor to tempt
Stanhope here with a few invitations of my own. Perhaps the theatre? I would like to pursue my acquaintance with you both. You make a charming couple."

Certainly it was only Freddie's solid presence by her
side that restrained their guest from favoring her with
another of his long perusals designed to leave her
feeling naked and soiled. She suppressed the urge to
shiver under the cold promise in his words.

"Thank you. Either will be entirely up to His Lordship." She managed a pleasant but neutral tone with
effort. "Would you mind if I borrowed Lord Stanhope
for a moment? He'll be back to bid you farewell in a
thrice."

"How could I refuse such a softly worded request?"
Jameson bowed and stepped closer to the front door
even as she drew Freddie across and into the doorway
of her private salon.

"Is everything all right, Maura? I am surprised you
have not yet retired. You must be fatigued after all

your preparations." The concern in his voice was so
genuine, so appealing. As was the warmth in his eyes
after the hardness in Harold Jameson's.

She seized the small chance to keep him safe from
the other man's influence, if only for this time, and
broke her only rule in their relationship. "Stay with
me tonight."

Freddie froze. His gaze fixed hers in the space of a
single heartbeat. She couldn't help but smile at the ardent look on his face.

"Maura—"

"I hope you will understand if the baron joins us
this evening, Mrs. Fitzgerald." Jameson's invitation
drifted back toward them, brazenly repeating his en-
ticement for what was surely a night of debauchery in
her very presence.

Percy and two of the other young bucks emerged
from the card room.

"Wait here." Freddie squeezed her hand and
stepped out into the foyer once again

"I appreciate your invitation, Jameson, and I cannot
say I am not . . . intrigued. But I'm afraid I already
have plans."

"How disappointing, but not entirely surprising,"
Jameson intoned archly.

"And Percy, my friend, did you not promise to help
me host this night of frivolity organized in your
honor? How can you desert me?"

Maura peeked discreetly around the door in time
to see Percy's crestfallen expression and Jameson's casual shrug.

"Perhaps the offer will be repeated at another time.
Shall we be off then gentlemen?" Harold Jameson
ushered Lord Longford and his other pirated guest
out the door Gerald held open.

Tension sluiced from Maura as he left, even as she
worried about Freddie's other two friends. At least

Freddie had displayed enough sense to pull Percy back. She stepped up to join Freddie and his remaining guest.

Percy swayed in the gaslight for a moment as if trying to grasp what had just happened, rather like a child who had a promised treat snatched away. He obviously had imbibed too freely, even with watered drinks, to make any rational decision. After a moment more of swaying, he shrugged and put his arm around Freddie's shoulder. "Come on, my lord. Once more into the breach. This chap Lynch's won most of my pin money for this quarter. I'd like a chance to earn it back from him."

"As you wish, my friend. One more round."

As they turned back into the gameroom, Freddie leaned down toward Maura. "You meant what you said?"

"Aye, my lord." She breathed the words to him, happy to have rescued him from Harold Jameson's pursuits this time at least, and relieved despite herself that this small drama had succeeded in pulling her thoughts away from the dangerous path they trod while she looked through her ledgers.

Dangerous was definitely one way to consider Garrett Lynch despite his appealing demeanor. So like the hawthorns of which he reminded her. Familiar, green, and inviting, but beware the thorns that lurked beneath. She had enough to handle right now, as she tried to rearrange her life and finances so that she could provide for those she loved, for those who depended on her, and yet establish herself independently. She was almost there. Almost free.

There was no room for yet another man in her life, especially one who could see her only in the role she had established for herself—a rich man's pastime. *Eyes of green to steal a woman's soul and hair of midnight ebony*, not withstanding. There was no place in her life or future for Garrett Lynch or any of his kind. When she and Freddie parted, she had no intention of being a kept mistress ever again.

She needed to hold on to Freddie's affections for just a little while longer, if only to keep him safe from Jameson's machinations. She hoped the man would grow bored and move on to likelier targets in whatever game he played.

Guilt twinged. Having Stanhope stay the night would no doubt offer him hopes along lines she knew were doomed. Still, he was surely safer occupied in ardent pursuit of her than trailing after things that might get him into far worse trouble.

"I'll await you in my chamber," she promised.

"Then it shall be a very short round."

Footsteps sounded on the grand staircase even as Garrett maintained his careless posture sprawled on Mrs. Fitzgerald's dainty, satin-tufted settee. He dare not react lest he alert the footman set to keep an eye on him.

His back ached, and he longed for a good stretch and a hot cup of coffee. Both would have to wait. Mrs. Fitzgerald's manservant had spent most of the night dozing on a stool opposite the door. Long practice and his own current deception had proven such appearances often misleading. Still, if this fellow was merely posing in his apparent slumbers, he had proven himself eminently believable and as such could be a useful recruit at some later date.

The descending steps were light, soft, and quick. Definitely not the tread of Stanhope's dress boots or the jingling shuffle of the housekeeper and her keys. Perhaps one of the upper maids dared flout the practice of most well-ordered households by utilizing the main stairs in favor of less direct service steps to hasten the completion of whatever errand she was about? The one who greeted him at the door last night had been a pretty little package.

Slitting his eyes open a fraction, he peered toward the partially open doorway. A shift in the footman's posture as his chin rose and his shoulders straightened signaled not only his alertness but either that he hoped to impress the maid in question or that the person descending to the foyer was the portly man's employer.

A distant clock had chimed the hour just a short time ago. The earliness of the descent surprised Garrett as much as the notion his unknowing hostess might be up and about her business when her *business,* in the form of her patron, presumably still lay abed upstairs.

He had a hard time conceiving how any man would allow such a woman loose from his bed any sooner than absolutely necessary. Images of Maura Fitzgerald's wide gray eyes, long dark hair, and enticingly genuine smile hovered in his thoughts.

The kind of smile to warm the darkest corners of a man's soul. The oddly romantic thought that sizzled through him when he caught her in the doorway last night still disconcerted him. If he had any soul left, it was hardly that of a romantic, let alone where another man's nesting grounds were concerned.

Still, the creamy white skin promised by the neckline of her gown last night and the memory of her in his arms, smelling of spring roses and fitting against him so perfectly, had haunted him through the dark of a night spent in her utterly feminine yet unfrilly private salon—a contradiction in design matching the woman decorating the premises.

Most men's mistresses flaunted the jewels and wealth showered on them. Her attire last evening had been alluring but eminently tasteful. The rooms she'd

opened for the card party were well appointed but
had more the feeling of a family home than a sensual
love nest. She wore scant makeup and arranged her
hair in an easy manner that bespoke a country picnic
rather than a night of entertainment.

Stanhope's mistress was indeed a sweet package of
contradictions, worth puzzling over under other circumstances. He could well understand the attraction
for Stanhope; not for the first time since entering the
door of this house, he felt a pang of envy for the
baron. But not enough to ignore the direct request of
the young man's grandfather to separate him from
this woman.

"Good morning, Gerald."

While Mrs. Fitzgerald's dulcet greeting confirmed
one set of his assumptions, it still surprised him that
any man who took Maura Fitzgerald to bed would let
a prize like her ever leave it, let alone after such a
short night. Perhaps Stanhope was not so enamored
of her as he let on, despite the mooncalf looks he'd
given her whenever she was in the room last night.

"Good morning, ma'am," the footman answered as
he stood up stiffly.

"You had a late night last night, Gerald. Why are
you not still abed?" Garrett's attention sharpened as
she continued. She spoke more like a concerned
friend than an employer. "I thought Mrs. Kelly instructed all of you to take this morning off and let the
temporary help handle the cleanup?"

"I asked him ta stay on." Mrs. Kelly, the housekeeper,
jingled into the foyer from the direction of the back
hall. "One of yer guests had the devil's own luck last
night." She made a small sound of disapproval. "He felt
unsafe leaving with his winnings in the darkness. Said
the city was rife with footpads and lowlifes and he had
need of his pot to stave off creditors."

"Really?"

"*His Lordship* said it would be all right." Disapproval rippled through the heavyset woman's voice as she spoke to her employer far more familiarly than tolerated in most households, disapproval Garrett had received last night when this formidable woman had confronted the fact that he intended to stay the night. She probably thought he planned to make off with the silver service after ransacking the butler's pantry. Only Stanhope's insistence that she allow him to stay when the other stragglers left had held any sway.

He'd stood his ground or, more accurately, purposefully lurched his way through his point with Stanhope's unwittingly generous support to give her the impression he was as foxed as his host. Having sent Daniel off to track whatever mischief Jameson and his cronies were plotting last night, he'd be pressed to perform the shadow work on Stanhope on his own until he could get in touch with some relief. He'd gotten the distinct impression Jameson would not have done much if he'd made up part of the company who left earlier in the evening. Jameson seemed to prefer younger, more gullible pockets to pick.

"Oh dear. I suppose safeguarding large winnings is sensible, although I do hope he's gone before anyone on the street is out and about enough to notice him leaving. I cannot have them wondering at his presence." Mrs. Fitzgerald's worry piqued Garrett's interest. Imagine a mistress who worried what the neighbors thought.

Through his barely open eyes, Garrett could make out little beyond a few shadows in the foyer. It took all his willpower to remain casually draped on the delicate furniture when every part of him strained to listen to the conversation on the other side of the door.

Maura Fitzgerald intrigued him. She had the look of an innocent, the lifestyle of a jade. She'd played the discreet hostess last night, greeting her guests then withdrawing so the men could pursue their brandy, cigars, and play unrestrained. Then she'd shown up at just the right moment to prevent Stanhope from leaving with Jameson. There was definitely more to her than the pleasing exterior she presented to the world.

Now here she was, up and about her day when most mistresses, or even wives, would be resting on their laurels after putting themselves out so thoroughly. What was she about?

"If ye ask me, which ye needn't, sense had nothing ta do with it." The housekeeper's keys jingled. "He was too far into his cups to know the way home."

"See if you can get him to leave as soon as possible. I'm likely to have my hands full enough if anyone remarks on Freddie . . . His Lordship's departure without having to deal with a second gentleman's overnight stay."

"Don't fret, I'll see to it yer guest's on his way before His Lordship stirs, even. He'd jest better not have put his dandified pumps all over yer new brocade, that's all I can say."

"Who is this impromptu guest?" Mrs. Fitzgerald sighed. "And which one of the guest rooms did you allot him?"

"That Mr. Lynch." More disapproval etched Mrs. Kelly's tone. "Handsome as the day is long, but there's more ta him than meets the eye, if ye ask me, which ye didn't. He wouldn't even consent ta take one of the guest chambers . . ."

The housekeeper sounded as thoroughly scandalized at this impropriety now as she had last night. He'd wanted an excuse to spend a few more sheltered hours awaiting young Stanhope's departure inside the household rather than lurking in the bushes, but a bedchamber limited his options for a quiet exit on the lad's heels so he'd insisted on not disaccommodating anyone by having a chamber aired.

". . . said he'd be perfectly all right waiting ta slip out come daylight. Well, daylight's come and he's still here." That seemed to make his imposition all the worse. "I set Gerald here ta keep an eye on him."

"Exactly where is Mr. Lynch?" Amusement softened Maura Fitzgerald's question.

"He's in yer private salon."

This elicited a long-drawn-out sigh from Mrs. Fitzgerald. "Gerald, would you see if my hackney has arrived? I need to be on my way early this morning."

"Yes, madam."

The footman clumped across the marbled foyer, and the door clicked open.

"Wait until I've been gone a good five minutes or so and then send Gerald in to wake Mr. Lynch."

Her voice was nearer. Garrett closed his eyes before he got more than a glimpse of her silhouetted in the sunlight spilling through the foyer. He swallowed his disappointment and imagined the veriest hint of roses wafted to him through the doorway. "If need be, send Gerald with him if he is still concerned about his safety."

"Yes, ma'am." The housekeeper also sounded closer. "And what about His Lordship? Surely he'll be wondering where ye are when he rouses."

Another sigh. "I left him a note. Make sure Cook has plenty of coffee ready when he rings. I'll speak to him about inviting guests to stay in my home. The neighbors barely tolerate my presence here as it is without giving the appearance I am setting up a bawdy house. This is not the sort of neighborhood that suffers my sort of circumstances lightly."

"Damned hypocrites, the lot." Mrs. Kelly snorted. "If ye ask me—"

"Which I didn't," Maura finished with a laughing fa-

miliarity that made Garrett wonder anew at the contradictions that seemed to define this woman. "This
house suits me. And a move right now would be in-
convenient, don't you think?"

"As ye wish." Mrs. Kelly sounded skeptical. "I'll fetch
yer potion and ye can be off."

"There's no need for the potion this morning . . ."

Garrett wondered what sort of potion she required.
Was she ill? Was she taking some kind of restorative
that would account for her ability to entertain guests
both below and above stairs all night and still arise for
an early morning outing?

". . . Lord Stanhope barely got his boots off before
he was snoring," she continued. "Mr. Lynch is not the
only one who was in his cups by the end of last
evening. I won't be a bit surprised if I find Mr. Masters
curled under a bush in the front lawn."

"That's fer sure." The housekeeper snorted. "Even
the colonel's officers could not swill so much in one
sitting as those so-called gentlemen last night."

Their voices moved away from the doorway. "Could
you send something calming over for the new girl
they brought in the other night?" Garrett had to
strain to hear Mrs. Fitzgerald's soft tones. His nerves
were suddenly taut; all concerns over maintaining his
pose of sleeping guest fled. "She's still so frightened.
Anytime a man approaches her, she screams hysteri-
cally."

"Which surely upsets yer other customers."

"Not to mention . . ."

He lost the rest of the conversation as the front
door opened. Her hackney must have arrived, just
when the discussion had turned to matters of greater
interest.

What on earth compelled Lord Stanhope's mistress
to leave so early in the morning, and what was this
about a frightened girl? And customers? He could not

think of any legitimate connection, and the illicit ones were too numerous and discordant for him to recognize in the gracious hostess of last night's festivities.

There was definitely more to Maura Fitzgerald than her ever-so-appealing outer shell allowed the casual observer to see—something he dared not trust when placed beside all the other questions regarding her present circumstances and future plans. Either she was a consummate actress or he was very much maligning her in believing her the worst of jezebels.

The sooner he got the earl's grandson out of Maura's clutches the better. No matter that she had *the kind of smile to warm the darkest corners of a man's soul.* The fires of Hell were reported to be quite hot as well.

He leveraged himself off the settee and tugged his jacket and waistcoat into place. Emerging from the dimly lit salon, he blinked in the blazing light in the foyer as the housekeeper and footman spoke quietly by the open door. A haunting whiff of roses lingered in the air. Despite himself, Garrett's gut twisted with a sense of loss that he had not caught a single true glimpse of Maura Fitzgerald's trim figure, her gray eyes, or especially her smile.

"Well, sir, Mr. Lynch. I see ye've roused yerself." Mrs. Kelly stepped forward with the footman on her heels. "Can Gerald fetch ye a cuppa coffee?"

"Thank you, no. I'll take my hat. I believe it's past time I seek a change of clothes and the company of my banker." He patted his pocket. "Please thank your employers for their extended hospitality."

"I'll convey your gratitude to Mrs. Fitzgerald once she's arisen, sir." The housekeeper barely slid her eyes away as she lied through her teeth. "Would ye like Gerald here ta escort ye home?"

"I believe I shall be safe enough now the sun has risen. Thank you, though." He accepted his hat from the footman and followed the man to the door.

Chapter Four

There was no sign of a hackney as Garrett descended the steps to the quiet residential street a block in from bustling Baggot Street. Thankfully there was not much other activity either. No one to notice a gentleman exiting the house and then lurking in the bushes to await Baron Stanhope's departure. No one to remark on any of the doings at the neat town house he'd just left.

Maura Fitzgerald had made good her escape, not that he had really expected otherwise. What hysterical young woman was she so interested in calming? What customers concerned her? How was Stanhope involved, if at all? All questions he would have to wait to answer. As soon as he could manage, he'd have to free up a man to check on the background and activities of Mrs. Maura Fitzgerald. That much was clear. That much irritated him out of measure.

The neighbors barely tolerate my presence here as is . . . her worry echoed. Although why that should matter to him escaped him at this point. Still, he checked again.

A maid laden with a basket of fresh fruit scurried down one side of the cobbles. The footman at one of the establishments already polished the marble steps. At another, a groom tried calming a prime gelding awaiting an early morning ride. And the smell of roses wafted from the trellis of the house next door.

From one ornate Georgian doorway to another, the homes on this street bespoke genteel respectability.

Stanhope's mistress was right: this was hardly the usual neighborhood where Dublin's gentlemen kept their paramours. The soft rendition of a redstart echoed from the bushes covering the entrance to an alley across the way. Garrett hid a smile and shook his head. Good thing most citizens would not recognize the call of birds that seldom ventured into the city.

"Daniel sent word ye might need some relief." Dressed in a bricklayer's apron and cap, Seamus brushed sand across the bricks just inside the shadows cast by the houses looming on either side of him.

"Good man. Did you see a woman emerge from the house a few minutes before me?"

"Aye." Seamus nodded. "A real trim looker that one. Told the driver ta take her ta Shoe Lane."

"How odd."

And close to home. Mulligan's Pub House was one of the Green Dragon's favorite meeting spots, as Seamus well knew. The warning bells surrounding Maura Fitzgerald rang loud and clear. His interest in the nature of her early morning errand had grown from mere curiosity, to unease, to true alarm.

Now the question was, should he send Seamus, who'd gotten a better look at her turnout this morning and who would have far less explaining to do if she spotted him, or go himself?

"Describe her outfit." All of his men were experts at noting key details.

"The young woman had on a deep gray barouche coat with three rows of black trim on the bottom hem. Similar gray serge skirt. Gypsy hat tied with a black ribbon. Would she be Mrs. Fitzgerald's abigail?"

"No, that would be the lady in question herself." The one with the smile to warm a man's soul. Or would she consider using it on a hackney driver as a waste?

Seamus cocked an eyebrow as if he heard not only Garrett's answer but also his inner thoughts. While he kept his focus on the simple task he performed, strengthening the brick alleyway, Garrett knew his man was already thinking a half-dozen moves ahead. Seamus was a champion chess player.

"Can you keep yourself occupied here long enough to make sure Stanhope returns to his lodgings from here? Or see if he meets up with anyone?"

"Aye." Seamus nodded. He sprinkled more sand on the bricks and continued sweeping. "I should be able ta stay here right enough. With any luck the households on either side will think the other hired me. If worse comes to worse I'll lay the cost at the Lord Mayor's feet."

"Good." There wasn't one of Garrett's men who was not a master at blending into the city backgrounds. Each had proven himself time and again. "I'll see if I can trace Mrs. Fitzgerald's movements, then catch up with Daniel and see what Jameson's game was last night. Shall we all meet for a pint at The Brazen Head? Usual time."

Seamus nodded. "We certainly have our trenchers full with Sean away."

"That we do." Garrett turned to leave.

"My cousin works at Greer's two doors up from Mulligan's, on the corner. If she alights anywhere in the neighborhood, he'll know. Michael's got quite an eye fer the ladies."

Garrett flipped Seamus a half crown as if giving him a tip, lest anyone noted the strange gentleman talking to the tradesman. He made his way through the streets and alleys to the quays along the Liffey until he reached the Tara Street Baths around the corner from Shoe Lane.

The sky overhead was gray with smoke and clouds. The street crowds, growing with the city's inhabitants, had shifted from cartmen, servants, and even the ambitious gentleman of a business or two heading about their day to dockworkers, seamen, and shopgirls. Maura Fitzgerald's early morning errand to this end of town, with its twisting alleys and warren of little-known shops, seemed all the more mysterious. Or meaningless.

He thought of Seamus's observation. Full trencher indeed. Sean and Liam had yet to report any progress on the admiral's missing daughter, Rourke was needed at his father's stronghold in Galway, the wolves circling the High Lord's latest heir had yet to bare their teeth, and even without their menace to Stanhope, Jameson's crowd gave all the indications of being up to no good in general.

His certainty that Jameson and his cronies were connected to the latest rash of Orangemen's activity in the countryside grew with each new report of Jameson's inroads into the underside of Dublin even as he maneuvered himself through the ranks of the elite. Garrett's men and their network of contacts were stretched to their limits trying to track all these new lines of interest, notwithstanding their usual activities in trying to mitigate the supposedly repealed Catholic suppressions as they played out in Dublin's environs.

So what am I doing trailing a slip of a lass with stone gray eyes and a smile to stop a man's heart through the streets of Dublin? Stanhope was certainly part of the answer, but not quite all. Something about Maura Fitzgerald had his senses on the alert. Something beyond her charms.

Although he had more than enough to occupy his time without taking on the baffling behavior of Stanhope's mistress, he hadn't come this far as the Green Dragon without paying attention to nagging details.

Years before, his tutor had often remonstrated that the devil was in the details, and the years had proven the old goat right more often than even his lofty self-opinion could have guessed.

Garrett strolled the two blocks of Shoe Lane past Mulligan's and entered Greer and Son, a saddle and harness shop, half-expecting to see His Lordship's mistress shopping for a gift for her patron. Expecting, or was that hoping?

"Can I be of service ta ye, sir?" A wiry man with a long leather apron stood up from a workbench situated near the front of the shop. He put his punch and hammer aside, wiped his hands on his apron, and stepped forward.

The shop had the comfortable scent of oil-worked leather. Under other circumstances, Garrett would have liked nothing better than to peruse the wares hanging from hooks in the wood beams overhead or resting on railings that ranged across the small shop. But the location of the craftman's bench afforded him the best of the light filtering in from his mullioned windows along with the view from them and his open shop door.

"My friend Seamus sent me here." Garrett extended his hand. "Said you tooled the finest saddles this side of the island. His cousin Michael works for you."

"That would be me, sir. I'm Michael Greer." The man wrung Garrett's hand with his own leathery fist as he beamed at Garrett. "Though why ye'd listen ta the likes Seamus Granger is beyond me. He's the biggest liar and scoundrel ever come out of County Kildare. Save meself, I suppose."

Garrett shook his head as they both laughed. "So you don't sell the finest saddles?"

"Oh no, that we do. We craft the finest saddles and harnesses in the whole of the island, truth be told."

Michael chuckled at his own joke. "The Greers and Grangers have been working with Irish horses and their trappings since the days of the High King. I knows me business right enough. So does Seamus. How may I be of service ta ye, sir?"

"Today, I'm looking for a bit of information." He reached in his pocket and pulled out one of the sovereigns he'd won last night. "A lady gave the lane as her destination to a hackney driver earlier this morning. She would have arrived within the last half hour or so. She's a young woman, dressed in dark gray."

"A young lady, ye said? Dressed in gray?" The man wrinkled his brow for a moment, even as he waved away the coin Garrett offered. "And Seamus sent ye?"

Garrett nodded as the man contemplated his answer.

"I'll take that ta mean yer intentions is honorable, sir. 'Cause the woman I'm thinking ye seek is a regular angel and I'd hate ta be the cause of any worry fer her."

"I mean the lady no harm." The leather merchant's caution surprised Garrett more because he recognized the urge to protect Maura Fitzgerald. Despite the suspicions her activities aroused, there was a part of him that felt willing to do almost anything to keep the light of laughter in the depths of her eyes and the smile on her lips.

"Well now, that would most likely be Mrs. Eagan, proprietress of Eagan's Drapers." The man nodded toward the street. "Three doors down on Hawkins Street. Next ta the wine shop. She was a tad early this morning, but she comes by hackney near every day."

"Eagan? A draper's?" What use would Maura Fitzgerald have for a calming potion at a draper's? From the elegant charm of her home's reception room, she did not appear to have the sort of taste that would send a fabric and household goods merchant into fits.

So the woman Greer described was almost certainly not the woman he sought after all. Had Maura Fitzgerald changed her mind regarding her destination or had she been aware she was being watched and deliberately misled any observer. A hysterical girl, customers and evasion. Could her behavior be any more suspicious?

"You're sure the name is Eagan?" he asked.

"Aye. Came here from Meath after her husband's death and opened a shop and apprentice program." Now that he'd decided to trust Garrett, Seamus's cousin proved a fountain of information. "Keeps a real neat shop and even gave my wife a nice discount on some table linens last winter on account of us being practically neighbors."

The widow Eagan could not possibly be Maura Fitzgerald. Still Mrs. Eagan's former home in County Meath begged further consideration given a slender connection to the missing Jane Fuller. Garrett worked to keep his concern from showing on his face as he thanked Greer and sauntered casually toward Hawkins Street.

He passed a whitewashed storefront with a simple, carved, wooden sign proclaiming it as Eagan's Drapers. On one side was a bakery, and beyond was a wine merchant. If he could have thought of a single reason to go inside and confront the owner of the drapery, he would have done so.

He most certainly would look out of place in a drapers, especially still dressed in his evening wear. He might have pulled off a coincidental meeting in a saddle shop, but however would he explain his presence in a draper's?

On the off chance that Mrs. Eagan was not another name for Mrs. Fitzgerald, he would wait until he had a chance to confirm or refute his suspicions. Or find out what kind of game she was playing. But in the grand scheme of things he had to place time and manpower on priorities and deviling as she might be. Maura Fitzgerald was not yet one, even with her connection to Stanhope.

He rubbed his chin. It was well past time he returned to his lodgings to bathe and dress for the day ahead. He hoped there'd be some word from Sean regarding his search for Jane Fuller and Daniel on the late-night exploits he'd shared last night after leaving the card party. Following their meeting at The Brazen Head, he'd set Seamus to scouting out Eagan's under cover of his cousin's shop and try to figure out how best to extricate Stanhope from his mistress's grip without completely stripping the lad of his manhood.

"Here ye go, Mrs. Eagan. A nice cuppa tea will help put ye ta rights."

Mrs. Polhaven bustled into Maura's office carrying a steaming kettle in one hand and a dainty blue cup and saucer in the other. Her gray-sprinkled curls bounced below her lace-trimmed hat, and a broad grin creased plump cheeks even as a pair of discerning blue eyes fixed on her employer.

Maura smiled in return as she pushed back from the long oak table that served as her desk. She wasn't getting much of anywhere looking at the list of fabric purchases Silas Polhaven had prepared for her approval. Too many other thoughts crowded her mind—Freddie, finances, and a surprisingly persistent set of green eyes. A cup of tea might prove just the thing to clear the cobwebs from her attic.

"You spoil me, Mrs. Polhaven. You have your hands full enough with the girls. You know I am perfectly capable of fetching my own tea."

"Course ye are." Katherine Polhaven nodded as she set the cup and saucer down on the far edge of the table and filled it. "But it doesn't cost me anything ta show ye a little kindness now and again after all ye've done fer Mr. Polhaven and me. Not ta mention my sister and my girl."

"Well thank you. I must admit I have been a little overset these past few days. I cannot seem to concentrate." And she hadn't been sleeping well either. Those eyes, and the kindness in Garrett Lynch's voice, haunted her with surprising depth. Not to mention the sensations that seemed to course through her anew with the thought of his hands on her arms, of being held so close and feeling so safe in the embrace of a stranger.

She was hardly some innocent chit to be mooning over a man she had met but once. She refused to count the fleeting glimpse of a man she'd caught walking past the shop windows the morning after their encounter. It was too impossible. Too schoolgirlish.

She'd banished the nosegay he'd sent to thank her for her hospitality to the back of the others from her guests, almost out of sight, although she couldn't quite bring herself to instruct Teresa to toss them into the ash can.

She accepted the teacup from the older woman and took a tentative sip of its savory contents, trying to order her thoughts.

"Ye have a lot on yer mind. Especially as ye try ta handle it all on yer own."

"Nonsense." Maura shook her head in denial. "I have you to help with the girls. Dorothy runs my house and Mr. Polhaven the store."

She had help and advisors for every aspect of her life save the one for which she really needed guidance. The well-meaning sisters helped her run her house and her school, but there was no one she could turn to for counsel on her private affairs. No guide for wayward mistresses looking to avoid both heartbreak and loneliness.

The card party she'd hosted for Freddie two nights ago had shown her how ready she was to leave that part of her life behind her, but at the same time such bad elements as Harold Jameson ready to pounce on the new Baron Stanhope's naïveté left her reluctant to break all ties with him, as though she alone could steer Freddie through all the pitfalls life had to offer.

She'd managed to avoid any further intimacies with Freddie since before his trip to his grandfather's. Besides being too floored to do more than snore against the pillows their first time back together, he'd escorted his aunt to a musicale evening the first night after the party. She'd pleaded her monthly indisposition when he'd come to supper last night.

He'd stayed late into the evening playing chess with her by the fire. He'd been so charming as he entertained her with stories about his grandfather she'd almost relented a second time and let him stay the night. But in the end, common sense, and her "indisposition," prevailed. She'd sent him on his way just before he launched into his latest marriage proposal.

Her need for companionship could not be allowed to drag him down. She cared too much to let that happen. She'd always cared unwisely, and that fault had set her feet on this path in the first place.

"Ye don't fool me—"

Maura started and nearly sloshed tea into her saucer. She'd forgotten Katherine Polhaven was still in the room. Yet, there she stood, one hand still gripping the kettle and the other on her hip.

"—nor any of us. Dorothy is already beside herself because ye've hardly eaten a bite in three days."

Katherine glanced about and then put the kettle down on a tile holding correspondence that Maura usually used for just that same purpose. She folded her hands across her apron and fixed a knowing look on Maura. "Ye do know ye gave Mr. Polhaven permission yesterday to purchase whatever he recommends from the list ye've been staring at this past hour or more, don't ye?"

Heat crept over Maura's cheeks. She was more scattered than she realized. Dorothy Kelly had fussed at her in much the same manner only a few hours before. Once she had a plan she'd feel better. Once she could see her way clear in a way that would not harm Freddie. She owed him that much at least. "You and your sister worry about me too much."

"Well, with my Angela settled into her new life in America thanks ta ye, we have the luxury of giving ye the benefit of our attention."

Maura bit back the observation that having both of their eyes fixed on her hardly felt like a benefit. She'd been too alone and too vulnerable when she'd arrived in Dublin not to value their loyalty and concern.

"How is Angela?" Perhaps she could divert Katherine's attention. Changing the direction of your life seemed much more difficult under close scrutiny, even from well-meaning friends. "Did you get another letter?"

"Aye." Katherine's answer was accompanied by a genuine grin. As usual, mention of her daughter successfully distracted her. There'd be no such relief when she returned home to Dorothy Kelly, but that was hours from now and she'd worry about answering to her housekeeper then.

"She's settled into her job with that new family in New York." Katherine beamed her satisfaction. "With three daughters to marry off in the next few years and more ta come down the road, she has enough work to need an assistant. And the family even lets our granddaughter sit in on the tutor's lessons for their younger children."

Hearing how well Angela fared always warmed Maura and firmed her convictions the work she did was worth the other part of her life. Angela had been Maura's first student, the first young woman Maura had been able to help after the poor girl had been turned out of her position without a recommendation when the mistress of the house found out her eldest son had impregnated her.

Angela had sought shelter with her aunt Dorothy and in turn given new meaning to Maura's own life and the choices she'd made. Angela's success at starting her life over with a self-supporting skill as a seamstress had inspired Maura to purchase the draper's shop and the house on the other end of the courtyard as a haven for girls in service whose employers had taken advantage of them.

The Polhavens gave up their dry goods store to come and help with the project. Part of their work involved establishing the young women in new positions far away from the shame that would attach to them if their pasts as the cast-off playthings of the nobility were ever revealed. Angela had chosen to accept placement in America as a widowed mother. The swell of pride on Katherine's face was surely reflected on Maura's right now.

"I'm so glad for her. And how is the young woman who came to us last week. Has she spoken to anyone yet? Did Dorothy's calming potion help her?"

"Nay, poor thing." Katherine sighed, her shoulders doing a slow rise and fall and her eyes taking on a hint of mist. "She jest sits and stares most time. Unless of course she catches sight of Mr. Polhaven or the doctor. Then she screams fer hours. The echoes can still be heard clear into the shop even though we moved her to the backmost bedroom. She was ill used, that's all I know."

"Is there anything else we can do for her? Anything she needs?"

"Jest time." Katherine shook her head. "The doctor said it might be good to get her outside fer a bit of fresh air. So one of the other girls and I tried the courtyard, but she went rigid when she saw the sunlight yesterday afternoon."

Maura stood and moved over to the window that overlooked the courtyard. She pulled back the lace undercurtains. There was grass and a nice, tall oak tree to provide shade. A small natural haven in the midst of the city. Plenty of room and a peaceful spot for the elocution exercises she had planned for today. "Perhaps I could hold lessons outdoors and you could try again while the rest of the girls are outside, too. That might make her feel safer."

"Very good, ma'am." Mrs. Polhaven stood and picked up her kettle. "I'll tell the girls ta assemble in the courtyard directly after luncheon. They can bring their chairs."

"And the children, too," Maura added. "Perhaps Cook could supply some lemonade and sweetcakes. We'll make it a party. No one is threatened by a party or children."

"No one save their natural fathers." Katherine sniffed her disapproval. About half the girls in residence at the Eagan School had bastard children by their former employers. "Sounds like a fine party and jest the thing that may coax poor little Mary out of her waking nightmare."

"Mary?" That was the name of Katherine's granddaughter in New York.

"Aye, I couldn't keep calling her 'poor wee thing' so I named her after my own *garinion*. I'd like ta think if something happened to Angela's girl there in America, someone would take her in and be kind, too."

"I think that's a good name for our newest student. I'll look forward to seeing her after lunch." Maura blew a stray wisp of hair from in front of her eyes. "Until then I'd best move on from Mr. Polhaven's list to something more productive."

"And I'd best get back ta the school and make sure the girls are ready fer their afternoon." Katherine closed the door behind her as she went about her duties.

Maura sat back at her table and picked up the order list again: bolts of damask and silk, linen and wools, all listed in orderly rows. Already approved. If only her own life could be so simple and orderly. As simple as it had been before she'd stepped outside the bounds of society, before she'd taken her position in the colonel's household, before her Da had passed away.

"I am certain I can find the way myself."

A commotion on the steps leading from the shop below her office broke her reverie. An irate customer? Not many got by Silas Polhaven. Not many had need to. The shop part of this enterprise seldom gave her pause thanks to his honest dealings with their customers and suppliers. She picked up her cup of tea for a bracing swallow before dealing with whatever was about to occur.

"My business is with the shop's owner." The man's voice seemed oddly familiar, but she could not place him from among the local tradesmen or fabric merchants she dealt with from time to time when Silas Polhaven thought it prudent.

"Really, your shopgirl said I might find her at the top of these steps."

The next thing Maura knew, her office door swung open and the arresting face that had haunted her since the card party peeked in at her. Garrett Lynch.

"Mrs. Eagan?"

For the first time since opening her school, her two

worlds collided. The shock of it froze her in place as she gazed up into dark green eyes flashing an angry contradiction to the pleasant tone he employed.

"Mrs. Eagan? If I might have a moment of your time, I have an offer for you."

Chapter Five

"Sir, sir." The elderly gentleman peered at Garrett over tall stacks of colored fabric puffed high along the table in front of him. "May I help you?"

"I'm here to see Mrs. Eagan." Garrett answered without stopping as he wove his way between a half-dozen tables similarly stacked and headed toward the stairs at the back of the shop. Fueling his speed was the realization that a bit of his heart yet held on to the hope his men and the information they had gathered had been wrong—that the woman he'd observed the other night had been just what she'd seemed, genuinely attached to Stanhope and not a practiced deceiver who could conduct herself in this manner. He would know for certain in a moment.

"Mrs. Eagan? Oh, sir, ye canna interrupt her without an appointment." The older man's voice trailed off in unhappy protest as Garrett ignored him and took the steps two at a time.

Seamus's time spent sweet-talking one of the shopgirls yesterday to learn the routine and who worked in what area at Eagan's Draper Shop would provide Garrett the element of surprise and a little privacy. Confronting her alone in her office was preferable to accosting her on the street or within the bosom of her home, whatever way the conversation led. If it turned out truly to be her.

Right up until the moment he opened the door and saw her behind the long table piled with ledgers and papers, calmly sipping tea, Garrett hadn't realized how very much he'd hoped Seamus Granger had been wrong. The woman posing as Mrs. Maureen Eagan, widow, late of County Meath, was indeed Maura Fitzgerald, current mistress of Frederick Vaughn, newly named Baron Stanhope and heir to the Earl of Clancare.

Yet there she was. Anger sluiced, white hot, and unexpected.

There she was in the flesh—the proprietress of a thriving draper's business on Hawkins Street backed by a discreet courtyard with a second building providing shelter to a variety of young women few of the neighbors knew anything about.

"Mrs. Eagan?" He managed the inquiry in an even tone despite his reactions, even as his mind poured over the information his men had gathered during their discreet investigation of the surrounding streets. Again and again, this woman had been described as honest, kind, and generous to a fault. The ideal businesswoman and neighbor. And easy on the eyes to boot. His fists clenched at his sides.

Their inquiries unearthed the little-known fact that the saintly Widow Eagan ran a school of some sort for girls in reduced circumstances, taking them in and teaching them a trade. Maura Fitzgerald or Maureen Eagan, or whatever she styled herself, was a paramour, draper, and schoolmistress? He could have laughed. Just what exactly was she teaching the girls she took in out of the goodness of her soul?

Rage swirled within him, barely held in check, as he confronted proof of her deception. It was unreasoned. It was unnecessary. It was uncharacteristic. And it was almost beyond his control. Dare he call her the name by which she'd already been introduced or should he partner in her deceptions and pretend he never met her? Either option galled him out of proportion with the task at hand.

Which would she choose?

At least she possessed enough grace to blanch white and stay perfectly still in the breathless minute after their gazes locked. Small comfort there, and it did nothing to vanquish his reactions.

He drew another breath finally and struggled to keep anger out of his voice.

"Mrs. . . . *Eagan*?" He hesitated deliberately, stressing the name again slightly, as if stunned at seeing someone unexpected. He did not want her to realize he possessed any clue before he ascended the stairs who might be waiting at the top.

"If . . . if I might have a moment of your time, I have an offer for you." Attempting to appear as if he were recovering himself after a shock, he doffed his hat and placed it in the crook of his arm as he awaited her reaction.

"I am so sorry for the interruption, Mrs. Eagan." The shopkeeper had managed to catch up with Garrett, paunch and age notwithstanding as he gasped for breath.

"Please, sir." He put his hand on Garrett's sleeve. "If ye'll accompany me to my office below, I'm sure I can assist ye. Or ye can make an appointment to return and meet with both Mrs. Eagan and myself at a more convenient time."

"I really need to speak to Mrs. . . . *Eagan*," Garrett insisted, pausing to highlight her use of this different name once again.

"Whatever your business with our shop, I can assure ye I am authorized ta make all decisions or accommodations deemed necessary. I am ready ta offer ye the full range of services Eagan's can provide."

Although clearly outmatched, the man also looked ready to throw himself physically between Garrett and his employer if deemed necessary. Garrett's eyebrow edged upward as he looked from the man to Maura Eagan–Fitzgerald.

"It's all right, Mr. Polhaven. I will see Mr. Lynch. You have no need to worry." She stood up.

"Please come in, Mr. Lynch. This is an . . . unexpected . . . pleasure." Her tone struggled to make her greeting ring true.

"Would ye like me ta stay, Mum?" Her protector cast a sharp eye on Garrett. "Or I can send fer Mrs. Polhaven?"

This brought a smile to her lips as she shook her head. "Really. I will be all right in this gentleman's company. I do not need a chaperone. I know you are very busy taking inventory. Pray do not trouble yourself any further on my account."

"Very well." Polhaven looked less than satisfied as he retreated toward the steps. "Ring if ye have need of anything. One of us will be up in a whipstitch."

"I will." Her eyes stayed fixed on the point where his head disappeared as he returned to his duties below.

"Anything." Polhaven's determined voice echoed back up the stairway for emphasis.

She took a deep breath. The set of her shoulders and the firm line of her lip when her gaze met Garrett's again told him she meant to brazen things out for as long as possible. He couldn't help but admire her spirit despite himself. Meeting him head on showed character.

"Thank you for seeing me without an appointment, Mrs. . . . ?" He left her title dangle, forcing her to acknowledge her deception one more time, trying to knock or keep her off balance.

"*Eagan*, Mr. Lynch. I use Eagan in connection to my business affairs." The faintest hint of color stained her cheeks as she gestured to the pair of rushed armchairs on the opposite side of the table from her work area. "Please, will you sit down and tell me what brings you to my shop?"

The rushes squeaked a protest as he settled on the offered chair. He stripped off his gloves and placed the pair and his hat on the edge of the table in front of him.

Folding his hands together, he looked at them for a moment as if trying to collect his thoughts after receiving the shock of meeting someone he knew, in such an unexpected place. With a deliberate grimace, he then fixed her with a piercing look.

"This is very awkward. Had I . . . had I . . . realized . . . I should probably take up this matter with Stanhope."

Her eyes narrowed as he stumbled along with his tongue-tied pose.

"But even he and I are barely acquainted." He let out a deep sigh and let his shoulders sag ever so slightly.

"Baron Stanhope has nothing to do with this enterprise," she assured him in a even tone as she took her seat.

Sunlight from the window caressed the top of her braided chignon, bringing out the chestnut highlights shining within its dark depths. She certainly knew how to use her assets to distraction. Her crisp white blouse enhanced the creaminess of her complexion. The deep Mexican blue of the work apron she wore gave a steely glint to her gray eyes. Her rose-colored lips were enticing, despite the firm line she set them in.

She leaned forward and folded her hands on the desk. "I can assure you, whatever you have to say can be said to me. Stanhope knows nothing about choosing fabrics for upholstery or drapes, let alone lesser household goods."

"Lesser goods?"

"Tea towels. Table linens. The aprons your servants

wear. Someone has to provide them to Dublin's households. Eagan's is striving to become one of the major sources. From curtains to bed linens. What can we supply for you, Mr. Lynch?"

Looking the way she did, and running the sideline business he suspected, he was quite certain she should not have included mention of bed linens in the recitation of her inventory. Images of the entertainments she could offer within that line of wares sprang too easily to mind. Or perhaps that was part of her pitch, dangle the thought and then see if the customer was interested in exactly that sort of pursuit?

In either case, it was wasted on him despite her personal appeal. Most nights, like last night which he spent bedded down in a barn avoiding English patrols, or the one in her drawing room two nights before, he never even saw a bed, let alone needed linens. And women had been few and far between, an unfortunate side effect of his Green Dragon responsibilities.

"I believe you are mistaken in my intent." He fumbled in the breast pocket of his jacket and pulled out a handkerchief to mop his brow. Then he met her frowning gaze once more.

"I am here to make some inquiries regarding your other enterprise."

She continued to frown. Storm clouds gathered in the depths of her gray eyes. "My . . . other . . . enterprise?"

He nodded once.

Her jaw worked for a moment. "Is that why you wanted to involve Stanhope? Because you wished to discuss my . . . other enterprise?"

She stood, her chin raised and shoulders straight, clasping her hands in front of her. "I fail to see what you would have to discuss with me that might involve Baron Stanhope."

She schooled her voice very carefully. Her self-righteous indignation was almost believable as a result. "I have made all my own decisions for quite some time."

"I meant no offense. I just assumed . . . given the nature . . . given your relationship . . . that—"

Her gaze narrowed further. "—that I depend upon him in all things? That may or may not be so. The nature of my relationship with Baron Stanhope is no one else's business but the baron's and mine."

She really was indignant. And headed in the wrong direction for today's conversation. The earl's dictum to separate his grandson from his mistress notwithstanding, today Garrett was concentrating on the girl she had mentioned to her housekeeper.

Whether Maura Fitzgerald had Stanhope in fact by the leading strings, as his mother and grandfather feared, was a lesser concern than exploring every avenue toward finding the admiral's daughter, no matter how far-fetched. Mrs. Fitzgerald's ties to Stanhope would be broken in due course. Jane Fuller and the release of the prisoners in Newgate Gaol were his current priority over rescuing Clancare's heir from a pair of scheming arms.

"Again, I apologize. I truly meant no offense. Especially since we are apparently talking at cross-purposes." He mopped his forehead again. "I've been so overset since I got the news."

"What news?" She folded her arms in front of her as she eyed him through suspicion.

He took a deep breath as he rose to his feet to face her across the table. "My poor little cousin. She's run away from her home in County Meath. She's only seventeen."

She took a breath and looked at him for a moment longer. "Oh, I am sorry. How very unfortunate."

Genuine sympathy softened the mistrust in her eyes. He nodded. "One day she sent her grieving parents a note saying she was bored with country life and was going to the city to make her fortune. They haven't heard from her since."

"Does your cousin have any other relations or acquaintances here in Dublin who could have offered her shelter?"

He shook his head. "She knows no one here, save myself. And I am but the merest whisker of a relation, being a second cousin to her mother."

"I do not wish to sound harsh over what is obviously a family tragedy." She unfolded her arms and moved a step closer to the end of her table. "But what has your cousin's disappearance to do with me?"

"Surely you can understand how frantic her parents must be." He raked his hand through his hair. "And living the life I do, I know all too well the dangers that lurk in the city. Especially for the young and innocent. I have done my best to seek her out for them."

"I have no way of knowing the life you lead, but that still does not tell me why you are here." Another step left her just a few scant feet from him. The tantalizing scent of newly opened roses drifted to him.

Here goes. "I'm at my wit's end. She is but seventeen. How can a child of her years survive in the city? I was about to write to her family to expect the worst. Then someone told me of a woman from County Meath who owned a shop on Hawkins Street, a draper who sometimes took in girls to teach them a skill."

"Which brought you here? To see if your cousin was among my students?" A look of concern flitted across her face. "Not many people know about my school."

Did Stanhope? Perhaps that was the impetus for her earlier upset. The man paying her bills had no idea how she was putting his funds to use?

He took a deep breath. "I realize how outside the normal borders of society this is, but would you please let me see if my cousin is here?"

She was already shaking her head. "I am sorry. I cannot."

"Cannot or will not?" Anger touched his voice despite himself.

"Both." She admitted readily enough as she continued to study him.

"You would take away my last hope? How can you be so cruel?"

"For many of the same reasons you fear for your cousin." She turned away from him and stepped over to the window to look toward the rear of her property. "Most of the girls who make it to this door have not had a good time of it. Some have been forced to work under intolerable circumstances. Some have been beaten. Others cruelly used, then coldly turned aside."

She looked back at him. The sunlight in the window framed her face and gave it almost an ethereal glow. If it was a calculated effect, it was working. "No one who comes looking for them is allowed to see my students."

"Not even their family?" He was nearly dumbfounded. Could she really be running so noble an enterprise so quietly that he had never heard of it? Impossible.

"Not all family should get a second chance, and not everyone who claims a familial attachment actually holds one." That truth hit very close to home when it came to his supposed cousin. Had she guessed?

"This school," she continued, "is their haven, a place to heal and work for a new chance at life."

"But surely—"

She held up her hand. "When they are ready, they contact their families if that is their wish. Some are reunited. Some move on to new lives."

"But her parents are in an agony of waiting." He moved around the corner of her desk and joined her at the window. "Is there not some way?"

He looked down into the courtyard. A line of young women dressed in modest gray or light blue gowns, white aprons, and caps carried chairs into sunlight.

"Some of my students . . ." She spoke so quietly he had to strain to hear her despite being so close. ". . . choose to lose touch with their families because of the poor choices they made. Because of shame."

She looked up at him. Tears shimmered in the stormy gray depths of her eyes.

Understanding surged.

"Is that what happened to you?" He could hardly credit that he had asked such an intimate and surely unwelcome question. Something about this woman, her surprising honor despite her role in Stanhope's world, reached deep inside him and brought out the oddest reactions.

Her tears hovered a moment longer before spilling over to streak dual paths down her cheeks. She looked horrified. Her gaze fled from his. "No. Yes. For a time."

She shifted to face the windows, one shoulder pointed toward him, and he could see her troubled profile. She swallowed several times.

Sympathy twisted inside him. If she was trying to disarm him, it was working. He knew far too many people suffering similar fates through no fault of their own. It was the reason he followed the path he was currently on.

"Does your family know where you are?" He touched her arm.

She nodded as she looked back at him. "Now. Yes. They know about the shop and something of the school. But they did not . . ." She sighed. ". . . they did not know about . . . the other choices until long after I made them. My first choices."

"Did you have a choice?" He had no right to ask.

He had no reason. But he asked anyway as the anger he'd been feeling and the concern he couldn't stem collided.

"Aye." She nodded. "I had a choice."

He could see how hard it was for her to answer. He knew instinctively she rarely talked about herself, that he was receiving the rare gift of her trust. A gift he didn't truly deserve.

"I was one of the lucky ones." The tears glistened again in her eyes. "I was lucky."

Her gaze returned to the courtyard below. "Some of the girls down there have not yet celebrated their fifteenth birthday. I was seventeen when I accepted my . . . first post."

Her first post. It sounded like an ordinary position.

Maura drew in a long, quavering breath. The heat of Garrett Lynch's hand on her shoulder spread warmth and unexpected reassurance through her. She could hardly believe she was speaking to this man at all, let alone so intimately and so personally. She hadn't talked to anyone like this in years. But he'd brought the sudden and unexpected collision of her private and public worlds when he walked into her office. Now she couldn't seem to stop herself from telling him everything.

Why him?

All she knew of Garrett Lynch was that he was a gambler who lived, for all anyone could tell, by his wits and his winnings. Or so Stanhope had related during their evening of chess last night. Perhaps that was the appeal. A man who knew what it was to live on the edges of acceptable behavior.

She looked down at the girls in the courtyard. They were giggling and jostling one another as they finished setting up their chairs for their lesson. One took a knotted handkerchief out of her pocket and tossed it in the air, and soon several of the girls were engaged in a game of *Imithe Coinnigh* while others formed a circle to watch and clap their encouragement. Shrieks of carefree laughter echoed skyward as they kept the bit of cotton and lace aloft and out of one another's hands.

I was lucky, isn't that what she'd just declared? She knew she had been because, unlike many of the girls, at the very least she'd had a choice. Having dangled that tidbit, she felt compelled to at least give a minimal explanation. Perhaps it would give him hope for his young relation as well.

"I came to Dublin as a nurse–governess for a cavalry officer, Colonel Whyte, and his wife. They were touring the countryside with their two sons and infant daughter when Mrs. Whyte took ill. My father was desperately ill. Money was very scarce and opportunities even more so. I knew how lost and alone those children felt. What I didn't know was how lost their father would feel. How alone I would be."

"He took advantage of you?" The deep timbre of Garrett's voice held no condemnation, no judgment. It shivered through her, giving her the acceptance she needed to go on with a story she had never related before.

She shook her head. "Not in the way you fear for your cousin. He was so lonely, especially as his wife's illness progressed. I was so homesick."

She gulped another breath and condemned herself with the truth. "We gave each other what comfort we could. Two lost souls trying to escape the horrors of our lives if only for a few stolen moments. What we shared was more consolation than passion."

Tears streamed her cheeks. Not tears of shame for freely admitting her adulterous affair with her employer's husband, but tears for the grief she'd felt when the news came of her father's death, when she'd known she would never be able to go home to her mother and brothers and take up her life again, and for the colonel when he'd finally arranged to transport his wife's body home to England. She had felt far older than her youthful seventeen years at that point.

She still did.

Garrett Lynch handed her his handkerchief, and she smoothed the tears from her cheeks.

"Still, you were Whyte's responsibility. He took you from your family. How could he abandon you?"

"He paid the lease on the house for an additional six months when he resigned his commission and took his children home to Suffolk. And he arranged for Sir Reginald to look after me, to provide me with references and help me secure either a respectable position or a suitable marriage."

At some point, Garrett had moved his arm across her back to brace her other shoulder. His strength flowed through her, accepting the scandalous behavior she was relating so matter-of-factly with a gesture where words would surely have failed.

"I held no illusions that marriage was an option for me after the colonel and his family departed. I could not deceive a future husband regarding my behavior. I possess neither birth nor fortune that might allow a man to overlook the truth, even if I were to wish an alliance with someone whose standards were for sale."

Silence lay between them for a moment.

"Any regrets?" he voiced softly.

She shook her head. "Not on that count. Neither of my parents would have wanted me to be so dishonorable. Sir Reginald became my friend first as we tried to decide what sort of position he could recommend for me—governess or companion. Unfortunately my age and my . . . appearance worked against me. Eventually we settled on his becoming my patron."

It sounded so much colder than it had been, so much more deliberate. Her arrangement with Sir

Reginald had saved her from the edge of despair and given him comfort and unexpected joy as he had assured her throughout their time together.

Garrett's grip on her arm tightened. She could feel the steady rise and fall of his chest as he pulled her closer. There had been less than a handful of men who had ever been this physically close to her, all save her father had ended up in her bed, but she sensed no danger of such persuasion in Garrett Lynch at this moment. Only unimagined support and open compassion.

"That would be Sir Reginald Manchester, the late barrister?"

She nodded.

Memories of Sir Reginald brought a smile to her lips as they always did. True, he'd been her second lover, the one who really made her into a member of the demimonde by setting her up in her own house and providing for all her needs including funds she could send home to her mother and younger brothers, to help provide after her father's death. But he had been so much more. Confidante, friend, tutor, and benefactor—his untimely death had left her very bereft and alone.

"His generosity allowed me to help the first girl who needed me. She was my housekeeper's niece, turned out into the street without references when her employers discovered she was pregnant. The fact that the family's eldest son was the father made no difference to them. She would have been forced into prostitution to support herself and her child."

She glanced up to see Garrett's gaze intent on the girls below, his mouth a grim line. She turned slightly in his arms, and his gaze bore into hers. "So you have no regrets on his account, either?"

"Sir Reginald's legacy allowed me to purchase this shop and adjoining house. He gave me the means to help other girls find a way out of impossible situations, just as he helped me. I cannot regret the consequences of my choices when they include such a result."

"And what of Stanhope?"

This question came so quietly she was not sure if Garrett had spoken or if it whispered from her own conscience. Somehow it did not matter. Like the tears that had flooded her eyes, she could not hold back the last of her sordid story, not at this point.

"When Freddie first arrived on my doorstep, it was as bearer of the news that his godfather, Sir Reginald, had died after a brief illness he had kept hidden from me and from most of his friends. He had no family."

Garrett held her securely in his arms. She felt as oddly safe as she had when she'd stumbled into him the other night. "Reggie had tried to take care of me in every way. Leaving me the title to the house I occupy and enough money to remain independent."

Wordlessly, Garrett reached under her chin and gently pulled her face up so he could look at her directly. *Eyes to steal a woman's soul.* Her tears kept falling, wetting his hand as he cupped her jaw and traced his thumb over her cheek.

"I think he was doing the same for Freddie," she repeated. "Not with money. But he was in his last year of schooling, very naïve and lacking direction. His elder brother had just died in a sailing accident. His father had passed away only a few months before. He needed a friend."

"The way you had when Sir Reginald entered your life." A statement not a question.

"This was before the accidents and illnesses that claimed his two uncles and three elder cousins and left him heir to the Clancare title and a legacy he never aspired to. He was very sweet and fun. He made me laugh."

"So you fell in love and lived happily ever after?"

For the first time she caught a hint of condemnation in Garrett's gaze. Perhaps not condemnation, but something hard enough to make her pull back and step away from his embrace.

"Not love."

Her denial sounded hollow even to her own ears because for a time she had allowed herself to believe she loved Freddie Vaughn. The knowledge still hammered at her guilt over the depth of his attachment to a woman so totally unsuitable to become his wife. She did love him, in a way. But for a brief time before his meteoric rise in social status, she had indulged herself in the illusion of a future much as Freddie still wanted to believe was possible.

She felt uncomfortably bereft outside the circle of Garrett Lynch's arms, bereft and vulnerable as she had not during all of her gushing confession. What had possessed her? Whatever it was that had made her pour out her sordid descent to this man shook her to her core. Her head ached, and she had the distinct feeling she was about to be ill.

She grabbed the bellpull and tugged it vigorously. Silas Polhaven or his wife would surely be upstairs in no time.

"If you will excuse me." She didn't trust herself to even look at him again. If she burst into tears she'd be hard-pressed to prevent either of the Polhavens from ringing a peal over his head at the very least.

"I will send someone to give you a limited tour so you can ascertain for yourself if your cousin is here."

With that, she scooted around the far side of her worktable and fled the room.

Chapter Six

"Here ye go, Mrs. Fitzgerald. A nice tea tray ta fix ye right as rain in no time."

Teresa entered Maura's salon bearing a silver tray laden with enough food for three women. Obviously, Dorothy Kelly had taken one look at her employer as she came through the door at this uncharacteristically early hour and decided she had returned home in search of sustenance besides the tea she had requested.

"Mrs. Kelly says ye're ta eat every bite on these plates or she'll be in ta have a word with ye jest as soon as she returns from the greengrocer's." The maid set the tray on the Pembroke table by the bow window overlooking the back garden.

"Seems the last two batches of taters he sent round were spoilt at the bottom of the crate. And she means ta have a word with him herself." Teresa busied herself setting out the afternoon tea as she talked.

Maura looked at the feast being spread before her. "I cannot possibly—"

"Mrs. Kelly says I'm ta remind ye of the last time she had a word with the greengrocer, should ye kick up any kind of fuss over eating this here tray." Teresa interrupted Maura's protest.

She stifled the urge to giggle over the exaggerated roll of the little maid's eyes or the way she wagged her eyebrows as she related the housekeeper's dire warning. If this was anything like the last, there could very well be a slight . . . delay in the timing of Mrs. Kelly's shopping trips, just to remind the greengrocer just who shopped from whom and paid for what.

"She did get a little carried away with her umbrage last time," Maura admitted when her inner mirth subsided.

The pounding in her head had not subsided in the hour since she'd fled her office at the draper's shop. Despite letting her hair down, shedding her shoes, and changing out of her stays and work clothes into a soft blue Indian muslin day dress, she found the headache made doing anything else, including resting, impossible. "Perhaps a little something to nibble with my tea would be in order."

"Good thinking, missus." Teresa nodded her endorsement. "I would not wish ta be the next one in Mrs. Kelly's sights when she's through with him."

Maura sighed. "Well, there is no way I will be able to finish an entire plate of sandwiches, crème horns, and biscuits with preserves by myself. Could you be persuaded to join me? I could use some company, and an extra mouth, if I'm to dissuade Mrs. Kelly from the need to reform me."

"Oh, I shouldn't." Teresa looked longingly at the crème horns, her favorite treat. "Ye spoil me as it is, missus. And I still have linens ta fold. Mrs. Kelly will have me in her sights if I don't finish stacking the laundry in the upstairs service chests."

"But if you take a small break from your duties to distract me with one of your stories, I am sure she will relent. After all, they might prove just the thing to perk up my appetite, although I will never be able to finish all this bounty."

Teresa had a wonderfully expressive voice and face. Everything she felt or thought showed when she talked. Maura had done more than enough talking

herself for one day. Perhaps listening to someone else
would distract her from her troubled contemplations
for a few minutes and allow her some peace. "Please
help me by eating at least one of those horns."

"If ye insist." Teresa's broad grin belied the reluctance she voiced. "I do have one tale I heared taday
when I went ta the baker's."

Teresa poured a piping cup of Bohea for Maura
and then passed her the plate of sandwiches before
helping herself to the sweets and settling onto the
edge of a brocaded chair opposite the settee Maura
occupied.

"More adventures in derring-do for your Green
Dragon?"

Teresa nodded. She never failed to report the latest
adventures from her hero, always with breathless be-
lief that each detail was true. Maura settled herself
comfortably against the cushions anticipating just the
sort of distraction she had hoped for when she'd invited her maid to join her.

Legends recounting the exploits of the Green
Dragon had been around for generations. To accomplish all that was attributed to him, he'd have to be
well into his second or even third century, but that
did not stop Teresa. She attributed his feats to ancient
magic like tales of the Fian of Old or the even more
ancient Tuatha de Danan, the first people to settle in
Ireland.

"Sheila, the baker's shopgirl, her uncle works on
the mail coach. He's a driver fer the Belfast route.
And he saw the whole thing whilst on a layover at The
Red Lion just outside Bardsgate."

Teresa stopped to nibble her treat. Maura knew from
past experience not to try and rush her in the telling of
her tales. There was a rhythm and order to the recounting; questions only threw her maid off the flow.

"Do ye remember me telling ye of the young man I

saw standing on the bridge the other week when I had my day ta go and visit my mam?" Teresa wiped a smear of crème from the corner of her mouth with her fingertip.

"He was unusually handsome and handing out pamphlets?" Maura dimly recalled the incident.

"Aye." Teresa sighed. "He had a head of red curls and eyes so green ye'd think he'd sprung straight from a mountain pasture."

How Teresa, who'd never ventured beyond Dublin's city boundaries, would know what a mountain glen looked like Maura refrained from asking. Her role was to listen and supply only the answers she was called upon to give. And try not to remember another pair of green eyes, all too determined to remain in her thoughts.

"Turns out he was arrested that very day. Thrown right into Newgate Gaol over by the Royal Barracks fer handing out Catholic literature. Seems he wishes ta become a priest, more's the pity. But lacks the funds ta travel abroad and get his training. Charged him with sedi . . . seduction?"

"Sedition?" Maura offered.

"That's the word." Teresa pressed her lips in a line and then nodded. "Sedition and agitation. Sheila says he'd been in trouble fer the very same thing up north so the soldiers was takin' him there the other day ta stand trial fer his crimes."

She stopped and fixed Maura with a probing look. "Do ye know what the punishment fer sedition or agitation is, missus?"

Maura shook her head.

"Neither me nor Sheila either, although the baker himself said it was most likely hanging or transportation. Imagine hanging fer wanting ta be a priest." She shook her head in disbelief. "There's reason enough there ta marry."

Maura doubted threat of death would persuade the truly religious to so completely abandon their beliefs. And this man sounded like a true believer. Why else would he have been standing on a bridge in the middle of the city making himself a target?

The Catholic suppressions of the past might have been officially repealed years ago, but the English still ran Ireland and there were stories aplenty of the horrors practiced against those who did not conform sufficiently to their rule.

"In any event, the soldiers taking the man ta Belfast stopped fer a pint or two at The Red Lion jest the other side of Bardsgate and left him tied up in the stables with the horses and only one of them to guard him. Ye'll never guess what happened next."

"He overpowered the guard and escaped?" Teresa's tales almost always had a happy ending.

"Worse." The maid shook her head in denial. "Them Orangemen what's been harassing good folk of late, showed up and took him fer themselves. There was close to a dozen of them all wearing the orange sashes and masks."

"The soldiers did not stop them?"

"Nay, they didn't utter so much as a protest. Sheila's uncle said they jest shrugged and got on their way back ta Dublin quick as can be. Sheila says her uncle thinks they was in on it. He says the more of us they takes, the less they have to deal with."

"How shameful. What happened to the prisoner?" Maura wasn't sure she really wanted to know, but she asked anyway, putting her faith in the righteousness of Teresa's tales.

"The men that took him planned ta give him a pitch cap."

Maura sucked in her breath. She'd heard of this brutal practice, putting a pitch-soaked cap on a man's head, then setting it aflame. Horrible.

"They took him ta a glade a little ways from the tavern," Teresa continued. "And invited all ta come and witness what happened ta them what went against king and country."

Not for the first time, Maura wondered if the king on the other side of the Irish Sea had any idea of the horrors invoked in his name.

"They had a big bonfire going in the center of a ring of trees. Out of sight of the road, probably ta cut down on the chances of being discovered. Not that there's many what will go up against a mob armed with muskets and pistols and out fer blood. The prisoner jest kept praying, loud as he could fer his soul, and fer theirs."

"Remarkable."

"Indeed," Teresa agreed. "If it was me I'd be cursing them. The leader took his pistol butt and whacked him ta shut him up. Then they threw water on him so he would be awake when they killed him. He looked doomed fer sure."

Maura leaned forward. "But?"

"But." Teresa smiled. "Jest as they was fixin' ta put the cap on him and set it aflame, out of the trees rode—"

"—the Green Dragon."

"That's right, missus." Teresa's eyes shone with excitement. "The Green Dragon and his men rode out of the trees. They fired their pistols in the air and ran straight at the bad men holding their prisoner by the scruff of his neck. Sheila's uncle said there was a terrible fight. Pistols, knives, and fists 'til ye couldn't tell who was what. Some of those Orangemen grabbed the pot of pitch and tried ta toss it straight on the prisoner, the Green Dragon, and whoever was in their path."

Teresa brushed a few crumbs from the bib of her apron as she paused for breath. "Sheila's uncle got a large gob on his cheek. He got a welt ta prove it, too, she says, from scrubbing it off. But the Green Dragon, he reached down and pulled the prisoner up in front of him on his great black steed and rode off with him."

"How do you know it was the Green Dragon?"

"Sheila's uncle saw his ring, missus." Teresa nodded her head once for emphasis. "Gold with a emerald dragon carved in the center. He rode off and his men followed, leaving the Orangemen to cart off their wounded."

"I suppose your red-haired preacher is halfway to Europe now." Maura speculated. "He should be able to study for the priesthood there if he wants."

The housemaid nodded. "So Sheila's uncle believes. More's the pity."

"But you wanted the man rescued by your hero, did you not?"

"Oh, aye," Teresa sighed. "I'm right glad he's not in a gaol, nor suffering those horrid burns. But making a man that handsome into a priest is surely a waste."

Maura could have laughed out loud at that remark. She looked down and surprised herself to find the entire plate of sandwiches had disappeared, along with her headache.

"I'd best be getting on ta folding the laundry now, Mrs. Fitzgerald." Teresa stood up and took the plate back to the tray. "Thank ye fer the crème horn. Would ye like me ta freshen yer cup afore I take this back to the kitchen?"

"Aye, thank you. I will take this to the desk and get to some long overdue correspondence." The shadows in the garden were starting to lengthen. She wasn't expecting Freddie to call this evening so she'd have as much time as she'd like to write to her brother. He was in his third year at school and seemed to look forward to her letters, and the cakes Mrs. Kelly usually sent along with them.

"Mrs. Kelly will be so pleased." Teresa handed her back her cup, sounding thoroughly pleased herself. "She thought a little distraction would prove jest the thing ta get ye to eat more than a nibble or two."

With that, the maid picked up the tea tray and sailed out of the salon with a springy step, leaving Maura wondering if the latest tale of the Green Dragon's adventures she had just heard had been nothing more than a well-intentioned diversion, a true tale, or a little of both.

Garrett scanned the interior of The Brazen Head as he entered its smoky depths. This was a man's world: dim lighting reflecting on highly polished brass railings and gleaming oak counters, the chink and clink of glass and pewter, the scraping of stools and benches on worn floor planks. He took a deep breath of the tobacco and spirit-laden air, then flipped the tapman a crown for keeping his usual corner open and ready for the game to come.

He took note of each cluster of men inside the tavern, who was with whom, who was alone, who was a regular, who a stranger. He'd track each one throughout his stay, not looking so much for the ebb and flow pattern of the pub trade, but for that which did not fit in. Each of his men would do the same as they entered and made their way to the corner. So far, this alertness had paid off, allowing them to maintain the pose of a group of card-loving comrades as they discussed their business.

"Hullo, luv." Dana, the tapman's niece, greeted him by plunking a pint of stout on the table in front of him as he settled into his seat. "Ye're here a little early. Got plans fer later this evening?"

"Not if you'll clear your dance card for me," he answered, then took a sip of the foaming brew in his mug.

"If only ye meant it, I'd be sorely tempted." She flicked the table with a rag, chasing away imaginary crumbs. For the rest of his time in The Brazen Head she'd make a show of refilling his mug, but he'd never actually drink more than this first one.

"Whatever would make you think I'm not serious? There's nary a man in the place that wouldn't lay the city at your feet if you'd but snap your fingers."

With her blond curls and wide brown eyes, Dana was one barmaid who looked good to her uncle's patrons even before they were in their cups. But her uncle kept a strict eye on her and never let things get out of hand. Anyone who laid a wayward hand on her or even grew too bold in his remarks was shown the door.

She snapped her fingers and looked around the pub with a laugh. "Ye're full of bog gas, Garrett Lynch, and that's a fact. I see the first of yer mates is about ta join ye. Enjoy yer game."

Dana swished back to the bar with an exaggerated sway to her hips that set her curls bouncing as they peeked out from under her lace-edged cap. Sure enough, there in the doorway, enjoying the show just as she'd intended, stood Seamus Granger. He made his way to the bar and picked up a pint before joining Garrett.

"I see you managed to get an early day from your new employer." Garrett greeted Seamus who'd spent the last days helping out in his cousin's saddle shop as he made his inquiries regarding Eagan's. "Did you get a message to Daniel?"

"Aye, he should be along by the time the Christ Church Cathedral bells ring." Seamus flexed his fingers, then took a healthy swallow from his mug. "I'd forgotten how unforgiving leather work can be, that's fer sure."

Garrett pulled a deck of cards from his pocket. "Shall we try a practice hand while we wait?"

They each stacked some coins on the table. Garrett lit a cheroot while Seamus shuffled and dealt the cards.

"So how did you make out at the draper's today?" Seamus asked as they played their first cards. "Is Stanhope's fancy piece running a finishing academy after all?"

Stanhope's fancy piece.

Hearing Seamus state Maura Fitzgerald's role in the baron's life so baldly startled Garrett. He had to force himself to maintain a calm demeanor. After listening to her pour out the details of her story earlier, and seeing for himself the good she was trying to make out of a bad situation, he had no stomach for the ribald humor or lecherous envy that usually accompanied discussion of another man's mistress.

"No." He blew out a cloud of smoke and laid down a winning hand. "For what it's worth, looks like she's really trying to help young girls escape a life like hers. According to the shop manager's wife, the girls that find their way to them are given shelter and taught a trade, and then they help find them new positions."

"In truth?" Seamus gathered the cards and shuffled them once more, his brow furrowed.

"To all appearances." Garrett scooped his winnings back to the modest pile in front of him.

They both knew only too well how false appearances could be. Too few coins on the table made the game look staged, too many at stake garnered too much attention from the other patrons. It was a delicate balance, but he and his men were well practiced. The taverns changed, as did the players, but the information exchanged and plans made were always vital.

"Stanhope's a fortunate man." Seamus drained the dregs from his mug. "Poor fellow."

Garrett nodded and studied his hand. Seamus was right on both accounts. Stanhope was both lucky and to be pitied.

Having held Maura Fitzgerald in his arms, having felt the warmth of her smile, having witnessed the good she was attempting to do, Garrett could see how the young baron had been led to declare his intentions to flout society's dictums by marrying his mistress. But knowing the lad's grandfather as they did, Garrett and Seamus both knew Stanhope would never see that wedding day. The *Ard Tiarna* would never allow his heir such liberty.

"May I come in on the next hand, gentlemen?" Daniel McTavish slid onto the bench next to Seamus. "I believe I have time for a quick one."

"Ahhh, Longford. Plans with your new cohorts?"

Daniel grimaced before nodding. "Aye. Jameson is promising some sport in a different vein this night, thankfully. I doubt he would believe I swilled too much to perform this night as well. I barely made it out of his priory the last time with my pants on."

The entertainments Harold Jameson offered to entice Stanhope and his guests away from the card tables the other night turned out to be so depraved that even a man of Longford's reputation as a ladies' man had blanched and declined to participate, which spoke volumes against the older man. It also sharpened the question of why he was seeking out Stanhope and the other young men of his circle. What did he want from them? Seamus dealt the next hand as Dana arrived with a fresh mug and a pitcher. She set the pitcher on the table in front of Seamus and winked.

"It's good to see ye again, sir." She put the mug

down and favored Daniel with a bright smile. With his sandy brown curls, chiseled chin and light green eyes, Lord Longford received the same greeting from most women he met whether he was in the lowest tavern or the finest drawing room.

"You too, lass." He returned her smile enough to reveal the dimple in his one cheek. Whenever he did that, the ladies always swooned. Causing that type of impression, Lord Longford was not much use for stealth work, but he more than proved his worth as he gathered tidbits of information from the many women who fawned over him in Dublin's drawing rooms.

True to form, Dana blushed as she filled Seamus's empty and sauntered away after a final lingering look at Daniel, accompanied by a long sigh.

"Any clue what Jameson has in mind?"

"Not really. He hinted at something out of town. We're to bring our horses and wear dark clothes. We gather at The Crown before dusk unless it rains. If the weather turns foul, we'll have our fun tomorrow."

Daniel looked at his cards and threw them down on the table. "Stanhope and Masters also received invitations."

"Seamus will trail you once you leave The Crown. With that large a crowd, you should be fairly easy to follow. I suspect this will be a pretty tame night, more a test of your taste for mischief than real trouble. If I'm wrong, get Stanhope out of there no matter the costs. The *Ard Tiarna*'s heir is your priority."

Daniel nodded his understanding. He would protect the next High Lord with his own life if need be. They all would. The fact that Lord Longford was also Stanhope's boyhood friend would serve to make him all the more vigilant.

Garrett flicked his eyes to Seamus. "Take Ailin with you. When you get a fix on the direction they are heading, send him back to The Blue Boar for the rest of our available men. I will join them if I can."

"Aye, sir." Seamus showed him the cards he held, then claimed the pot. "That Jameson's got all the markin's of a bad 'un. Pity the baron does not have as good a taste in friends as he does his women. No offense, Longford."

Daniel waved one hand as he took a long pull on his stout.

"Stanhope is young. He will learn. This role as heir to Clancare is not one he was ever expected to take on." Garrett scanned the pub's other patrons; no one appeared interested in the card game in the far corner. "And in the meantime, we will keep watch over him. He shows promise."

Garrett had paid close attention to Stanhope the other night. Much about a man can be told by how he approaches games of chance. Stanhope had been cautious in his betting and alert to the nuances of play from others at the table. At the same time, the lad had kept a wary eye on his flighty friend, Masters, holding him back from the second party Jameson had proposed. It was only after Jameson left, when he appeared to be celebrating, that the young baron had overindulged in his drinking.

"Any word from County Meath?" Daniel asked as they all anted up for the next hand. "I had no luck with the rest of the potential suitors list. All are accounted for.

"Only that there has been more than one young woman who has vanished over the past year."

Daniel traded in two of his cards. "Usually it is the lads who go missing, off to seek fame and fortune."

"I am not sure who would keep track of such, but according to the bishop at Christ Church Cathedral, most young women who leave home unexpectedly usually leave with a man." Garrett kept the hand he

dealt himself. "Liam's message said four others. All
from different villages."

"Has there been a rash of elopement sweeping the
country?" Seamus folded. "My brother came to town
on business last week and related how two girls had
gone missing from Cashel. Two in two months. Their
mams are frantic. One was set to wed but a week from
the date she disappeared. And my cousin Ray says a
neighbor's girl out in Wicklow was lost a couple of
months ago coming home from choir practice."

That made seven, not including Jane Fuller and her
maid—not an overwhelming number, but unusual
enough given their quest for the admiral's daughter.
That two of the girls were from Cashel struck very
close to home. His resources were stretched very thin
at the moment, but when he could spare someone,
he'd see if there was something they could discover
on the matter.

"Speak of the Devil—"

Garrett glanced to the doorway. There stood Sean
Talbot scanning the interior before he made his way
to their table.

"Deal me in, fellows, and pass the brew. I have had
a hard ride."

Sean looked as if he hadn't slept a wink since the
night they'd spent at Marnock. His dark hair was tousled, his chin and cheeks covered with three days'
stubble. He took the mug the ever-vigilant Dana had
handed him as he passed the end of the bar and
drained the contents in one long swallow as he sat
with a thump.

"You look like hell." Daniel spoke for them all.

"Any word?" Garrett asked. They couldn't sit here
just looking at him. Too many heads had followed his
progress across the pub.

Sean shook his head and rubbed a hand through
his hair. "No. Miss Fuller . . . and her maid . . . were

last seen going off toward the river to pick berries for tarts. Their bucket was found more than a mile away in the opposite direction."

He reached for the pitcher to refresh his mug. "There've been stories about strange riders in the area, dressed in black and riding at night. Mothers are keeping their children close at hand, but Jane Fuller wouldn't let that stop her, more's the pity."

"Surely, even English women are not so foolish as ta go out at night ta pick berries?" Seamus asked.

"No, it was just after luncheon." Sean shook his head. "But she could at least have been cautious enough to take a footman or one of the stable lads with her."

"Perhaps that makes the case for an elopement stronger?" Garrett observed as he reached in his breast pocket for another cheroot.

Sean shook his head. "There's no other indication. And more important, no groom in the offing."

"Besides you."

"*Diabhal.*" Sean's gaze slowly rose to meet his. "We have got to find her."

"It may already be too late to save either of you."

"*Diabhal.*" Sean swore again.

Devil indeed.

Chapter Seven

Garrett stood on the doorstep and hesitated for a moment before lifting the heavy knocker and letting it fall. The sound resonated both inside the stylish townhouse and down the street.

With twilight approaching, the street behind him was all but deserted. Lights shone in the windows of the neat townhomes and cast oddly shaped shadows on the cobblestoned street.

The neighbors barely tolerate my presence here as is without giving the appearance I am setting up a bawdy house. Maura Fitzgerald's worry echoed unexpectedly. Were any of Maura Fitzgerald's neighbors looking out of their front drawing room or bedroom windows and taking note of the gentleman at her door?

It was late for a call to anyone, let alone the mistress of another man. Knowing Stanhope was engaged elsewhere made this visit easier on one level and far more dangerous on several others.

He did not have the luxury of indulging those other levels, but he could not deny the woman's appeal, both physically and through the intriguing glimpses of her character afforded him so far in their brief acquaintance.

"Good evening, sir." The footman who had guarded the household from him through the night opened the door partway.

"Gerald?" Garrett pulled off his hat. "Would you ask Mrs. Fitzgerald if I might have a word with her?"

"I don't believe Mrs. Fitzgerald is receiving visitors tonight, sir." Gerald opened the door a little farther so the light from the foyer behind him could illuminate Garrett's face. His own remained in shadow, giving him the advantage. Had Stanhope changed his plans and even now was enjoying the comfort of his mistress's charms? The images that arose with that notion disturbed Garrett. He squelched the flash of jealousy that rushed through him.

"Would you please inquire anyway?" Garrett took a step, testing the footman's resolve to block the entrance. He remained firmly in Garrett's way.

"Or allow me to leave a note with these?" Garrett thrust forward the nosegay of roses he had brought with him. "I am Mr. Lynch, I was a guest here the other night."

"I recognize ye, sir." Gerald retreated enough as he accepted the flowers to allow Garrett a toehold in the entrance. Garrett admired the footman's resolute protection of his mistress even as he wished she employed a less strong-willed gatekeeper. "Mrs. Fitzgerald is not at home to anyone tonight. If ye leave yer card, I'll see she gets it first thing."

"Then if you will allow, I will write her a note. I wish to speak to her about a matter of utmost importance. It has to do with her school."

"If ye leave yer card, I will give her yer message, sir."

Gerald was vigilant and determined, skills Garrett normally looked for and admired in a man. At the moment he found them frustrating as they formed a roadblock to vital information he sought.

His brief conversations with Sean earlier had brought to light the depth of a problem with girls disappearing from the Irish countryside in recent months. His gut told him the ones they had heard about represented but the first blooms on a thorny bush. No one cared about a few missing Irish women. No one, except possibly Maura Fitzgerald, and now the Green Dragon.

"If you could fetch me some writing materials, I will leave a note." He reached into the inside breast pocket of his jacket. "Please give it to your employer as soon as possible. As I said, the matter is urgent and may concern the students at her school. She allowed me to tour the premises there earlier today. Then she left rather abruptly before we could conclude our interview."

He could have sworn that the footman sniffed as he supplied far more information than the man needed. Experience had shown that such action frequently allowed servants to feel superior and thereby more likely to grant requests.

Gerald looked unimpressed. "Mrs. Fitzgerald retired some time ago; she arrived home with a headache well above her usual hour. I will relate yer mess—"

"Gerald?" Maura Fitzgerald's voice sounded from the interior of the house. "Show Mr. Lynch to my salon. If he deems the matter urgent enough to call like this, the least I can do is listen."

"As ye wish." The footman immediately stepped backward, allowing Garrett to enter the foyer. The expression on his face remained impassive as Garrett paused for a moment to let his eyes adjust to the interior lighting.

From the gaslit sconces on the walls, polished marble floor, gleaming chandelier, and carved stairway at the far corner, this foyer bespoke wealth and privilege. Garrett still found it amazing that a woman who was so pampered would spend her days laboring to run a business and school.

"If ye'll follow me, sir." The man handed Garrett his flowers in exchange for his hat and gloves.

They walked to the doorway of the small salon

where Garrett had spent the night under the watchful eye of his current guide.

"Mr. Lynch, madam." The door swung inward as the footman made his announcement and stepped out of the way.

Maura Fitzgerald stood by the mantle at the opposite side of the room. That damnably uncomfortable settee he'd sprawled across the other night stood between them. She had a paisley shawl wrapped around her shoulders and her hair hung loose down her back. He had thought her beautiful before, as both the poised and attentive hostess and the efficient businesswoman, but seeing her like this she was stunning.

"Will that be all, ma'am?" her footman inquired.

"Perhaps Mr. Lynch would like some brandy?" She posed the question to Garrett by fixing her gaze on him. He nodded. "Please bring the decanter and two tumblers."

"Very good, madam." The footman disappeared, leaving the door ajar.

It was a small gesture toward propriety, especially considering his employer's lifestyle, but seeing how young she looked with her gleaming dark tresses, pale skin, and simple attire, Garrett could understand the effort.

"Thank you for seeing me at this hour, Mrs. . . . ." Her name dangled awkwardly. Should he keep calling her Eagan as he had this afternoon or switch back to Fitzgerald? He was in her home, where she used one, but he had come to discuss a matter more connected to the other.

"Maura. You may just call me Maura." The ghost of a smile flitted across her lips but did not touch her eyes. She hugged her shawl close and stepped around the settee. "We both know the use of Mrs. is a courtesy only for women in my position."

"Maura, then." He strode across the room and proffered his bouquet. "I apologize if my visit to your office this afternoon upset you. I was quite concerned when you left so abruptly. Your man mentioned just now that you were unwell."

"How lovely. And thoughtful." She took the roses and inhaled a deep breath from their fragrant depths. This time the smile she favored him added sparkle to her eyes. "And totally unnecessary. I am perfectly fine as you can see."

That he could.

She wore a simple blue dress that brought out the blue hints in her eyes and set off her long dark hair as it curled invitingly down her back. The golden fringe of the shawl she wore swept across her hips with a teasing invitation to watch its tantalizing dance against the blue folds of fabric. That her feet were bare only added to her innocent allure. She looked so young and pure, unaware of the appealing picture she presented.

How could this current appearance be real, given all she had revealed this afternoon? Could this be a deliberately seductive pose from a woman who knew her sensual enticements? Suspicion haunted him as he pulled his thoughts into line. She was Stanhope's mistress—a woman who supported herself by being beguiling.

The rattle of glass on a metal tray signaled the footman's return.

"Just put the tray on the table, Gerald. I will pour." She was already gliding over to the bow window that reflected the room's interior in wavy lines against the darkness that had fallen outside. The blue of her dress scattered across the panes, a blue beacon in the night.

She waited as the footman put the refreshments on the table by the window. "And if you would, please take these to Mrs. Kelly in the kitchen and ask her to take care of them for me."

"Aye, madam." The footman took the bouquet for the second time. "I'll be nearby when the gentleman is ready ta leave. Just ring and I'll be here."

"Will you sit down, Mr. Lynch?" she asked as she handed him a tumbler with his brandy. She had been generous but not liberal with her spirits. She carried her own glass with a much smaller portion and sat in a delicate Queen Anne chair beside the spot she indicated.

"Garrett." His emerald signet chinked against the glass as he settled himself on the tufted settee. "If I'm going to call you by your Christian name, perhaps you should reciprocate?"

She shook her head. "I do not think I am comfortable with that. After all, you are not the one with two identities. I'll stay with Mr. Lynch, at least for now.

If only she knew how wrong she was. Very few people suspected that the gambler and sycophant they knew was anything other than his carefully maintained façade allowed them to see. The reward for the capture of the Green Dragon currently stood at five thousand pounds, a fortune for most poor Irishmen, but since his efforts aided them as they tried to scratch out a living while surviving the whims of the English who ruled them, he had little fear of betrayal from those he served.

"Whatever makes you comfortable." He took a sip of the liquid fire in his glass. Stanhope had excellent taste in liquor as well as women. Although the brandy slipped smoothly over his tongue, the last thought tasted oddly bitter.

"You were telling Gerald your business was urgent?" She had yet to sample the contents of her own glass as she kept her attention fixed on him. "That it has to do with my school. Did you find your cousin among the students?"

He shook his head. "Jane was not among them. It was a long shot, at best."

"I am so sorry. I had hoped you had come to tell me

she was found." Genuine sympathy radiated from her. "What is it you want from me that seems so urgent?"

"I was hoping you would let me return to Eagan's tomorrow. I would very much like to talk to some of your students. Especially those who are newest."

"Two visits in as many days will surely raise some alarms." A line of concern furrowed her brow. She rested her glass on her knee. "If your cousin is not there, what do you hope to gain by such interviews that you did not see when you met the girls today? I would not like them to be alarmed by a second day of questions."

If she refused his request, what would he do? He doubted he could bluff his way past either of the Polhavens. He took a breath and prepared to be his most persuasive. "In the first place let me assure you, your Mrs. Polhaven was most insistent that I not disturb the girls. She allowed me to observe them from within the confines of the front building while they were in the yard. So they should not be alarmed at my return."

He pressed his lips into a line and let his reassurances sink in. "And, of course, either you or Mrs. Polhaven should be present when I talk to the girls. That should reassure both you and them."

"You still have not told me what makes this so urgent." She leaned forward slightly, fixing him with the full intensity of her gaze as she tried to discern his sincerity. At least she hadn't refused him outright.

"In searching for Jane it has come to my attention that there are other girls missing."

Her eyes widened with that revelation.

"Not enough from any one village or county to warrant attention from the authorities it appears." He pressed on. "But enough to create a disturbing pattern for anyone who pays attention."

She took her first sip of brandy and closed her eyes. "How dreadful."

"It is a slim chance any of the girls you are working with knows of these matters but . . . " He let the end of this statement dangle.

Her eyes popped open almost immediately. "Of course you may talk to my girls. Dreadful must not even cover what the families of those others must be going through. Even a slim chance is better than none."

"Thank you."

She put her tumbler down on the small table by her chair. "How many?"

"Like I said, I would only need to speak to the newest of your students. Unless of course you already know all of their stories about how they have come to Dublin."

She shook her head and rose from her seat to pace across a soft gold Axminster carpet to her desk. Despite his better intentions he couldn't help but be fascinated by the soft sway of her dress as she moved. He couldn't afford the seductive distraction this woman offered so effortlessly. He couldn't seem to ignore it either.

"They tell us what they want us to know. When they're ready." She spoke with her back to him. The soft glow of the lamp there outlined her slender form, leaving her almost in shadows. "Some never tell us everything. Some never tell us much of anything."

"But that is not what I meant." She turned to face him. Still, the lamp's backlight made her features, her expression, difficult to discern. "How many girls does it take to ring an alarm? Perhaps they are runaways, off to make a new life. Perhaps they do not wish to be found. Perhaps something awful has happened or perhaps something innocent. What is it that alarms you about these girls?"

What was behind these sharp questions? Only a moment before she'd been all concern and sympathy. "I don't know how many girls; it just seems odd the ones I have learned about disappear from their small villages without any warning to their families."

He put his glass on the table beside hers and stood as well. "One was just a week shy of her wedding. Another was set to take a new position; a third was trying to arrange placement in a convent in Nice."

"You said your cousin had left her parents a note. So she is not like these others. Why do you care what happens to them?" There was just enough suspicion in her voice to gall him, even as a part of him admired her spirit. She was neither a weak woman nor one easily fooled. Yet another reason to be cautious around her.

"Why not?" He answered the honesty of her question with his own and paced forward to join her by the desk. He could not gauge the direction this conversation was taking without looking at her more directly.

"Why not?" He asked again in a deliberately soft voice. He searched her face for clues as she swallowed hard and raked him with her own intense scrutiny.

"You are hardly the sort of man who rescues damsels in distress," she said at last. Something in her eyes tried to soften the harshness of her words. "By your own admission you lead a life that leaves you privy to the dangers and lures of life in the city. Seeking your relative is admirable, but why would a man like you go out of your way for a handful of country lasses?

"Given your circumstances"—she took a deep breath and, if it was possible, studied him even more intently—"why do you care?"

He couldn't tell her the truth and he couldn't offer an evasion he was certain she would not detect. She was one of the most intriguing and intelligent woman he'd ever had dealings with. He waited the space of several heartbeats before answering in the only way he could think that would not involve lying. "Given your circumstances, why do you?"

She sucked in a sharp breath and looked as if he'd slapped her. Given all she had revealed to him only a few hours ago, and her reaction to that vulnerability, he knew his turning her question back to her would hurt. Until it was hanging in the air between them though, he hadn't realized just how insulting it would sound.

Her face grew still as stone. They'd been engaged in a conversation of equals and he had suddenly cut the floor out from under her feet, reminding her of her status outside the bounds of polite society. She couldn't possibly hate him more than he hated himself at this moment. He reached out and touched her hand, trying to soften the harshness of the exchange.

She pulled away as if his touch burned and would have stepped back but the desk blocked her. She steadied herself and stood her ground. The gray depths of her eyes hardened to granite. "So it is all right for a self-professed gambler and wastrel to care about the less fortunate, but not a fallen woman. Mistress or whore, it makes no difference what title you give us. We are not allowed to have a heart, to have feelings beyond our role in a man's bed?"

"I never meant . . . I didn't . . ." He'd so obviously struck a nerve he had no idea how he could recover, how he could make things right.

"If my circumstances change, perhaps then I would be allowed to have concerns beyond my own well-being." Her tone was bitter, her features flat. She was gazing down at her hand as she leaned against the desk—her left hand.

If my circumstances change . . . Alarm bells pealed. Had he upset her enough to have her reveal her intent in a completely different game? Did she have intentions of taking up Stanhope's foolish proposal? His other obligation kicked into play.

"You cannot marry Stanhope." The words came out bald and ragged and far harsher than his previous comment.

Her head came back up sharply. "What makes you think I would? What makes you think he would?"

There was a dangerous light glittering in her eyes. He'd pushed her hard just to get her to reveal what she had already. He'd have to push harder to get the whole truth from her. "He asked you, did he not?"

"That is no one's business but our own." She practically spit her reply. She curled her fingers into her palms as if preparing for a true fight.

He closed the distance between them.

"Business?" he goaded. "If you think of his proposal as business, how much would it take to lure you away from Stanhope?"

She blew out a quick breath as her eyes hardened and she pressed her lips into a firm line. He'd hoped to throw her off balance with the rapid changes in their conversation, to force affirmation or denial from her.

He swore that although she certainly looked ready to slap him as he so richly deserved, she did not appear on the verge of revealing her plans. Somehow he was not surprised by her resistance, or even at his admiration of her for not immediately spewing the rage she so clearly held at bay over his insulting offer.

What did surprise him was the depth of his concern over her answer.

But he needed that answer. He placed both of his hands on her forearms. "I am prepared to be extremely generous."

She bit her lip, lifted her chin, and tried without success to pull away. Her shawl slipped from her shoulders, revealing the creamy softness of her skin above her dress's modest neckline. He could not allow her appeal to distract him.

She struggled for only a moment before freezing him with the coldness in her gaze. She did not, however, cease from resisting, and he gripped her harder to prevent her pulling free.

"Despite your luck at the card tables earlier, I find it hard to believe you are making such an offer on your own. Who do you represent? His mother, Lady Helena? Or . . . his grandfather."

The last was not a question. She closed her eyes and shook her head as though she had already read the truth in his eyes. "Please tell the *Ard Tiarna* that I am not interested in his money."

"I would rather tell him you were not interested in becoming the next Countess of Clancare, that you have no future interest in his grandson."

She barely took a breath as she studied him for what seemed an interminable minute. Her contempt was as palpable as his hold on her arms. He did not blame her. He could barely stand to be in his own company.

"I know why this matters to the earl. Why does my future matter to you?" The disdain in her almost-whispered question cut him to the quick. Her eyes flashed with anger and indignation. He hardly blamed her. He had jumped from concerned citizen seeking her aid to insulting and intrusive in the space of only a few phrases.

"Why indeed?" Anger heated his own question.

"Does my future matter at all?"

He looked at her, her eyes glittering with the rage and hurt he'd put there. Her fair skin was pale, her hair tumbling with abandon over her shoulders as she asked a question that seemed to rock the very world around them. "More than you know."

Then he surprised them both by pulling her against him and kissing her.

A startled gasp escaped her lips, parting them. She did not struggle or push him away. It wouldn't have mattered at this point if she did. She fit too well against him, felt too right for him to back away.

He deepened his possession of her mouth as fire raged through him and scorched his very soul. He slid his hands from her forearms to her shoulders and cradled her even closer. The softness of her breasts pressed against his chest. The warmth of her breath fanned his cheeks. His desire for her flared hot and immediate.

The silken feel of her gown felt cool under his hands as he threaded his fingers through her hair and tilted her head back to claim her more completely. Her lips parted further as he traced their inner and outer rims with the tip of his tongue, over and over, out and in.

He darted his tongue inside, then pressed her lips harder with his own to force them to open further so he could seek her tongue. She moaned softly and greeted his invasion with her own parry, the first sign that she was anything but passive in his embrace.

Triumph roared through him.

Her hands slid up his chest to rest just below his shoulders as she returned his passion, clinging to him, demanding more, giving more.

Primal satisfaction pounded through him. She was his. Her touch, her answering kisses left him breathless.

He braced her with one arm while his other hand sought the warmth of the satin-smooth skin at the nape of her neck. Her pulse was rapid, wild. Her skin every bit as soft as it appeared as he traced the neckline of her gown.

He rained small kisses over her cheek and back along her jawline before claiming her lips again with a deep kiss as he dipped his hand to brush and caress her breast.

Beneath the layers of gown and chemise her nipple greeted his touch, hardening as he stroked her with his thumb, back and forth, even as he plumbed the depths of her sweet mouth, in and out.

He was nearly mad with his need to possess this woman. All of her. Right here. Right now. There was no time for thought, no need for consideration. She was his, and he meant to claim her.

He cradled her fully against him, letting her feel just how much he wanted her, enjoying the fact that she wore no stays, that only a few scraps of fabric stood between them.

The pounding of his pulse in his ears turned into an insistent knocking on the salon door.

"Mrs. Fitzgerald?" her footman called. "Are ye all right? I have a message jest delivered fer ye."

They broke apart, both breathing heavily. She steadied herself on the edge of the desk as she gulped for air. He walked over and snatched up his glass, then strode to the table by the window to refill it.

"Madam?" The doorknob rattled. The door was still slightly ajar, but the servant would not enter unless summoned or unduly alarmed by their continued silence.

"Please bring the message here, Gerald." She attempted to smooth her hair and bent to retrieve her shawl where it had fallen on the floor.

Garrett watched her wavery image in the window's dark reflections. He needed the diluted perspective to put some distance between them and what had almost occurred. Over what had occurred.

What had come over him? What had come over her? She had practically declared a very mercenary intention to wed another man then very nearly allowed him to make love to her. What kind of woman was she? He hated the obvious conclusion.

"Is there . . . is there anything I may do for you, Mrs. Fitzgerald?" Gerald handed his employer a sealed envelope.

"Thank you, no. I will ring if I need you." She opened the envelope and read the contents as he left them alone once more.

"Oh God." She dropped the letter and buried her face in her hands.

He turned to her immediately. "What is it?"

She lifted her head. There was an incredible amount of pain in their depths. "You must leave at once. Stanhope is on his way. He arrives within the hour."

Her declaration hit his gut like a sledgehammer. He had no claim on her. The man to whom she belonged was on his way. He was dismissed.

"We have—"

"There is nothing we need to resolve this evening." She hugged her shawl around her and turned away, placing her lover's note on her desk.

"Nothing?" The ground tilted beneath his feet. She was right. He had no right to treat her the way he just had.

"Leave now, Mr. Lynch, or Gerald will escort you out. You may badger me about my personal life tomorrow when you come to my school, if there really are some missing girls you wish to find and not just a fat reward from the earl for scaring me off."

He left then, turned on his heel and strode into the foyer, unsure of how he felt for the first time in a very long time. How would he face her tomorrow knowing what was about to take place here? Knowing what had almost taken place between them? How could he not?

Gerald was standing by the doorway to his anteroom, Garrett's hat and gloves at the ready. He accepted them and was partly down the steps before he could put a name to how he felt.

Betrayed.

Chapter Eight

As the door clicked shut behind Garrett, Maura sank onto the settee. Nausea swirled in her stomach and pain pounded once more in her head. In all the time she had been in Dublin, she had only felt this dirty and ashamed once.

Not when the neighbors gave her the cut direct in front of their wives, or when they winked at her behind their wives' backs. Not when most of the servants quit rather than serve in a house of ill repute after Colonel Whyte departed for England. Not even when some of Sir Reginald's closest friends had paid their calls within days of his passing, claiming concern for her well-being, but all the while hoping to claim her.

Garrett Lynch had achieved something she had vowed would never happen to her again. He had molded her to him like putty in his hands and turned her into the very whore her own mother branded her. She was suddenly very cold despite the shawl she hugged about her while trying to cover her shame of welcoming, nay, practically begging for him to paw and fondle her.

She reached over to the table and snatched up her tumbler of brandy, emptying the contents in one fiery swallow as she tried to burn away the memory of her mother arriving in her widow's weeds, with the message burned into her very soul that knowledge of his only daughter's adulterous behavior had carried her father off to his grave.

To ensure her shame would not reflect on her brothers, she was instructed never to come home again. And lest she think she was free to go on her selfish and self-indulgent path to hell free of obligation, she was still expected to contribute to her brothers' educations and her mother's welfare.

Maura had understood that day how the despoiled and despairing could be prompted to throw themselves into the River Liffey. She tried very hard to sustain her family and use her resources to help other girls in less fortunate circumstances. To hold at bay the shame for the path her life had taken and her sense of self separate from what she did, despite her mother's condemnation.

Now, Garrett Lynch, with his piercing gaze and surprising quest, had led her to abandon all of her defenses and believe her mother had been right all along.

Was she nothing more than a wanton?

He'd thrown her completely off guard by his pose of concern for a matter so close to her heart. He'd made her so angry with his questions and offers on behalf of the earl, and then completely disarmed her with a mere touch. How could she have been so foolish? So weak?

From the first brush of his lips she had practically melted into him. She'd shivered in his arms and reveled in the power of the passion she'd awakened in him, evidenced by the tight passion he had poured into her with the demands of his lips, and the hard desire he'd pressed against her softness when he'd cradled her against him so intimately.

Another moment or two and she'd been certain he was going to sweep her desk clean and claim her right there in her own salon.

And she had wanted him to.

She had all but begged him to.

It had been mindless. Powerful. Overwhelming.

And a sham.

He'd staged the whole seduction to destroy her hold on Freddie.

Freddie.

Oh God, Freddie would be here in just a short time. Having practically betrayed him, however would she face him? She knew she looked a wreck. Garrett's purpose could still be achieved and he didn't even need to be there. Freddie had been her friend long before he became her lover. Surely he would know as soon as he looked at her that things were not as they should be. Pleading illness would be her only course, if only to spare him. She sat down instead

She started toward the salon door.

"Maura? I hope you do not mind my calling on you so unexpectedly." He was here, entering her salon without knocking, so sure of his welcome despite his disclaimers. She wanted to sink right through the cushions. But there was nowhere to hide.

"I told Gerald I would announce myself." He stopped a few feet in from the door as she raised her eyes to greet him. She sat down instead.

"My God, dearest. Whatever has upset you so?" He rushed over and knelt on one knee beside her. "Gerald said you had been feeling unwell earlier."

Freddie's gaze was so kind, so loving. He reached into his pocket and pulled out a handkerchief. "Say something, sweetheart. Shall I send for a doctor? Would you like Mrs. Kelly to make you a posset or some tea?"

He gently wiped her cheeks, drying the tears she hadn't fully realized had been streaming from her eyes. How long had she been crying? She shouldn't be crying, at least not tears of self-pity. She didn't deserve the comfort of tears. She didn't deserve Freddie's solicitude. She shook her head.

He gave her a little smile despite the alarm still filling his eyes. "That's a little better. At least you realize I am here. You do not have to bear whatever is bothering you alone."

He eased himself onto the settee beside her and pulled her gently against his shoulder and into his embrace. She could feel his breath on her hair, the rise and fall off his chest against her cheek, and hear the steady beat of his heart. She didn't deserve this respite. But despite the cost it would impose later, she welcomed it.

Dear Freddie, it would be so easy to take what he offered, to give him all that he asked of her—to be allowed to love and honor her. But he deserved more, so very much more than she could ever give him.

He held her close for several minutes, allowing her time to regain a measure of her composure, to try and draw her scattered thoughts together and determine what she was going to tell him and how best to put it.

"I know I told you not to expect me." He tried to draw her out again. He brushed his lips against her hair. "But I missed you."

"I missed you, too, my lord." *And I believe I will miss you for some time to come.* She sighed.

"You know, on my way up the street I could have sworn I saw Garrett Lynch."

Her heart skipped a beat. She swallowed. Hard. "Who?"

"Lynch. Garrett Lynch. You met him the other night at the card party."

"Oh yes." She pulled away from Freddie's arm and turned herself so she was sitting next to him instead of against him. "Did you . . . did you talk to him?"

"He tipped his hat and mumbled something about an appointment. I failed to catch it all." He took her hand in his. His fingers were warm and reassuring. "Did he call here? Looking for me? I canceled an appointment with Daniel and Percy to be with you instead. Perhaps Lynch was to be part of that group, too. Although I do not think he and Jameson care much for one another's company."

He was trying so hard to fill the awkward silence, bless him. Given the company he could be keeping at this moment, she should be grateful he'd decided to come to her. But she was just sad—sad and sorrowful. She'd never realized the differences in those words before she'd been called upon to break her first heart.

She drew a breath. Time to begin. "Mr. Lynch was here. He is making some inquiries about missing girls from the countryside."

"What on earth has possessed him to begin such a search, let alone seek you out?"

"I do not know what motivated his interest in these missing girls, but he wished to speak to me about my school." She offered him the easiest answer she could, at least on this point—the truth.

"Your school?" Freddie straightened in his seat and looked at her. "Whatever could have led him to discover your connection to the school you sponsor?"

She shook her head. "I have no clue."

Freddie jumped to his feet and paced across the carpet, turning to face her when he reached her desk. "Is that what had you so overset when I arrived?"

He paced back and knelt with one knee on the carpet before her again, bringing his eyes level with hers. "You should be proud of your work, of what you do for those poor girls. I have never understood why you felt the need to keep your name from being associated with either your business or your school."

How could she explain it to him? She had wanted to keep this project separate from her life as a mistress, as a willing playmate or plaything for wealthy men. She had wanted something that was just hers.

He cupped her cheek with his hand. "When we are wed, you might not have the time to devote to them that you do now, but you certainly will have enough funds to help as many girls as you can find. And you will have no reason to hide your good deeds."

She felt the tears gathering at the corner of her lashes as she looked deep into the eyes of this man who loved her. She hated the tears, hated what she was about to do. But her mother's condemnation echoed. She was selfish and self-indulgent. She had allowed his courtship to go on for too long, knowing it was doomed, knowing he was destined for more than a life of shame with his former mistress.

The warning she had taken from the offer Garrett had brought from Freddie's grandfather, and the lengths he had been willing to take to accomplish his ends, made it clear that if she had any hope of dissuading Freddie on her own, she would have to act.

And fast.

Perhaps if he could lay the blame for the end of their liaison solely at her feet, he would be able to take comfort from his family, to accept their support without blame and recriminations. She owed him that much at least. She hoped it would be enough to keep him from the likes of Harold Jameson or even Garrett Lynch, men who preyed on the weakness or vulnerability of others.

"Sweetheart, please tell me what is wrong. You are so distracted." Freddie knew her too well. "I love you. Talk to me. You can tell me anything."

"You must not speak to me of love." She jerked her face away from his caress. She slipped around him and walked a few feet away. "It is neither right nor fair. You must not love me."

"Maura. Maura." He followed her and tried to take

her in his arms. "Of course I love you. I love you as you love me. We are going to be married."

She stepped away before turning to look up at him. "No, that is a dream." She shook her head. "That is your dream."

He just stood there, looking at her. As if she spoke in a language he didn't understand.

"Marriage is your dream. Not mine," she said again.

"Then we will just keep on as we have been a little longer. Until you are ready."

She could see the shift in his gaze as the reality of what she was saying, and what she was not saying, finally sank in. She shook her head ever so slowly.

"Maura?" His gaze shifted from the half-filled decanter and tumbler of brandy on the tray by the window to the empty one on the table by the settee. Then he raked her with his eyes, the blinders beginning to fall away. "Why was Lynch here tonight?"

The directness of his question startled her. She was sure her surprise showed on her face "I told—"

"Why, on a night when you thought I was engaged elsewhere, would you entertain another man?" His gaze darted to the decanter and back. "If I had not sent you a message from my mother's, what would I have walked into this room and found?"

The woman you love in the arms of another man, at the very least. She was a coward. She couldn't bring herself to confirm his suspicions, to tell him that whatever he imagined either was true or had very nearly been so. Her guilt was surely stamped on her face. She looked at him mutely.

He pulled her to him. His fingers dug into her shoulders and his gaze hardened as the realization grew that she was offering no defense because she had none.

"Maura." He said her name as if it was distasteful, a bitter mouthful.

She'd known breaking things off with him would wound him deeply. She hadn't realized how much it would hurt her as well.

His grip tightened further. His lip curled. His eyes narrowed into those of a stranger. He opened his mouth to say something. She steeled herself for the invective she'd earned with her betrayal, for the anger she'd brought upon herself. She felt certain she'd already cried as much as she possibly could in one day.

He released her so abruptly she nearly fell. He strode from the room without another word and slammed the salon door behind him. As the front door followed suit in what seemed like the space of only a few heartbeats, she sank to her knees on the carpet.

Like so much else in this day, in her life, she'd been wrong about the tears. She'd thought she had no more left to shed.

The Crown was crowded tonight—standing room only and all abuzz with conversation and raucous good humor following a cockfight at a nearby warehouse. The winners were celebrating and the losers commiserating. Harold Jameson saluted them all through the amber depths of his whiskey glass.

Winners or losers were all alike to him—pawns to be maneuvered or sacrificed to suit his game.

The young bucks he'd invited for the night's midnight frolics were nearly all assembled. They enjoyed their spirits and some fine cigars in the convivial atmosphere of the private parlor he had secured for them. He preferred the more ribald company of the tap. He remained outside in the public room ostensibly awaiting his guests, but in truth he had little patience for the inane conversations and baseless boasting of the future scions he sought to catch in his net.

That Clancare's heir would not be joining his little party tonight after all was a minor source of irritation. He took another sip of his whiskey, savoring the raw burn of cheap spirits. He wanted control of that lad, or more exactly, control over the lands and influence he'd one day claim.

His more immediate purpose in casting his lure at Stanhope could just as easily be accomplished by Longford or even that feckless fool, Masters. But it was Stanhope he wanted firmly under his thumb. That the baron seemed so thoroughly wound around the oh-so-dainty finger of his mistress made him all the more of a challenge. He liked challenges.

As if in answer to his summons, the young baron strode through the door at that minute looking as if he were ready to choke the first man to cross his path.

"Over here, Stanhope." Jameson stood and waited just long enough for the baron to catch sight of him before retaking his seat. The more dismissively or offhand the quality were treated, the closer they swarmed.

Stanhope frowned but pushed his way through the crowd. From the careless way he jostled the dockworkers and warehousemen aside he either was looking for a fight or just had one. Perhaps the estimable Mrs. Fitzgerald's charms had a chink after all.

"Have the others already left?" Stanhope continued to rake the room, looking for a familiar face. How timely.

"The rest of our party awaits us in the back parlor enjoying their brandy. I felt the need for something a bit less refined at this point of the night." Jameson gestured to the chair opposite his. "Will you join me, my lord. Or can I show you to the parlor."

"Less refined?" Stanhope fixed on the whiskey bottle. His lordship appeared to be in quite a sour mood. All the better. "Suits me perfectly."

Jameson could have said the same.

The ever-vigilant barmaid placed a fresh glass on the table before Stanhope was even seated. Just the sort of service Jameson required, as the slut well knew. He expected all of those who served him not only to meet but to anticipate his desires. All who did realized there were consequences should they fail.

He poured a healthy portion of whiskey from the bottle into the baron's glass and topped off his own. "*Slainte.*"

Stanhope nodded as he grabbed his glass, then drained the contents without so much as a sputter. Interesting. A lover's quarrel by all appearances. The night was getting better and better.

"I hear congratulations are in order," he observed as he poured the younger man another and raised his own glass in salute.

"Congratulations?"

Stanhope fixed him with the first bit of clarity he'd shown since joining him at the table. It was a grim, cold clarity rooted in bitter truth. Jameson recognized it well, recognized and knew just how to exploit it.

"Only if you mean for my timely escape." The baron gulped this drink as well.

Jameson poured him another. "Then to your escape."

"Aye." After a first sip, Stanhope paused to stare at the contents of his glass, the effects of so much drink so quickly finally pierced the shield of his distress. He scrubbed a hand over his face and closed his eyes. "My escape."

Jameson took a sip from his own glass. The two of them might just as easily have been alone for all they sat in a crowded tavern. The party that awaited them could wait a little longer. The ones he already controlled would see to the contentment of those he had on the hook.

Much as he would love to seek all the details of however Mrs. Fitzgerald had fouled her nest so he could use them to his advantage, he knew better than to rush things. Stanhope, like most men, would be all the more grateful and far less suspicious if allowed to let his story unfold at his own pace.

And there was always a story to be told.

"I would have laid the world at her feet . . ." Stanhope began the litany of his trials. Jameson was all ears as the whiskey and self-pity flowed.

He could not say he was shocked to learn that Maura Fitzgerald had lost her chance to become a countess, and in such a classic way. She was but a woman after all. All women were weak.

Despite their denials and coquettish refusals, most merely lacked a strong guiding hand when it came to both fidelity and knowing how to please their man in all things. Maura Fitzgerald merely ran true to form. And Stanhope was certainly not man enough to give her the guidance she needed.

While his purpose was better suited by her banishment from Stanhope's sphere, under other circumstances he would not mind teaching the young lord how to ensure his woman's loyalty. Perhaps with his next mistress.

His own taste did not usually run to women of her sort—save as a means to an end or for quick satisfaction. Most men's fancy pieces prided themselves on the pleasures they could offer through artifice and pretense. He preferred to teach his conquests how to please him unencumbered by previous experience or expectations.

Given her status as Stanhope's mistress, however, Maura Fitzgerald had surprised him the other night. She possessed a naturally sensual appeal not easily forgotten or ignored, despite the outward devotion she had practically poured over Stanhope to keep him in her thrall that night. Although he'd heard Stanhope was not her first lover, there was an unspoiled quality about her he found intriguing. She had seemed to lack the deceit of others of her ilk.

That she was open to the advances of another when she so clearly had Stanhope in her grasp he could have predicted given the aura of ripeness she exuded. But that she would risk everything Stanhope offered for a liaison with a man such as Garrett Lynch was disappointing. Her behavior only served to prove his point over the weakness of women.

Still, it was a rare woman who surprised him once, let alone twice. Perhaps when he had guided his latest recruits to his quest for power through this particular thicket he might consider paying her a call. He had one or two surprises of his own he would like to try with her. If that meant he might be poaching on Lynch's property by that time, so much the better.

". . . so I left. She never even answered me. So I left." Stanhope looked forlornly at his empty glass, finally finished with his litany of sorrow.

If he started blubbering, Jameson would be hard-pressed not to cast up his accounts. Young bucks who believed there was such a thing as love, and that they had lost it, could be quite tiresome.

"Perhaps your lady was too flabbergasted by the accusation to be able to form an answer," he offered, taking the more sympathetic tack of the possible options open to him. Stanhope might vilify his mistress himself, but he was probably not yet ready to hear a word against her from another's lips.

Stanhope shook his head. He was tipsy enough to be careless but not quite in his cups—the best state for manipulation.

"Nope. She's guilty," he assured his glass. "I failed to

see it at first, but she had the look of a woman who had been thoroughly kissed and left wanting more. Not that I have ever actually seen a woman like that. But her lips were all puffy-like. So were her eyes. But that was from the crying."

"Enough." Jameson clapped his soon-to-be protégé on his shoulder and pushed his chair back. "Our friends and a little night air outside the city will help you put all of this in perspective. Perhaps you'll see things from a fresh eye in a day or two and be able to straighten this all out."

"Do you think so? Really?" A flare of hope brightened the baron's face as he looked up. A few more of those lit and extinguished with the fool's paramour and Lynch's unwitting cooperation and Stanhope would be his. How delightful.

"Of course. Let us go seek the company of other men and eschew all women this night." He grasped Stanhope under the arm and helped him to his feet as he stood. "Allow yourself a little time and perspective."

"Let us away then, good friend." Stanhope made his way with exaggerated care toward the back room.

Jameson smiled. His trap was nearly sprung. Soon he would have enough influence in the southeastern portion of Ireland to match that which he had already manipulated in the north. The truth of his birth might preclude the quality from including him in their exclusive social circles should they ever learn that truth, but he would always have a place in the back rooms and inner circles of power.

The rest of his assembled guests greeted his arrival in the company of Stanhope with cheers. This young man carried a great deal of sway within his set; snaring him would go a long way toward achieving his ends.

"What are we about tonight?" Percy Masters's irritatingly high-pitched question broke through the chatter.

"Come with me, gentlemen. I trust you have all

brought your mounts and are prepared for a bit of fun?"

Their interest whetted with several hours of drinking as they waited, and their enthusiasm for the night's entertainment fired by the ones among them already loyal to his cause, Jameson led his marks out into the street through The Crown's back entrance.

Once they were well outside the city environs he called a halt after passing through a hedgerow into an open pasture. Darkness enfolded them. The night air was crisp and clean. The ride had sobered some of the spirits out of his party as they gathered around him, just as he intended. He wanted to keep them off balance.

The only sounds were the mating calls of the summer crickets and the blowing and whickering of the horses.

"Thank you gentlemen for joining me on this little expedition. I know that I promised you some fun with a different kind of sport, so let me begin by apologizing for luring you here under false pretenses."

There was a murmur of questions, but no protest rang clear. Rabbits in his snare. He plunged ahead. This oration got them every time.

"Who among us is not a loyal son of Ireland? Who among us would deny our king our sworn duty?"

The murmurs swelled.

"Who among us does not pay taxes on our lands and revenues to support and defend our king and country? And who among us does not try his very best to keep food on the tables and roofs over the heads of our tenants."

He paced his horse past the gathering of present and future followers. He had them in the palm of his ever-so-deserving hand. "If any of us does not do these things and thank God that he can, then let him ride across this green soil of Eire, through our native hawthorns and back to the city."

"But if you love our people, our king, and our native soil, let me hear from you now"

The shouts ringing across the meadow were gratifying, as always. This was not the first time he had delivered this speech, nor would it be the last. It worked because each time he gave it, he believed it.

When the shouts died out he continued. "Not far from here lives a man who does not believe as we do. He preaches sedition to the children in his school. He undermines their loyalty to the king, to Ireland."

He paused long enough to get his point across. "This man encourages his students and their parents to finance his cause rather than pay their rightful rents and taxes. What say you to this man?"

Boos and hisses echoed across the meadow, along with calls to teach this man a lesson, to stop him. Mobs were so easy to create, to manipulate.

"I say it is our duty—as loyal citizens, as true Irishmen, and as Christians—to visit this man and help him to understand the error of his way. Who's with me?"

The shouts were deafening.

He waited a moment, relishing the power, before claiming their attention once more. "While some of you may be carrying weapons for self-protection, Bart here will hand out pistols for you all. These are ready to be used, but I hope you do not; they are for defense only. We don't wish to harm anyone."

His disclaimer was met with agreement. He pressed on, determined to bring them all completely into the fold. "To avoid detection we have party masks, and to readily identify one another, Charles will hand out sashes that show up with ease, even at a distance or in the dark."

Bart and Charles began handing out their bounty from the sacks they had brought along for this jaunt.

"Ooooooohhhh, costumes!" Percy Masters's squeal echoed.

Jameson grimaced. Masters was such a fool.

"Again I say." He raised his voice to be heard above the clamor of preparations. "If any of this makes you uncomfortable, if you are not with us, Ireland's truest sons, you are welcome to leave now. But if you want to protect your king, your country, and your God, then take your equipment and let us ride."

A roar of approval swelled amongst the recruits as he wheeled away and began to canter across the meadow.

Chapter Nine

"They were doing what to a *priest*?" Sean kicked off the coverlet and swung to a sitting position.

"Partial hanging. Gruesome." Garrett handed his friend one of the mugs of coffee his landlady had just brought up. "We provided the distraction and Daniel got him out of there."

"Still, what would possess anyone to bring back such methods? They were banned back in Wolfe Tone's days." Sean scrubbed a hand over his jaw and then through his hair, tousling his curls to even wilder abandon than a night on Garrett's sofa had afforded him.

"Aye." Garrett took a sip from his mug and sat down in his chair with a sigh. The sofa Sean had used last night looked far more comfortable than the couple of hours of sleep he'd gotten in the church nave after delivering the priest they'd saved into the hands of his brethren. The coffee's welcome warmth washed through him.

"The military may have stopped, but those Peep O' Day Boys from last century have turned themselves into the Orangemen of today. All hell has broken loose." Three facts linked together to bother him: the viciousness of the act, the research evident in picking the target for last night's raid—a teacher and priest, no less—and the company riding out to catch and torture last night. "Not that it's ever been far away despite the repeal of the Catholic Suppressions or passing the Act of Union."

"What do you know of the Devil's Club?" he asked Sean as his friend shrugged into a shirt.

"*Saofoir.*" Sean took big gulp from his mug and shook his head. His use of the Gaelic alerted Garrett to the depths of his disgust. Perverted indeed.

"Their club headquarters, as they like to call it, is just a cover for a bed-house where perversions abound, " Sean said. "They claim roots to the old Hellfire Club, without the devil worship. Why?"

"Daniel reports most of the young men up to mischief last night were also recently invited to indulge themselves at the Devil's Club."

Sean's gaze sharpened as he met Garrett's. "What is the connection?"

"Jameson. Harold Jameson organized both *entertainments.*"

"*Diabhal.*" Sean's knuckles blanched white as they gripped the mug.

"I can only speculate he derives some pleasure in pandering to the baser side of the young bucks he invites, that he gains power from corrupting them, either for use today or down the road. Which would explain his interest in Stanhope."

"*Diabhal.*" Sean jumped to his feet and paced away to the window.

"What is it?"

"I have heard rumors of secret meetings far outside Dublin, a rite of passage and an initiation that . . . that involves virgins."

Garrett's stomach knotted. "You are not thinking—"

"Jane." Sean grimaced. His free hand clenched tight.

He looked out the window with unseeing eyes. Worry etched his mouth as he spoke. "We talked to the mother of the maid who was with Miss Fuller the day she disappeared. She was adamant her daughter would not have willingly left the area. Her elder sister was expecting her first child any day. The girl was very excited."

"That alone does not preclude her from accompanying her mistress if she did indeed elope or run home to England after her father banished her to the country." Garrett tried to offer a more dispassionate view of the situation as he joined Sean at the window.

Sean glanced over at Garrett and shook his head. "Liam spent some time in the admiral's kitchen talking to the housekeeper. Seems the first thing the admiral did was send word to all the ports he could reach. There was no sign of either girl. They searched his daughter's personal effects thoroughly, and there were no missives from any particular beau or evidence anything was missing from her personal effects save the clothes on her back."

"What led the admiral to focus his concerns on your possible role?"

"Something she wrote in her private journal." Sean shook his head again. "She must have written something about the incident at the Hamilton's."

"Ahh yes, the dousing." Garrett recalled the belated report Sean had delivered after his meeting with the admiral. The incident apparently had a significant impact on both parties involved. Another Jameson connection. The fellow was turning up far too often with too many aspects of their business of late. "It never ceases to amaze me the amount of information Liam can extract from the kitchens he visits."

"Broken-down traveler never fails." Sean agreed. "This time he damaged a curricle axle."

"Country folk are nothing if not hospitable to those in need." Garrett agreed. "So if Miss Fuller has not left home of her own accord—"

"She is either dead at this point or trapped in some sort of living hell." Sean looked back out the window, his tone harsh and grating with whatever guilt haunted him. "I think it is time to visit Jameson and try to pound some truth from him."

"That may feel good, but also could tip the scale and force him, if he has any connection at all, to drastic action. Daniel appears in place as one of his marks along with Stanhope. We'll set Seamus to shadow Jameson's every move from here in case Daniel was observed slipping the priest to us last night."

Sean scrubbed a hand through his hair. "I cannot just sit here and do nothing."

Garrett clapped a hand on his friend's shoulder. "I have something important I need you to handle this day. I cannot be in two places at once."

Sean took a moment to pull his personal anxiety inside. His ability to focus on the task at hand was one of the many qualities that made him so valuable. When he met Garrett's gaze he was ready to give his all to whatever was asked of him. "What do you need?"

"I was to meet with Admiral Fuller today, at St. Michan's." He pulled a letter sealed with his signet ring from his breast pocket. "He will be told to come to meet at the rear confessionals at noon, during Mass."

Sean took the letter and weighed it in his hand. "Will be told?"

"Seamus will deliver his instructions giving him an hour to make the meeting. You take the last alcove, he arrives, and you slip him the envelope. Once he has read our price for locating his daughter—"

"Our price? You intend to haggle price with him in return for finding Jane?" If the edge on Sean's voice sharpened any further Garrett would be flayed.

"If I just accept his terms for the prisoners at Newgate"—he explained, swallowing back any remonstrance about getting involved with someone attached to one of their missions. It would do little good at this point. Sean was already more involved than he even knew—"he may realize how important they are. He thinks of me as the worse kind of fraud."

"A scoundrel masquerading as a folk hero." That was the official description the authorities used when posting updates to the growing reward offered for the capture or unmasking of the Green Dragon.

"Exactly. I do not want him to be surprised. Men of his caliber, when surprised, take closer looks. So I am, or rather you are, going to live down to his expectations and demand a handsome reward for locating his daughter. He may sputter, but he will accept."

"What happens to Jane if he refuses?"

"He won't." Faced with the skeptical look Sean shot him, Garrett emphasized his assurance. "He won't."

He clapped Sean's shoulder and strode over to the table where he'd set his mug. "You will be in the deep shadows, with a curtain between you. Take a slouch hat and one of my greatcoats. And the Green Dragon's ring."

He pulled the square-cut emerald from his finger and laid it on the table. It rocked for a moment against the dark wood, and the emerald winked in the sunlight. He was passing it to Sean now, as he would one day for good. The *Ard Tiarna* approved his choice for who would succeed him with the Green Dragon's ring and sword.

"Keep your voice low and flat so he will think it sounds enough like mine to pass. Just as he gets ready to leave, tell him he is to go down the street to Newgate and get those prisoners released as a sign of his good faith. Seamus and Liam will make sure he does not have an escort. Wait until one of them knocks and then exit when the noon Mass is over."

Sean strode over and picked up the ring, weighing

it in his palm for just a moment before sliding it on his finger. "But really. If he stalks out?"

"We will keep looking. That is my other appointment. I am going to talk to the girls Mrs. Fitzgerald is housing at her school."

Bleak determination flitted across Sean's eyes. He compressed his lips into a grim line as he twisted the ancient signet onto his finger.

"What was her reaction to the news that not only is your cousin missing, there are others?"

She practically allowed me to make love to her right there on the desk in her salon.

His lips twisted at the thought. He understood all too well how difficult it might be for Sean, feeling his way along the unfamiliar labyrinth of his attraction for Jane Fuller and his duty to their cause. Somehow, Maura brought out a protectiveness in him. He wanted his friend to think well of her. Her concern for her girls was real enough; he could comfortably discuss that with others without revealing their wayward behavior at the end of his visit.

"She promised to do all she could to assist us. She insisted."

"What did I tell you? Stanhope has excellent taste in women. Beautiful, intelligent, and willing to look out for others. Too bad she is unsuitable to be his countess."

Garrett knew the baron must be grappling with this very dilemma. Daniel had reported he'd shown up with Jameson for last night's adventure looking three sheets to the wind, with a wild hopelessness to his actions and a refusal to answer any inquiries regarding the cause.

Had she told him of their visit? Had Stanhope surmised what had nearly happened between his mistress and her guest last night? Things could not have gone well between the lovers if he'd behaved so recklessly.

"She is well-meaning enough. But there is only a slim hope any of the girls currently in her care will have had contact with the Devil's Club spawn."

"True. But we will never know if you fail to ask." Sean sounded better now he did not have a stretch of empty time yawing before him. "So I get Mass and a meeting with a cranky old bastard who would like little better than to arrest you, or me since I'll be taking your place, while you spend the day with a beautiful woman and a group of schoolgirls."

Garrett shrugged. "Some of us . . ."

". . . have all the luck." Sean finished their old joke. "Do you think he will really be able to set the men he promised free?"

"We will know soon enough. But I have to think that as a truly desperate father, he will do all in his power to live up to his promise. When we get the financial reward, we can donate it to a worthy cause."

"Perhaps to Mrs. Fitzgerald's school?" Sean took his turn as quizmaster.

"Aye. Perhaps. She appears to be trying to achieve some good with her life, at least."

"Aye." Sean agreed as he turned and headed to the door. "I will fetch hot water from the kitchen or neither of us will be much good this day. Do you mind if I borrow a clean shirt?"

"Have I ever denied you anything?"

Sean favored him with an appreciative wave and was out the door without another word.

Garrett scrubbed his hand across his chin. He at least would need a shave besides washing up. He didn't want to frighten the Eagan students.

Or Maura.

His thoughts had not been far from Maura Fitzgerald since he strode from her house. Questions plagued him. He'd spent the better part of the night fighting the urge to rush back and pry her from Stan-

hope's embrace. Counter to all logic and his oath because his mentor, the Earl of Clancare was counting
on him to steer his heir away from such choices, it
hadn't been until after he had learned from Daniel
the baron had been among last night's riders that his
tension had eased.

As he and Sean readied for the day ahead, his
thoughts and questions cycled. How would Maura react
to today's visit to the draper's shop? Would she even
allow him entrance? Would any good come of it? All
would be resolved as soon as he arrived on Hawkins
Street, the sooner the better.

But how would she have reacted to his return last
night? Would she have allowed him entrance then?
And what would have come from such a visit? Could
he have, would he have, convinced her his offer on
behalf of the earl had nothing to do with his kiss?
None of those questions would be easily answered.

Worse still was the knowledge it was not even the
questions that plagued him most in connection to
Maura Fitzgerald/Eagan. It was the rightness that had
accompanied taking her in his arms, the softness of
her lips under his and his reaction to her passion
when she had finally opened herself to him. Never
had a woman haunted him so.

"Well, Garrett?"

He blinked and turned to see Sean—scrubby
beard, slouch hat, battered coat, and all. "Your own
brother wouldn't know you."

"As if the likes of himself would 'ere be caught inside a place such as St. Michan's." Sean affected a
peasant's cadence to his speech. "And ye make a
fine figure of a man yerself, if ye don't mind me
sayin' so."

"*Thus we are arrayed and armed?*"

"Aye," Sean bowed with a flourish toward the door.
"After ye, sir."

* * *

"Mrs. Eagan?" Silas Polhaven stood in her doorway. "That Mr. Lynch is here again. At least this time he asked if ye were ready ta see him."

Maura closed her eyes. She'd thought of little else since Freddie stormed out last night. Shameless. The stern voice of her mother echoed. She agreed. She both longed for and dreaded this meeting, her first sight of Garrett Lynch since he kissed her last night.

She opened her eyes. Only last night? It felt like a lifetime ago. She hadn't even been sure he would show up now that his goal of forcing her out of Freddie's life had been all but accomplished.

"Show him up, please. And would you send word to Mrs. Polhaven we will be over to interview the girls in about five minutes?"

"Yes, ma'am. Would you like me ta stay this time?" Mr. Polhaven's chin tilted down and he perused her over his reading spectacles. "The man upset you something fierce yesterday."

"No." She smiled and shook her head much as she had done when Gerald had offered to escort her to and from the shop this morning. "I'll be fine. I just want a word with him before we go over."

"Very well." The older gentleman's fatherly gaze lingered just a little longer. "But I'll be nearby if ye need me. The whole visit."

He turned and trudged down the steps. For a dour, taciturn man, he really was very sweet.

Was she ready to face the man who had ripped her carefully constructed façade away so easily? Make that plural. She had tried so hard to see herself as more, but with his devastating kiss Garrett had shown her not only that she was indeed the woman of easy virtue her mother condemned but that her plan to save

Freddie from himself had been a sham, more selfish than selfless. She was a fraud.

Footsteps on the stairs. She straightened some papers on her desk and tried not to think about the feel of Garrett Lynch's lips on hers, claiming her heart, her mind, her soul. She tried not to think of how lost she had felt when he left her last night. How soiled his offer on behalf of Freddie's grandfather had made her feel. How contradicting were her feelings about the entire mess.

Then he was there, filling her doorway. He looked very handsome in his well-tailored Corbeau broadcloth coat, buff trousers, and Wellingtons. The green of his jacket set off his eyes to perfection. He held his hat in his hand, and his gloves dangled carelessly from his pocket.

"Maura?" Just her name, but both his penitent tone and the softness in his eyes hit the right notes of hesitation and apology. A small kernel of warmth inside her longed to respond. She resisted. He was good. He was very good.

She stood up. "I prefer to be called Mrs. Eagan here."

He kept his gaze fixed on her but didn't say anything. She rushed to fill the void. "This is my place of business and I find the use of my formal names garners a better response from both my customers and my students."

"Very well." He inclined his head. "Mrs. Eagan."

"I . . . I . . . wanted to speak with you before we meet the girls to make sure you will be sensitive to their situations." She stepped around the corner of her table. "They are here seeking fresh starts, trying to forget the mistakes they made or the ones forced upon them. We treat them with respect."

"Of course."

"If they get upset, you must let me handle their questioning."

"Agreed." So amenable.

"If you mean that, it will help if you let me know exactly what you are looking for."

Something in his gaze shifted as though he were considering what to tell her. And yet he seemed sincere in his desire to find his cousin and these other missing young women. After a moment, he nodded and squared his shoulders. "Similarities in behavior. In what happened to them. Were they abducted or coaxed? Was this by a stranger or recent acquaintance? Where were they? Do they remember locations? Anything may help, no matter how small or insignificant it seems to them."

"You really are looking for someone, aren't you. Jane is real."

He nodded without flinching from her bald questions. "I am not a total cad. I really am trying to find her. And I am sorry if I offended you last night."

She shrugged and struggled to ignore the pain welling inside her. "A woman in my situation gets used to the insults, the slights. You merely helped me to remember the impulse that got me involved in this life in the first place."

His cheek ticked. "Maura, I never meant . . . what happened—"

"What happened accomplished one goal for you." She interrupted him with a wave of her hand. "I hope we can as easily dispose of this one and you can be on your way. And, I would like to remind you, I prefer Mrs. Eagan here."

Even to her own ears, and knowing how she wished she could just crawl under the table, her answer sounded steady, mature, focused on the girls and not on herself. She'd be more than pleased if she could carry off the rest of this agonizing visit with such aplomb. Pleased indeed. Best to get moving before her knees turned any further into jelly.

"I apologize, Mrs. Eagan. I will not forget again." His expression was solemn. His tone sincere.

"Then let us be off." She offered brightly as she advanced toward the doorway he still blocked. "Please follow me. Mrs. Polhaven has cleared her office in the other building for us to use. She will send in our most recent residents, one at a time."

An hour later they had interviewed almost all of the new girls, to little avail. Only one claimed to have been approached by a stranger inquiring into the status of her virtue, and he had been scared off when he learned she already had a beau. The incident had also taken place more than a year ago."

The last girl knocked tentatively on the door. "Mrs. Eagan? I brought ye one of the handkerchiefs I've been working on. I was wondering if ye might check the stitching on the monogram and see if it's fine enough ta pass."

"Let me have a look at it, Caitlin." She took the square of striped cotton from the girl as she sat in the chair indicated for her. She was a short brunette with wide, freckle-flecked cheeks and an even wider smile.

"The stitching is beautiful," Maura exclaimed. "The hems are straight and even, and you have got a real knack for the embroidery. Is this a special order?"

Caitlin beamed, then looked suddenly worried. "No, Mrs. Eagan. It's jest somethin' I've been working on in my spare time. If ye'll allow I'd like to send it ta me grand-da. His birthday's next month. I can pay ye from me nest egg."

"Nonsense. You send this to your grandfather. I bet he would be thrilled to get a present you made yourself."

"Thank ye." Caitlin beamed. Then she glanced

shyly up at Garrett as he perched on the corner of Katherine Polhaven's desk.

"Caitlin, I would like you to meet Mr. Lynch. He is going to ask you some questions about what happened to you before you came to us."

Cailtlin's soft blue eyes rounded. But she nodded. "I don't much like ta talk of such things."

"Perhaps you can start by telling me about your nest egg?" Garrett smiled. He looked so innocent and charming as he attempted to draw the girl out. Maura had been very relieved throughout the interviews. He hadn't pressed any of them. He'd managed to hit the right note with each one, to get information without making the process painful. He had stopped his probing as soon as there had been any sign of distress or it was clear there was no connection to the cousin he sought.

"Our nest egg's the money Mrs. Eagan pays us fer our stitchin'," Caitlin explained, eager to be helpful. "We spends a goodly portion of the day cutting and hemmin' and working up ta fancy pieces. She keeps it on account fer us, and we get it ta help us move on when we're ready."

"Their work is sold in the shop. The profit goes to them," Maura said as he turned to her.

"Commendable." He smiled. Maura's stomach did a rebellious flip. "You teach them a skill, give them a fresh start. What else?"

"There's plenty more ta what we do. Mrs. Eagan helps us with our speech, and some of the girls are learning ta read. Mr. Polhaven teaches us sums so we'll be able ta manage on our own. Mrs. Polhaven sees ta everythin' else. She helps us care fer our clothes, leads us in prayer each mornin' and night, and takes care of us if we're feelin' sick or sad or afraid."

"Do you ever feel afraid, Caitlin?"

She shook her head. "Not since I came here. The priest what found me brought me to Eagan's."

"Found you?"

"Aye, and I thank the Lord fer him every day. I was going ta throw myself in the river and he caught me. The man what brought me ta Dublin had left me flat soon's I told him 'bout the babe. I couldn't go home. I had no money, no food, and I couldn't do what my landlady wanted me ta do."

"You have a child?"

The haunted look left Caitlin's eyes. "Oh, aye. My little Jenna. She's a real sweetheart. *Mo muirnín.* She's why I aim ta learn as much as I can here. So I can give her a good life, with a good mam, not one living from one man ta the next. On my own."

"Good for you. Your Jenna sounds like a lucky girl to have you for a mother." Garrett was doing a good job of keeping the disappointment from his demeanor. It had to be there though. All the morning and no closer to even a slender connection to his missing relative.

"Thank you, sir." Caitlin smiled. "And thanks to Mrs. Eagan. I never want my Jenna ta go through whatever that poor Mary had to suffer."

"What poor Mary?" He squared his shoulders.

"Aye, wretched soul." Caitlin sighed. "She sits so quiet most of the time, like she's someplace far away where no one can touch her. And when she does rouse it's either with shuddering screams or repeating the word *diabhal* over and over. Sometimes with the word *sliabh,* most times not."

"Devil and mountain." Garrett repeated. "Devil and mountain. Thank you, Caitlin. Good luck to you and your daughter."

After getting a nod of permission from Maura, Caitlin rose from her seat. "Thank ye, sir. I hope ye find what ye seek."

Before the door had clicked shut behind her, Garrett was on his feet. "I need to speak to this Mary."

Maura shook her head. "You cannot. She is in very precarious health. There is only a very slim chance she would know anything of value, and even less chance that she'd be able to tell you."

"I still need to see for myself. To at least try."

Maura shook her head. "She cannot bear the sight of any man. She is still terribly frightened by whatever happened to her."

"How did she come to you?"

"The same priest who brought us Caitlin. They had found Mary wandering the road outside Bray in Wicklow. They were going to send her to a home for the insane and Father John intervened. Even Mrs. Polhaven is afraid we may never be able to reach her.

"Wicklow, you say. That is something at least. Although very far from where Jane was last seen. Please let me try to talk to her. I will keep it very brief."

"What would you ask? You cannot ask her about what happened to her. It is far too frightening."

"I would ask about Jane and if she has any idea where she had been before she was found. Any information, no matter how small, may help."

Maura thought for a moment. He was urgent in his request and his eyes gleamed as though he were close to what he wanted. If Mary had information, how could she not help? Maura blew out a quick breath.

"I could ask your questions for you."

"Agreed." He nodded.

Several minutes later, Maura crouched by the chair where Mary rocked in the sunshine flowing through the window. Her unseeing gaze was fixed on a point where the wood held the glass panes in place. She looked so very young. How could anyone have thought to hurt her, to treat this scrap of a child as if she were a woman grown. The doctor had confirmed the fact she had been terribly abused by some man, or men even. The very thought sickened Maura.

"Mary." She covered the girl's hand with her own. "Mary, I want you to remember you are safe here. That no one is going to hurt you or make you do anything. You are safe. If you want to talk, when you want to talk—or not—is up to you. One step at a time."

The girl's gaze drifted over to rest hazily on Maura. The slightest of smiles played about her lips. Did she understand? Maura plunged ahead, praying she could ask the right questions and not disturb the girl overmuch in her efforts. "I just want to know if you remember another girl who might have been wherever you were. A girl named Jane."

Mary's soft brown eyes focused.

"Jane," she repeated not as a question. "Jane saved me."

Tears shimmered in her eyes.

"Jane saved me." Certain, even if voiced in a tremulous tone.

"From where *muirnín*? From who?"

But the horror was already building in the girl. She went rigid, and her gaze focused on things she should never have seen, memories she shouldn't have to carry. "Jane. *Diabhal. Sliabh. Diabhal.* Jane. Jane."

"Jane and Devil's Mountain?" Maura squeezed Mary's hand as the words she repeated became a litany and the litany came faster and faster.

"We will find her, Mary. We will save her too." Maura squeezed Mary's hand. "We will find her. I promise you."

Katherine Polhaven was already bustling into the room from her post in the hall with Garrett as Maura turned. She was not about to leave the girl alone. Not while she was so rigid. She feared Mary might have another screaming fit.

"There ye go, lamb." Katherine was using her most

soothing motherly voice as she drew near and nodded for Maura to leave. "Ye passed on the information, now ye need yer medicine and a good rest. Ye did well, lass. Don't fret yerself."

As she exited the room she could see the girl reach out to Katherine, tears streaming down her face as the older woman gathered her into a hug. She wasn't screaming or ducking back into her haze immediately. Perhaps she had taken another step in her recovery.

Garrett was waiting down the hall. She could see he was deep in thought. "Have you ever heard of Devil's Mountain?"

He shook his head. "Chances of her Jane being the one I seek are so slim. Wicklow, if that is the right place, is pretty far from Meath."

Was he regretting his search? If so, something had to be done. "Do you know where I might hire someone familiar with County Wicklow to act as guide?"

"Why?" The sharp intensity of the suspicious gaze he fixed on her took her breath.

"I promised I would find her friend. I have to at least try. It's not as if there is anyone who will miss me if I go out of town for a few days.

"You cannot go." Finality etched his tone as he took a step nearer. For a moment she was certain her would grab her again as he had last night. But he fisted his hands at his sides.

"You cannot stop me." She retreated a step. "I gave my word."

"So did I." His gaze held hers for a moment; she could almost see his mind twisting the situation through. She held her ground, determined not to back down when he restarted his argument. Finally, he took a deep breath. "Then hire me."

Impossible. The thought of going anywhere with this man was impossible, no matter that he'd sur-

Emily Baker

prised her with the offer instead of trying to convince her to stay.

She opened her mouth to tell him exactly how impossible the idea was. "It must be strictly business between us."

Her answer should have stunned her, but it didn't. Anything to do with Garrett Lynch seemed to turn out entirely different from her plans. "Strictly business and nothing more. We look for the girl and that is all."

"Agreed." He nodded and his hand touched hers.

She glanced down at their hands as a quiver of anticipation went through her. What had she just gotten herself into?

Chapter Ten

"And then he tied her bag to the back of the mount and they rode away. Neither of them saw me down the block. Mrs. Kelly, the housekeeper, would only say she'd gone out of town and would be away for at least a few days." Baron Stanhope looked on the verge of tears as he signaled the bar girl to bring him another ale.

Harold Jameson could only have been more pleased at the smooth turn of events if he had manipulated them himself. But then he had always possessed the very luck of the devil. He'd recognized a formidable foe in the shapely form of Maura Fitzgerald when it came to claiming the future Earl of Clancare. He thanked providence, divine or otherwise, for leading her to throw the baron over for the likes of Garrett Lynch, a card-playing wastrel.

"In my experience, women are fickle. Fickle and weak, my lord." Harold took a long pull on his cheroot and let the words sink in. "They do not know what is best for them. They depend on us for guidance, for steady vision, a firm hand. In all things, but particularly the calls of the flesh."

Stanhope's jaw worked. "So, you are saying I lost Maura because I let her wishes hold too much sway?"

"You still are. After all you have done for her, all you have given her, look how she repays your generosity. There is no man who could repay such loyalty, such selfless devotion by giving his loyalty to another, not if he has any claim to conscience."

The bar girl delivered the ale. Jameson grabbed her and pulled her onto his lap. He grabbed her chin between his fingers and turned her lips to his. She resisted, the position was certainly uncomfortable enough to warrant a struggle, but he dragged her around for a thorough kiss complete with a twisting grope for her breast while he held her fast.

After a few seconds, her struggles ceased and her nipple hardened from his deliberately brutal plundering of her charms. When he released her, she stayed in his arms breathing hard and looking dazed. He slid a coin from the table to her. "There's more for you later if you keep up such service."

She scooted off his lap clutching the coin with a speculative gleam in her eye.

"See that? Whore or maiden, it matters little; all a woman really wants is to be shown what is expected from her and she will comply. Her first reward should come from pleasing the man claiming her. Anything else she gains is secondary to the pleasure she must give him first."

"What if she is unwilling to give . . . to give in?"

"Then that is where the man's guidance, his vision, takes over. He must show her how foolish she is being whether it is for a night or for a lifetime. Pleasure is fluid—it passes from one to the other, like the tide turning."

Another satisfying pull on his cheroot sufficed while the younger man absorbed the lesson. "Remember, a man's desire is by far the stronger, more true compass than a woman's. Go where you want and the woman flows with you."

"That is not . . . that is not—"

"Not the way your father talked to you about sharing a bed?" Jameson chuckled. "None of our fathers talked of such beyond respecting the woman and begetting heirs. Trust me, sir. The wisdom I have is hard-won through experience."

He leaned forward, pouncing on the uncertainty he detected in the young baron's dazed look. Watching his mistress ride away with another man had shaken him to his core. He was ripe for the picking.

"If you do not mind my boldness, my lord—when was the last time you and the lovely Mrs. Fitzgerald were . . . intimate?" He knew he had just gone way beyond the bounds, but he was hoping for a big payout.

Stanhope looked shocked. Then guilty. A flush of pink streaked his neck above his collar. He swallowed hard. "Nearly a month."

No wonder a woman as lush and ripe as Maura Fitzgerald had jumped so readily into the arms of another, even one such as Lynch. If he'd only known.

"There you are, Stanhope. No wonder you can barely think. She has had you to heel for too long. Imagine a woman denying you for a month so she can take a new lover. You have definitely got to change your outlook on the fairer half of our race and their role in your life. In your bed."

Stanhope looked absolutely miserable. He'd reached a low point. Time to build up his new protégé. He almost chuckled aloud at the dual meaning. "If you might allow me to prescribe a cure, I know just the place to show you exactly what I mean. Help you find yourself so you can guide your next woman."

Make a man of you, was his implied message. By the time Maura Fitzgerald came to her senses and realized how little Lynch had to offer, her baron would be immune to her charms. Perhaps he could persuade the lad they should share her for a night or two, just to humble her. The possibility tantalized.

He'd not take Stanhope to the Devil's Club this

night. But he did know a discreet place that specialized in biddable girls adept at a number of skills to open up the baron's taste for dominance, for being the leader in pursuing pleasure. That should go a long way toward enticing him to participate in the initiation scheduled for next week. Hell, he might even move the date up, depending on how readily the lad took to his tutelage.

Stanhope took a deep swallow from his glass. He put it down with a loud slam. "Why not? Lead on, Jameson. I have been celibate too long."

"Good man, Stanhope. Good man." He clapped a hand on the baron's shoulder. "You are in for a rewarding night. A real eye opener."

"There is a sight."

Maura pointed to a group of children cheering in a circle as a fierce cricket match took place in the center of the field they approached at the edge of the city. The batmen for either side stood head and shoulders above the rest of the boys at play. Sean and Liam.

Garrett whistled the redstart's call, and both turned their attention immediately to the road. They handed their bats off to other players and headed over at easy paces.

Sean arrived first. He kept his surprise at seeing Maura sitting on a horse beside Garrett's to himself, pretending to be winded.

"Good day to you, ma'am." He tugged his cap in between gulping air. "Garrett."

Liam puffed up just then. "What did I miss?"

Garrett could have gladly strangled his two men for the speculative gleam in both their eyes, but he wanted to get started before any more of the day was lost and he wouldn't have time to seek replacements.

Take A Trip Into A Timeless World of Passion and Adventure with Kensington Choice Historical Romances!
—Absolutely FREE!

Enjoy the passion and adventure of another time with Kensington Choice Historical Romances. They are the finest novels of their kind, written by today's best-selling romance authors. Each Kensington Choice Historical Romance transports you to distant lands in a bygone age. Experience the adventure and share the delight as proud men and spirited women discover the wonder and passion of true love.

Get 4 FREE Books!

We created our convenient Home Subscription Service so you'll be sure to have the hottest new romances delivered each month right to your doorstep—usually before they are available in book stores. Just to show you how convenient the Zebra Home Subscription Service is, we would like to send you 4 FREE Kensington Choice Historical Romances. The books are worth up to $24.96, but you only pay $1.99 for shipping and handling. There's no obligation to buy additional books—ever!

Save Up To 30% With Home Delivery!

Accept your FREE books and each month we'll deliver 4 brand new titles as soon as they are published. They'll be yours to examine FREE for 10 days. Then if you decide to keep the books, you'll pay the preferred subscriber's price (up to 30% off the cover price!), plus shipping and handling. Remember, you are under no obligation to buy any of these books at any time! If you are not delighted with them, simply return them and owe nothing. But if you enjoy Kensington Choice Historical Romances as much as we think you will, pay the special preferred subscriber rate and save over $8.00 off the cover price!

We have 4 FREE BOOKS for you as your
introduction to
KENSINGTON CHOICE!
To get your FREE BOOKS, worth up to $24.96, mail
the card below or call TOLL-FREE 1-800-770-1963.
Visit our website at www.kensingtonbooks.com.

Get 4 FREE Kensington Choice Historical Romances!

YES! Please send me my 4 FREE KENSINGTON CHOICE HISTORICAL ROMANCES (without obligation to purchase other books). I only pay $1.99 for shipping and handling. Unless you hear from me after I receive my 4 FREE BOOKS, you may send me 4 new novels—as soon as they are published—to preview each month FREE for 10 days. If I am not satisfied, I may return them and owe nothing. Otherwise, I will pay the money-saving preferred subscriber's price (over $8.00 off the cover price), plus shipping and handling. I may return any shipment within 10 days and owe nothing, and I may cancel any time I wish. In any case the 4 FREE books will be mine to keep.

Name_____

Address_____ Apt._____

City_____ State_____ Zip_____

Telephone (____)_____

Signature_____

(If under 18, parent or guardian must sign)

Offer limited to one per household and not to current subscribers. Terms, offer and prices subject to change. Orders subject to acceptance by Kensington Choice Book Club.
Offer Valid in the U.S. only.

KN055A

PLACE
STAMP
HERE

KENSINGTON CHOICE

Zebra Home Subscription Service, Inc.

P.O. Box 5214

Clifton NJ 07015-5214

"Mrs. Ea . . . Fitzgerald, may I introduce The Honorable Sean Talbot and Mr. William Murphy."

"Good afternoon, ma'am." Liam touched his cap. "Most folks call me Liam."

"I answer most readily to Sean."

"Then you must call me Maura. I am pleased to meet you both and grateful you were available on such short notice to join our quest."

The smile she gave the men chased some of the haunted look from her eyes, a look he'd put there last night when he spoke on the earl's behalf. That she conversed so easily with Sean and Liam grated on his guilt, especially since she had hardly spoken to him at all during the hour they'd negotiated their way out of Dublin.

"Get your horses and gear." Garrett brought the exchange of pleasantries to a halt. "We have a ways to go before nightfall."

He didn't blame Liam or Sean for being surprised at his including her in this trip. As far as he knew, no woman had ever joined the Green Dragon on an actual mission. But she had been so determined to go in search of the Devil's Mountain, he could not dissuade her.

"Exactly where are we going? And why is the lovely Maura Fitzgerald in our company?" Sean edged his chestnut gelding up to pace beside Garrett as they headed south.

"We are in search of Devil's Mountain. There are four such mountains on the island. The nearest seems to be in the Wicklow range."

"So your visit to the school paid off?"

He nodded. "There was one girl at the school who may have provided a clue. She fit the description of Miss Fuller's maid."

He hesitated, searching for the right way to prepare his friend without adding too much to his anxiety level. They each would need to have clear heads to deal with what they might find.

"Did she mention Jane . . . Miss Fuller?" Sean's sharp question spoke volumes. "Is she all right? Is she at this Devil's Mountain?"

"Easy, lad." Garrett shook his head. "The girl has not had a good time of it. She was found hysterical and wandering near Bray, where we are heading first. Won't let a man near her. She's been sadly used and could only speak a few words as yet."

"Sadly used, you say?" Sean's jaw worked, his lips set in a grim line. "What did she say?"

"*Devil's Mountain.*" He hesitated just a moment and decided to tell him the whole of it. "And, *Jane.* She said Jane saved her."

Garrett allowed his friend a few minutes to chew on what they might find if they managed to locate Jane Fuller before answering the other part of his question. "Mrs. Fitzgerald travels with us so we can prevent her from blundering into our investigation and rescue."

Sean shot him a puzzled frown.

"The realization others girls might be in danger struck a chord in her." Garrett shrugged. "She was very set on hiring men and setting off on her own."

"So you persuaded her to hire us?"

Garrett nodded. "At least this way we have the means to keep some control over her activities. Matters with Stanhope seem to have come to an abrupt end and mayhap she is seeking some diversion by concentrating on the other aspect of her life."

"And it would not pay to have her drawing attention to our inquiries by being reckless." Sean finished the line of logic that had led to the formation of this particular company. "Plus, it is the best way to keep her from getting into trouble herself."

"Exactly."

A quick hoot of laughter showed Liam was doing a

fine job of occupying their guest while his two com-
patriots talked business. Coming from a large family,
Liam had a gift for evoking laughter with his tales of
their various antics.

"Think he has gotten to the one about his gaffer
and the wolfhound yet?" Sean asked, his own mood
lightening just a tad.

Another peal of laughter carried up to them.

"I would say so." Garrett picked his pace up enough
to put a few more yards length between Sean and
himself and Liam and Maura.

"How did you make out at St Michan's?"

"Just as you predicted. The admiral agreed to all the
terms and left immediately for Newgate Gaol. Seamus
is keeping an eye on things at that end, but I imagine
our men should be free even now."

"Good work. This gives us even more reason to re-
store his daughter to him."

"I have to say, her disappearance has taken a visible
toll on him. Even for a craggy-faced old sailor he
looked haggard."

Relief that at least part of the load they were carrying would be lifted soon eased some of the tension
in Garrett's gut. The key men would be free and
could be whisked into protection. They had yet to ful-
fill their end of the exchange, but he felt certain they
were on the right course now. He seemed to have
managed to separate Stanhope and Maura as the earl
had wished, but he was afraid the action would provide the lad with impetus to seek far worse company.

He glanced over his shoulder at Maura and Liam.
In her deep blue riding jacket and skirt with a pert
blue bonnet on her dark hair and the breeze putting
roses on her cheeks, she was a lovely sight. But it was
her loveliness of spirit that called to him. The genuine
concern and care she showed to those less fortunate
was rare in any circle and far beyond expectation for

women who were considered fallen by ordinary standards.

That she had been able to confess her history so openly, accept the consequences of her choices, and then turn them toward helping others was beyond remarkable. It was a pity the earl and society judged her based on one aspect of her life alone. Stanhope would have been lucky indeed to have her for a wife. Any man would.

He dropped back and signaled Liam to join him.

"Sean will fill you in. We head to Bray first."

"If that's our destination, I know a shorter way than the regular roads. My cousin Raymond runs an inn just below Bray."

"Is there anyone on the island that either you or Seamus are not related to?" He shook his head and laughed. "Lead the way, but have a care. She is a city-bred lady, probably not up to much in the way of jumping hedges and streams. Keep the path smooth and the pace slow."

"Aye, city folk are not much fer riding neck or nothing. 'Tho there's something to be said for learning ta ride dodging passersby and leaping over the greengrocer's cart." Liam winked.

"What was that about city-bred riders?" Maura joined them. "I will have you know I nearly grew up on the back of my father's horses. He was a breeder and we could ill-afford lads to exercise the stock. I imagine I could take either of you in a race."

"Ye're on Maura." Liam's eyes danced with anticipation. He'd been horse-mad since birth to hear any of his relatives tell it. That's how Seamus had found him, hanging on the railing at a race meet. "First open pasture we find."

Garrett caught Liam's eye and gestured with his chin for him to ride up to the front with Sean.

He dropped back to keep pace with Maura and

make sure they maintained a discreet enough distance to allow Sean to let Liam know the details of what they planned.

"Mr. Lynch?" she inquired. She had a firm grip on the reins and certainly had the seat of an experienced horsewoman.

"Garrett." he corrected. "Don't you think that if the rest of you use Christian names, we should as well?"

It surprised him how very much he wanted her to use his first name again—as if that would signal a measure of forgiveness for how badly he had hurt her last night in the aftermath of their kiss. It was a kiss that had promised, and very nearly delivered, so much more. Never had he come so near to mindless passion, so lost to control. He did not regret the kiss so much as the consequences for her. Those may have worked toward his goal, but he had not intended to act so directly and cause her unnecessary pain and doubt. A bigger part of him than he cared to admit wished they had not been interrupted.

"You know a great deal about me, Mr. Lynch. But I do not feel I know you well enough to call you by your Christian name." There was just enough sparkle of challenge in the clear gray eyes she batted at him to let him know she had forgiven him, or at least been able to put aside most of her rancor for the purposes of this trip.

"There is not much to tell." He shrugged. They guided their horses off the main road and followed Sean and Liam onto a much narrower wooded lane.

"Come now, Mr. Lynch. Even a veteran gambler and all around ne'er-do-well such as yourself had a childhood. Grew up somewhere. Have you always lived in Dublin or its environs?"

"I grew up in Tipperary, near Cashel." He never spoke of his history. Not to anyone. The less people know about you personally, the safer you remain.

"See?" She flashed him a bright smile. "You come from Cashel. That was not so terribly hard. What about family, parents?"

"I am an orphan. My father died before I was born, my mother giving me life. My foster parents took me in from birth. They had no one else."

"You must have been the light of their lives."

He wasn't sure whether he detected a twist of irony in her words or not.

"They were good to me."

That much was true, the love they had lavished on him made their betrayal seem all the worse when he'd finally learned the truth. He hadn't known he was not their natural child for years. They never told him. They had been English immigrants, inheriting an estate from a distant connection and settling into their new land just before he joined their family.

"But then I grew up and moved to Dublin to make my own way in the world."

As a child, he'd never questioned the visits to his godfather at Clancare Manor or the annual visit the earl had paid their household. Despite their personal Protestant faith, his parents had been advocates of Wolfe Tone's propositions for religious equality and harmony. The two faiths, Catholic and Protestant, even shared the same church building in Cashel. The prejudice the English ruling class carried against the Catholics mystified him to this day, particularly as hatred fostered under the guise of religion. That much he had taken away from his upbringing at least. His hands tightened on the reins.

"Garrett?"

If she used his name to draw him back to the conversation, it served her purpose and more. Even now he wanted to hear his name on her lips just as he had when he kissed her neck last night, when she'd felt so right in his arms.

"I asked if you saw them very often? Your foster parents. Do you miss them?"

"My mother is dead."

Her face transformed into immediate sympathy. "I am so sorry. Is it recent?"

He shrugged. "I was eighteen. Set to go to England, to Cambridge, as the man I thought was my father had done, and his father before him. I learned just before her funeral that we were not truly related."

"Oh?"

The fact that she commented without prying made it easier for him to add, "My father and I have been estranged ever since."

He'd found the man he still thought of as his father drunk in the chapel the night before his mother's funeral. He'd confessed it all then—how his real father had been hung by the English soldiers, sending his real mother into early labor and then to the grave, leaving his life in doubt as well. They had fostered, but not adopted, him at the request of the Earl of Clancare who entrusted the infant son of his friend to them. They had been planning to tell him all of it and let him decide if he wanted an adoption to go forward once he came of age.

He'd reacted badly. With the arrogance of youth, he'd accused his father of lying to him all his life and stormed off to the city to drown his sorrows. Six months later the Earl of Clancare dug him out of the gutter and set his feet on his true father's path, to take up the Green Dragon's sword.

No matter how he regretted his parting from his foster father, he had not gone back, not apologized or tried to reconcile. He wanted there to be no connection between them should he ever be discovered as the Green Dragon, no repercussions visited on the man to whom he owed so much already.

Even now there sat a box of letters, tied together

but unopened, in a lock box in his desk. He received
three such letters a year, sent via the earl from his foster father. One on his birthday, one at Christmas, and
one on the anniversary of his mother's death. He'd
opened the first few. He knew his father worried because he never answered, that he not only understood
the cause of their rift but that he sought forgiveness
as earnestly as he offered it. But Garrett could not put
the man at risk as long as he was fulfilling this part of
his pledge. Sean or Daniel, should they ever inherit
the title, would not have that luxury, but he did and
could protect his da in this one way.

The woods opened up to an expanse of rolling hills
covered with green pastures criss-crossed by deeper
green hedgerows.

"Now's yer chance ta show us yer stuff, Maura,"
Liam called. With a laugh she set off, and in a few
minutes they were all letting the freedom of a good
gallop liberate them from their worries.

"The tinker and his family found the girl here," Ray,
the innkeeper at the Forked River Inn just outside Bray,
pointed to a spot on the map. "Here, between Rathdrum and Glendalough. They were going to turn her
in for confinement as a crazy woman until Father John
took her off their hands."

"Then we will split up and make inquiries at those
towns on the morrow." Garrett studied the map of the
towns at the feet of the Wicklow Mountains.

"Agreed," Liam said. "There's Devil's Hill near one
and Devil's Peak near the other. Seems right that one
of these must be near what we seek." He clapped his
hand on Ray's shoulder. "Thank you, cousin. Ye've
done very well by us. A delicious meal in yer finest private dining parlor, comfortable beds awaitin' us, the
information we need—"

Garrett raised his glass to salute their host. "And the best whiskey this side of the island."

After they drained their glasses, the innkeeper blushed at the praise and shrugged. "What else can I do? Ye're family. Now, if ye don't mind I've got other guests ta tend to. Enjoy yer evening. I'll see ye all in the mornin'." With a cheery wave, he left them in the alcove of his bustling tavern and turned his attention to a patron who looked about to throw a fist at his companion.

"We'd best get back to the parlor and fill in Sean and Maura."

"Aye," Liam said. "Afore the furnishings start ta fly, too. Ray's never been one ta back down from a fight."

Garrett could not resist making the observation plaguing him since Liam mentioned his cousin. "Ray is not a name usually associated with an old Irish family name like yours."

"Aye. And his tavern is nowhere near a river. What's yer point?"

Liam's laughter joined with Maura's as he opened the door to the dining parlor their host had set aside for them. He headed straight to the decanter still on the table. Maura and Sean were sitting opposite one another in front of a peat fire. Sean was leaning forward in his chair and she was curled in the corner of a caned settee with her feet tucked under her and her hair down.

"That was a wonderful story. I never had a nurse who told me tales of olden days. My mother read us the Old Testament at bedtimes. Do you know any more?"

The delight in her voice and the sparkle in her eyes made an arresting display. Garrett halted in the doorway. Her appeal and his jealousy that it was Sean who received the benefit of her smiles clashed.

Sean caught sight of Garrett and his eyebrow edged

up. "Ahh lass, my tongue's grown weary. But here is Garrett. He had a nurse that stuffed his head with the same tales when he was a lad. Mayhap he will favor us with the legend of the Green Dragon."

"The Green Dragon." She looked at Sean, then Garrett, then back to Sean. "My maid favors the tall tales told about him. No outlaw can be that good or that noble. If he exists, he is but a man."

"If he exists?" Sean and Liam's amused reactions were sure to make her suspicious.

"And therein lies the beauty of his story, or so my nursery maid insisted." Garrett strode over to the hearth and poked the peat fire to a better flame while he talked. "In the days of old, when the three kingdoms reigned, the King of Desmond had three knights pledged to do his bidding in a fealty beyond that of his other loyal clansmen and allies. The Black Knight, the White Knight—"

"And the Green Knight?" she supplied.

He glanced over his shoulder as she turned and rested her head on her hands at the edge of the settee's arm. "Aye. Only now he is known as the Green Dragon because of the signet ring he wears and the mighty sword he wields in battle."

"A ring with a carved emerald dragon on a field of gold? And a sword hilt fashioned like a dragon's tail?"

"That's them. So far your maid strikes the legend true."

He kept his attention focused on the glowing flames in the fireplace, not the look in her eyes. "The titles were reduced to ceremony only after the Normans came to our shores. As were the times of the High King. Titles changed, families dwindled and died out. Only the Green Dragon's fealty remained constant: to obey his lord and protect the people from terror, plunder, and all enemies. To help the less

fortunate, rescue those in peril, and serve the cause
of justice."

He straightened and hung up the poker. "The title
passes with the ring and sword wherever the High
Lord directs, but the fealty remains."

"Thus we are arrayed and armed." Sean supplied.

"Aye. The motto from Amergin's chant, rooted in
the before times."

"Garrett. She's fast asleep."

He turned. Sure enough her eyes her closed, her
breathing soft and even.

"Get the door."

He scooped her into his arms, shushing her as she
made a very sleep-laden protest. She fit there like she
had been made just for him.

The last thing Maura remembered from one of the
most oddly enjoyable days she'd ever had was being
laid gently down on a soft bed with a coverlet pulled
over her and a soft brush of lips on her temple.

As the door clicked shut, she snuggled into the pillows and smiled. "Thus we are arrayed and armed."

Chapter Eleven

Soft Irish grass spilled in every direction, curving and sloping in lush variegating shades of green bordered by dark hedgerows twined with honeysuckle and clematis. The Wicklow Mountains dominated the horizons, purple on blue, scattering the lazy clouds drifting in the sky near their summits.

Maura took a deep breath of the rich air. There was nothing like the open countryside. Peaceful, constant—rife with memories of childhood and freedom. Of innocence. How she did miss it.

"Over there." Garrett's voice drew her attention back to him and the small glade where they would await his men. "We can tether the horses in the trees. The shade will lower our chances of drawing unwelcome attention while we await Sean's report. Here's hoping they had better luck than us."

She nodded, and they cantered to the spot. They were early yet. Their own inquiries had proved maddeningly fruitless. She could only hope Sean and Liam would find more information in the village they visited. The scope of the search they would have to mount if they needed to stretch farther away from this point was daunting.

Time stretched in front of them until full nightfall. She was unused to so much time on horseback since she'd left her home to go to Dublin. Dared she hope for a few hours' respite? Images of an afternoon spent with Garrett under the trees, as if they were some heathen king and queen of old, guarded by loyal men while the fate of their country rested in their hands flitted through her mind.

She rubbed a hand over her forehead at the fanciful thoughts that must hold their roots in the tales they'd told her last night. She had to be far more exhausted than she'd imagined. That's what made her so susceptible to their charms, to his.

She had hired this man and his friends because it had seemed the most expedient course given the urgent nature of her quest. Nothing more. Theirs was a business arrangement. That was the way she wanted it. That was the way he wanted it, too. With the exception of simple directions, he'd barely spoken to her since they'd revealed so much of their backgrounds to one another.

They reached the trees and he reined in his mount. She followed suit. A light breeze shivered through the trees, and the leaves whispered and chattered together overhead.

"Stay here." He didn't wait for her nod of assent. He dismounted and walked away, sure of her compliance. How could he be so sure of her when she was so full of questions about him? He'd told her of his childhood, but he remained a mystery.

Garrett scouted the area within and without the glade, peering into the hidden depths of darkened tree branches and thick trunks. From this distance, with his back to her, she could study him without making him uncomfortable for the scrutiny.

He worked so naturally and efficiently, as though his actions were part of his everyday routine; she was intrigued despite her determination to limit her interest in him. When this inquiry was done, when they had found the girl and reported what was going on to the authorities, they would have no need to see one another.

Still, he was a fine figure of a man as he crouched to look around a rocky outcropping. He stripped off his gloves and dipped his hands to catch water from a small wellspring at its base.

He was far different from the proper, well-dressed gentleman who had filled her hallway the night of Freddie's card party only days before. Had that really been such a short time ago? Lifetimes seemed to have come and gone since then. He looked just as at home on horseback, or assuring their safety in a hidden glade. He carried so many layers of mystery.

Too many.

She should not have indulged herself by studying him as he studied their meeting place. She sighed and rubbed her head again.

Garrett turned at that moment and his gaze caught hers. He smiled an easy carefree smile that hid so much. "Weary, are you?"

Again, so thoroughly observant.

"Come with me." He approached her mare with an easy stride and held his hands up to her. "You have time for a rest before my . . . friends return with any news from their inquiries."

The slightest of pauses, but she clearly heard the unspoken word *men.* "There's a goodly patch of grass within, just awaiting your company. The water is fresh and clear."

His lips curved upward in a charming smile. Desire curled in her stomach and tightened her breath. Too easily he sparked these responses in her. Too easily and too frequently. Did he know how he affected her?

She forced out her breath and leaned forward slightly to rest her hands on his shoulders. Just a touch. Then his hands were at her waist. So firm. So secure. Despite the dangers, she wanted to surrender herself—into his arms, into his bed. Did he know how much she wanted him? There was no logic. No good could come from such surrender, but the desire was still there, still simmering from the other night.

Her desire was like fine wine, aged to perfection, rushing through her without direction, with only one purpose: to chase away all reason. Did he know the havoc he wreaked on any claim she once held to common sense?

He pulled her from the roan's back as though she weighed less than nothing. What was he thinking behind his mesmerizing eyes?

She closed her own eyes and slid into his arms.

Her breath hitched, like an untried girl experiencing passion for the first time. What was wrong with her? She'd never felt this breathless in a man's arms before.

Her feet touched the ground after what felt like a thousand rapid heartbeats.

"Thank you." Her thoughts scattered like leaves. He did not release her. She could think of nothing beyond the heat of his hands on her. The scent of hawthorns twined with the breeze. Her lips tingled with the memory of his mouth against hers.

"Thank you," she repeated and looked up into his unreadable dark gaze.

"Indeed." He offered one word only. Low and filled with unnamed emotion.

Almost imperceptibly his hands squeezed her waist. She was certain he would kiss her again, in the raw magic of this secluded glade. Her heart leapt, her body tensed in anticipation. Waiting. Wanting.

After a timeless moment, he released her. She reached out and supported herself with a hand on her mare's saddle for support.

Disappointment stung, abrading her pride. She almost laughed. She'd come within a whisker of giving herself to this man a second time, a man she barely knew, giving herself with no commitment, no promises. His rejection had been as unexpected as her unspoken offer. Did he know? Did he realize how foolish she felt?

She pushed away this line of thought, determined not to dwell on things that obviously were not meant to be. She turned to him again.

"As long as we have time on our hands, tell me more about the stories your nurse told you when you were a child." Those stories of the Fian of old must be the basis for her fanciful thoughts earlier, of an ancient band seeking shelter in this very spot.

"As you like." He held out his arm to escort her to the aforementioned patch of grass as though they were still in her townhouse and not amidst green Irish splendor and uncertainty.

She sat, her skirts billowing outward around her and he leaned on an elbow to begin his tale.

"Your turn. I have told you of my childhood . . . tell me something of yours." He asked a half hour later, after he set her giggling at his exploits as he had rounded up the village lads and had them storm the garden wall of the rectory in imitation of one of the Fian battles.

"Mine?" She sobered almost immediately, wondering if he'd acquiesced to share his story all along only to lead her into subjects she'd rather not discuss. Her youthful past was her own.

"Aye." His dark gaze was intent on hers. All of Ireland's best greens were locked in that gaze, as though the very heart of Erin beat inside of him.

"Are you looking for the sad tale of my past, Mr. Lynch?"

"Aye, if that is the tale you wish to tell. You already told me about Dublin. But what about before? What about your childhood? What haunts the back of your eyes and makes them sad?" His answers and questions were soft. No demands. No intrusions. Just a willingness to listen. And a too-astute guess regarding the location of her darkest moment.

"It isn't," she told him, even as raw memories tore loose inside her. She could feel his gaze on her hot face and knew she wasn't handling the conversation well and was hiding nothing from that all-too-observant perusal. She'd told him far too much already. She wasn't ready to share her father's death, her mother's disgust, and the firm distance held between her and her younger brothers. Not with him. Not with anyone.

"I . . . it just isn't," she ended, repeating herself.

"Aye." Quiet acceptance. "Here I am scorching you with questions when I know all you really need is a wee bit of rest."

He shrugged out of his jacket and bunched it together. "Lie back, Maura. Rest your mind and your spirit. It has been a very long day. I'll fetch you a drink of cool water, shall I?"

She had taken off her gloves and bonnet earlier when they had sat. The cool softness of the grass beckoned. He placed his hands on her shoulders and that betraying burn of fire flamed to life in her belly. She couldn't look at him.

Don't look; it is better if you don't.

Then his gaze was on hers.

She could spend her life in that gaze.

The sadness of that thought burned a trail over her already hot skin.

"Rest," he said again. "All will be well."

He pressed gently, tilting her backward.

She went without resistance as he coaxed her down onto her back amidst the scents of green grass and dark earth. Her head rested on his jacket suffused

with the deep scent of man and wool. Her heartbeat
quickened further. The dark green of the whispering
leaves overhead made a perfect backdrop for the vibrant, glinting green of his eyes as he leaned over her,
bracing his arms at her sides.

"Ah, Maura Fitzgerald." Her name escaped him in
a sad whisper. "Truly."

"Truly what?" She whispered softly in order not to
disturb the tension throbbing so eloquently between
them.

"You make it hard for a man to think." One corner of
his mouth drew up in a self-deprecating grin. His smile
tore at her heart, at the raw emotions he'd somehow
drawn from the secret corners she'd tried to lock them
in. She wanted him. And if she truly was a wanton as
her mother so surely believed, what was there to hold
her back?

She slid her hands to his arms, so staunch and firm
on either side of her and pushed them slowly upward.
He didn't move. The sparkle in his eyes brightened.
Emboldened she slid her fingers to his mouth, tracing
the firm fullness of his lips—remembering them,
longing for them against her own.

"Then don't think," she whispered and cupped his
cheeks. "Don't think."

Wordless, she tugged at him ever so slightly. He
bent toward her, his gaze never leaving hers, waiting
for some sign that she meant exactly what she indicated. He was a gentleman, despite her open offer.
He was the oddest mix of action and gentleness, determination, decorum and demand. And she wanted
him desperately.

"Garrett." His name whispered from her on a satisfied sigh as he closed the final distance between them.

At last his mouth touched hers, hot and firm. She'd
never wanted a man more than she did at this very

moment. She never wanted any man as she did this one. Her body fairly sizzled with desire.

For a long moment he did naught but kiss her, soft firm pressure. Their breath mingling as the trees rustled above them.

Then he groaned and pressed his tongue to her lips; she opened for him on an answering moan, tasting him as he tasted her, open and reckless in a flash of wild heat that threatened to reduce her to cinders. She was out of her element, spinning out of control far from anything that would help her manage the situation.

At this moment, control didn't matter. Nothing mattered but this man, this time, and the need burning so hot to life inside her.

His mouth slanted over hers. She'd never realized a kiss could be so intimate, so complete, as though their very souls touched in the mating of tongue to tongue. Rigid barriers she'd held for so long were melting inside her. Waves of exquisite heat and desire undulated deep within her, firing her blood.

She slid her fingers into his hair. She wanted to be his with a depth she had never felt with any other man. She would be his in a fresh and different way—deeper, hotter, more complete, as though in truth he would be the very first to touch her.

He made short work of the buttons on her riding jacket and blouse with her assistance. No stays stood between them in anticipation of the day or more spent in the saddle.

Cool air spread over her skin, followed in quick succession by the heat of his palms as he cupped her through the silken softness of her chemise.

"Too beautiful." He whispered the words against her mouth. "Too damned beautiful."

She kissed him, long and hard as pleasure surged through her. His hands tangled in her hair as he cradled the back of her head and returned her kisses, pulling her curls free.

He kissed a hot trail over her neck before blazing down to her breasts. He tugged free the ribbon that gathered her chemise neckline and exposed her flesh completely. Without preamble his mouth closed over her nipple. She gasped at the feel of him, tugging and suckling, enjoying her so fully even as he trapped the other breast in his hand to roll and tease.

Passion sizzled over her nerve endings. He turned slightly, pulling her half atop him so she was feeding him her breast, her hair spilling around them. She could do naught but arch her back and enjoy the white hot desire simmering through her as her hands clutched his shoulders.

He transferred his attentions to her other nipple, leaving the first bared and wet, throbbingly sensitive and open to the air as he concentrated on the second. She bent and pressed kisses along his hairline.

"Mmmmm." His moan vibrated against her skin as his fingers trailed over her side and down beneath her bunched skirt and petticoat. With unerring accuracy his fingers slid above her stockings to find her very center. She went breathless with anticipation.

She was wet and open to him as his fingers slid against her skin, slid inside her.

"Oh Garrett." She couldn't move, couldn't get enough of him as he caressed her. All the while he suckled her breast—pulling and teasing, laving her nipple with his tongue.

Back and forth, back and forth, he used her own moisture to massage the swollen aching part of her nether regions. Long, slow, expert strokes coaxed and teased, encouraged and demanded. He continued his ministrations unchecked, undaunted, so slow and deliberate that her breath caught over and over again.

Then in a sudden rush, pleasure spilled through

her, ripe and hot and overwhelming. She shuddered in his arms, again and again, hearing her own cries echo into the treetops. He released her breast and she collapsed against his shoulder.

She had never experienced anything to compare with what he had just done to her. No man had ever cared enough to have her find pleasure before he sought his own. She was stunned and speechless. She raised her head to meet his gaze.

"Lovely." He growled the word up to her. "Absolutely lovely."

"Garrett, I—"

"Shhh, darlin'. I'm not done with you just yet." He turned her onto her back, tugging his jacket under her for a rudimentary blanket.

She lay still and replete, with her skirts bunched around her thighs, her breasts rosy and throbbing from his attentions; she was limp and satisfied yet already anticipating renewed desire.

He pulled off his shirt and cast it aside, offering her a glimpse of his muscled shoulders, his strong forearms, and flat stomach. She couldn't get enough of the sight of him, of the look on his face when he looked at her. She moistened her lips with the tip of her tongue, already aching for his kiss.

He brushed his palms over her thighs sending whorls of expectation spinning through her in their wake. Coaxing them apart, he lifted her skirts higher still until he had exposed the dark hair between her legs and the damp, sensitive skin he had just pleasured with his fingers.

"I want to see you. All of you." Heat poured over her cheeks as he spread her legs farther still, enticing her knees to bend and open, splaying her before him.

Cool air drifted over her damp core. She shivered.

"Lovely," he repeated, and then he dipped his head

toward her. His tongue touched her flesh, and she almost screamed with the unexpected wonder.

Softly, gently he lapped her, tasting her with slow, deliberate strokes as his hand slid beneath her thighs to cup her bare buttocks. He squeezed and fondled them in the rough heat of his hands as he continued to taste her so intimately. Her hands scrambled for purchase in the soft grass as she gave herself up to the sensations and the man. Her very center whirled, and she could think of nothing but him and the magic he invoked within her.

No man had ever done such a thing. She considered herself experienced in the pleasures of the flesh, of the intimacies that passed between a man and a woman. And yet no man had ever dipped his head between her thighs to taste and tongue her at his leisure.

His tongue darted inside her, and she groaned over and over, urging him on, unable to stop herself as he made such intimate love to her.

In, out, and around, his tongue laved her. She slid her fingers into his hair, groaning as he licked her. In out, in out. She arched her back and groaned as he squeezed her buttocks and suckled her, drinking from her depths.

He tipped her still closer to him, her legs spread. He could do whatever he wished and she would do naught to stop him. He tongued her deliberately, first fast then tortuously slow, pushing deep into her, rasping his teeth against her sensitive flesh, suckling the wet response she gave him.

Then he focused on the swollen flesh he'd pleasured so recently with his fingers. He sucked the full bud into his mouth and began to gently nip, suckle, and lick until she was writhing against him, crying wordlessly until again the white hot rush raced through her, over and over, rippling through her soul to leave her drained.

She was panting, breathless, and nearly senseless when he lifted his head from her. "So you liked that then, Maura?" There was a wicked gleam in his eyes as he teased her.

"Oh, aye." She breathed back to him, finding it hard to focus on him. Her body had never felt so alive. Every muscle, every inch of her skin, seemed alive and humming his name. "Aye, Garrett. Very much."

"And we are not done yet," he promised her. "I want to feel myself deep within you. To feel you clench around me and fill this place with those sweet sounds again."

"Aye."

He rubbed his hands gently over the length of her legs and pushed up onto his knees. When had he removed her stockings? When had he shed his boots and pants? Could she have been so lost in her own pleasures? She was awed and dumbfounded; she never lost such control, never lost herself so completely. She wanted more.

He poised his full and throbbing length between her legs, ready to give her more, ready to surge into her and seek his own pleasure at last. And she wanted to give him that pleasure, to gain from him the very cries he sought from her.

He lifted her legs and slid her ankles over his shoulders, keeping her open and wide for him as he lowered himself between her arched legs. Her knees rested over his shoulders as he bent and kissed her deeply, fully. She could taste her own sweetness on his lips, revel in the power of his tongue as it met hers, welcome the caress of his hands on her breasts. And all the while she quivered, awaiting his ultimate possession.

"Now, Maura. Right now, you are mine." The words

came low and vibrant against the pulse point on her neck as he suckled her there.

"Aye."

As he had claimed her with his words, his engorged, manly length filled her at last, sliding deep within her sensitive aching flesh.

"Oh yes," she groaned. With each new release she'd been certain the pleasure he gave her couldn't get any better, but now, sensitized by the repeated orgasms he had wrought, her body sang at his invasion.

Rich, sweet friction ached and throbbed inside her. She'd never felt anything like it. Each thrust filled her completely, touching her very womb with his manhood as he withdrew and thrust, withdrew and thrust. Twin gasps and groans twined in the early evening air as his body claimed her and her body clenched around him.

He kissed her deeply. His tongue tangling with hers as their bodies strained together in an ageless struggle he had somehow made new all over again.

With her legs straddling his shoulders and his flesh deep within her, she was open and filled as never before. She clung to his arms and kissed him back, taking all he had to give her and demanding more.

"Mine," he repeated, his gaze pinning hers.

"Aye." Nothing mattered but this man, this moment.

"Maura."

"Aye." This man.

"Mine." He affirmed his complete possession.

His movements grew in strength and quickness, thrusting quicker, faster, hotter, harder. She was lost to the rhythm he demanded, lost to the pleasure he gave and took as he loved her.

And then the pressure building and building inside could hold no longer. She cried out and groaned, bucking against him as the waves rippling over her took control. He joined her in the aftermath, shuddering against her as the hot flood of his satisfaction spilled inside her.

She'd never known such lovemaking. Tears pricked at the backs of her eyes as their panted breathing mingled with the whispering leaves overhead.

Lovemaking.

The word brought home to her the truth that she was out of her depth. She'd made love with a man with no commitments. Nothing lay between them except the pleasure they'd given each other and the words he'd spoken to claim her in the midst of their passions. It was both frightening and liberating.

What incredible freedom came from making love to a man purely because she wanted to—not because she was beholden, not because he could help her financially, but because she wanted him. Somehow that freedom made her more vulnerable than she had been before.

Even resting beneath him, in the green grass of the glade, was different from lying with any other man. She didn't mind the feel of him atop her, still within her. In fact, she enjoyed the feel of their bodies still joined together in the aftermath.

After a moment she heard him chuckle, weakly.

He was laughing. She couldn't help but smile. That indeed was a new reaction.

"What are you laughing about?"

"You," he told her, then lifted his head to beam those incredible green eyes down at her. "Me."

"Why?"

"Because I had no intention of seducing you when I offered you a chance to rest. And I cannot believe you feel the tiniest bit rested. Do you?"

She smiled too, and then laughed. Her body clenched around him with the movement, and she had the pleasure of watching him groan and sigh in reaction.

"Actually," she told him truthfully, "I feel much better, thank you."

"Ah. So now you wish maybe to thank me for the suggestion?"

"Indeed." She smiled up at him and traced her fingers over his brow. "Do you offer this to all weary women of your acquaintance?"

"Nay, love. Not all." The words were spoken softly and with surprising intensity. "Just you."

He dipped his head to kiss her and something inside her heart broke open as though the barriers he'd breeched with his first touch had disintegrated completely, leaving her vulnerable in ways she hadn't been in many years. It was frightening and overwhelming and something she wasn't ready to deal with. Not just yet.

He lifted his head.

"Garrett, I—"

"Shhh." He placed a finger over her lips. In the distance they could hear the sound of multiple hoofbeats, horses drawing nearer by the second. "We are about to get company."

He pushed to his feet, leaving her almost painfully empty. He held his hand out to her. For a moment she was tempted to stay right where she was and just admire the sight of him—tall, lean, muscular, and naked—but sanity prevailed. She accepted his hand. He pulled her to her feet.

"Lovely as you look, Maura, you had best get dressed."

"And you." She arched a brow as her skirts settled to her ankles.

She bent to retrieve her blouse and jacket, and he reached around her to pluck them from the ground. He pulled her back against his chest. Heat from his

skin suffused her. His breath was hot against the back
of her head. His hands cupped her bare breasts for
just a moment.

Then he turned her in his arms and dipped his head
to kiss her one more time. "Time is just too short."

"Aye." She shrugged into her clothing and struggled to adjust it as he made short work of his own. In
moments they were dressed and smoothing the last
telltale wrinkles from their clothing as the horses
thundered to a stop beside the glade. A whistle rang
out into the air.

Garrett winked at her and returned the sound.

Chapter Twelve

The redstart's call cut the early evening air just as the approaching hoofbeats thundered to a stop next to the glade.

Garrett turned to smile at Maura before offering the greeting in return. He'd never felt such profound regret at the arrival of his men. His time with Maura had been far too short.

Under other circumstances he would have been grateful for his men's adherence to rendezvous timing.

Maura Fitzgerald was a woman to make a man forget all of his responsibilities, big or small. Making love to her had obliterated everything but the responsive feel of her body and the passionate sounds of pleasure she made beneath him. Echoes of those sounds hummed on inside him as the trees overhead whispered with the secrets they'd just witnessed.

He bit back a sigh.

This was not how he should have been with her. Here in the open with no time and no finesse to make love to her as thoroughly as she deserved. Quick heat in the woods, interrupted just at the finish, should have been reserved for a woman less . . . less . . . important. There was a thought startling enough to give him pause. Somehow, when he hadn't been watching, Maura Fitzgerald had become important to him.

He managed not to glance back at her as this realization took hold and Sean and Liam approached.

"Garrett. Maura."

Sean nodded to them both as Liam brought up the rear. Garrett had trained these men himself; they habitually observed their surroundings and the company they joined. Sean was a master. Garrett could see the speculation gathering behind both of their eyes. He shook his head, telling them the question was not open for discussion.

Sean cocked an eyebrow, but other than a quick exchange of glances between them, neither allowed their thoughts to show on their faces.

"What did you discover in your travels?"

"Well . . ." Liam held out a bag he had slung over his shoulder. "For one thing there's a fine batch of apples to be had at McGillan's farm. And the cheese to be had from Mrs. McFinn is something to speak of as well."

He opened the bag to produce said apples and cheese.

"Oh." Maura's appreciative reaction coincided with the immediate grumble of Garrett's stomach. Neither of them had eaten and this looked too good to pass by.

"Obviously an important report." Sean noted as he appropriated the bag from Liam and offered the apples and cheese to Maura.

"Thank you." She took them and offered an apple to Garrett.

Garrett crunched into his apple with relish. It was sweet and tart and would go perfectly with cheese. He nodded and gestured for them to continue. "What else?"

"That is about it for food stuffs other than the wine."

"Oh yes, the wine." Liam pulled a small jug from another sack.

"Wine fit to be shared, I'm assured." He popped the small thick cork and took a swig before offering it around.

Maura's gaze danced over the bottle rim as she drank deeply. It was quite obvious this was not a dining venue she was used to, but she seemed to enjoy it nonetheless.

The sight of her swigging wine straight from the jug, munching into her apple with a piece of cheese in her palm, without the slightest bit of pretense at nicer manners, warmed him straight through and made him wish once more for just a wee bit more time without interruption.

She was disheveled from their lovemaking. There was no denying that. Dark curls were still loose from her hastily rewrapped chignon. They dangled about her neck and along the pale curve of her cheek. And despite her careful sweeping movements to smooth her skirts and bodice, there were wrinkles and bunches in evidence. He could only imagine the co-inciding dishevelment evident in his own appearance. What a pair they must make at the moment. Bless Sean's and Liam's discretion.

Her deep gray gaze shimmered up to his, and he wondered what she was thinking.

"—in town, but that did not seem to get us any-where either. I think it bears looking into from a closer perspective."

"Aye, we need to examine this property from all an-gles," Sean said. "Something stinks in that general di-rection. And as my old nurse was so very fond of saying, 'If somethin' stinks ye canna leave it be' or it will just get worse."

"Oh, I can well imagine her saying that in regard to ye." Liam may not have had the advantages Sean en-joyed, but he was bright and self-educated.

Garrett realized with a start he'd lost all track of the

report he'd asked for. He had no idea what they were talking about. With a mental shake he turned his gaze from Maura and focused once more on Liam.

"I'm sorry, what stinks?"

"Well, obviously Sean stinks or his old nurse wouldn't have had anything to reference in the first place. Where did ye lose us?" Raised eyebrows and an ultra-polite tone accompanied the question.

For a moment Garrett was tempted to thrash the two of them where they stood—raised eyebrows, controlled smirks, and all.

"Somewhere just before Sean began to stink." He offered in a tart tone as Maura handed him a wedge of cheese.

"Right. Well after riding the countryside in search of various types of wine and cheese—"

"—and apples."

"Aye," Sean started again. "We questioned a variety of people in Rathdrum. The priest, the dry goods store owner and his wife, the tapman who happened to be at the farrier's, and various tenants and dairymen along the way. Except for the usual stories of highwaymen, raiders, and another missing girl . . ."

"One of the dairymen's daughters," Liam supplied. "She's but fourteen, missing about a week after taking biscuits to her gran's."

"The best information we got was in the tavern we found halfway between Glendalough and Rathdrum. It's not far from here—The Wild Boar. Several patrons mentioned strange doings, comings and goings at odd hours and people they didn't know. It all comes back to an isolated hunting lodge up in the midst of the Wicklow Mountains. And hear this, Liam forgot to mention this earlier. The property is located just beyond the turn toward a mountain in the range known locally as the Devil's Peak.

That perked up Garrett's ears. That was one of the

locations they sought. Maura must have been thinking the same thing. Her hand touched his forearm.

"I was getting there," Liam spoke up. "The tavern's
regulars mentioned the place at least a couple of
times. You'd swear they wanted to cross themselves at
the mention, though. No one seems to know who
owns the property or what they use it for, save the occasional party. Even the servants there keep to themselves."

"Isolated. Few if any neighbors. Far enough from
Dublin, but not too far. Add to that the proximity to
the Devil's Peak." Garrett spoke his thoughts aloud.
"It is a start. Good work. We will have to at least go and
look at the place. Ideas?"

"Well, it sounded like they only hire certain people," Liam started. "No locals."

"Just those known to be able to keep things to
themselves," Sean chimed in.

"So there's not much likelihood that we'll be able
to get anyone hired in as help in order to search the
place. Which leaves—"

"—broken-down travelers," Sean finished.

"Not the most reliable way of searching a property."
Garrett frowned as he mulled their report.

"If this place has any connection to Jane's disappearance, time must be running out. It has been so
long." Sean's worry broke through. "What other options do we have?"

"This is a long way from where she disappeared."

"Broken-down travelers?" Maura passed him the
bottle of wine.

He took a quick drink before answering. "Aye.
Broken-down travelers is a plan in which we proceed
to this hunting lodge, pretend to have had some
kind of trouble with our coach."

"Axle trouble," offered Sean.

"Or harness trouble," Liam supplied.

"Either works well. So does breaking a wheel. It would be bad manners to turn us away completely. No one turns away travelers who come to his door for aid. Not unless they have something to hide."

"And what happens when they realize we don't really have any trouble with our coach?" Maura's brow had furrowed with concern. Garrett had to remind himself that she wasn't a regular member of the Green Dragon's men and therefore had no experience with their exploits.

"No one really questions the trouble. What matters is that for whatever amount of time our unsuspecting host allows us to be on his land we will be able to take a good close look at this hunting lodge and determine if it is the place we are searching for."

"Oh." She nodded and nibbled her lip for just a moment. "We do not seem to have a coach."

"No problem there, Maura. We'll go back into The Wild Boar and hire theirs."

"It will be dark by the time we get there tonight." Sean looked at the sky. "So we'll stay the night at the inn and set off for the mountains in daylight. The inn was small but looked clean and comfortable enough."

Maura's gaze flew to his as Liam and Sean continued to flesh out the plan for the coach and the best approach to take in order to reach the lodge. Garrett was lost in her gaze, so smoky and beautiful. He knew those eyes now, knew the hazy glow of pleasure, knew the deep softness in the aftermath. There were promises in those eyes, promises that could be acted upon in the comfort of the inn so easily proposed in the planning just moments ago.

"Done," he said, bringing an end to the conversation. "We will go back to the inn. If it is small, perhaps Maura and I should pose as husband and wife?"

He watched her face as he made his proposal, waiting for some sign that what had happened between them had been merely a thing of the moment and not something she wanted to repeat. She nodded almost imperceptibly save for the soft springy movement of the curls gracing her cheek.

"And we will be your servants." Sean bent to pick up the jug and the bag of apples. "We already mentioned we'd been sent scouting property in the area for our master and his new bride. We can join the company in the tap once more and see what other details we can find."

"Right," Liam affirmed. "We'll get the horses, Garrett?"

"Aye." His gaze was still locked with Maura's as the men turned to go about their duties.

"An inn sounds . . . restful," she offered quietly, but there was soft glow in her eyes that promised anything but rest.

"Aye." He closed the distance between them and took her hands in his. "I am sorry to—"

"Please do not apologize. Not for anything." She leaned up and pressed her mouth to his.

"It is merely the imposition and the supposition that I apologize for, Maura." He pulled her into his arms and planted a more thorough kiss on those soft and willing lips. "All else is far too grand to need apology."

"Imposition and supposition?"

"Aye." He kissed her again, taking whatever advantage he could of the few moments it would take Sean and Liam to gather the horses. "I am imposing on your goodwill by taking you to the inn without asking. I am supposing that you will agree to masquerade as my spouse to accomplish what needs to be accomplished. For this I apologize." He kissed her again. "But aside from those things, I fully intend to take you to the nearest bed and make long, slow, thorough love to you. And for that I will make no apology."

"Ahh, then your apology is accepted. But only because of what you hold out as my reward."

Two hours later, as a full moon rose into the soft, ebony depths of the sky, they were safely ensconced as overnight guests at The Wild Boar at the foot of the Wicklow Mountains, midway between Glendalough and Rathdrum.

Sean and Liam were below at the bar amidst the other visitors and the employees at the inn enjoying a pint of home brew with their ears alerted for any useful information. Normally he would have spent the night much as they were. But tonight was different.

He turned from the open window.

Maura stood before him awash in moonlight. A tentative smile curved one corner of her lips. The supper they had shared below, stew and bread, had been brief and filled with long silences. Then they had retired. He'd hung up his jacket and pulled off his boots and awaited her return from the necessary.

Now, in the quiet of their borrowed room, he couldn't help wondering if she regretted what had passed between them in the glade. Had their lovemaking been as satisfying for her as it had been for him? Was what they shared more than hot coupling? No other woman had ever touched him this way. Never before had lovemaking mattered beyond the satisfactions of the moment.

"Maura—"

"Garrett." She stripped off her jacket and took a step toward him. "Supper was . . . satisfying and this room appears . . . acceptable. But I find the evening somewhat . . . lacking up to this point."

"Lacking?"

"Aye." She came closer and slid her fingers into her hair, loosening the pins that held it until it flowed over her shoulders in long, dark waves. "You made certain . . . promises earlier this day. Promises I find myself anticipating. Eagerly."

After another step closer, she looked beyond him to the window, then over to the bed. "Although the room is comforting to have instead of the open wood, I am still suffering anticipation, instead of—"

"Satisfaction?" His mouth went dry. She was so lovely. And willing to meet him more than halfway. Why did he still hesitate?

"Aye." Her fingers worked the buttons of his shirt as a peat fire crackled in the hearth. She spread his shirt open by sliding her fingers over his chest. "Mmmmm, that's a start."

She leaned up and pressed her mouth to his. "Make love to me, Garrett. Love me as I have never been loved before."

"Aye."

Questions crowded his mind, but now was not the time to ask them. He pulled her closer and took her mouth with his.

She was so damned soft, tasting of wine and spices, tasting of Maura. And she would be his, all night, without interruption. That was enough to burn away any questions and concerns that might linger. He worked the buttons and tapes of her blouse and skirt as he kissed her. She kissed him back and helped, until her garments draped the floor about her feet, leaving her in nothing but soft, creamy skin and moonlight.

He cupped her buttocks and drew her against him as he kissed her again, deeply. Her hips cupped his erection. She fit perfectly against him. Her breasts pressed to his chest, full and round and tempting. He leaned back and then sat against the window seat; she came with him, her legs parting to slide against his as she sat in his lap.

He groaned at the pain and pleasure of having her

fit so intimately against him with naught save his trousers to keep them apart. He cupped her breasts and bent his head to taste them, nibbling and licking her taut nipples as he fondled her.

"You are beautiful," he told her, meaning every word. "So very beautiful and so very soft."

"Garrett." She whispered his name as her fingers slid into his hair to cup him to her as he tasted and suckled her. "Oh Garrett."

She squirmed atop him, responsive to his touch as he laved her nipples and rasped his teeth against her tenderness. He kneaded her buttocks, pulling her more tightly against his hardness. He felt near to bursting despite the fabric barrier between them.

She was naked and in his arms—his to do with as he pleased.

He slid his fingers between her legs, down into the dark triangle of her hair to find the wet heat he'd enjoyed earlier that day. She sucked in a gasp at his touch as he found her slippery softness and massaged her.

"Oh yes, oh." She squirmed against him as he rubbed her and suckled her. Her pleasure cries became wordless urgings as he parted her soft, wet folds and slid his fingers into her hot velvety sheath. She groaned and squirmed and groaned again as he began to stroke her deeply.

"I'm going to fill you," he told her, watching her flushed face as he stroked her. "Over and over. Again and again."

"Aye." She groaned again. "Oh aye."

"And then I'm going to watch you as I watch you now. I'm going to enjoy each little gasp I pull from you."

"Garrett . . . oh, Garrett . . . please."

He bent his head, teased her breasts with his teeth again as he increased the invasive movements of his hand. In moments she began to shudder in his arms and cry out wordlessly in surrender.

She was too beautiful for words. His throat was dry and his chest tight with desire. She squirmed in his lap, rubbing herself against his burgeoning erection, teasing him even as he wrung the cries from her.

"I lose such control of myself." Wonderment touched the words so very softly voiced as she rested her head on his shoulder, her body trembling against him, her breathing fast and warm against his neck. Her taut breasts grazed his chest enticingly.

"Aye, it's one of the things I like best about making love to you." His own voice came still harsh and tight with the desires she drew from him.

She gave a breathless little laugh that ended on a half-moan. "Then enjoy it well, Garrett Lynch, for it happens only with you." Open honesty etched her words, cutting them deep into his heart.

Heat thundered through him. With so few words she had thrown the men who had been her previous lovers between them and disposed of them as nothing of consequence, because only with him did she lose control of herself.

Only with him.

"Dear God, woman, you drive a man to distraction." He caught her lips with his, tasting total surrender, total passion in her response as her tongue did a slow dance against his own. For now, for whatever totally unknown reason, she was his—his completely.

"That would be the point," she whispered, a smile lighting those soft gray eyes.

"Come, sir, you have me at a disadvantage." She pushed to her feet to stand bold and beautiful in nothing but soft, satiny skin. Her hair rippled long and dark and springy over her shoulders, caressing the length of her arms, her breasts, the rounded curve of her hip.

"A disadvantage?"

"Aye." In a quick, graceful motion, she knelt before him and began unbuttoning his smalls.

"I am fully as naked as God intended. Yet, you have not so accommodated me." Her smile mesmerized him as she worked the fastenings and spread the fabric open. He sprang from the confines, rigid and aching.

He couldn't breathe.

"And this you have kept hidden from me. For shame." She teased him as her fingers reached out and traced the length of his shaft. Soft, teasing fingers.

Surely she would drive him out of his skull. Pleasure shuddered through him as she traced him up and down and up again. He couldn't move. He could only watch her and enjoy the power she had over him.

She dipped her head toward him. Blood thundered in his veins as her mouth touched him. Her soft, full lips parted to engulf the aching head of his shaft.

"Oh God." He pleaded for sanity as he tilted his head back and closed his eyes, lost to the feel of her warm mouth covering him. He gripped the window seat

"Maura." He could do naught but name her as she murmured her pleasure. The sound filled his ears, humming against his flesh and deep into his very core.

"Dear God, Maura."

She traced his length with her lips, her tongue. Up, down, up, down. Maddeningly slow torture. Pleasure he could neither stop nor deny.

He slid his fingers into her long silky hair, very lightly cupping her head as she continued her slow, mesmerizing ministrations. She was sucking him, taking him so deep into her mouth, licking and tasting and enjoying him. He traced her shoulders and slid his hands downward to cup and weigh the resilient flesh of her breasts.

"Mmmmm." She moaned again as he fondled her, and his own groan echoed hers.

Pressure built higher and hotter inside him. He'd never known such pleasure as the feel of her lips on him, the unselfish giving she offered. Her fingers slid lower to cup him. He groaned again as she fondled him and massaged him so intimately.

"Maura, you'd best not continue or . . . or . . ."

He couldn't seem to finish the warning as she began to quicken her movements. Up, down, up, down. Her tongue flicked over him, laving and darting as she suckled him and rimmed the aching head of his shaft.

"Aye." She whispered her breath against his tip, and then her mouth consumed him again.

She knew. She knew he would not be able to stop himself from spilling into her mouth and still she continued. Her fingers were nimble and quick, caressing him with gentle pressure as her mouth sucked and licked and sucked and licked.

"Ahhhh." He lost himself to the pleasure she wrung from him, unable to stop as she pulled him deeply into her mouth. Hot seed spurted from him as overwhelming pleasure consumed him so he could do naught but shudder over and over again.

Stunned and drained, he felt his blood pound in his ears as she lifted her head from him. She smiled a satisfied womanly smile full of knowledge and power. She'd just made him lose the same self-control she had lost.

Incredible.

Even more incredible, he could already feel the first distant stirrings of renewed desire. He'd never wanted a woman the way he wanted her.

He lifted her to her feet as he pushed to his own. She melted against him as he bent his head and pressed his lips to her forehead. Her arms twined around his neck and he swept the length of her slender back with his hands. God, she was soft and warm and his.

He lifted her in his arms and carried her toward the bed, determined to take advantage of the big four-poster. He let her legs slide down against his own when he reached the edge. Her body slid so intimately and completely against his. She fit in all the right places.

"I'm going to love you all night," he promised as he lifted his head to meet the sparkle in the depths of her eyes.

"All night. That sounds just about right," she offered back to him.

He drew her onto the bed with him. Wide and soft, it cradled them together as he kissed her and touched her.

He was determined to love her slowly. He lay her back against the quilted coverlet and let his gaze roam the length of her body as he smoothed his palm over her soft skin. "You are so very beautiful, so very soft. I could never get tired of touching you. Every sweet inch."

He bent his head to taste her lips again and then to kiss a long, slow path down over her neck, her breasts, the curve of her stomach, and into the dark warm vee at the juncture of her thighs.

She sighed and parted for him, allowing him to dip his head to taste her. He tongued her slowly, and she sighed. He nipped and nibbled and tasted her, enjoying the intimacy of having her so open and ready and willing for whatever he wanted to do.

He thrust his tongue into her and sucked her sweetness as she moaned and moved against him, so very responsive to even the tiniest flick of his tongue. She was aching and ready when he lifted his head, determined to prolong the pleasure for both of them. She writhed against the coverlet as he blew a light breath against her parted womanly folds.

"Oh Garrett."

"Aye, love." Then he turned her onto her stomach.

She rolled without resistance, presently the lovely sight of her pale, well-rounded bottom—her smooth back, her long dark hair fanned across her. He coaxed her legs wide apart so that he could see her slick folds glistening between her pale thighs.

"So very lovely," he told her as he trailed his palms slowly over her calves, the backs of her knees, and up the backs of her thighs.

She shuddered as he brushed his thumbs against the damp heat between her legs, massaging, prodding, teasing, even as he ran his hands upward to fondle her lushly rounded bottom.

He cupped her, weighing each lush cheek and then sliding downward again to prod his thumbs against her—teasing, testing, dipping into her heat and then back out again to repeat the process. She squirmed as he caressed her, and he smiled, knowing her pleasure would be all the sweeter for the wait.

He bent toward her and began to kiss and nibble one fully rounded cheek as his fingers continued to dip and tease. She squirmed against him and a moan escaped her as he nipped her flesh with his teeth and then dipped his head to tease and taste her damp folds.

His own desire rose and thickened with each of her pleasure moans, each sigh she released. Her response to each touch, each taste, made hot blood rage in his veins.

Still, he held back.

When at last she was writhing at his every touch, begging him for release, he lowered himself against

her. He pushed his swollen heat deep into her softness as he pulled her hips up to meet him.

She closed around him, clutching his shaft deep inside her. A long shuddering sigh of satisfaction escaped her. He nearly burst right there and then.

Twin groans split the air as he filled her and withdrew, filled her and withdrew, teasing them both further by refusing to give in just yet to the need for
rhythmic movement. She pushed back against him
as he thrust into her, forcing him deeper.

He groaned and ground himself against the soft
cushion of her buttocks as he slid his hands to grip
her hips, feeling himself so deeply sheathed inside
her.

"Faster, Garrett, take me faster," she begged, both
plea and a demand in one.

It was enough to force his control over the edge.

He gave into the need driving them both as he quickened his thrusts, taking her faster, deeper, harder.

He slid one hand up to cup her breast as he
pumped himself against her softness again and again
and again. She cried out and shuddered beneath him,
her body bucking against him as her sheath clutched
and rippled around him.

Then he followed her into the welcoming abyss of
dark, satisfying pleasure.

In the aftermath, they slept, still cradled together.

Chapter Thirteen

Morning's earliest gray light edged beneath the curtain and flowed across the length of the bedroom's dark wood floor. Garrett was instantly awake and alert.

Too many years spent in the open, with lives dependent on his awareness and his ability to react, prevented him from dozing too peacefully, soft downy bed or no. Immediate memories flooded him, giving value and depth to the warmth and softness snuggled at his side.

Maura. Maura Fitzgerald.

Images from the previous evening burned into him as clear and vibrant as a brand. He had loved her and been loved in return until they exhausted themselves, only to dream and then wake in the dark depths of the night locked once more in each others arms, hungrily satisfying the ardent demands of their bodies.

He smiled and glanced down at her. Shadowy sleep yet hovered over her features, making her seem somehow even softer, defenseless. Her vulnerability reached inside him and lodged in his chest with a bittersweet mixture of pleasure and pain.

Each time he touched her tightened the need inside him to touch her again. Feelings he'd never thought to have for her, for anyone, swam just below the surface. Now was not the time to involve himself with a woman, any woman, on a permanent level. And yet . . .

He should rouse himself. He should dress and join his men below. There were plans to be addressed. But he couldn't bring himself to leave Maura's side. Not just yet. With a slow sigh, he lay back against the pillows and savored the warmth of her curled against him. Even asleep as she was now, she fit perfectly against him, as though she comprised the missing parts of him.

He had never sought to feel this way about any woman, especially not now, when his commitment to being the Green Dragon was at its zenith. The Green Dragon's ring and sword could pass from man to man as injury or other obligation required. But he knew he was not meant for managing estates or a family, so he had never sought the regular company of women beyond the physical need for satisfaction. If the time was right and the woman willing, he'd not turn down a little companionship. But Maura was different.

The redstart whistle from the small country inn's courtyard below drew him from this thought. Duty called, putting a hasty end to further speculation.

He reluctantly slid from the bed, padded to the window, and returned the call. Liam smiled up at him, his red hair looking brighter as the pink of dawn joined the gray light. The man offered a quick salute. Garrett nodded in return before turning back toward the bedroom.

First, he would need to find his clothes, discarded so carelessly the evening before. He glanced toward the bed to find a pair of solemn gray eyes watching him.

"Garrett." Soft color washed over her cheeks as she sat up a little in the bed, clutching the coverlet to her. Was it his imagination or did his name sound especially sweet whispered over her lips.

"Aye." He padded back to her and dropped a gentle kiss against her brow. She was soft and warm, and he longed to slide back into the bed beside her. He resisted.

"What are you doing?"

"I have got to dress and then we will be on our way."

"What?" She pushed upright in the bed. The quilt slid to her waist, baring her breasts beneath her hair rioting around her in glossy waves.

"Ah, *muirnín.* You make it all too difficult."

The color in her cheeks washed to a rosier hue, but she smiled and drew the sheet up against her. "It is your fault. I have nothing to cover myself with."

"Aye? I seem to recall you managed the disrobing for us both. I merely went along with your scheme."

He pulled his trousers on and fastened them, trying not to remember the feel of her fingers on him last night after she had completed the unfastening.

"You cannot go without me." She pushed to her feet, dragging the bed linens with her. Her standing in naught but a quilted coverlet and sleep-tousled hair did nothing to quell his memories of the night before or the desires already stirring to life this morning. He struggled to clear the tightness from his throat before answering.

"We will return for you once we have finished ascertaining that our destination has anything to do with our search."

"No." She crossed to stand in front of him, determination evident in every line of her body despite her disarray and the attractive length of leg revealed by her inadequate covering. "If you find your Jane, or any other woman, you may have need of another woman—of me. She will have been through a nightmare, Garrett. Think of Mary."

"You have a point." He sighed and kissed her very briefly as he finished buttoning his shirt. "And more than once, both about my teasing and the likelihood of anyone we find needing a gentle smile and unthreatening touch. But I cannot like having you placed in any danger."

"This is my expedition," she told him, her firm tone belying the alluring image standing before him.

"That it was. That was before."

"Before what? Before we made love? Before you decided I could not take care of myself? I would like to remind you, Garrett Lynch, I have been taking care of myself for quite some time now."

"Aye." He couldn't fault her there. As soft and vulnerable as she had looked only a short while ago, curled in sleep, she had been a woman on her own, taking care of herself and providing help to others long before he met her. She was capable and intelligent. So why did he have this overwhelming need to shelter her from harm?

"If we are right, I need to be there," she repeated in a softer tone that was no less firm.

"Aye."

He stroked his fingers over her cheek. She was so fiercely passionate in her need to protect this unknown young woman should they find her, just as she was with the young women already under her care.

He was accustomed to dealing with men—men at all levels of competence. Men united with a common need to help others, the same need that burned in her. He should not let his own selfish need to protect her stop her.

"You had best get dressed."

She nodded, a smile lighting her face as she bent to retrieve her clothes from the floor where they'd fallen as she'd shed them last night.

The enticing glimpses of the thigh and breast he caught as she rushed to comply only served to remind him why he had wanted to leave her here where she was safe—leave her to keep her safe for him.

"I'll order breakfast," he threw over his shoulder as he strode out the door. One more look at her and he'd be tempted to lock the door behind him.

"Just tea for me, please," he heard her ask despite the door between them.

At the bottom of the steps the tavern owner's wife waited. He smiled at her.

"Thank you, Mrs. Doyle" He accepted the coffee she held out to him and sipped. Hot and strong.

"I hope ye find what ye're looking fer, sir. But don't let yer men take ye ta that place in the mountains. There's a lovely stud farm fer sale not too far outside Glendalough. There's a lake, the beauty of the mountains and a new stable and training paddock—jest the thing fer ye. My brother works there. Ask fer Tim, Tim Martin, and tell him Abby sent ye."

"It sounds eminently suitable, Mrs. Doyle. But tell me, why is the property nearer the mountains not equally desirable?"

"There's rumors about that place. Strange doin's, if ye ask me. That's all I know. Steer toward Glendalough." Her eyes darted up the steps. "Yer lady is here."

She nodded toward the stairs, and he turned to see Maura at the top, chignon tucked regally into place, bearing her now severely wrinkled skirt and jacket with a grace sure to be envied, every inch the lady the innkeeper's wife expected her to be.

"I am ready." She accepted a cup of tea from their hostess.

"Aye. So you are." He fought to stifle the warnings ringing inside him over taking her along, but he was willing to trust her. She said she would keep herself safe, and he would believe her.

She finished her mug of tea quickly, and he escorted her out into the yard and around toward the stables where Sean and Liam were waiting, leaning in seemingly negligent repose against the coach they'd borrowed for their plan. Liam straightened as they approached and nudged Sean without preamble.

"Ah, top of the morning to ye both." Sean's buoyant greeting was accompanied by a full-bodied smirk.

"And to both of you as well," Maura answered before Garrett could come up with anything sufficiently quelling. Her even tone managed to disarm his teasing intent before it could blossom in full.

Amazing.

"Are we ready?"

"Aye. The Doyles are allowing us use of the coach. And we've sent the stable lad back to Dublin to roust the others. They should be in this vicinity by nightfall."

"That works well." In their experience most successful rescues came off better at night. At this point, although they assumed they were going to very soon be working a rescue mission, they had yet to determine they were even targeting the right location.

"Shall we be off?" He turned to Maura and offered his arm. She placed her hand on it and allowed him to lead her to the coach. Sean opened the door; Liam waved his hand with the flourish. She smiled at their nonsense and stepped up into the coach.

"And now?"

"Now, lady, sit back and enjoy the ride. It will take us an hour or two to reach our destination."

"Very well." She nodded and settled back against the cushioned interior.

Sean climbed up into the coachman's seat and Liam fetched his horse, intent on taking up the rear position. Garrett would join Sean overhead. Giving in to impulse he stepped up onto the coach steps and leaned inward.

"We will warn you when we approach."

"Thank you."

"Maura—"

"Aye?"

Asking her to stay behind one more time hovered on his tongue. He bit the urge back, closed the distance between them, and gave her a long, slow kiss.

Maura smiled to herself as he closed the coach door and was gone before he could say anything further. What a contradiction Garrett Lynch was proving to be. A strong leader, compassionate, but determined. A man of passion and convictions. Where was the man she'd expected when he was first invited to Freddie's card party? The wastrel and drunkard?

He was not that man.

A quick shout set the coach to rolling, and she rested her head back against the cushions. Images swept over her in varying degrees of heat. Their lovemaking last night had been so very satisfying in ways she had never experienced before. Satisfied hardly covered what she had felt, or what he had made possible for her to feel.

She'd always taken pleasure in the act. If she'd not been able to enjoy the relations she had allowed, her life up to this point would have been a small, well-furnished corner of hell.

But she never suspected the passion and fire, the incredible feelings, inherent in making love to a man purely because he wanted her and she wanted him in return. There was no thought, no planning, no deliberation, nothing between them except the desire to please and be pleased.

She shifted against the seat cushions as swirls of lingering sensation cascaded over her. Her eyelids drifted closed as she remembered Garrett's every touch. His kisses. His smiles. And so very much more.

No planning. No responsibility.

The realization hit her quite suddenly. Not only was she no longer in Dublin, no longer Freddie's, or anyone else's, mistress, she was far from the potion she took so religiously from Mrs. Kelly's hands each morning.

An icy chill swept over her, wiping away the warmth of her reverie over yesterday's extraordinary encounters with Garrett Lynch. Mrs. Kelly's potion of herbs and tea kept her from conceiving a child. Among the many rules that had made it possible to conduct her life with a minimum of guilt had been Dorothy Kelly's assurance that the women of her family had used the very same potion for generations and had never had an untimely pregnancy.

But here, far from Dorothy's herb closet, she'd given in to the passion she felt for Garrett without thought or planning. In the overwhelming seductive freedom of choosing him, she had forgotten the need for caution.

Each passionate encounter sifted through her mind. Five, six times? Or was it seven? They'd made love over and over again and not once had she considered the possible consequences to what they were doing with such abandon.

She groaned, feeling the press of time and the narrowing window of safety afforded to prevent something she wasn't ready to face. Edges of panic attacked her nerve endings. How long would it take them to determine if the lodge they were heading toward was even the place they were looking for? And if it wasn't, what then?

She blew out a slow breath and turned her gaze outward to the gradual passing of scenery, deep green hills sloped into the nothingness of the early morning fog. She had time yet, surely. Time to return to Mrs. Kelly, drink the potion, and not worry. If she knocked on the stage coach roof or called through the little hatch designed for occupants and coachman to communicate with one another, if she went back to the inn and road through the day and into the night, if she abandonded the girls she feared were being abused nearby, left Garrett—

Enough—she was a woman, not some green girl to panic over pregnancy the very first time she lay with a man. For all she knew, after all this time, she wasn't even capable of conceiving a child.

A child with dark hair and vibrant green eyes.

His child.

"Enough!" The protest escaped her aloud. They hit a bump and she bit her lip. She was used to dealing with any number of problems on a daily basis. This possibility would have to get in line. She would see to this problem when they all returned to Dublin, until then she needed to concentrate on the problems ahead—whatever they were.

Two hours passed, leaving her restless and unsettled. Her mind still churned with possibilities despite her resolution to let the problem be, or rather the potential for a problem be. Deep in thought, she startled when the coach began to slow. Garrett swung down out of the seat above as they rumbled to a stop.

"Hello." Deep appreciation sparkled in those unfathomable green eyes. That she could spend the rest of her life in that gaze struck her again, just as surely now as the very first time she looked a him.

She caught back a sigh.

"Hullo." A second face joined his at the window, and then a third.

"Maura." Sean touched his hat.

"Are ye ready to play a broken-down traveler, Maura?" Liam rubbed some dirt across his cheek, simulating his efforts to fix the broken whatever on their coach.

"Ye'll need to appear a bit overset." Sean sprinkled dirt on his jacket and then turned to Garrett.

"Aye." Garrett coughed as a cloud of dust rose from Sean's efforts.

"And somewhat impatient with the lot of us." His normally refined tones slid into a soft lilt with surprising ease and authenticity. "Do ye think ye can manage such a tall order?"

She couldn't help but smile. Managing to seem overset at the moment was not going to be as tall an order as they supposed.

"I believe I can manage, gentlemen."

"Proceed." Garrett gave the one-word order over his shoulder as he levered himself into the coach beside her, all trace of the lilt gone. "From here we go forward on foot."

"On foot?"

"Aye, the coach will be within easy reach of the lodge if anyone cares to check our story. We're taking off one of the wheels right now. We'll make a break in a couple of the spokes, and that will be our excuse for needing repairs. If they have something to hide, it is more than likely they will not allow us inside. So we'll have to do our best to observe and question from the outside."

He took her hands in his. "There is the outside possibility that you might be able to gain entrance. If you are very, very careful."

"I will be."

He gave a smile that was part grimace and shook his head. "Somehow I knew that would be your answer."

"Then we're ready, except for this." He leaned toward her and took her mouth in a gentle soul-searing kiss that poured molten heat through her.

Everything inside her still dwelling on her concerns for the past two hours melted into a warm pool of desire. "I have needed that," he said.

"I have too." She breathed her answer back to him.

"Ahh, don't look at me that way, darlin', or we'll need to postpone the entire day." He traced his fingers over her cheek. "And I don't know if the Doyles can spare their coach a second day."

"Think how disappointed Liam and Sean will be if we don't get to play broken-down traveler today." She smiled. "They have talked of little else since yesterday."

"Come then. I would hate to disappoint *them* above all else." He answered her smile with one of his own and her heart did an odd tumble. "We must be off."

Within moments they were walking a rutted path that led up a slow incline into a thickly wooded area, not a path often traveled apparently.

Sean rolled the huge carriage wheel along beside him. There was something grim and determined in the set of his jaw despite the easy way he rolled the wheel, the teasing tone he'd maintained in the two days of this expedition.

Liam's face also showed determination and concentration. Maura transferred her gaze to Garrett. "What is the best you hope for here?"

"Enough information to assure us this is the place we're looking for. If it is, we'll come back tonight with the rest of our . . . friends."

"Aye, friends." Sean smiled and offered her a wink, his mask of casual carelessness firmly in place once more.

"Surely, this is a matter best given over to the authorities, to the army even," she argued.

"We've a great many, experienced friends who will give us whatever help we need in order to accomplish this mission." Liam spoke with assurance. He did not sound boastful, just confident.

Garrett nodded. "Enough to complete the job."

Again she was struck with the differences. This

man, this man that had somehow worked his way into her heart, was not the same man who had played cards, visited her draper's shop, and offered information about a supposed missing niece.

And the men around him were as changeable as he was. Now they moved together, focused on the goal of obtaining information. They made frequent reference to this broken-down traveler guise as though they as a group used it often. She had thought of it as youthful sport, a game from their younger years. But it was somehow more serious, more important. Then there was the unspoken, but recognizable acknowledgment that Garrett was their leader, that he had been for some time.

What did all this mean?

They topped a rise and entered woods. Deepening shadows spread in all directions. The mountains surrounding them disappeared, hidden by the treetops.

The woods gradually closed around them. Tall trees stretched upward to the sky, blotting out the sunshine. With little breeze it was eerily quiet; even the distant rustling of the leaves overhead seemed to whisper of secrets best not known. Garrett's hand took hers. She was grateful for the pressure of his fingers against hers, and grateful she was not alone amidst the gathering gloom. This place didn't feel like a good place.

The road grew even more rutted and uneven, almost as though the wood and shadow, the unwelcoming road, would deter all but the most determined of visitors. For the first time a shiver of dread crawled over Maura's back. Would they truly be believed as travelers in need of aid?

She wasn't sure whether to hope her growing fears were baseless, all in her head, or to hope they were approaching the right place after all.

"This is it." Sean's announcement came short and

tense as they rounded a slight bend in the rutted path. Up ahead beyond a large field of tall grasses, Maura could make out the outline of a large structure squatting solid and heavy amidst the tall dark trees. It looked to have been there for a very long time. She shivered.

Garrett squeezed her hand again and she turned her gaze to his. "You don't have to—"

"I am all right," she told him quickly. "I think my imagination is holding sway. This place looks . . . it looks . . ."

"Aye. Ye've hit the same thing we did, Maura. That's why we're here." Sean managed a wink despite their surroundings. "Don't ye be aworryin' yer head too much. We've plenty of experience with nasty places."

"And nasty folk as well." Liam tugged his hat farther down over his brow and slouched.

"Maura." Garrett squeezed her fingers again.

"I will be fine."

"Forward then?"

"Aye."

They approached the lodge as she tried to quell the concerns rising inside her. She could too easily imagine Mary trapped here, along with a number of the other young women who had come to Garrett's attention recently.

Dear God, if there was yet one more young woman, or a group of them, within these dark and foreboding walls she would do whatever she needed to do to help them get out.

As they approached the small circular drive and columns that somehow seemed out of place with the rest of the architecture, the front door opened and a woman stepped out. Maura thought she could see someone else standing in the shadowy depths behind her.

"Greetings, good neighbor." Sean's smile broke

forth with the warm geniality he seemed able to conjure at will. "We are mighty thankful to see ye. Our employers have had trouble on the road. Would the master of this household be about?"

"Trouble?" The small woman's gaze ran over them as her hands smoothed her apron front. "What kind of trouble?"

"Our coach wheel broke a few spokes, Mum." Liam helped Sean heft the wheel up as evidence. "We're in sore need of repairs. Can ye offer us a hammer and a few wee nails?"

"We'd greatly appreciate any help ye could spare, good lady." Garrett's tone lilted. "My wife is weary from our travels. We are hours late trying to make it home to Naas and she is not well."

"We are expecting our first child." The words popped out of Maura's mouth before she realized. Her hands slid protectively over her flat belly.

Garrett's gaze, along with Sean's and Liam's, shot to hers as hot color filled her cheeks.

She offered him a shy smile, hoping she appeared as a shy, young wife to the woman still hovering in the doorway.

"Aye." Garrett nodded and turned his gaze back to their possible benefactor without missing a beat. "And it has been a long walk in search of your aid. She would appreciate a moment of rest before we continue on our way, even if you cannot aid us with our repairs."

"Of course I can give ye poor folks some aid. What am I about? We do not get many visitors out this way." The faux pregnancy seemed to have unbent the woman's stiffness enough to allow her to comply with their request, though was still far from welcoming. If Garrett was correct, that meant they were indeed in the right place.

"Oh, thank you so much. Darling, could you help

me?" Maura leaned heavily on Garrett's arm as he helped her up the few short steps to the portico.

"Yer fellows will find the tools they need in the stables around to the back. Don't touch anything else. The master is most particular about who he allows about his property. And ye'll have to be quick about yer work. There's a party tonight, and ye'll want to be well clear of here afore they arrive."

"Thank you so much." Garrett's tone still held warmth as though her offer contained all that they needed instead of just barely allowing them to remain.

"I'll take care of yer wife." The gnarled woman blocked the entrance to the lodge. She was nervous but unwilling to budge. Her hands ran repeatedly down the front of her apron. "Ye'd best see ta them repairs."

Her hard-worked hands were at Maura's elbow and shoulder, almost bodily taking possession as Garrett relinquished his hold. He managed a reassuring squeeze just before releasing her.

"Thank you very kindly."

"Aye."

Maura's heart sank as he retreated back down the steps and her hostess stewarded her into the lodge's shadowy interior. It took a few moments for her eyes to become accustomed to the dimness within the house. She was not prepared for what she saw, not if this was the site of a party in the making.

Chapter Fourteen

As Maura's eyes became accustomed to the dimness inside this menacing lodge, she found the darkness held little promise of any ordinary party preparations, that much was clear.

Her reluctant hostess held fast to her arm as they stepped inside. The heavy thud of the door closing made Maura acutely aware she was cut off from Garrett, and his men. Their easy comfort and familiarity with what they were attempting here bolstered her nerve.

Now . . . she drew a deep breath and tried to concentrate on the task at hand. What would they need to know when she rejoined them? How many details could she absorb and remember to report back to them?

"Did ye feel the need of a wee drink, then? I can scare up a little watered spirits ta settle yer stomach."

The room to the right of the hall they stood in was wide and spacious, though sparsely furnished. From ceiling to floor, the wood-paneled walls were only broken by the occasional stuffed deer head, some chairs, and a long table still covered with a sheet of heavy cotton. Not a welcoming place. Maura struggled to keep from shuddering.

"Anything would be greatly appreciated, thank you." She tried to infuse the same note of warmth Garrett has used to address her hostess.

"Ye have nice manners, that much I'll say fer ye."

The woman nodded her gray head once. "Come along then. I'll give ye a drink in the kitchen. Can't be too much harm in that, can there?"

The question didn't appear to need an answer. Maura made some agreeable noises.

The woman released Maura's arm at last from her tight grip. "This way, stay close ta me. I canna have ye wandering about."

She spoke almost more to herself than to Maura as she led the way down a narrow hall with rooms leading off in different directions. The doors were all closed. The woman's steps were quick and light, making little or no sound.

All of the doorways remained closed as they made their way into the depths of the shadowy interior. Maura strained her ears in an effort to hear anything that might give her a clue that someone waited even now behind one of these doors for any hope of rescue or relief.

She felt ineffectual at best. What was she looking for? What would help aside from this woman's obvious reluctance to have anyone enter and her need to rush Maura through whatever reluctant hospitality she could manage to provide?

"This is a much larger place on the inside than out." Maura's comment seemed almost to be swallowed into the shadows. For a moment she wasn't even sure her companion heard her. She was about to repeat herself when they reached a bend in the hallway.

The woman turned, her wizened face coming close to Maura's. There was fear in her gaze. Her breath smelled of stale cheese.

"Please, ye must be quiet. There's no need to disturb . . . to disturb"—her gaze darted away as though searching the rest of her sentence—"to disturb the peace. There will be disturbance soon enough, and I'll not be responsible for it starting up aforehand."

Her whole manner during this odd discourse was enough to set the fine hairs on the back of Maura's neck on end. "Disturbance?"

"Aye. Come this way please, and do not dawdle." She turned off to the left. "Drinks and travelers, they never said anything about that. What's a body to do?"

"I'm sorry, Mrs. . . . Mrs. . . ."

"It doesn't matter what my name is. Don't worry yerself about that. This way." She ducked her head as the hallway sloped downward. In a few moments, after another twist or two, they entered a rather gloomy-looking kitchen. It was large and open with the simplest of accommodations, as though having dinner parties and guests were the least of concerns to the owner of this odd place. "Here we are."

With deft movements the woman poured a draft of ale into a pewter cup and handed it to Maura. "This will have to do. There's naught else. Don't know what I was thinking. Tea takes too long fer yer stay. All that boiling."

"Why . . . thank you." Maura took the cup and sipped carefully. It was palatable. She moved toward the broad hardwood worktable taking up the center portion of the kitchen. One chair was positioned next to it.

"May I sit for a moment?" She sat as the question left her lips, guessing the answer would not be positive.

Silence held.

"Suit yerself." Her hostess's lips pursed together in displeasure.

"Oh, thank you." She sighed and rubbed her back as though to soothe an ache.

The silence descended, heavy with unease, as Maura searched her mind for a topic of conversation.

"Yer first?"

She nearly started out of her chair as the woman spoke first.

"Aye. My first," she agreed. "I must admit to being a bit unnerved by the whole idea."

"I thought as much. Ye dinna have the look of an experienced mother. But ye've broad enough hips, and it's clear yer man has a care fer ye. Ye'll do fine."

The tiniest bit of warmth infused the woman's voice. Obviously this would be a good topic.

"Do you really think so?"

"Oh, aye. The way a man looks at his woman tells ye everything. There's them what don't care about a woman any more than their horse. Maybe less." She snorted. "Then there's them what think ye're some kind o' treasure. That's what ye got in yer man."

There was envy and resignation in her tone.

"I appreciate your kindness. Does your husband work here with you?"

"What?" The woman snorted again. "Don't have a husband, dearie. If I did I wouldn't be here, ye can be sure of that. This isn't the place for a decent woman. Not one with a family. But sometimes ye canna be too choosy about where ye find the money to get yer own bread. The master provides fer me, and I mind me own business."

"The master? Can you tell me his name so we can write and thank him for this hospitality?"

"Oh no. I can't tell ye that. He values his privacy, fine-spoken gentleman he is. Although I canna vouch fer his friends and his parties."

"His parties?"

"Aye, has them about every month. Supplies come outta nowhere along with a note tellin' me to ready the place. Very demanding he is. But he pays well. I stay here in the meantime so I have a roof over me head, money enough to see to my needs when I'm too old ta work. I know when to keep me mouth shut."

"I'm sure he appreciates that."

"Indeed. Ye know there's not that many who could do what he wants and keep their mouths shut. It's a bit lonely sometimes because I canna talk with the loonies he leaves behind. But . . ." She trailed away as though having realized she'd said more than she should have.

"The loonies?" A chill shivered down Maura's arms again.

"Aye. But ye don't need to hear about that. I can tell ye're far to refined ta care about the likes of them. Less ye know the better ye'll like it."

The woman peered out her sink window. "Have ye finished yer ale? Do ye think yer menfolk are finished their repairs? Ye'll all need to be getting on yer way before the master comes. He don't take on with people he don't know. And visitors have to have approval."

"Of course." Maura pushed to her feet. "I do not want to cause you any difficulty after all your hospitality. I will be happy to hurry my husband along."

"Right." The woman scooped up Maura's used cup and strode to the basin by the grubby window where she dunked it quickly in water and set it aside to dry. Erasing any evidence of a visitor?

"Come along then. The sooner ye're on yer way the better."

They started back down the winding hallway with the closed doors.

"There are so many rooms." Maura offered the comment in a louder tone and gained an instant reaction.

The woman turned back to her with consternation clear on her homely features. "Hush. I told ye not to disturb 'em."

"Them?" She lowered her tone obligingly. "Who are we disturbing? I thought there was no one here but you."

"Aye, well there might as well be for all the help I get from those great hulking buffoons he's got guarding the place. I'm here with the loonies. I told ye that."

She waved a hand to encompass the row of closed oaken doors. "They carry on something terrible at times, and at others they try their best to convince me they're as right as ye or me. Peace is few and far between when ye have to care for them. Today is one of their quiet days. I told 'em his lordship . . . I told 'em the master would be returning tonight with his friends. That was enough to settle 'em down. Along with a sleeping draught. Can't have another of 'em go missin', now can I?"

She snickered into her hand as though drugging the *loonies* under her care were a great joke.

Cold fear coiled in Maura's stomach, souring the ale she'd drunk. One of the loonies had gone missing? Mary?

"Most of the time he don't let me drug 'em," the woman continued. "But when he's coming for the night with his company he wants 'em rested and ready fer his guests."

She shrugged and ran her hands over her apron again. "Least it gives me a nice quiet day ta get ready. Even the guards take it easy, ta rest up. That's the only way ye got this close. They takes care ta turn most away."

Maura's mouth was dry, and she struggled to keep up her end of the conversation as if she were just idly curious. She let her gaze fly from one door to the next. "These loonies . . . are they . . . are they . . . dangerous?"

"Oh, la no. They're harmless as lambs at the moment. I wouldn't trade places with 'em. Not on yer life. But it's a livin' and sometimes that's all a body can ask fer."

This woman knew what was going on here. She knew and it didn't matter to her. Maura was convinced to her marrow that she knew, too. Behind each of these doors, some poor young woman who'd been stolen from her family or lured with the promise of a future might be sleeping, resting for the rigors to come. Dear God.

Unlike this woman who knew for sure, Maura only had her suspicions. The walls swayed for a moment. The fear of waiting, of dread, hung heavy in the stale air.

"Come along. We canna dawdle here."

The clawlike grasp was on her arm again, hurrying Maura back down the gruesome hallway. She went without protest, knowing she had more than enough information for Garrett and his men.

They would have to mount their rescue immediately. There was no time to lose if indeed there were plans for some kind of party tonight with poor hapless girls at risk. Nausea swirled in her stomach at the thought.

"Maura?" The call came from in front of them down the hallway. "Maura, where are ye?"

"There's yer man now. I told ye his care was true." The woman dragged her forward. In the light spilling from the open doorway Garrett stood silhouetted.

"Is yer wheel fixed?"

"Aye, thank you for your kindness."

"Here's yer lady." She released Maura's arm. "As I told her, I'll tell ye. Ye need to be gone as quick as ye can. The master don't like having strangers about. I hope ye left the stables as ye found 'em."

"Aye, we did." Garrett nodded and his hand snaked around Maura's waist. She was grateful for the contact, drawing strength from his warmth. Her knees had begun to quaver as the enormity of the situation around them came home to her.

"Then yer welcome to what ye needed."

"Thank you again." He turned Maura back out the door.

Air.

She took a deep breath of freedom and realized just how close and discomfiting the house had been. Dark and gloomy and confined.

"Oh, Garrett, it's . . . it's . . ."

"Shhh, not yet, love. Let's put a little distance between this place and our backs before you tell us anything of what you saw."

She was only too grateful to comply. They walked quickly with Sean and Liam, falling into step behind them. None of them spoke. All that she had to relate swirled through Maura's mind over and over again. Fear and anger twisted inside her. They needed to get those girls out of there. They needed to do it now.

A dip in the path took them downward and then to the left.

Finally Garrett stopped, and she turned to him. "We have got to get them out of there. We have got to. Oh Garrett, I don't know how many of them there are or who they are, but she knows. She knows what is going on in that place and does not care."

"Take a breath, Maura." He reached for her shoulders and pulled her close. As his hands spread over her back, she shuddered.

"It is an awful place. Awful."

"Aye." He soothed his hands over her again and again.

"Tell us what ye heard." This from Liam, but in the gentlest tone she'd ever heard him use. "We need to know anything ye can remember."

"Aye. And everything you saw, even the smallest detail." Sean's tone was equally earnest. There was a quiet desperation in his gaze she hadn't seen before. A haunted look. "Think carefully."

She pushed back from Garrett's arms to find his gaze intent on her face. "I am sorry you are so overset."

"Do not be, please. I am just so angry and . . . and . . ." she stopped and blew out a long breath. "I am all right. I . . . I . . . this is the right place. This must be, and tonight they are planning on having guests. She kept making references to the master of the house and guests and . . . she talked about the girls who are being held there. She called them loonies. One of them went missing. Perhaps Mary?"

All three men wore identical frowns. Concern tempered with steel. She felt oddly reassured. "I have no idea how many of them there are, and I am not sure where they are, but there was a long, winding hallway that slanted downward. There were rooms leading off that hallway on either side. All of the rooms were closed, and there was no sound coming from anywhere. I think she drugged them. From the way she spoke it seemed this is a regular occurrence."

She pressed a hand to her stomach as the nausea swelled once more.

"Anything else?" Garrett asked.

She nodded and gulped a breath. "There may be other people there, but I didn't see anyone. She made mention of some men who help her with the . . . girls."

"Confirmation," Liam stated in a flat tone.

"Aye." Garrett's jaw tensed. "You did very well, Maura. You got far more information than we did. We saw no one else either."

"What now?"

The men locked gazes for a quick heartbeat. "We wait for the rest of the men Sean and Liam sent for. We will need force on our side."

"But surely it would be better to get the girls out now before anyone else arrives. Before anything could happen to them. Before any—"

Sean made a strangled noise and paced away.

"We know how you feel." Garrett squeezed her shoulders gently. "But rushing in without adequate people and a solid plan not only will leave us open to unknown circumstances, but in all probability will not save the very people we are trying to help."

He spoke with firm conviction, with the voice of experience, as though he'd been on many other rescues. Her mind whirled. Who was this man? Who were the men who seemed so willing to follow him?

"When we return to the coach you will have to give us detailed sketches of the interior. And tell us everything you saw, from doorways to furniture. You will remember more than you realize once you've had some rest."

"Come on then; Mrs. Doyle did us a kindness in packing us a luncheon," Sean called. "Food and rest are in order. We will all need our strength."

The casual tone returned to his voice, but his hand gripped the coach wheel so tight his knuckles were white.

She sighed. There was something going on between the three men, something unsaid just beneath the surface.

They continued down the path in silence, questions vibrating in her mind.

Hours later, as darkness thickened and began to pour from the depths of the woods around the lodge, Maura was no closer to the truth about the men whose company she kept. She hoped they were closer to resolution for the young women inside that awful place. As twilight fell the woods were suddenly full of redstarts. Garrett's friends gathered around the coach they had pulled off the road and into a small wooded copse, to watch and wait.

In addition to Garrett's friends arriving, a number of carriages and coaches passed them by, following the rutted path into the woods. Fine carriages and coaches, equipage she recognized from Freddie's circle of peers and her own neighborhood. She prayed Freddie and Percy were not among the group arriving for this evening's hedonistic entertainments at the lodge.

Garrett walked over to the coach where she sat as the time for them to begin the rescue surely came nearer. Sean was a pace behind.

Garrett's gaze locked with hers. "Maura, you must stay here."

It wasn't a question, but it wasn't quite an order either. It was a request, almost a plea. She appreciated the subtle respect.

"We will bring anyone we free to you. Be ready. I am leaving Seamus behind to tend the horses and carriages. You may need to be ready to vacate this area in a hurry."

She nodded. A knot of mingled tension and fear tightened in her stomach. He was tense enough; she had no desire to add any further concern to the assault on the lodge he had organized.

"Good." He gave her a small smile and turned his attention elsewhere.

"Garrett." She touched his arm. He turned back to her immediately. "Please be careful."

A slow smile tilted his mouth. He leaned in toward her and brushed her lips with a quick kiss. "Aye, we will all be careful."

"Take this, just in case." Sean stepped forward. The haunted look still loomed in his eyes. In fact, it had grown with each carriage that passed them by.

Cold metal pressed into her hands. She looked

down to find a small and lethal-looking pistol in her lap. Gooseflesh pebbled her skin as the knot in her stomach tightened still further.

"Oh . . . I . . ."

"You will probably not need it." Garrett explained Sean's gift. "Take it for my peace of mind if for nothing else."

"I do not even know how to use such a thing."

He smiled again. "Point it at anyone who menaces you and pull that little lever if they come too close. I'll hear you."

She nodded again.

"I will be back soon." He closed the coach door. "Lock this." His tone was low and deadly serious.

She did as he asked.

As he turned from her she heard the clear, high song of the redstart close to the coach. And then in the distance a repeat, and again farther on.

Fear shivered over her again. It had begun.

Garrett made his way into the darkness with the distant whispering of trees and bracken for company along with the men he'd spent so much time with. The moon was hidden by overhanging branches. Well enough. They would be invisible in their approach. The men inside were probably not expecting anything to disturb their fun. If this place had been in operation for as long as various reports had given them to believe, they would be expecting to be undisturbed and well secreted away. So much the better.

Sean was at his side, his face hidden in shadow, but Garrett could feel the tension pouring from him. It had crossed his mind a couple of times to tell Sean to stay behind with Maura instead of Seamus, but he hadn't wanted a mutiny on his hands. The man was far more affected than he wanted to admit. His caring for Jane Fuller was like a beacon in the darkness. It might cause him to take unhealthy risks.

Garrett recognized the depth of his friend's involvement and fear because he would feel much the same if Maura was in danger. At least if he kept Sean close, he stood a better chance at keeping him safe. Left with Maura and the coach he'd be just as likely to tear off on his own.

"Sean."

"Aye." Sean's voice was tough and determined.

"We will get her out safely."

"Aye, that we will." More promise than agreement. Although he'd held himself together with admirable restraint during the intelligence-gathering mission preceding this rescue attempt, Sean's fear for Jane was plain.

Within moments they reached the outer grounds of the lodge, surely the country haunt of the Devil's Club. Garrett blew out the call of the redstart. This was the signal to surround the perimeter of the building and for a smaller group to surround the stables and cut off that avenue of escape. It would do them little good to scare the vultures from their nest within only to have them scatter to the winds.

His men moved with quiet, practiced stealth, spreading into the welcoming darkness to encircle their quarry.

He glanced at Sean again. A haunted, angry gaze stared back at him.

"All of those coaches—"

"Aye."

"They are animals. No better." Raw hatred and contempt laced Sean's voice. "Taking women for no reason save to serve their own debauchery. Jane could very well be in there."

"Aye, lad." He placed a hand on Sean's shoulder. "Steady."

"She does not deserve any of this."

"None of them do. We will get her out. We will get them all out."

"I know we have a plan, Garrett. I know it up here." Sean tapped his forehead. "But my gut is another matter."

"Your gut and mine as well. Stay with me. We await but one more call."

They moved forward, closer and closer to the building. Although light glowed from the edges of the windows, all of them appeared to be heavily curtained to keep out prying eyes. More evidence they had arrived at the right place. What sort of hunting lodge possessed such in the midst of the country where prying eyes would be few and very far between and first light welcomed a new day's hunt.

"Garrett." Sean spoke low enough so that he wasn't sure he'd heard him at all.

"Aye."

"What if we are wrong? What if Jane is not in there. What if she never was?"

"Then we will free whoever is confined here and keep looking for her elsewhere."

"Aye."

Creeping up toward the windows, he and Sean both took up a position that would allow them to peer inside. A quick glance between the edge of the curtain and the window ledge at first showed nothing.

Then as Garrett's eyes grew accustomed to the candlelight blazing within he could make out a large room, empty of guests and sparsely furnished just as Maura had described. There was a long table in the middle of the room and chairs scattered about, but they were not drawn up to the table. This was not a dining table.

"*Diabhal,*" Sean whispered through his clenched jaw.

Garrett's gut churned, and he could imagine the

thoughts going through Sean's head. This table, complete with leather straps, appeared to be the area wherein the Devil's Club members would complete their *sacrifices*. Daniel McTavish's limited investigations into the actions and the purposes of the Devil's Club had provided rumors of a group of men engaged in monthly high sacrifices—young, virginal females used and abused by as many men as cared to take part in the act.

Sean's explanation to Liam when the gruesome details first surfaced echoed back to Garrett, and their friend had sought a reason for such depravity.

"I would think that would be fairly obvious." Sean had spoken in a hollow tone that day. "They enjoy the idea of taking unsuspecting, innocent young women and subjecting them to their debauched ideas of pleasure. It's not the sex, it is the power."

He'd allowed Sean the truth of his point that day. But deep in his gut he couldn't sway the feeling, the certainty, that there was another, more evil, purpose. He'd spent the evening playing cards opposite Jameson that night in Maura's town house. He'd watched the man's face as he played. Watched him in his discourse with young Stanhope and his feckless friend, Percival Masters. Each bit of conversation, whether jest or serious point, seemed carefully constructed to build on the last, to gain from these young men exactly what he wanted from them.

Jameson intended to drag them to this club. His question from that night remained, why? Aside from whatever pleasure he might derive from bringing new converts to the altar of his perverted pursuits, what plans did Jameson have for Stanhope, Longford, and Masters?

Were they among the night's company? Was Jameson? His gut churned harder.

There was more here than just depravity.

But what?

Perhaps they would gain an answer once their rescue began. Where was that last call? When would they begin?

Chapter Fifteen

"Excellent, truly excellent." Harold Jameson, entrepreneur, statesman, puppeteer, surveyed his image in the heavy gilt mirror with burgeoning satisfaction.

Tall and slender, wearing the best clothes fashion could imagine and coin could purchase, he made a fine figure of a man. No one would know to look at him that he was the bastard son of a marquess. No one would even suspect that he seethed with anger over the whims of fate that made him a bastard, without prospects or status, especially within the bosom of his family.

He was the eldest son; as such, he should be the one with the financial backing, with the lands and the recognition that would enable him to manipulate through position and respect alone what he now accomplished through his own hard-won and unending machinations.

No matter. His trials had made him the man he was. He smiled at himself, watching the familiar sparkle light his pale hazel eyes. He smoothed his hair into place.

He deserved the power he carefully maneuvered over lesser men. He'd been careful and calculating in his moves across the grand chessboard of life, gathering allies, foiling enemies. His fascination with new experiences, with the pleasures to be had from women and supplied to other men, had certainly aided him in gaining his present position.

And there were no little bastards littering the landscape in a pale string of rejection behind Harold Jameson. He knew better than to beget some unwanted chattel to envy and steal everything he wanted from life. He'd learned early on how to take his pleasure and leave no lingering traces.

He cast a quick glance over his shoulder as the scrawny servant woman who managed this place in his absence presented herself. He caught back an impatient sigh at her interruption and spoke with the warm cordiality she was used to.

"What is it, Enid?"

She bobbed a grotesque mockery of a curtsey. "I just wanted to let ye know, jest to bring to yer attention."

She wrung her hands over her apron. She was a repugnant little woman, colorless and without imagination, only too ready to treasure her position in his household. He in turn treasured her loyalty and her ability to keep to herself out in the wild and lonely countryside. She might annoy him with her appearance, but her service was above reproach.

"Yes? Come, Enid, do not dawdle; what is it you wish?"

"Well, sir, there were some travelers as stopped here earlier today. They had a broken wheel and needed to make repairs. I couldn't turn 'em away."

He frowned at her, more concerned about her apparent worry over the situation than about any stray travelers stopping at a lodge for help.

"And?"

She twisted the apron again. "That's all, sir. I jest wanted ye ta know."

"Indeed." He studied her in silence for a moment. Thin nondescript hair, scrawny whipcord leanness, dull complexion—there was naught to recommend her outwardly. However she was steady in her temperament and as reliable as a rock. Her nervousness over this incident was such that she needed to bring it to his attention before the evening's festivities began? That alone was unsettling.

"Are you sure there is nothing else, Enid?"

He took a step toward her and caught her bony chin in his hand. She didn't flinch from his touch. He'd never been anything but good to her. Although she held full knowledge of the activities that took place beneath the roof, she didn't fear him in the least. Another quality he appreciated in her.

"Aye, sir, they did nothing but repair their wheel."

"But it worried you?"

"Aye." She looked up at him with the placid eyes of a devoted mongrel. "There's not many coaches that come by this way by accident."

Indeed, she was quite correct. The lodge was quite a bit off the beaten path. It was one of the reasons he purchased this land ten years ago and had taken the time to build according to his own specifications. Never leave anything to chance that can be addressed through intelligence and thorough consideration.

He pondered her a moment longer in silence. She waited patiently, certain he would address whatever needed addressing.

"Who were they?"

"I don't know, sir. They gave very little information aside from the fact they'd thrown a wheel. There was a gentleman and his wife and two servants."

"Ahh." He pondered that a moment longer, glad he had taken the time to question her. The presence of the woman in the party helped set his mind at rest. Any law enforcement officials checking into the situation here would not have included a woman in their midst.

He knew there were groups attempting to locate his

current prize, but those too would not have included a woman.

Still . . . he released his hold of Enid's chin.

"Send Bart to me," he told her, requesting the man who headed his own small security detail.

"Aye, sir." Relief lit her pale features as she bobbed another curtsey to him and disappeared back into the dimly lit hallway.

Moments later Bart Cargill muscled his way into the room. There was truly no other way to describe it. The man was one large muscle from his beefy-looking feet up to his thick neck. Arms like tree branches hung at his sides. Here was another example of the type of loyalty Harold so prized. Bart wasn't the smartest man Harold could have chosen to guard his back from all comers, but the man was loyal to a fault and had proven his worth over and over again in the depths of Dublin's seamier streets and alleyways.

Harold really had no need of intelligent, second-guessing individuals in his employ. He required people who would do his bidding without question and respond always with loyalty uppermost in their hearts and souls. He'd surrounded himself through the years with just those types of people. They had been ridiculously easy to find and recruit into his service.

"Evening, sir." Bart offered respectfully.

"Good evening, Bart. Thank you for arriving so quickly. Our dear Enid has informed me we had some . . . unexpected guests this afternoon."

"Here, sir? At the lodge?"

"Yes." Not quick, but loyal and that was all that mattered.

"Who?" Bart bristled, his fists clenching and unclenching, as though ready to do battle with whomever might be lurking in the shadows of Harold's room.

Harold stifled a chuckle. "That is a very good question. Enid is not sure who they were. The entire incident may turn out to be nothing more than what she claims. Three men and a woman stopped here this afternoon, requiring repairs to a coach wheel. They were not here long, just long enough to upset our Enid. And you know she does not upset easily."

"Aye, she's a good woman." Bart nodded emphatically. He had developed somewhat of a tenderness for Enid over the years, which Harold found both disgusting and endearing at one and the same time. He held back a shudder.

"Indeed, she is. My concern is the possibility that they were not what they seemed. I would like you to have your men check the grounds and keep themselves alert for anything out of the ordinary."

"Ye think they'll be back, sir?"

Harold pondered that a moment. "No, no I do not. But I also think it never hurts to be prepared for all outcomes. I have anticipated this particular evening for some time and I do not want it interrupted if we can avoid it. Have your men check the grounds, then come back to me with a report."

"Aye, sir, I'll do that right away."

"Thank you, Bart. You may remain for the festivities when you have completed your duties."

"Oh, thank ye, sir. Thank ye very much." Bart's small dark eyes and eager smile reflected his anticipation. The man was very easy to please. He was a voyeur. Allow him to stay and watch the occasional party festivities and he remained grateful in the extreme, loyal to a fault.

Deflowering Admiral Fuller's daughter should prove a very entertaining evening to be sure. With young Lord Stanhope earmarked to be the guilty party, Harold would have not only the baron but also his grandfather and the admiral falling neatly under his control very shortly.

He would also have the pleasure from the coming

tender night of sexual education that would make proud, opinionated Miss Fuller into a more amenable and thoroughly educated bride for Stanhope. Perhaps then, with Stanhope otherwise engaged and Mrs. Maura Fitzgerald newly without protection, Harold Jameson could engage Mrs. Fitzgerald to be his mistress for a time. That particular scheme would offer multiple satisfactions of its own.

He'd watched Stanhope and his puling adoration of her, watched her carefully manipulate Stanhope into withdrawing from the first night of pleasures he'd offered. He could only imagine the ordinary, carefully respectful sexual relations they engaged in on a regular basis. Staid and boring, like Clancare's heir.

But Maura Fitzgerald was an earthy beauty who demanded fuller, more satisfying sexual pleasuring. He could read her needs in the bewitching glow of her stormy gray gaze, feel what she could offer in the frankly sensual aura that surrounded her and beckoned men into her web. She was a woman begging for his personal tutelage.

And he would be only too happy to be the man to introduce one such as her to the variety of pleasures and possibilities he'd learned and engaged in over the years. He might not keep her long—it was not his habit or his want to tie himself to any woman—but he would enjoy schooling her thoroughly for as long as he chose before bestowing her on some half-wit, only too glad to take his leavings.

"Yes, indeed." He smiled at himself again. And now as Bart spent his time securing the outer grounds before his guests arrived, it was time to stop in and pay a short visit to his prize.

Miss Jane Fuller herself.

Would this extra month spent in sweet Enid's care, wondering about her fate, have taken any of the starch out of Jane Fuller? He dearly hoped not. It would be all that much more entertaining to watch her degradation if she was still just as full of herself as she had been the last time he'd visited with her.

On their initial meeting he had wondered at the admiral's choice in allowing such a beauty to retain a spirit and intelligence that would make her a difficult sale on the marriage market. But now, after acquainting himself with her and anticipating the coming evening, he was thankful for the admiral's mistake.

Harold stopped in the hallway before Jane Fuller's assigned room. There was silence from within. Apparently she hadn't broken down into a fit of weeping as so many virginal females did at this point before the proceedings. Good. That promised a more interesting evening.

He turned the key in the lock, twisted the knob, and let himself into her room.

She faced him standing. She was a young woman with long golden curls shimmering over her shoulders, spilling about her slender frame. She was petite, invitingly so. The whisper-thin muslin gown he'd provided her did more than hint at her womanly charms—if anything, it enhanced them.

Her small stature did not diminish her curves. She possessed full, high, well-rounded breasts, a tiny waist, and lushly curved hips. If it weren't for her usability as a pawn in his grand chessboard he would have been more than willing to have her for his own before his guests.

But sometimes a man had to override his own needs and desires in the short term to focus on long-term outcomes and desires. Now was, regrettably, one of those times.

She had obviously turned as he entered the room, evidenced by the gentle swing of the white muslin above her small, bared feet. He liked the idea that she faced him so boldly; he liked it even more that she must have been pacing the room in fear and anticipation before he entered. It made her more human, more conquerable.

He thought back to the kiss he had pressed on her in a moonlit garden. It had been sweet and surprising, especially when he'd ended up in the fountain. But for that fool Talbot he'd have taught her a lesson in compliance that night that would have spared her this night's humiliation.

Her eyes widened as she realized his interested gaze rested on the region where her thighs joined. She sat on the one chair available, gathering the folds of the gown about her as though to hide herself from him.

What a treasure she was.

"Jameson, this will avail you nothing." Her tone was tense with dislike and a pulsing undercurrent of fear. Oh, but he did enjoy the initiation of virgins with a little bit of the spitfire in them.

"Indeed?" He closed the door behind him and watched her eyes widen ever so slightly as it clicked shut.

"I do not know what you plan in regard to my father, but he will agree to nothing, and neither will I." Her chin lifted over the last statement and her eyes flashed blue fire at him.

Ah, a spitfire indeed. Desire kindled low in his belly. Perhaps he would sample her after all, just a small taste without the actual deflowering, to let her know what lay in store—a little teaser to whet her fear.

"Really? I would beg to disagree with you, but then it is not my reputation that is at stake." He walked across the room, enjoying the sound of his booted feet against the bare floorboards.

She paled but didn't move from her seat. The muslin gown, clutched against her sides, dipped low over her breasts and fluttered with her rapid breathing. Did she have any idea of the beauteous image she presented, practically begging for the lessons he could give her? Any man, no matter how principled and proud, would be hard-pressed not to take advantage of the temptation she presented.

She was an excellent choice, truly one of his better selections if only for her beauty. The political advantages she offered by her birth would prove a bonus. Stanhope would be well-blessed with a pleasing woman and the handsome brats he could get upon her. *He will owe me a great debt.*

He stopped beside her, his eyes delving into the depths of her natural cleavage for a delicious moment before he took her chin in his fist. Unlike his stalwart Enid, she flinched at his touch. "You are quite lovely, Jane. I have always thought as much. But then I imagine you know that."

She glared up at him, wide blue eyes filled with dislike and fear. "Am I supposed to be flattered by your interest? I assure you, I am not."

He chuckled and stepped closer still, enjoying the stiffening in her posture as she forced herself not to flee his advance. She wanted to run. He could smell her fear and it was intoxicating. Only her will alone held her in her seat.

"You should be, my dear. But overall it matters very little to me if you are flattered or not. You are lovely. Soft. Virginal. All the things I prize in a woman. Your feelings are of little consequence."

"I will never agree to anything you ask." She flung her defiance at him.

He stepped closer still, placing a booted foot firmly between her own much smaller, bare feet. She nearly jumped. He shifted his weight, and the pressure of his leg pushed her knees apart. "Your agreement matters even less."

He slid his fingers into the silky mass of her hair

and pulled, tilting her head back so that she looked up at him like a supplicant. The long column of her neck sloped downward to the fullness of her breasts. "Your willingness matters not at all."

With that he bent and took her mouth with his, swallowing her protest as he plundered her. His free hand slid beneath the thin muslin to weigh and fondle the soft resilient flesh of her breasts as his knee wedged tight against her stomach to stop her from fleeing his assault.

She gasped as he knocked the wind out of her. He took advantage of the weakness to thrust his tongue deep into her mouth to possess her more fully. She struggled against him, her protest futile as he fondled and tasted her.

It would be all too easy to bend her to his will and be the first man to thrust himself into her tight, untried body. What a pleasure it would be to impale her and watch her face as he enjoyed her to the tempo of his body's needs heedless of her protests.

He pinched her nipples to hardened points, deliberately bruising her so that when the next man touched her there, when Stanhope took her, she would be reminded of this moment through the haze of her degradation, deflowered for all to see.

"Ahh. Very nice, very nice indeed. Your body is every bit as soft and tempting as I suspected. But I haven't the time or the inclination to fully initiate you into the world of fleshy delights. More's the pity."

His taunts came thick with his desire for her, but he restrained himself as he straightened his waistcoat and put a bit of distance between himself and the disheveled maiden he'd so thoroughly and pleasurably explored.

"I have chosen another to be the recipient of your virginity. But rest assured, my dear, I shall be there, with a host of others, cheering him on and sampling what little delights come our way. Perhaps he will share when he is done with you."

"You are a fiend." She defied him still, but her tone was shaky as the words rasped from her.

She pressed her hand against her kiss-ravaged mouth. Tears glittered in her eyes, but she refused to shed them. Oh, but he did admire that. Even when threatened with multiple rape she managed not to break down into wailing and weeping. It gave her promise for the future. He had chosen very well.

"As much as I have enjoyed our time together, I am certain my guests are as anxious for tonight's entertainment to begin as you are."

"A vile fiend," she repeated, anger shaking in her voice. "It does not matter what you plan. You can attack my body, but you will never hurt me."

"Ah, a lovely sentiment. I truly admire your spirit. But they are empty words, my dear." He unlocked the door as he smiled at her. "Trust me in this, if in nothing else. We will plunder your delights very thoroughly, and nothing you can do will prevent it. When you have lain beneath twenty men, served their needs, we will talk again about what may or may not hurt you."

He chuckled to himself as her eyes widened and fear showed clearly on her lovely features.

With that promise ringing in her ears he closed the door and locked it behind him. Now to get his report from Bart, and then the evenings festivities could truly begin. He rubbed his hands together. There was nothing he liked better than the culmination of his plans. This particular plan had proceeded thus far with added bonuses in the way of personality and possibilities.

It was going to be a very good night.

He ducked his head into the parlor where the men involved in tonight's delightful proceedings were relaxing over a brandy and anticipating their pleasures as only young men could.

"Jameson." A chorus of greetings rang out.

"Hello, gentlemen. I am sorry to have delayed myself for so long from your company. I hope you will forgive me for just a few more moments."

"Not a problem at all, old man. We have waited this long, and you must have heard that old adage about anticipation whetting the appetite?" Percy Masters sniggered at his own joke and elbowed young Stanhope, who appeared to be caught between his friend's humor and his own uncertainty about just what he'd gotten himself into. It had taken a great deal of persuasion to get the new baron to attend this party and finally fall in with his plans. Thank goodness they were away from town and there really was no place for Baron Stanhope to retreat. The young man was essentially trapped by his own curiosity and inability to say no to his friend.

A true pleasure indeed.

"Jameson, if things are not turning out as you'd intended, perhaps we could wait for another—"

"Not at all, not at all." Harold interrupted before Stanhope could finish his ridiculous attempt to end the evening prematurely. He couldn't afford to have this man unsettling the others and destroying his plans when they were so very close to fruition. "Do not fret yourself. It is merely my own attention to details that has your waiting here. Enjoy the brandy and anticipation. I shall return for you in a thrice."

With that he closed the salon doors behind him. Anticipation had been exactly the right note to hit in order to get Masters started. He could already hear that young man launching into his own exploits in the boudoir and his plans for the evening.

Nauseating, but necessary.

Now, where was Bart?

* * *

As the front door swung open, Garrett's men blended into the darkened scenery. With bated breath they waited and watched in the shadows. In a moment a large silhouette filled the light spilling from the open doorway.

Garrett held his breath and could feel Sean doing the same beside him as the large bulk bled out into the darkness followed by a host of smaller but equally lethal-looking shapes.

So Jameson had brought additional forces beyond the two Maura had warned them about to guard his iniquitous den—not really surprising given the people who assembled inside. He thought quickly. If they took out this force of men now, they would no doubt tip their hand to the men inside. There was no knowing if the troop that had exited the building was the entire security force or if there were more men inside.

Better to wait and blend quietly. His men knew better than most how to become part of rock, bush, and tree. Garrett forced his tense muscles to relax as he touched a hand to Sean's shoulder in silent communication. He could almost hear Sean's unspoken rejection of his plan and then in a moment the acceptance that was part of his respect for Garrett's leadership and authority.

Garrett tilted his chin down and closed his eyes, slowing his breathing and opening his ears to wait for the search.

Harold Jameson paced across the foyer, anxious to be about his business. He forced himself to take even breaths as he crossed to the unpretentious bar taking up one corner of the room where his plan would unfold. It blended into the background almost as if it weren't there. Exactly as he'd planned. There was nothing to distract his guests from their pursuits. Nothing in the slightest. It all worked to the good. The liquor and the sparse accommodations would focus their attention on the purpose of their celebration. Their mutual presence and the masks he would distribute would free them from individual responsibility as they turned into a lustful mob ready to be led as he directed.

Damnation. What was taking Bart and his collection of oafs so long to check out the grounds?

He stopped before the large hearth which hissed and crackled with a satisfying fire. Heat poured over his legs. Behind this massive stone edifice lay the escape route he'd built in anticipation of unexpected guests. Should anything untoward happen he would be out of the building and far away before anyone was the wiser. He patted the stone tigers decorating the massive hearth. One quick twist of the wrist and freedom and safety would beckon. But that wasn't what he wanted. Not tonight.

He poured himself a short dram of whiskey and knocked it back without giving the appropriate respect it deserved. It burned its way down his throat and into his stomach without remorse. In moments a warm flood of exhilaration flooded through him. Much better.

Heavy footsteps interrupted his reverie.

"There ye are, sir." Bart, at last.

"Your report?"

"There's nothin' out there as shouldn't be, sir. We checked the entire grounds. There's not so much stirring as a few blades a grass and the tree leaves."

"Excellent, Bart." He patted the hearth one last time and stepped away. Secure.

"Let us begin."

Chapter Sixteen

"Enough, Garrett, we cannot wait any longer." Sean's urgent whisper carried barely restrained panic. The redstart's call from behind the house sounded at last.

"Let's go. Remember the plan, Sean."

"I won't forget. I have got to get Jane out of there. Before . . . before . . . I kill Harold Jameson with my bare hands."

"Let's go, lad."

He repeated the call of the redstart and heard it answer back. The men around the other side of the building would begin pouring in through the rear door as they entered through the front.

Between the two sets of men they ought to be able to stop anyone from exiting, save the girls, and bring Harold Jameson to an immediate stop. What happened afterwards to the young lordlings and upstarts who were willing to go along with Jameson's plans was another matter—one to be sorted out another day.

They opened the front door on silent hinges. Inside there was an almost palpable sense of anticipation. As they proceeded into the darkened building, light spilled from beneath a pair of pocket doors to one side. Voices could be heard within.

"—present our lovely sacrifice of the evening."

A chorus of aroused male appreciation could be heard in response.

"*Diahbal,*" Sean cursed.

Garrett held a finger to his lips as they inched toward the door.

"Aye, she is lovely indeed, is she not gentleman? And a true virgin. Waiting to be awoken to the full blossom of her womanhood. Untried and untested by any man. Until tonight."

Dear lord, the man was a showman! He touted this young woman like a gypsy at a carnival. Garrett's anger kindled higher.

"She shimmers with untapped sexuality, just waiting to find fulfillment with the aid of your manly rods. Tonight we will give her the education a jewel like she deserves, eh?"

More appreciative murmurs could be heard.

Garrett and Sean had reached the door. With a nod they edged the doors open far enough to be able to judge the room and its occupants.

Inside were approximately twenty young men in masks. Arousal and anticipation, layered with the strong scent of heavy drinking, hung tight in the air. He could not pick out Daniel or Lord Stanhope from the ranks, but he was certain they were both there.

Strapped to the table in the center of the room like some living human feast was a young woman dressed only in the sheerest of nightgowns. She was small and perfectly proportioned, her arms stretched over her head, legs spread, her body open to the view of every man's hungry gaze.

Jameson stood at her head in his glory, his hands slowly fondling her helpless form as she shivered and strained to escape his touch despite her bonds. She was gagged and masked, whimpering beneath his deliberate invasions. Blond curls scattered in wild array around her.

"Jane." Anger seethed from Sean in hot waves.

"See how responsive she is?" Jameson crooned as he pawed her. "I assure you, she will be well compensated for this night. She will play her part in our games well."

Sean started forward.

"Focus on the enemy." Garrett managed to edge the words between his teeth. He could well identify with what Sean was feeling. If anyone were to touch Maura that way . . .

He forced his thoughts to examine the situation. Aside from the young men in attendance and Jameson, there was a large brute of a man standing off to the right. From his sheer bulk he had to be the silhouette they'd seen just then leading the search of the grounds before this shameful fiasco began.

There didn't appear to be any other guards in attendance. That meant the rest of the force searching the grounds was somewhere else in the house. He could only hope the contingent of his own men he'd sent to the rear of the building were making short work of the lot of them.

"The man with the longest straw won the first go at her. Step forward and claim your prize before your envious fellows. She will accommodate any or all of us afterward. Plus you all have your room keys for the private delights that await you there."

Jameson unlaced Jane Fuller's gown, displaying her more fully to the gaping, lascivious gazes of his guests. "Let the games commence."

They were out of time. Garrett pushed to his feet. Sean was there ahead of him.

"Stop!" With a roar of anger Sean burst through the doors. "Release her immediately or by God you will answer to me."

Stunned, the masked young gentlemen turned toward the door, horror and guilt warring openly in their partially hidden expressions.

"Bart, protect!" Jameson's short order set the huge bulwark of a man into action. He moved surprisingly fast for a big man. In two great strides he was at the doors, swinging two giant fists at once. Before Sean could duck he was clubbed harshly with once massive blow that sent him sailing into the opposite corner of the room.

Shielded from view by the doors, other guards rushed to join the brawl as Garrett's men surged through the doors behind him. Garrett pushed forward past the dismayed gentlemen who moments before had been intent only on their own enjoyment at the expense of one very helpless young woman. Daniel MacTavish quickly pulled off his mask and stepped forward to release Miss Fuller from her bonds.

Garrett almost reached his side when a great hand grabbed him from behind and yanked him backward with enough force to lift him completely off the ground. He sailed into another fist and landed hard on the ground. Blackness and stars enveloped him.

Chaos reigned around Garrett as men shouted and his head spun. He fought to hold on to lucidity. He couldn't fail Sean, couldn't fail that poor lass. The room swirled around him as he scrambled to get to his feet.

"Bart, come!" Jameson shouted in the distance. The big man's feet shook the floor as he rushed to do his master's bidding.

Garrett struggled to stand upright and focus in the direction of Jameson's shout. His vision blurred for a moment, and he could see only a flash of sheer nightgown and a flurry of limbs.

When his gaze cleared he could make out the struggling form of Jane Fuller tossed over the massive shoulder of Jameson's giant. The bodyguard ducked his head beneath the mantelpiece and disappeared into the massive fireplace. There was no sign of Jameson. In a moment, the blazing fire took up the space the giant had filled just before.

He shook his head as nausea rushed over him.

"No!" Sean swayed to his feet, looking equally as confused. "Jane!"

Daniel also stood, looking dazed as he rubbed his skull.

Garrett signaled Liam, stepped forward, and took Daniel by the arm to lead him from the room. The two of them would organize a thorough inside and outside search of the rooms Maura had described and free the prisoners before they too could be whisked away.

Sean pushed forward, elbowing the cream of Dublin society out of his way as he headed to the hearth. These young men were no threat to anyone; they stood looking shamed and defeated, wishing themselves anywhere but there while the rest of Jameson's guards were subdued.

Let them suffer the writhing of their own consciences for a while, if they were sincerely sorrowful and not just sorry their fun had been spoiled or they had been caught. The Green Dragon would deal with each of them in turn, when other matters were less pressing.

Sean reached the mantle. He pounded a fist against the massive stone. "Open, damnation. Open!"

"There's some sort of trigger on the side." A lone voice among the group of shamed young men spoke up into the sudden silence. With a quiet dignity at odds with the rest of his fellows, one young man stepped forward. With a heavy sigh he removed the dark mask covering his own features.

Stanhope.

"What did you see?" There was no quarter in Sean's voice as he turned on Stanhope.

"I am not quite sure. This is Harold Jameson's lodge. I am sorry I ever came here."

"As well you all should be." Garrett stepped in before Sean could throttle the young baron.

Bashing Stanhope, while satisfying, would not get them the information they needed. "What did you see?"

Stanhope's brows knit together as he turned and walked to the hearth. He ran his fingers over the carved stone. "He pushed something or twisted something and caused the hearth to swing open like a door. They disappeared with that poor woman into what looked like a tunnel."

Sean's gaze met Garrett's filled with renewed fear for Jane Fuller. Garrett focused his attention back on Stanhope.

"Help my man get this open again."

"But, I—"

"You know more than you give yourself credit for. We have got to follow them for that girl's sake. We are losing precious time."

"Aye." Stanhope swallowed hard as he avoided Sean's gaze.

"Now." Sean grated the word out with enough menace to incinerate any lingering hesitation on Stanhope's part.

They went to work probing the mantle with Stanhope providing everything he could remember about Jameson's actions.

Garrett turned to the waiting room.

"Remove your masks." Some had already stripped away the offending dominoes. The rest did as he directed without complaint.

"Know now that I am the Green Dragon. I have marked each and every one of your faces. I know who you are. I know who your families are. I know where to find you. You should all be ashamed of yourselves, conspiring to debauch an innocent girl."

He let that sink in for a moment as their faces paled and many feet shifted restlessly against the barren wood floor.

"You will leave this place and never speak of it again. If anything that happened here tonight becomes common knowledge or if any of you ever engage in such activities as you intended here, I will know and I will come for you when you least expect me. If you are tempted to stray, imagine that young woman you were so set to exploit was your sister."

He ran his gaze over the lot of them, letting them mark the seriousness of his intent. "Do you mark my words and know them for the truth?"

"Aye." Many heads nodded as one. "Jameson said she was a prostitiute. That this was a game."

"Jameson lied to you. You are all fools. Make haste and get out of my sight." Garrett enjoyed the small satisfaction of watching them scramble all too eagerly out of his presence.

He blew out a long breath. There were times when he felt so very much older than most of the men who might be considered his contemporaries.

He turned his attention to what was left of his men. They had successfully bound the guards and gathered them into a misshapen cluster.

"There are a number of young women still here in the house. I'm not sure how many. See who you can find and free. Use care with them—they may have been poorly used and may not react well to men in masks."

With nods of understanding, they turned to leave.

"There was another woman here," he called after them. "An old crone who worked here. See if you can find her as well.

"Aye." They filed out of the room.

"Here!" Sean's voice rang with renewed urgency.

Garrett turned back toward the hearth to see Sean's fingers pressed against the stone. The stone gave beneath the pressure of his fingers.

"This has to be it, but nothing is happening!"

He hurried to Sean's side as Stanhope stood aside. "I told you he twisted it. Or turned it. Damnation, I wish I knew."

Garrett placed his hand over Sean's, feeling the pressure points that gave into the carved stone. He ran his gaze over the intricate carving, then gritting his teeth, he twisted the points with his and Sean's fingers still pressed hard against the stone. With a harsh grating sound that filled the silent room, the stone swiveled.

In a moment the hearth, complete with the still blazing fire, swung inward, groaning against its massive hinges. A rush of cool damp air passed over them.

"Yes!" Stanhope was excited. "You got it right! I knew there was a twist or something. I knew—"

Sean's gaze snapped to him, and Stanhope trailed into immediate silence. Sean stepped into the passage. "Mark my words, boy-o: keep this evening silent, even in your memory."

Stanhope nodded, his hair swinging forward, disheveled from running his hands through it in frustration.

"I do mark your words, sir. Let me come with you. Surely you can use another pair of hands."

There was no time for lengthy discourse. He was right. The more hands willing to help, the better. What better way for the baron to learn the consequences of thoughtless actions than by working to rectify them?

"Come then." Garrett followed Sean toward the cold, dark tunnel. It was impossible to see the way. Jameson must have taken whatever lantern or candle was there for his flight. Once the hearth closed they would be pitched into total darkness.

"If you fall behind, we will not wait and we will not come back for you." Threat as well as promise filled the words Sean grated to the younger man as he joined them.

Stanhope nodded. "I will keep pace."

"We have wasted enough time already."

In quick strides, Garrett grabbed a single ladder-back chair near the hearth and broke it against the stone. He handed a wooden leg to Sean, then one to Stanhope before lighting his own in the hearth fire. Each man followed his lead. With that they plunged the darkened confines of the passageway.

Stale air passed over them as they hurried into the tunnel. The sides were close and the ceiling low. They had to bend in order to fit. He could only imagine this would have been an impediment to Jameson's giant bodyguard, especially burdened with a less than cooperative Miss Fuller.

"They are so far ahead." Despair twisted Sean's worry.

"Liam and Daniel have already begun the search from the woods. We will find her."

He didn't put voice to his main concern. He knew Sean's thoughts were already there anyway. Having failed at his ploy to enlist the sons of Dublin society to ensure Jane's disappearance remained a secret, Jameson's next best course would be to get rid of her and disappear. They quickened their pace.

The tunnel went down and down and down. Then it twisted to the left, running level for some time. Another twist to the left brought them to a steady, slow incline.

To the best of his reckoning, Garrett felt that this passage was leading out and away from the lodge. If he was right, they were heading toward the wild grasses that edged the woods. If their course held true, Jameson, his guard, and Miss Fuller were even then headed parallel to the rutted lane leading to the lodge.

A chill shivered over his spine. If the tunnel emerged in the woods, Maura would be almost directly in their path, ready to provide easy escape in the form of their borrowed coach. Garrett prayed his direction was wrong, that Jameson had left nothing to chance in his escape plans and had provided transportation for himself at the end.

He should have left more men with her. In trying to provide as much manpower as he could for the rescue, Garrett had left her vulnerable to the unthinkable. Even with Seamus there to guard her, she was practically alone in the woods with no idea she might be in trouble.

"*Diabhal.*" He remembered the reluctant look on her face when Sean handed her the loaded pistol. A quick prayer broke from his lips that she would use it if the need arose.

Maura sat in the coach, trying to calm her nerves by gazing out at the serene moonlight filtering the landscape around her. She had long ago placed Garrett's pistol on the floor of the coach by her feet. Pray God she would not need to touch the thing again.

They had been gone for so long already, and she had no idea how much longer they might be.

"Enough." The inaction was getting to her. Her fears were getting to her. There had been a deadly seriousness clinging to every action of Garrett and his men this evening, something far more than what she thought she had hired when she had asked for his help.

She fumbled with the lock on the coach door and paused for a moment as Garrett's parting words came

back to her. *Lock this. I'll be back soon.* The deadly seriousness of his tone had shivered over her then, and
did so again at the memory. He'd suspected she
might be in danger out here so far from the lodge.
She sat back against the cushions again, only to have
her thoughts cycle back into the same rut they had
run in for the past hour. Where were they? How much
longer?

She couldn't stand this confinement any longer.
How had those girls in the lodge survived being
locked in with their fears?

"Just for a moment, Garrett. I will stay alert to my
surroundings."

She fumbled again with the lock and breathed a
sigh of relief when it clicked open. Seamus was right
there.

"I need to stretch my legs," she explained. True, but
not in the way he assumed from the look he gave her
before stepping out of the way.

"Don't go more than ten paces from this coach.
I'll . . . I'll be keeping the horses quiet as I have been.
The ones by the dogcart are a flighty pair. Call out
if ye have need of me."

"Very well." They had gathered a ragtag caravan of
coaches, three gigs, and the dogcart to help carry
away any victims. Seamus had his hands full with the
horses for riders and carriages without her adding to
his burdens.

Pushing the door fully open, she scrambled to the
edge of the coach and then out into the high grass.
Standing again after sitting still for so long was a
pleasure.

With Seamus busy and no one else to witness any
unladylike display she gave into the urge and
stretched her arms as high as she could. Soft breezes
blew over her, calming and soothing. This was much

better than being closeted in the dark coach to wait and worry.

Garrett's warning repeated in her mind. He'd sounded so certain, so determined.

"Very well. Just a quick circuit around the coach."

With a nod to the spectral Garrett frowning in her head, she set out. Once around. Twice around. She felt better with the blood pumping through her veins and the kinks worked out of her system. She had faith in Garrett and in the men so obviously loyal and respectful to him.

With a reluctant sigh she opened the door and hiked up her skirts. Getting into and out of a coach demanded a little bit more concentration when one did not have a steady arm to help, but she was up to the task, if somewhat awkwardly. She felt reluctant to summon Seamus away from his other charges, especially as a nervous whicker split the air just after the thump of a limb falling from a tree right outside the circle of vehicles.

She pushed up and into the interior and pulled the door shut behind her. Her fingers had just twisted the lock back into place when an arm shot out of the darkness through the coach window and cinched her wrist in a tight grip.

"Unlatch the door, my dear." Low and angry, despite its conversational tone, Harold Jameson's voice threatened her.

"No." She twisted trying to free her wrist from his grasp. The pistol Sean had given her, now a necessity, lay discarded and out of her reach on the far side of the coach floor.

"Seamus!" she called. "Seamus!"

Jameson's grip tightened further and wrenched her flesh. She gasped at the pain he inflicted. "We have no time for pleasantries, Mrs. Fitzgerald, not even introductions. Your erstwhile guard has met the end of my compatriot's pistol butt. Open the latch or I will break your lovely wrist and open it myself."

Was Seamus alive or dead? She hesitated a moment longer and won another wrench of pain for her efforts.

"Now, dear lady. My patience is in an even more limited supply than the time we have."

She lifted her fingers to the latch and turned it, hoping he would release her wrist to open the door. Instead he transferred his grip from one hand to the other as the door swung outwardly, forcing her to lean forward as though greeting him eagerly.

"Ah, Mrs. Fitzgerald, a vision as usual." He smiled up at her through the open doorway, then bent to retrieve a lantern at his feet, pulling her even farther forward. "So eager to greet a man no matter where he may find her. It could lead to an interesting discussion about why you are where you are so conveniently, but first we must away."

She wished she had kept hold of the pistol as Garrett had requested.

He cast a glance over his shoulder. "Bart, hurry along. The sooner we quit these environs, the better."

"I'm comin', sir." A voice called out of the darkness beyond her vision. "But she's astrugglin' somethin' fierce. She's a might slippery in this gown."

"Then cuff her man. Enough to take the struggle out of her for the moment. We don't have time to waste."

"Aye, sir." There followed a quick squeal of protest, the sickening smack of flesh against flesh, and a sudden silence.

"Well done, man." Jameson beamed his approval. He released Maura's arm and shoved her into the coach. "Now get her into the coach with this other one I found."

The shuffle of feet through the grass preceded the arrival of a very large man. He more than filled the coach doorway. Maura sucked in a breath of fear.

Over his shoulder, an unconscious young woman draped in sheerest muslin hung limp and defenseless.

"One fer each of us, sir?"

"We will have to see about that later."

Where was Garrett? And the rest of his men? Fear tightened Maura's throat and brought tears to her eyes. Jameson's gaze roamed her features, she could almost taste his enjoyment of her distress against her tongue. She refused to shed the tears hovering on the edge of her eyelashes.

The large man elbowed his way against the coach and unloaded his helpless burden against the bench opposite Maura. Long blond hair and a domino mask obscured her face, although her gown did nothing to hide her nakedness beneath. She was masked, gagged, and limp. Maura was sick over the woman's obvious maltreatment.

"Now get up into the coachman's seat, Bart, and take us away from here."

"What about Enid?" A note of worry had entered the large man's tone.

"Don't fret yourself about Enid, she knows how to take care of herself." Jameson hooked the lantern into a holder and levered himself into the coach. "Get about it, man, no dawdling. We cannot wait here for those rascals that attacked us earlier."

"Aye, sir." Bart closed the coach door behind Jameson, smiled blandly at Maura as though nothing untoward had taken place in the last few minutes, and disappeared into the darkness. The coach tilted beneath his weight as he made his way up onto the coachman's perch and called to the horses.

Jameson sighed and sat back against the cushions. He turned his strangely light and dark gaze toward Maura. Fear moved over her.

Dear God, where was Garrett?

"Am I correct in surmising that you are with those

scoundrels who interrupted my . . . party . . . this evening?"

She didn't answer.

He grabbed her wrist again and twisted it hard. Pain shot up her arm, wrenching a moan from her despite her resolve not to give him the satisfaction.

"My dear, there is no point in saving your tongue. I will find out all I need to know either directly from you of your own free will or through persuasions you have never considered."

He smiled at her. There was nothing but cold satisfaction and anticipation shimmering in his eyes.

"Witness our winsome companion." He jerked his head to indicate the prone form of the young woman he had brought with them. "She has not always agreed with me either. It makes little difference, for she has done, all along, exactly as I wanted her to do."

He leaned toward Maura and jerked her toward him as though he would share some secret with her. "Even tonight's interrupted entertainments would have seen her a willing participant at the end. They have all been so. Willing or not at the beginning, your gender always learns the error of their ways by the end. You too will be meek and pliant, willing to serve whatever needs I require."

His breath was hot on her face and stinking of whiskey. With a quick dip of his head he pressed his mouth on hers. She jerked away and scrubbed at her lips.

"Ah, so fiery. I appreciate that in a woman. Up to a point, of course. I am quite certain young Stanhope never fully appreciated you. If he even knew you for the true woman you are. I, on the other hand, shall appreciate ever nuance of pleasure you will give me, every inch of your delights."

"Never," she gagged. His conceit was more nauseating than the waves of fear rippling over her. The carriage jolts kept throwing her leg up against his.

"I have no interest in pleasing you," she told him, grateful her voice did not carry the quaver she felt deep inside her.

He chuckled, undeterred. "You will, my dear. You will. Take off your jacket."

"No."

He released her wrist. "Very well. I will amuse myself with our young companion."

He trapped Maura in her seat by placing his booted foot on her skirt as it spread across the floor. Then leaned over and began to paw the unconscious girl, pushing and kneading her breast through the thin fabric of her gown. A moan escaped her gag as her body flinched instinctively from his assault.

"All right, stop." Maura's fingers were already unhooking her jacket.

Jameson sat back with a very pleased grin on his face. "You see how easy it was to persuade you. This night holds more than small promise."

Chapter Seventeen

"Up ahead," Sean called out as he ditched his makeshift torch. It clattered against the wall, the sound echoing back down the length of the stone shaft.

"Aye." Garrett dropped his as well.

Stanhope said nothing but followed suit.

In moments they broke into the open air. Mist hovered over the open grass. Dismay tightened Garrett's gut. They were almost right on top of the area where he left Maura in the coach.

Please God, don't let them have spotted her.

"This way." He ran through the high whispering grasses, his heartbeat straining against the certainty riding higher and higher in his throat. They ran and slid down a slight incline that spilled them out of the woods and into the open clearing.

Garrett came to a halt. This was it. He spun in a quick circle, taking in the other carts and gigs they'd assembled. The horses were hitched and tethered nearby.

"Where's the coach?" Sean's question echoed Garrett's. "Where are Seamus and Maura?"

"Exactly." His heart twisted in fear. Now Jameson had Maura as well to bargain for his escape.

"What is it? What's wrong?" Stanhope padded up to them, out of breath and sweating.

"We left a coach here." Sean's reply was terse. "He has taken it."

"Along with the woman inside."

"What woman?"

"A friend of yours." Garrett turned to Stanhope. "Maura Fitzgerald."

"Maura?" Stanhope's brows knit with concern. "What was Maura doing out here in the middle of nowhere?"

"The same could be said of you." He had no time to pander to the pup. "Let's get the horses."

"Aye." Sean had already turned to the tether line.

They left Stanhope to follow or not, as was his wish. The young baron followed in their wake. The longer he held his peace, the better Garrett would like it.

Fear and anger burned inside Garrett. He'd underestimated Jameson's planning skills when he'd considered the man for possible threats. He'd taken Jameson for a lecher with a desire to play puppet master with the young men he pulled in with his lures of dangerous hijinks and base behavior.

The escape passage, the array of guards, added to what he knew already about the man, changed the landscape of the enemy they faced. This man was no mere lecher intent on luring innocents into games of debauchery for the pleasure of his untried young friends. This man had a plan. Jane Fuller suddenly seemed less innocent pawn, more political chess piece.

They mounted and circled back to the clearing to see if they could pick up the coach tracks. The possibility that Seamus and Maura had moved the coach ended as they passed a moaning lump on the ground.

Garrett jumped down. "Seamus."

Sean hesitated then rode ahead to the tall grass. Stanhope lingered.

"Seamus." Garrett touched his friend on the shoulder. "Wake up."

Seamus sat up holding his head. "Where's the horse that kicked me?"

"It was two men with a girl. They took the coach. And Maura. Did you see which way they went?"

Seamus shook his head. "I saw stars and then ye was standing over me. Sorry, boss."

"Can you stand? Will you be all right?"

"My head aches, but I can ride."

"Stay here. Wait for the others. They should be here in minutes." Garrett was already back in the saddle.

Stanhope and he followed after Sean. As they reached the meadow, Sean was climbing back onto his own mount. There was a feral gleam in his friend's gaze as he pointed to the path he'd found. Now it was a hunt.

So much the better.

They knew who, and where. The coach, although sturdy, was not exactly the speediest conveyance around. If they could just catch up to the coach before Jameson had a chance to change vehicles they would be able to rescue Maura and Jane without further harm.

"What? Have you no sad tale to tell of the powerful employer who stole your maidenhead?" Jameson's voice held rich satisfaction. "Or was it some ham-fisted farmboy who first climbed atop you to break through your shield of virginity?"

He'd been baiting Maura almost constantly for the past ten minutes. Threatening, then cajoling. Menacing and then attempting to seduce her.

She'd tired of Jameson's games long since. Her concern for Garrett grew exponentially with each mile they placed between themselves and the lodge. Her fears remained fixed on the men who'd disappeared into the night and her unspoken prayer that the man who led them would discover her gone and come for her.

In the meantime she had nothing to aid her beyond her bravado and the pistol still lying on the floor of the coach, hidden in the sweeping folds of the muslin nightgown worn by the girl on the opposite bench.

Jameson chuckled again, thoroughly enjoying the power he seemed to possess over her, keeping her so frightened she couldn't speak.

"Pray say something, my dear. Keep me amused. Keep my attention fixed on you. Surely a woman such as you is quite used to changes in fortune and the need to get along with those in charge, eh?"

She turned her gaze back to him.

"Who is she?" She waived her hand toward the prone young woman.

"Ah, a spark of curiosity returns. That is a good sign. While I like my conquests to be humble, I rather enjoy the process of guiding them to that state."

He chuckled again and she clenched her teeth together to keep from raging at him. He derived too much pleasure from any of her actions, ineffectual as they proved.

"Wondering who it is that you have been struggling so valiantly to protect? Perhaps she should tell you herself."

"She doesn't appear to be conscious at the moment thanks to your coachman."

"Ah, a coachman. I believe Bart will relish that description. I shall have to remember to tell him. But must I remind you appearances can be deceiving."

"What do you mean?"

"Our young companion has been awake for the last few minutes. She has been listening and wondering who *you* are in fact. Is that not right, Jane?"

The prone form across from them blew out a deep breath and pushed upright to Maura's surprise. He noticed everything. Afraid to glance down for fear she would give its presence away, she prayed the pistol remained out of sight as the girl sat and her skirts swished.

With shaking fingers the young woman pushed away the black mask and gag that covered her features. The beginning of a dark bruise covered her cheek just below her left eye. A gift from the coachman. Long blond curls swirled over her shoulders. For all she must have been through, she seemed surprisingly lucid as she fixed an angry blue stare in Harold Jameson's direction.

"Yes, I am awake."

The girl's fingers carefully brushed her cheek before she turned her angry stare toward Maura. "My name is Jane Fuller."

"Maura Fitzgerald," Maura offered.

"Oh, this is delightful," Jameson purred as they jostled along in the coach. "The two of you offering introductions as if meeting over tea. Truly delightful. I do hope we can all be friends."

Jane lunged for him quite suddenly in a flurry of blond hair and whisper-thin muslin. Maura's jacket slipped to her lap. Jameson caught her before she could land so much as the first blow.

"Ah, sweet, fiery Jane. I wondered how long it would take." He dragged her hard against him and then twisted his body, forcing her hands behind her back and managing to pin Maura in place with the pressure of Jane's back against her.

Jane's breathing was harsh and frightened as he held her firmly in place. His hot breath fanned over her slender shoulders to blast Maura as well. Maura gagged from the stench, then struggled just for air with both of their weights pressing into her.

"You will not get away with this," Jane panted.

"So you keep saying. I believe you must be seeking lessons to the contrary." He leaned closer, his gaze going back and forth between Jane and Maura. "Quite a lovely handful this."

He dipped his head to plunder Jane's mouth with his. Maura squirmed but couldn't get her hands loose as Jane moaned a protest beneath his ravaging assault.

He lifted his head. Desire glazed his eyes bright in the lamplight. The coach lurched, pressing them even tighter together against the padded bench. "And an even more delectable mouthful."

"No."

Jane's and Maura's protests mingled and made his gaze burn brighter. He lowered his head again, going farther down to nuzzle his nearest prisoner's breasts through the thin of her gown.

"No!" Jane struggled to escape. "Stop!"

"Let her go!" Maura shouted, too. She and Jane struggled in unison.

With a laugh Jameson released them both so suddenly that Jane fell to the coach floor. Maura nearly lost her seat as well.

"Jane." Maura reached for the other girl and helped her regain her seat on the opposite bench. High color rode Jane's cheeks as she thanked Maura with a tight-lipped nod. Angry tears hovered on her eyelashes.

"Touching." Jameson observed.

"You have no heart." Maura tossed over her shoulder as she quickly retrieved her jacket. She slid the garment around the other girl's shoulders.

"Thank you, Maura." Jane offered her a tentative smile.

"You are more than welcome, Jane." Their hands linked across the width of the coach.

"Enough."

Jameson sounded angry. Satisfaction surged for a moment. She made no effort to hide the feeling as she returned the girl's smile with one of her own. The coach lurched over another deep rut.

Jameson reached forward and yanked the jacket from Jane's shoulders. Before either of them could react he tossed the garment out the window.

"I have no objection whatsoever to you disrobing, Mrs. Fitzgerald. In fact, I look forward to it. However, I see no reason for you to cover the pleasure of Miss Fuller's charms as you reveal your own."

"You are vile." Jane enunciated each word in tones overflowing with dislike.

"Your opinion matters so little, dear Jane. I am far more experienced in the world than you. What you see as vile, others view as experience and sophistication. What makes your dainty little toes curl with distaste, others view as the fine edge of true gratification. Everything is just a matter of viewpoint I assure you. I look forward to expanding your horizons."

"I agree with her." Maura spoke up as his lesson caused the light of fear to kindle anew in Jane's wide blue eyes. "She is so right. You are vile."

"While I might have hoped for better from you, Mrs. Fitzgerald, lack of proper training in your art has you espousing such opinions."

He put his arm around her waist and pulled Maura back on the seat, holding her fast beside him. "Trust me, both of you, when I am done with you, your educations will be complete and you will both thank me for showing you the error of your current opinion."

He paused, letting his threats sink in. "Thank me in any way I desire from you."

Silence held for the space of several heartbeats within the coach. Maura edged a glance toward the coach floor where she had left the pistol. In the ensuing struggle the pistol had been kicked out of sight except for the tiniest portion of its dark, smooth barrel. She drew courage from the sight of it. If she could just manage to distract Harold Jameson and get her fingers on the pistol once more she would shoot him without a second thought. Not to kill him certainly, but to put him out of commission long enough so she and Jane could make good their escape.

It took patience and keen eyes to go over a mist-laden meadow in search of evidence that coach wheels had passed a certain way. Normally that would have been just fine with Garrett, but this had been their third clearing and they could ill-afford to spend even a little bit of extra time to assure himself which direction they needed to go to rescue Maura, and Jane Fuller, from Harold Jameson's clutches.

In the distance he could hear Stanhope muttering to himself. The young man was out of his depth.

"Wheel tracks in the grass? What on earth was Maura doing out here?"

Poor devil was probably blaming himself. Convenient. But Garrett knew who to blame. He should never have left her with the horses. He should never have let her leave the inn. He should have gone inside the hunting lodge himself this afternoon.

"Here!" Sean's shout rang over the meadow.

Garrett raced to join him. Stanhope wasn't far behind.

"Do you see them? Running north?"

"Back to Dublin?"

"Bold as brass," Sean agreed. "Could he really be taking them back to town as though he'd done nothing?"

"It won't matter; we'll catch them before he so much as reaches the outskirts of Bray."

"Aye."

He and Sean swung back into the saddle in short order. Stanhope swung up as well.

Garrett took pity on the younger man despite his presence in the evening's events. "Stanhope, you don't have to come with us. Go home and rethink your future from there."

"Thank you for the offer, but I'd just as soon come with you. I have a debt to pay to that young woman and if Maura is out there, suffering at the hands of Jameson . . . well, she deserves whatever protection I can offer."

Jealousy burned quick and hot in Garrett's stomach. This man still saw himself as Maura's protector even though he'd ended their relationship. He ought to see the baron's position in a positive light. He could not, but he also could not allow his personal feelings to interfere with his mission.

"Very well. You may come."

"But do not dare get in the way," Sean added.

"I won't."

"What good can we possibly be to you?" Maura asked the only question she could think of to offer this monster the opportunity to pontificate on his maneuverings. She hoped he would be so busy puffing himself up he would not pay any attention her goal of retrieving the pistol.

He favored her with such a look of approval she could have gagged.

"I actually had good plans for our little Jane's future." He cast a quick glance at Jane before returning his attention to Maura. "Once initiated into the full pleasures of serving as a sexual vessel, in a most public, humiliating, and scandalous manner—guaranteed to force all involved to silence—I intended to wed her to your former benefactor."

Maura had stretched her foot out to see if she could catch the pistol with the toe of her boot. But the end of the sentence caught her attention, freezing her.

"My benefacter?" she inquired carefully as she turned her gaze to his.

"Why, yes. Did I not say former friend now that you so conveniently cuckolded him?" He smiled wickedly at her. "Dear Freddie Vaughn, our new Baron Stanhope, is the broken-hearted groom-to-be."

Freddie? A chill passed over her. What on earth did Freddie have to do with any of this? How could he have even considered such a vile plan, let alone fallen in with it.

"I thought you'd appreciate the irony." Jameson's light and dark gaze roamed her face. "Your dear Freddie was part of our little group tonight. In fact he was the guest of honor, so to speak."

He laughed then. It was a chilling sound. "Not that he was ensnared easily, I can assure you. Your hold over him was stronger than I originally gave you credit for. Brava, my dear. But with work, and your misalliance with that wastrel Lynch, I was able to tempt Stanhope into joining my country extravaganza."

Guilt swamped her at this news. Freddie was at the lodge and no doubt Percy was a part of the group as well. She couldn't bring herself to ask. The betrayal Freddie had feared had allowed him to be drawn into the circles she'd worked so hard to keep him from.

"When . . . when . . ." The question wouldn't form.

"When did he agree?" Jameson tapped his chin as though her question deserved serious consideration. "Thursday last, I believe. Although it could have been a bit before that. Or after. The timing does not especially interest me. The important thing was that he agreed so this particular plan could come to fruition."

"Fruition?" Maura's thoughts were spinning. If she hadn't broken off with Freddie just when she did. If he hadn't suspected what she had almost shared with that first passionate kiss with Garrett.

"Of course. I told you he was going to be the guest of honor. He and Jane. He was chosen to be the one to deflower, what he had been told was a willing participant, surrounded by the randy urgings of his peers, all of whom would then enjoy her charms for themselves. In return he would have gained her as a marriage prize." He offered her a sympathetic smile. "I realize you had hopes in that direction yourself, my dear. But truly Jane will make him a much more acceptable alliance."

"So your goal in all of this is to matchmake for Freddie?"

"Oh, dear heavens, no. You misunderstand me. He is merely another pawn in a much larger game."

"It doesn't matter what you would have done to me at your little party." Jane found her voice again. "I will never agree to marry any man who would take part in such horrendous acts."

"Tut, tut, Jane. You betray your ignorance again." He shook his finger at her like an indulgent father scolding a child. "And you interrupted. I will forgive you, later. Suffice to say you would have no choice, and you really should not blame the man. A little too much to drink. A pinch of some special encouragement I placed in his cup. The urgings of his friends, similarly fired up with my special mixture of spiced brandy, and he could hardly have resisted. Lust and mobs are very potent."

"How . . . how did you intend to get Freddie to marry Jane, after . . . after . . ."

"Ah Maura. Can you not even bring yourself to say the words? After he violated her? After he'd taught her the very essence of what it is all men require from women? After she'd been broken and tasted and ridden to ecstasy by every man present?"

His gaze narrowed on Jane's pale face. She lifted her chin and didn't answer his taunts. "That is the easy part. Stanhope, aside from this one wayward slip, has been the soul of honor. Why, he even treats his mistress with excessive respect as you can well attest."

Jane's gaze slid to hers. Sympathy, understanding, and a quick questioning flash cycled through her wide blue gaze in an instant.

"You would have found out eventually, my dear." Jameson's voice held that note of thick amusement once more. "This is your rival for your intended's affections, the woman he will always regret losing. God knows he blubbered as much to me often enough this past week or more."

Jane's glance wavered from hers, and Maura felt the hard sting of Jameson's words. So easily he would place a wedge between them to spite their mutual goal of freedom from him. He was a master manipulator. She maneuvered her foot toward the base of the pistol and waited.

"But I digress. After each of his friends had enjoyed your services in such a public forum, when you were slack and totally pliant from their lustful attentions, your mask would have slipped, revealing your identity to all. As your first, Stanhope would have been honor-bound to wed you. The circumstances would ensure silence from all concerned and a little fillip of power for the one who held the secret. Even the earl and your revered father would have complied with my requests."

Maura shivered. She had misjudged him. Jameson was evil incarnate.

"Hold." Garrett called out the command as a flash of something metal caught his eye. He swung down out of the saddle and picked up Maura's jacket. Fear for her twisted anew in his gut. Her soft rose scent clung to the fabric he clutched.

Sean and Stanhope reached his side.

"What is it?" Sean was barely keeping hold of his own tension.

"This garment is Maura's." He and Stanhope answered in the same breath.

Sean's gaze went back and forth between the two of them. "Right. Then we are on the right trail. They cannot be too far ahead of us."

"Aye. Let us finish hunting the bastard down."

The three of them remounted without further word and urged the horses to a still faster pace. There was a rise about a mile down the road. Anticipation tightened across Garrett's shoulders.

"Do not look away, Jane. Look at her. This woman will be part of your life for some time to come. You should fully acquaint yourself with the face that would have come between you and your husband in your marital bed."

Jane turned her face toward the window, ignoring his jibes.

He leaned toward her, intent on enjoying every bit of the verbal torture he spit at them and in tormenting them in other ways as well. One hand fell intimately against Jane's knee, the other gripped her chin and forced her gaze back to his.

"You must face your fears, Jane. Look at them directly and know them for who they are. For what they are."

He managed to sound sickeningly fatherly and lecherous at one and the same time. Maura's stomach lurched. Then she realized that, however unwittingly, Jane had managed to get him to turn his back to her. She would not get a better chance to retrieve Sean's pistol. She prayed she would be able to handle it properly once it was in her hands.

She levered her foot against the pistol and felt it move across the floor until it was directly between her feet. Then she dipped forward, and the cold metal filled her palm.

Was it heavy and solid enough for her to just thwap it against the back of Jameson's head? Could she hit him hard enough, or was shooting him the better course? There was no time to debate. She scooped it up and straightened to face him.

"Stop this coach, now." Her voice held firm resolve despite the quavering inside her.

He turned to face her, relinquishing his hold of Jane.

A frown flitted across his brows. His shoulders tensed as anger flashed in those strange eyes of his. Then he relaxed visibly and settled back against the cushions as though the loaded pistol pointed in his direction was of no concern.

"Now, Jameson." Maura repeated her order.

"Stop the coach?" He chuckled. "Now, here? In the middle of nowhere? With no one to help you? I think not, my dear, dear, Maura. I shall, however, remember this for later. There are consequences to every action, my sweet."

"And yours have just come," she answered. "Stop the coach, now or I will shoot you dead where you sit."

She prayed she would truly be able to carry out the threat.

His brows rose. "With that little thing? You might wound me, I'll grant you, which will make me . . . less amenable . . . than normal, but kill me?" He shook his head, managing to look disappointed with her lack of understanding. "You would do better to hand me the pistol and begin your apologies."

"Begin your own apologies." Anger tightened her

tone. "I will tell you one last time. Stop this coach or I *will* shoot."

Silence held in the interior of the coach with naught but the rumbling of the wheels over the rutted ground. She could feel his gaze weighing her resolve. She meant every word.

"Very well, my dear. If you are so determined to play this farce out, I will stop the coach as you requested." He eyed her again. "I will need to signal my man in order to give the command to halt."

"Then do so."

"As you wish." He half-turned on the bench seat and raised his hand as though to open the small hatchway that would allow him to communicate more easily with the coachman.

She realized her mistake as he leaned forward.

"Maura!"

Jane's shout jolted her just as Jameson's hand came down without ever reaching the hatchway in the roof. His fist closed around her wrist with lightning speed and twisted cruelly. Pain arced up her arm. She maintained her hold of the pistol with an effort.

"Release the pistol or I'll break that traitorous little wrist." He hissed the words between his teeth, his face all too close to hers. The stench of stale whiskey and tobacco from his breath sickened her again, intensified by the urgency of their struggle and the pain he was inflicting on her.

"No!" Jane launched herself at Jameson's back. "Release her, you fiend!"

He swung his elbow back, catching Jane full in the stomach and launching her backward into the bench seat she'd just left. Her head banged against the side of the coach and she lay there limp once more as the pistol went off in Maura's hand, firing her one shot harmlessly through the side of the coach.

Chapter Eighteen

Jameson leaned atop her, anger evident in the hot gaze boring into hers.

"You wasted your shot, my dear." He snarled the words at her. "And caused me considerable concern."

He twisted her wrist again, his gaze narrowing as he watched her.

Pain raced through her in a white hot spear that launched up her arm and ripped a cry from her. She dropped the empty pistol to the floor.

He slid his other arm between them and grasped her free wrist before wrenching both her arms up over her head. She gulped air in hot gasps as fear ratcheted higher within her. He gripped her hands together in one fist, freeing his other hand.

Satisfaction leered out of his gaze and curled his lip.

"I think you will begin your apologies for this misadventure right now."

"No." The plea whispered out of her, despite the anger and loathing warring inside her.

"Oh yes." He trailed his hand down her arm with deliberate slowness. She struggled trying to free her hands, longing to claw at his face. He held them tight. His face was only inches away, enjoying her panic.

The coach continued to slow, and he didn't seem to care. Lower and lower his hand moved, light and caressing, over her upper arm and then lower still. He stopped just above her breasts. A low satisfied chuckle burst from him.

"Anticipation." He enunciated the syllables carefully.

He undid the buttons of her blouse. As she tried to wriggle free, his weight and strength, the confines of the coach, made her efforts ineffectual. His fingers barely brushed her. In too short a time, cool air touched her skin, nearly paralyzing her with dread. Naught but her chemise covered her now.

"So vulnerable." Jameson's appreciative tone rasped her fears. "Quite wasted on fools like Stanhope and Lynch."

"They are both more men than you." She managed the taunt despite a shaky voice.

"How will you know until you have a true comparison? Shall we begin?"

His fingers caressed her once more, slow and deliberate, as if he had nothing but time on his hands. He stroked her underarm, her shoulder, and then circled lower. She sucked in a breath as his hand claimed her breast through the thin silk of her chemise, kneading and pinching her but with the gentlest of pressures.

"Mmmm. Very nice." He dipped his head, plumping her breast so that her nipple crested higher, as if offering itself to him. His mouth closed over her through the silky fabric, hot and wet. She could feel his tongue moving against her as he suckled more of her into his mouth.

"No." She struggled against him. He tugged at her nipple with his teeth, nipping hard and making her writhe against the seat. The foreign feel of wet silk separating them made his attentions seem all the more disgusting. She tried to twist away.

"That's it. Give me that fire that glows within you.

Fight me—it makes the pleasure of this conquest all the sweeter, for both of us."

Her stomach churned from his threat as his fingers dragged her chemise aside, baring her breasts.

His mouth covered her nipple once more, with nothing to protect her from his slick, wet heat. He suckled her hungrily, making obscene noises of pleasure as he did so, nipping and bruising her tender flesh deliberately. He pulled her arms higher over her head to keep her taut against him as he transferred his sordid attentions from one breast to the other and back again. She fought to keep silent, to stay still and not fuel his lust for power, to stop herself from pleading with him. She'd never felt so panicked, so helpless.

He moved his hand between their bodies, and began to hike up her skirts. She could feel the weight of his desire despite the layers of trouser and skirts still between them.

Higher and higher, cool air touched her calves, her thighs. *No, no.* The denial seared her brain but would not come out of her mouth.

She struggled again, and he bit her nipple hard enough to make her cry out.

The coach door opened behind him. He turned his head away from her for a moment but kept her held fast and helpless. She fought tears of frustration and fear.

"Are ye all right, Mr. —" The coachman gaped at them, his bright gaze moving over her bared flesh in appreciation. "I heard a shot."

"A minor infraction, which I am dealing with, Bart. Our guest must learn the consequences to rash actions. Nothing more." He hiked her skirts higher still, drawing the big man's gaze to her legs.

"Can I watch?" Eagerness framed his question. Maura was horrified. His was the type of degradation with which Jameson had taunted Jane.

Jameson's fingers dipped between her legs to massage her for the pleasure of his coachman. She tried, but failed, to shrink away.

"What do you think, my dear?" Jameson's gaze locked once more with hers as he continued to rub and stroke her. "Shall we let Bart observe your punishment? There is power in public humiliation. Perhaps you will think twice about threatening me again."

He dipped his head, not waiting for an answer as his mouth closed over her once more and he suckled her hard, pulling a moan of dread and pain from her depths. She closed her eyes trying to deny the truth of his threat, but the reality still burned bright in her mind, the leering gaze of the giant coachman did make the assault worse.

She arched her back, trying to buck Jameson off her, trying to free her hands, anything that might save her from his touch. His lips. His teeth. From the other man's slack-jawed enjoyment.

A fleshy weight hit her legs. She gasped, and Jameson chuckled against her, his fingers searching for entrance between her thighs. In a moment the weight moved, and he was pushing her legs apart. She squeezed hard, trying to keep her thighs closed to him, and earned another painful bite on her bruised and swollen breast. She swallowed her cry, but he gained enough leverage to force her legs to open.

She twisted and squirmed, wishing she could overset him. Wishing she had shot him first or thwapped him then shot him. Wishing Garrett would arrive and put an end to this interminable assault.

Outside the coach there was a shuffling noise followed by a loud grunt and a muffled curse. But she was too intent on the struggle inside the coach to take it in.

"Jameson!" An angry shout filled the coach.

He lifted his head and pulled his hand away enough to brace himself on the seat and face the door.

"Release her." The demand came from a man with a green mask covering half his face who now filled the coach doorway. She knew him instantly without having to wonder how she knew. Hope flooded her.

"I'm busy," Jameson growled.

There was a distinctive click, and a much deadlier-looking pistol was aimed at them. "Release her."

"Who *are* you?"

"That doesn't really matter, does it?" With quick hands her rescuer reached inside, grasped Harold Jameson by the scruff of the neck, and dragged him bodily out of the coach. He landed hard on the ground with a grunt of pain.

Maura scrambled to cover herself, her fingers shaking as she tried to redo the buttons on her blouse. Tears burned her eyes as the fear she'd held at bay while Jameson molested her rolled through her.

"Take them both and bind them together." Her green-masked rescuer tossed the order over his shoulder and turned back toward the coach.

"Maura." His gentle tone undid her. Tears poured over her cheeks as she launched herself toward him.

"Garrett, oh Garrett." She flung her arms around his neck and sought solace in his welcoming kiss. His mouth felt so good against hers as he held her tight against him.

"Where, how?" She couldn't form the questions she wanted to ask.

"Hush, love. I'll tell you everything you want to know." He smiled at her, his eyes aglow behind the green mask. "How is Miss Fuller?"

"Oh Jane." Maura left the shelter of his arms to turn back to the younger woman still prone against the corner of the coach.

She ran her fingers over Jane's scalp. "There's a bump."

"Move, will you?" Another voice demanded from behind Garrett.

A man in the same type of half-mask Garrett wore filled the doorway.

"Jane." The girl's name rasped out of him. He shed his jacket without a moment's hesitation and draped it over her. "Jane, answer me."

"I don't think—"

Jane's wide blue eyes fluttered open. She gazed up at the man looming over her with a dazed expression. "Who?"

He swept the mask from his face.

"Oh." Color flooded her fair features. She pushed upright, clutching his jacket around her. "Sean. What happened? Jameson? Maura? Oh, my head."

She pressed a hand to her mouth. "Oh Sean."

"Jameson has been dealt with," Maura offered quietly when Sean didn't reply. He seemed caught by looking, merely looking, at Jane.

"Aye, there is naught to fear at the moment," Garrett offered.

"Oh." Jane's gaze took in his green silk mask. "Why, you're . . . you're the Green Dragon, aren't you?"

Garrett's mouth tilted up at one corner. "Why yes, Miss Fuller. I am."

He swept her a short bow.

"I've heard so many stories. It would appear that they are true. Despite my father . . . my father not being one who believes in your veracity." She swallowed hard. Her eyes shimmered with tears. "I do not know how to thank you. I am in your debt, sir."

"There is neither need for thanks nor a debt to be repaid, I assure you." He bowed again with more of a flourish. As he straightened he swayed and caught at the coach door.

"Garrett!" Maura leaned toward him. "What's happened? What's wrong?"

He smiled at her though his face had gone pale beneath the mask. "I appear to have been injured. I—"

He slumped to the ground before finishing his sentence.

"Garrett!"

Sean knelt next to him and pulled him away from his slumped position in the coach doorway. As he laid Garrett out against the ground they could see a large stain of blood across the front of his shirt.

Fear exploded in Maura's heart. She jumped from the coach without waiting for assistance.

"Oh Garrett." She smoothed her hand over his forehead. "Garrett."

"There is more blood than damage, I think. We will have to take him for mending."

"Aye." She was grateful for the calm efficiency of Sean's voice. Despite owning a draper's shop and running a school whose chief curriculum was needlework she had no experience with wounds beyond the plasters her father had put on his horses or the bindings he'd wrapped on his own injured knee.

"But where?"

"There is a farm not too far from here and a magistrate within a day's ride from there. The farmers are friends, Maura, and will be able to tend his wound while we get this vile cargo off our hands."

Sean stood. He glanced into the coach that still held Jane. "Stanhope! Are ye done back there?"

The name caught Maura's attention. She straightened and turned to see Freddie come around the side of the coach. He stopped as his gaze met hers.

"Maura." Warmth and relief flowed from him even as his gaze took in her position at Garrett's side. "You are safe. I am glad."

"Thank you, Freddie. Thanks to all of you." She

blocked out the horrifying images of what had almost taken place. She blocked out the recriminations springing to mind over Freddie's part in the events that had made such an attack possible.

"Give me a hand here, Stanhope. We need to get him into the coach and be on our way."

"What happened?" Freddie hurried to do Sean's bidding. He looped his hands beneath Garrett's legs as Sean took his shoulders.

"Hold on man, we have got to move you," Sean told Garrett, who did not move so much as a muscle.

"Heave." With a strain and a twist they levered Garrett into the coach on the bench Maura had just vacated.

"Can you drive a coach?" Sean's dark gaze swept over Freddie in frank assessment.

"I . . . I have not done so in quite a while. But I have been known to appropriate the family coach in my younger days. I managed then. I am certain I can manage now."

"Very well, you have a job." Sean turned back to the two women. "If you will get into the coach, Maura, we will be underway. Jane . . . Miss Fuller, we will get you home as soon as possible."

"As long as I am free of that horrid man, Jameson, nothing else matters." Jane's chin rose a fraction as she convinced herself of the truth in her declaration. "This man's need for medical help outweighs my homecoming. I have been away for quite some time; what is one more day or so out of port."

"You are a brave girl." Sean reached up into the coach and touched her cheek with the tips of his fingers, almost as if he were afraid she wasn't really there.

"I will see to those blackguards." He stalked off toward the horses and the men who'd been their captors such a short time before.

Maura turned to the coach and the injured man

within. Freddie's hand was instantly beneath her elbow. Courteous and caring, gentle Freddie. However had he involved himself in the exploits of not only Harold Jameson but the Green Dragon on the same night? At least he had come out of this on the right side.

"Maura. I meant what I said. I was afraid for you. I am very gratified to find you safe."

"Thank you, Freddie." She leaned up toward him and pressed a kiss to his cheek. "I . . . I'm glad you are here."

Without further word he helped her into the coach and shut the door behind her. She settled onto the cushion opposite Jane, gently laying Garrett's head on her lap.

"*Diabhal.*" Sean cursed at top pitch.

Fear shivered back down Maura's spine. She leaned her head out the window as Jane's hand gripped hers. It was a relief to see Sean's angry but otherwise unharmed face loom into view as he pulled beside them on horseback.

"That fool." He cursed again and shot an angry glance up toward Freddie. "Did I not tell you to check them for knives?"

"What is it?"

"Jameson and his dog. They have escaped. The ropes were cut through. And they took the horses. Must have led them away like the sneaky little . . . it will leave us to hunt them again. Garrett's not going to be pleased when he wakes."

He cast a worried glance toward the coach's interior.

"I . . . I . . . have nothing to say. I obviously did not do a thorough job. I am sorry."

"Follow me." He tossed the command to Freddie. "Do not make me listen to those last three words from you again tonight."

"Aye."

The coach began to rumble along again with just the slightest change in direction. Maura leaned over Garrett and held his hand in hers. His fingers were so cold. The crude bandage Sean had fastened using Freddie's cravat was seeping blood through the tightness of the binding. They couldn't reach this farm fast enough. She wanted him tended and mended. And then she had some questions for Mr. Garrett Lynch.

Linen seemed to coat Garrett's mouth in thick wads—not the most inspiring experience, to be sure. His eyelids felt fastened shut, his head thick. He tried to move. Pain burned his side. Familiar pain. A knife wound. Not overly deep if he judged the pain correctly.

"Oh, ye're awake. They'll be so pleased." The warm motherly tone poured over him, soothing and soft.

"They?" The word croaked out of him, coated in the same linen that lined his mouth.

"Oh dear, do have a drink."

A cup touched his mouth and he sipped gratefully. Ale. He smiled.

"That's better. We've not seen such from ye since ye arrived a few days ago."

Another touch of the cup and more sips of the cool liquid slid down his throat.

"I cannot open my eyes." His voice sounded almost normal.

"Hold on." In moments a moist warm cloth wiped his face. His eyelids came unfastened, and he opened them to see Maeve Clancy bending over him with a smile.

"Much better," he told her. "You've a way about you, Maeve darlin'. I have always said so." He always enjoyed teasing a smile from her after that night long ago when they'd rescued the Clancy family from fire and destruction at the hands of some overzealous Orangemen. Young Bridget's family had proven a strong ally over the years since.

"Go on with ye." Maeve protested, but her smile broadened. "Ye've a full set of company downstairs. Waiting and pacing. Two women, one lovely and warm, the other a wee scrap of a thing. Sean's come and gone and come back again. And there's another, keeps ta himself but eager ta please if not more than a bit awkward."

"The first would be Maura?" He was not sure how long he'd lain here but he knew she had never been far from his side. Or his thoughts.

"Aye. She's most devoted ta ye. Hard ta convince her ta lay down herself."

"And Miss Jane Fuller," he continued. "The young man is Baron Stanhope."

"A baron!" She crossed herself quickly and her face paled as she sat with a thump on the chair beside the bed. "And me sending him ta sleep in the barn with our lads so the ladies could have their bed. No wonder he didn't seem too thrilled with the idea."

Garrett couldn't hold back a chuckle, even though it pained his side. She'd be even more horrified if she discovered the guest in her hayloft was the *Ard Tiarna's* heir.

"Don't ye laugh, Garrett Lynch." She shook a finger at him. "Ye'll bust yer side open again and then where would we be? Besides, it would have been nice of that Sean ta warn me ahead of time I was playin' hostess ta a . . . well, almost to royalty."

"A baron is far from royalty, Maeve. Don't worry your head about that."

"Aye, well." She didn't look convinced. "Did ye want me to fetch them?"

"No." Garrett pushed upright in the bed, gritting his teeth against the burn in his side.

"Ach! Don't move. Ye'll pull the sewin' I just did all ta pieces."

"Surely it wasn't that bad."

"Aye, well, perhaps not as bad as that. But I'd like to see ye rest a wee bit longer."

"I'll rest soon enough." He pushed to his feet and swayed, grateful for the shoulder she offered him. His breath hitched and blackness threatened. "Perhaps you are right, Maeve. Ask them to come here."

"Aye." She helped him settle back against the pillows and disappeared out the door.

In moments, Sean's face peered around the door frame. Not the first face he'd hoped to see, but welcome just the same.

"Still abed? I thought you would be fighting to get back into the saddle a half hour ago. You must be getting old."

"It is the injuries that get old. I believe this is my third carving."

"Old and slow, too, eh?" Sean sauntered into the room his pace belying the anxiety in his gaze. He gave Garrett a quick once-over. "You do look better than you did when we first brought you here. I guess that will settle for improvement. I had faith in Maeve's skills as a healer."

"Aye." Garrett nodded. His side felt raw. Breathing hurt, and he was weary beyond measure. He could not afford to waste his conversation in banter right now. He had many concerns and very limited reserves of strength. "Tell me what I missed."

"Well, there you are then. Enough recovery time. Jump right back into the fray. You would think you could not trust anyone else to see to things." A shadow passed over his friend's face.

"What is it, Sean? What happened? Is Maura all right? And Jane?" He tried to reassure himself that Maeve had said the two women were in her kitchen just now, but he knew guilt and worry when he saw it and Sean was full of both.

Sean scrubbed a hand over his face and sat on the edge of the mattress. The motion jarred his side, but Garrett tried not to grimace as his alarm mounted.

"We lost them." Sean sighed.

"What?" Garrett pried himself off the pillows and struggled to free himself from the coverings.

Sean shook his head. "Not Maura and Jane. They are below stairs trying to piece together a decent wardrobe for Jane. Jameson and his bear of a bodyguard escaped. We bundled you into the carriage, leaving them trussed next to the horses. When I went to retrieve them, their bonds were cut and they'd made off with two of the horses. He has the devil's own luck that one."

"So it would seem." Garrett panted as he settled onto the pillows once more. He'd not feel really settled until he saw Maura. He thought he might recall her sitting and holding his hand or wiping his brow, but he was not sure when or for how long.

"I should have kept a closer eye. I should have checked their pockets myself."

"Don't judge yourself or the lad too harshly. It was a night fraught with the possibility of far worse outcomes than we had. The rest of the rescue went all right, I take it."

Sean nodded. Garrett shifted his position searching for a better way to breathe. "We know enough about Harold Jameson to bring him down. We will find him."

"Aye." Sean was quiet for a long moment. Garrett knew him well enough to know he had something to say that did not sit well with him. Sean was his closest friend since he'd come to Dublin all those years ago, since the earl had brought him to his estate and begun both their training to be the Green Dragon.

"Garrett, I . . . well . . . I have to talk to you about Jane."

"Indeed?"

"Aye." Instead of launching into his speech, Sean scrubbed his face again.

Garrett pondered the nuances of what was said and not said by Sean's reluctance. An end to all they planned and experienced hung in the air between them. Life seldom turned out exactly as one would wish.

"Sean, say what you need to say. I suspect I will agree with you long before you reach the end."

"I wish such agreement was as easily mine." Sean ran his hand over the back of his neck and paced to the window that gazed out over the simple Clancy farm.

Garrett waited, in part to give his friend time and also to gather some scraps of his own strength.

Sean pulled in a deep breath. "Jane had been missing for too long. Her father, and those familiar with her status, already suspect me as being the culprit in her disappearance." He paused, then blew out a long breath. "I cannot see how she can face disgrace alone. I . . . owe . . . her more than that. We owe her father more than that."

Garrett dropped his head back against the pillows and eyed the long shadows striping the walls and ceiling. The burdens and responsibilities seemed too much at times.

"When I take her home to her father, I suspect the answer will be all too clear to both of them at that point."

Garrett met his friend's gaze. "As clear as it is to the two of us at this moment."

Sean nodded. "Better the scandal of a runaway match than the truth of what actually occurred. I ex-

pect to wed Miss Jane Fuller within the next fortnight."

"Aye."

Sean was to have been his successor, the next man
to wear the Green Dragon's ring, to carry the burden
of leadership along with the dragon sword. Sean's
marriage would put paid to that plan, as it had for
members of the Green Dragon's faithful band for the
three hundred years they had been in existence.

He would be obligated, as they all were, to provide
shelter and supplies when called upon. But the main
core of activity would no longer involve Sean Talbot
in any manner. This was the understanding held by
their oath of fealty. Single men took the risks, those
with families provided the support.

"There are more things twixt heaven and earth . . ."
The rest of the quote eluded Garrett at the moment,
but it seemed appropriate. "Your decision is truly the
only one you can make. And truth be told, she just
might not accept your proposal."

Sean shot him a narrowed glance, then chuckled.
"Aye, you are quite correct. It is entirely possible for
her to reject my suit out of hand.

"Or the admiral may well string you up from the
highest yardarm."

Sean nodded, the edges of his brows edging up at
the suggestion. "Better and better."

"Somehow I do not think the admiral will choose
that course," Garrett continued. "He is an intelligent
man. You may not be an eldest son, but your family is
well respected. He could do much worse for his
daughter, even without the breath of scandal blowing
hot on her heels."

Sean shook his head. "This is not what I planned."

"Ask Maeve for materials so I can write him an-
nouncing your return."

"Really? What will you write?"

"The lost is found. Sean and Jane are on their way to you."

Sean paled ever so slightly. "A bit bald, is it not?"

"The admiral is a military man." Garrett chuckled. "He will appreciate the opportunity to prepare for battle."

With far less certainty of Garrett's jest, Sean left to do his bidding. In moments, he returned with paper and ink. One of the younger Clancy boys would be dispatched to deliver the missive posthaste while Sean made preparations to take Jane home at an easier pace.

Garrett sighed back against the pillows and turned his head to see Maura silhouetted in the doorway. Light and shadow. He would have known her in the dark. When had she become so important to him?

"Mrs. Fitzgerald." His throat tightened.

"Mr. Lynch," she offered back softly as she entered the room in a graceful swish of skirts. "I am gratified to find you returned to the living."

"Indeed? I would not have known. I have felt positively deserted this past half hour or more." He took her hand as she sat beside the bed and laced her fingers with his own.

She smiled, pleased with the recovery evidenced in his humor. "You had business with Sean. I was never far away."

"I know." Just holding her hand was soothing. It hit him suddenly that she was more than just important to him. He loved her. An emotion he'd never expected, found in a most exceptional woman. Warmth spread through his chest, and he pressed the back of her hand to his lips.

She pulled away from him and fussed with the set of his pillows. She wouldn't meet his eyes.

"I am going with Sean as he returns Jane to her father. It will not be right for them to travel alone, re-

gardless of her recent circumstances. Freddie will also
join us. Then I'll go to Dublin."

She was leaving him. With Stanhope.

"To Dublin," he repeated dumbly. Why was she talking with such stilted politeness? Why wouldn't she
look directly at him? "Maura, what is wrong?"

"Naught that cannot be made right," she answered
softly. "You need to rest, to recover. Jane needs to go
home to her father. Freddie has his own responsibilities, and I am long overdue at my school. All of those
young women rescued so fortuitously along with Jane
will need support and compassion in the coming
months. That is where I fit in. I failed to meet them as
they were first rescued. I would like to be available to
them now."

She crossed to the window, taking the same steps
Sean had taken such a short time ago. Farewell hovered in the very air between them. *She was leaving him.*

"Maura—"

"Thank you for all of your help, Garrett." She
looked at him at last, but her gaze was flat. "I am quite
certain I would never have been able to rescue anyone. But then I had no idea I was hiring the Green
Dragon to prevail on their behalf. Had I known I
would have felt more certain all the way."

She smiled bravely, but it didn't reach her eyes. She
walked back to him with quick no nonsense steps that
echoed hollow against the bare wood floor.

"Thank you for everything." She bent over him and
brushed her lips very softly against his own.

He gripped her shoulders before she could turn
away. "Maura—"

"Let me go, Garrett." Her gaze held his. Pain shimmered in the deep gray depths, along with a chilling
resolve that shook him.

"Just let me go."

Chapter Nineteen

The farm receded in the distance behind them, wrenching Maura.

Freddie would escort her back to Dublin, then she would say her farewells to him, too. The hardest parting was already behind her. Leaving Garrett wounded in mind and spirit by her rejection had hurt her at least as much.

But it would be better for both of them. And certainly better for the people who needed him, who depended on him. A small sigh wrenched free of the tight control she was trying to keep on her shattered heart.

"Maura?"

Freddie had been the soul of solicitation since the other night. She knew his heart so much better than he had ever known hers. He was still quite certain that he loved her. Even in the face of the relationship he suspected between her and Garrett, his ardor had not seemed to cool.

She caught back another sigh.

"These have been tiring days. I shall be happy to reach home once more."

"Indeed." He reached over and pressed her hand. "A few days' journey and we will be there."

Her mind strayed far from the covered cart they shared with Jane and Sean. A coach would have been more comfortable given the distance they would be covering, but neither Jane nor she could bear the thought of entering an enclosed vehicle so soon after their escape. Instead they had padded benches, pillows and lap robes, and a carefully erected canopy to provide a modicum of privacy. Paddy Clancy would drive them in easy stages to County Meath, but none of these arrangements brought her much in the way of comfort.

She thought back to each time she had been in Garrett's arms. His touch, his kisses burned on in her heart. Even she knew the Green Dragon never married, was sworn not to give his heart to any woman. It was one of the aspects of his tale Teresa told with such relish.

That left her as just another comforting body to him in what was surely a long history of such women. Even still, that might have been enough for now, but eventually she would have hated not being able to gain access to Garrett's heart. She knew the way she felt about him needed to be reciprocated fully. It was better to end whatever they shared now while there was still a slim chance she had lost her heart alone and not also the security of her future.

The timing of her trysts with Garrett could not be worse. She, who never needed to worry about such things due to the infertility potion faithfully administered by Mrs. Kelly, had never considered the possible consequences when she had made such passionate, satisfying love with him.

Now, she faced at least another week of worry and concern. Two at the outside. She might very well be pregnant this very minute. Pregnant with the bastard child of the Green Dragon. The prospect chilled her

She had promised herself no children, sworn that her choices would hurt no one but herself. As happy as the thought of holding living proof of the love she had shared with Garrett might make her, it was selfish benefiting neither the child who would grow up with no father nor the father who would never get to know his child without the pain of betraying his solemn oath.

She just had to pray that she calculated wrong.

"We will be home very soon." Freddie patted her hand, and she let him.

It would be so very easy to allow Freddie back into her life, especially if she really was pregnant. A few weeks in her bed would easily serve to convince him any child she carried was his. She would deny anything had happened with Garrett, and Freddie would believe her because he'd want to. And he would marry her before she could draw another breath if she asked. Her child would be born the son or daughter of Baron Stanhope, heir to Clancare.

A tempting prospect, save for the fact that she could not imagine ever taking another man to her bed after sharing herself so completely with Garrett. Nor could she betray Freddie or her possible unborn child like that. The lie would eat into them, burning away whatever happiness they might try to claim.

She sighed, and Freddie patted her hand again.

She cast her gaze over to Sean and Jane. As solicitous as Freddie was to her every breath, the two people sitting across from them appeared to be totally unaware of each other.

She couldn't help but smile her understanding.

It was clear there was more than a passing interest on both their parts. Yet whatever they struggled against in their inner hearts precluded them from so much as glancing at each other.

She hoped that when Sean arrived at Admiral Fuller's home with his daughter he would not immediately have some price to pay for his part in returning her to her father.

It was late afternoon on the following day that they

passed the outskirts of Admiral Fuller's lands in Meath. Paddy's brother had brought word to the farm that this was where the admiral would await his daughter's return after receiving Garrett's missive. They had set out immediately after, and she had not gone back up to Garrett in all the time they had waited. One farewell had been wrenchingly enough.

If the two across the cart had been tense before, they were more so now. Maura's heart went out to them both even as she was looking forward to the lessoning of tension once they had left them at the admiral's estate.

"Two miles ahead." Sean's announcement fell into the cart like a leaden ball.

Jane's gaze turned toward him. "Yes."

She turned her gaze back to Maura and tried to smile despite the worry gathering behind her eyes. "Thank you so much, Mrs. Fitzgerald, for being so willing to stand as chaperone. And you as well, my lord."

Her gaze ran quickly over Freddie and back to Maura.

Maura leaned forward and pressed the girl's hands. "Do not worry so, Jane. I am certain your father will think only of your well-being and how happy he is to have you home safely."

"Yes," she said again, her gaze drifting outside the cart again to some place on the horizon. "That is what I am afraid of."

Admiral Fuller was a strong, brisk gentleman who reminded Maura of Colonel Whyte. She couldn't help but like him when they arrived at his spacious manor house. His joy in his daughter's return shone quietly in his eyes, though his speech was brusque and to the point. Early the next day Maura and Freddie took their leave and began the final leg of their own journey.

Jane clung to her in one last spontaneous embrace

trembling at the interview to come once she and Sean were alone with the admiral.

"You'll be fine. Write me," she whispered to the petite blonde.

"Write back." Jane gave her a final squeeze.

The ride back to Dublin was much longer than the distance allowed. She was all too conscious of Freddie's loyal gaze as they covered the miles and she prayed for this interminable travel to end.

All the way, her thoughts stayed fixed on Garrett, whose deep green eyes bespoke the very heart of Ireland. She could have spent her life in that gaze and been happy. But now . . .

Darkness fell and she dozed in a fitful sleep filled with guns, masked men, and danger at every turn. She woke with her heart pounding, her cheeks wet with tears. Freddie's concerned face hovered near her own.

"Dearest Maura, you are safe. Don't cry." He pulled her into his arms, and she clung to the reality of his warmth for just a moment. It was very late or very early as they traveled the darkened, deserted city streets at last. He soothed his hands over her back in long, slow strokes and she shuddered.

She'd dreamed of death and destruction, of Garrett in danger. He was the Green Dragon; he would always be in danger. She couldn't live like that. That truth devastated her.

"Thank you, Freddie." She pushed back from him, and he let her go with obvious reluctance. "You were always kind and good to me. Much more so than I deserved."

"You deserve so much more than you will allow me to give," he argued back. "I would give you everything, all that I have and all that I can manage to acquire. If you would marry me."

The cart rumbled to a stop. She was home at last.

"Sweet, Freddie." She leaned toward him and

traced her fingers over his cheek, falling back on the physical answer as she had so many times in their past. "Thank you for seeing me home."

He frowned at her but didn't press the point. In moments he helped her down from the cart.

She looked up toward the young man atop the coach. "Thank your parents for me. You make a very efficient driver. Do you have money enough for the journey home?"

"Thank ye, missus." Paddy Clancy grinned down at her. "Mam would have my hide if I accepted yer money. Ready, sir?"

He seemed all too anxious to put paid to the streets of Dublin and get back home to the farm.

"Your ride awaits, my lord." She curtseyed.

"Maura." He touched her hands as she straightened. "I will come by tomorrow."

"Don't. Just take care of yourself." She brushed her lips against his cheek and hurried up the steps before he could see the tears trailing her face.

A week passed.

And then a second, just to be sure.

But there was no mistaking the fact that her courses had not come—she, who had been as regular as the cycles of the moon. Her breasts were tender. Her mood even more sore. Her stomach queasy all the time.

"There's nothin' for it then." Mrs. Kelly brought her a tray in the front salon where Maura sat gazing out onto the street. Tea and just a few dry biscuits. Anything more bothered her stomach.

"Aye." There was no need for further conversation. Dorothy Kelly knew, just as she did herself, she was most definitely pregnant.

She took a careful sip of tea. Hot and strong, no sugar. For the past ten days she hadn't been able to abide sweetness in anything. Somehow that seemed a portent of things to come. She sighed and took another sip.

Freddie had been at her door almost every day. With flowers. Jewelry. Demands. Nothing worked. Gerald was ever vigilant in his guardianship of her front door. So it would be, so it would stay until Freddie eventually tired of the chase and moved on to something or someone else.

Garrett was another matter.

She felt a twinge of pain at the thought.

He came quietly, but with a persistence that set her teeth on edge. He always left as quietly, accepting Gerald's rejections without protest. She had taken to sneaking out to the draper's shop at odd hours or she dressed in Mrs. Kelly's outer garb, anything to guard against a chance meeting. But, knowing she was dealing with the Green Dragon, and quite possibly his men as well, had left her unsettled and skittish. She was certain she was being watched.

Either that or the pregnancy was making her feel overset at the slightest provocation. Ten young ladies had been rescued from Harold Jameson's clutches. Most had been restored to their families. Two were recovering at her school. Teresa had been only too happy to recount tales of this latest exploit, albeit with a slightly altered version than truth allowed.

How much longer would Garrett continue to haunt her door? How was she to be rid of him before she began to show? She could not sleep; she was too haunted by nightmares of his death.

Garrett finished another bout of conversational sparring with Maura's formidable gatekeeper.

He couldn't be entirely certain, but he thought he'd begun to detect the slightest thawing in the man's manner. Any advantage would be greatly appreciated. As it was, he was essentially laying a quiet and persistent siege to Maura Fitzgerald's townhouse. Eventually she would have to give in. She would have to see him.

And then, this whole nonsense would be settled.

No matter what denials sprang from those soft and beguiling lips, he'd seen the truth in her eyes, felt it in the response of her body. Nothing would dissuade him of that. He'd spent too much energy and too many years reading situations, reading people, to be uncertain now.

"Lynch!" A voice called out in greeting.

He glanced over to find Baron Stanhope, who actually looked pleased to see him.

"Stanhope."

"I . . . I've been anxious to talk to you."

"Indeed?" Garrett continued to walk, and Stanhope fell into step beside him.

"Yes, I am. I wanted to offer, well, to offer my services. If you would, consider—" His voice trailed off.

This was not the same young man he'd played cards with a little over a month ago.

"I know I am not experienced," Stanhope continued. "I cannot offer you all of the skills you may require. But I would be honored if . . . if . . ."

He trailed off again, managing to look young, earnest, and determined at one and the same time.

"Stanhope."

"Aye."

"I appreciate your offer. Come to The Boar's Head on Tuesday next."

"The Boar's Head? What shall I do there?"

"You will find that out when you arrive. Say four o'clock?"

They continued walking together, skirting the park on the opposite side of Merrion Street and passing the Rutland Fountain where a number of women gathered, waiting to fetch home one last bucket of water before dark. Although he listened only enough to remain polite, Stanhope was still thanking him for the faith he was showing in him, the chance he was taking and guaranteeing no regrets. *Too late for that one.*

They stepped on either side of an open coal shute in the slate walk when a figure stepped out in front of them. The huge man blocked their path. Arms like tree branches hung at his sides, fists bunching and unbunching.

"Stop." His tone low and clipped. To the point.

"Lynch." Behind them, the bored tones snaked forward, etched with menace. "And Baron Stanhope. You may wish to leave. Now."

Stanhope's gaze widened as they turned and took in the deadly looking pistol in Jameson's fist. He waved it to indicate which direction to take. The younger man's gaze turned to Garrett's, wide-eyed as apprehension and reality took the place of dreams and idealism.

"You can go." He released the pale baron. The earl would not appreciate it if some harm befell his heir simply because of a stroll down the street with the wrong companion.

Stanhope took a long, slow breath and seemed to straighten ever so slightly. He squared his shoulders. "No, sir. I will stand with you."

"As you wish," Jameson almost snarled. "I took you for a fool when I first met you. I see my ability to judge character is on target as usual. We are all given free choice. Even fools. Perhaps that will be your epitaph."

"What do you want, Jameson. State your business and be gone." Garrett weighed his chances of overcoming the man in front of him and avoiding the bulky bulwark behind him. As if sensing his thoughts, the giant stepped closer. Not good.

"My business?" Jameson gave a mirthless chuckle.

"You interrupted my business. It will take me some time to recoup and begin again. But I am not without resources. You have not stopped me, Lynch. You have merely delayed me. Trust in that."

"Enough people know of your scandalous pursuits now to send you scurrying off to hide in the dark where you belong."

Jameson's brows drew together. "You have made a thorough nuisance of yourself. But I have recovered from worse. And shortly you will no longer be a problem because I know your secret—the secret you will take to your grave. The great Green Dragon, gunned down in the gutter like a common thief."

Behind Jameson, off to the left on the opposite side of the street, Seamus was coming to meet Garrett to take the night watch over Maura's house. As long as Jameson had been on the loose, one or the other of his men had been nearby. Even if she would not see him, he could not leave her vulnerable to the kind of assault Jameson had almost pushed on her.

Out of long habit and training, Seamus sized up the situation in every detail of the street in the space of a single heartbeat. Seamus crossed the street and disappeared into the bushes of the Merrion Square Park.

Good man, Seamus.

If he could just keep Jameson talking for a few moments longer.

He forced a hoot of laughter. "That's rich. You think I am the Green Dragon."

"I did not come here for conversation. You will not stall for time. Farewell to a legend who turns out to be but a man."

The pistol in Jameson's hand exploded. Pain lanced Garrett's side.

"No!" Stanhope's shout sounded far away.

Everything in Garrett's world seemed to slow down and focus on the dull thud of his own heartbeat. He felt weightless and drifting as he fell to the ground. Sounds of a scuffle and Seamus cursing mingled together.

Darkness engulfed him.

For several days neither of her erstwhile suitors called. They both left her alone, finally.

Perversely Maura was unsettled by the lack of their attention. Where had they both disappeared to? And why at the same time?

She had a pang for Freddie, twined with relief that he might have found a way to move on. But Garrett's disappearance left a deep, painful wound that somehow managed to underscore all of the reasons for her decision to leave the Clancy farm and bar her door to him. Could he be in danger? Where was he? And with whom? The myriad of concerns for him plagued her as they always would, no matter where she settled, but at least she would not run the risk of running into him any time she emerged from behind her door.

She dressed to go to Eagan's. She needed to set things in motion to sell the townhouse to support her far from Dublin and to turn the draper's shop and school over the Polhavens and Mrs. Kelly. Between them all, they should be able to keep things going. She hated leaving, but it would be the only way for her to raise her child with any peace of mind.

As she descended the grand staircase, an urgent knocking sounded at the front door. A shiver went up her spine and she froze midway down the stairs. She knew no one who would pound so precipitously, demanding entrance. Not for any good reason.

Gerald frowned as he approached the door. He glanced up at her and she nodded. He opened the door the tiniest bit.

"Thank God!" Freddie's voice spilled through the

crack and the tension eased out of her shoulders. Just
Freddie, not bad news. Not the news she would dread
every day of her life. She had overestimated his ability to accept farewell as final.

"Let me in immediately."

"I am sorry, my lord. Mrs. Fitzgerald is not at
home." Gerald repeated the well-practiced line he
had been using for the past few weeks.

"Damnation." Freddie cursed with an urgency she'd
never heard in his voice before. This was not the desperation of a spurned swain. "Don't give me that drivel,
man. I know full well she is at home. Interrupt her!
Now! She's needed. She will want to hear what I have to
say."

"Let him in, Gerald." Maura descended the rest of
the way and met Freddie as he entered the vestibule.

"Maura!" He gripped her hands. His face was pale,
his clothes creased and his hair in disarray. She'd
never seen him in such a state.

She pulled free of his grip. Alarm raced through
her, and her hands moved instinctively to her belly.

"Freddie." She pressed her hand against his cheek,
wondering if he was feverish. He was cool, clammy to
the touch. "What is it? What has happened?"

His gaze ran over her quick and assessing. "Good,
you are dressed to go out."

"Go out? Freddie, please—"

"You must come with me, right now." He grabbed
her arm and tried to pull her toward the door.

"You are not making any sense. Go where? Why?"

In her heart of hearts she already knew the answer
even as he continued to simply try to hustle her out of
the house.

"Freddie." She dug her heels in. "I cannot go anywhere with you. Not anymore. We have been through
this—"

"Shall I throw His Lordship out, madam?" Gerald pulled Freddie away from her.

"This is not about me." He looked frantic and as if he hadn't slept in far too many days. "You have to believe me."

"Believe what? You have not told me anything."

"It's Lynch." His voice gentled although the urgency returned to his gaze. "You must come with me for him."

"Garrett?" Her heart dropped to the floor. Her knees threatened to buckle.

"He is injured, Maura. He was shot. I had him taken to my home. My personal physician attends him. But—"

"But what?" Alarm raced along her nerve endings. Freddie's personal physician? "What are you trying to tell me?"

"His condition is grave." Freddie blew out a long breath. "He may die. Soon. The doctor does not think there is any rally left in him."

"Oh." The word tore from her on a moan. She swayed as her vision darkened and nausea swirled afresh.

Freddie gripped her elbows and helped her to a chair. "He needs you. He has barely spoken, but the last thing he whispered was your name."

She focused her gaze on his.

His lips tilted in a half-smile though regret shadowed his eyes. "From the looks of you, you need him too."

"Oh Freddie."

His hands drew her to her feet. "Ready then?"

An agonizing carriage ride later they pulled to a stop in front of a prestigious-looking townhouse— Freddie's home.

He helped her alight as a footman took care of the

carriage. They ascended the front steps, and the butler opened the door as they reached the top.

"This way."

She followed Freddie inside grimly, her thoughts focused on Garrett and the injury that threatened his life. Dear God, let it not be so.

"Upstairs, first door to the left." Freddie told her as she paused, uncertain where to go.

"Thank you." She rushed up the steps as quickly as she could. Why had she denied her love? Why had she turned him away day after day. Why hadn't she taken the chance for what happiness she could find, not hidden out of fear?

Please. Please. Please. Let him live.

Incoherent prayer ran through her mind and shuddered through her heart.

She turned at the top of the steps and found a bedroom door that stood ajar. Fear gripped her at the silence within. She pushed the door open. There on the bed was a lone, very still figure. A lamp from a table beside the massive four-poster cast strange twists of light and shadow across the coverlet that was too smooth.

"Oh Garrett."

He lay there in the bed, so handsome her heart was breaking at the sight of him. So very still. So very still.

A young maid sat nearby. She looked startled at Maura's entry and started to protest until Freddie came to the door. In moments the maid was gone and Maura was at Garrett's side.

"Garrett." She touched his face and traced his jaw. She laced her fingers through his, slack against the counterpane. He was far too hot and so pale.

"Oh, my love." She pressed her face to his hand as tears burned her eyes. Her throat ached.

"Freddie, what happened?"

"Jameson." Freddie's answer was clipped. "Attacked

by that whoreson Harold Jameson and his beef-witted dolt. I was there, Maura. I was right there beside him and there was nothing I could do."

"Garrett."

"Jameson was caught. His days of manipulation and secrecy are finished, thanks to Garrett's man, Seamus." Freddie paced away from the bed. "Lynch's men have come and gone and come again. I have left my home open to them at any hour they wish. The doctor says there is nothing else that can be done for him. All we can do is wait."

He turned back to face her.

"I knew that if it was me lying there, all I would want is you." Sweet, honest, Freddie. "So I came to get you, for him."

"Thank you." She pressed a kiss to Garrett's hand.

Freddie studied her face for a moment longer, then crossed to her side and pressed his hand to hers. "I shall be right outside, if you need anything."

"Thank you."

He left her then, alone with the man who had displaced him in her heart. She would have been so very proud of him in that moment had her heart not been tearing in two within her.

"Garrett. Oh Garrett. Can you hear me?" A sob broke from her in the silence.

When the colonel's wife lay dying, he had insisted over and over again that she could hear him, even though she gave no sign. Maura remembered the long hours he would sit by his wife's bedside, talking to her about everything and anything and always repeating how very much he loved her.

And she had never told Garrett.

The thought burned through her like a light in the darkness. She rested her weight carefully against the bed, coming as close as she could without risking any injury to him. "It's me, Garrett. It's Maura. I love you."

Not the slightest flicker of an eyelash showed that he heard her. It didn't matter.

She stroked her fingers over his brow as her soul twisted within her. Tears welled hot and dripped over her cheeks.

"I'm here, I am with you. It's me. Maura. I love you. I always will. You, Garrett Lynch, and no one else. I am yours. You are mine. There is a future for the both of us." She took his hand, slack within her own and pressed it against her belly. "Inside me is our child. Our future. Our life together. You cannot leave me. You cannot leave our babe. You must live. For the babe. You must stay for both of us."

She stayed that way for the rest of the day and into the night, repeating herself over and over again. Telling him anything and everything she could think of. All about her past. Her mother. Her brothers. The grief and guilt she'd felt over her father's death. No detail was spared. She would share everything with him, open her soul to let him know how very much she loved him, even when she hadn't wanted to, and how very much she needed him to stay with her.

And always she circled back to "It's me. It's Maura. I am here. I love you."

"Oh God, please let him stay with me."

And then in a desperate whisper. "Papa, if you can hear me, if you see him, please send his soul back this way." The tears continued to drip down her cheeks unceasing through all those hours.

Seamus and Liam came and went. Daniel McTavish, too. No one interrupted her.

The maid brought her tea. She sipped a drop or two and spooned some into his mouth as well. Cool water in basins was always at her elbow so she could sponge his face. Sean was there for a time. Liam, Seamus, and a host of others. Silent and respectful, they too kept vigil.

"Garrett, it's me. I am here. I who love you."

In the wee hours of the night, exhaustion took over; she slept for a short time, clutching his hand, her head on the bed by his side.

She awoke with a start at the first rays of the sun. For a single instant she couldn't remember where she was or what had happened; then she realized she was curled against Garrett's side, and the night flooded back to her.

"Oh Garrett." She'd slept. She'd left him even as she'd begged him not to leave her. She lifted her head to begin her litany again. His eyes were open. Those lovely green eyes. That gaze she could spend her very life in.

A gasp shuddered out of her and the tears began anew in joy now instead of sorrow.

"Garrett—"

"Aye." His voice was rusty and his eyes rolled shut before opening to focus on her once again. "You love me even when you tried so hard not to. You're my Maura, the one with the smile to light the darkest corner of a man's soul and the will to wrestle him back from the devil."

She kissed his hand, her heart full. She'd talked all night and had no words now when he could hear her.

"We are well met, my love," he whispered. "For I will not have our babe born without me."

"Oh Garrett." She pressed a soft kiss to his lips as the sun continued to rise and spill bright light throughout the room. "You did hear me."

"Aye, how could I not?" His eyes shut again, but his skin was no longer burning with heat and his breathing was more normal. "I dreamed of you all through the night."

She held his hand and his eyes opened again.

"There was a man who asked me to tell you that he understands and gives you his blessing."

"A man?"

"Aye, with gray eyes like yours and a slight limp."

"Oh, that's . . . that's wonderful." The joy inside her lifted higher still.

Oh Papa, thank you.

"Going to rest, just a little bit longer." His voice sounded very sleepy. "Stay here. I like waking up to you."

"Aye, I shall be right here." She promised her heart so full she could burst.

"And Maura?"

"Aye?"

"I love you as well. I always will."

She brushed her lips against his cheek and fell back to sleep stroking his hair.

Epilogue

"Come here, Mrs. Lynch." Garrett pulled his wife into his arms and back onto the bed. She'd just finished feeding their son, and the babe, very cooperatively from his father's point of view, had gone right to sleep.

She fell back against him with a laugh, her hair spreading across the pillows in dark shiny waves that gleamed in the soft lamplight. She was more beautiful now than he'd ever seen. And she was his forever. He turned and propped his head on his arm so he could look at her

"You are a very demanding husband, Mr. Lynch." Her tone scolded, but her eyes shone up at him.

"Nay." He kissed a pathway from her temple down into the warm hollow of her throat. "I am a pliant one. I succumb too often to your lures."

"Oh really? My lures?"

"Aye, always looking so soft and touchable, with your begging smiles and pleading eyes. I am weary to the bone from keeping up with your demands."

"Oh." She giggled against his lips, then melted against him as he tasted her slowly. Heaven was right here, right now, in her arms.

As the first streaks of sunlight edged the sky, he stood at the windows and looked past the mews to the rolling green fields and paddocks now in his care. He

drew in a deep breath of contentment. He was a lucky
devil, indeed.

A year ago, who would have predicted this future?
Married to a woman whose love showed in everything
she did, father of a healthy son, reconciled with his own
father, and managing the lands he'd roamed as a child.
The wastrel and gambler, the adventurer and hero replaced by a staid family man who bred horses and
tended his estates. The *Ard Tiarna* had said it would be
thus, but he had never believed until he met Maura.

"Do you ever miss him?" Maura asked very softly
against his shoulder as she joined him to look out at
their home. Her hair was sleep tousled, her cheeks
still rosy with sleep. She wore nothing but a sheet
wrapped around her. How he loved her.

He smiled, knowing who she meant, the reassurance she sought. The Green Dragon. He flexed his
hand, wondering when he had stopped feeling the
ghostly weight of the heavy emerald signet ring on his
finger.

"He will always be a part of me," he answered hon-
estly.

"Aye." She fit so neatly against him as he drew her
into his arms. "So . . . do you miss . . . *being* the Green
Dragon?"

Being the Green Dragon.

There was so much more wrapped in that simple
phrase than could ever be fully explained.

"I am proud of the work I did. Glad I was there to
help the people we helped. But being the Green
Dragon was never mine to claim as my own. Just as we
protect the legacy, the legacy protects us—passed
from man to man, generation to generation, like the
ring and the sword. It is my honor to serve for life, but
my time has passed."

"We provide support and shelter—"

"—when called upon. There can only be one Green

Dragon at any time, and he is no longer me. I would not have it any other way."

He traced his fingers over her bared shoulder. "I would trade nothing. I yearn for nothing. Nothing could ever replace what I have right here."

She leaned back against him and ran her fingers over the empty spot on his hand.

"Who wears the ring now?"

"Mmmm." He kissed the edge of her neck. "I would have given the ring to Sean, that was always the plan."

"But he married his Jane."

"Aye."

"So . . . who?"

"The ring, the sword, the power, and the responsibility passed to the man destiny chose. It is his job now, as it was another's before me."

"But—"

"No buts. We work in the light of day now and within the bounds of the law, just as the Green Dragon works outside the boundaries. His identity does not matter as long as his work goes on."

She turned and smiled up at him, caught as she always was in that green Irish gaze in which she would spend her life. She could hardly believe her luck.

"I love you, Garrett Lynch. All that you were, all that you are, and all you are yet to be."

"Amen, my love." He pulled her against him for another satisfying kiss as the warm Irish sunshine spilled in the window and another day began.

The sounds of their son awakening pulled them apart. "We had best get dressed for the day ahead," he whispered against her cheek.

She linked her arm with his as they turned together to face the future she had never before dared to dream possible.

"Thus we'll be arrayed and armed." She answered.

"Aye, my love. Always."

About the Author

Emily Baker is the pseudonym for lifelong friends and writing partners, Susan C. Stevenson and Mary Lou Frank. They both grew up and continue to live in southern New Jersey.

Susan is a bank assistant vice president and Mary Lou works part-time as a grant writing consultant. Between them they have two husbands, seven children, and assorted pets to fill their lives with love at the times they are not creating stories about achieving your heart's desire through love's special magic.

Look for another romantic adventure set in Ireland by Emily Baker from Zebra Historicals in 2006.